BECOMING RAIN

BECOMING RAIN

a novel

K.A. TUCKER

ATRIA PAPERBACK

NEW YORK LONDON TORONTO SYDNEY NEW DELHI

ATRIA PAPERBACK
A Division of Simon & Schuster, Inc.
1230 Avenue of the Americas
New York, NY 10020

First Atria Paperback edition March 2015

ATRIA PAPERBACK and colophon are trademarks of Simon & Schuster, Inc.

For information about special discounts for bulk purchases, please contact Simon & Schuster Special Sales at 1-866-506-1949 or business@simonandschuster.com.

The Simon & Schuster Speakers Bureau can bring authors to your live event. For more information or to book an event, contact the Simon & Schuster Speakers Bureau at 1-866-248-3049 or visit our website at www.simonspeakers.com.

Cover design by Anna Dorfman
Cover photographs © Marcel Jancovic/Shutterstock (woman), Kenny1/Shutterstock (alley)

Manufactured in the United States of America

10 9 8 7 6 5 4 3 2 1

Library of Congress Cataloging-in-Publication Data is available.

ISBN 978-1-4767-7420-6
ISBN 978-1-4767-7422-0 (ebook)

To P, for answering every last one of those texts.
All 752 of them.

Such a precious sun it is, the one that
shines after a cold, harsh rain.

BECOMING RAIN

Prologue

∎ ∎ ∎

CLARA

It's a modest Seattle suburban home, with two stories, steep gables, and cream-colored siding. A row of artless bushes lines the walkway, courtesy of the builder's unimaginative landscaping. It looks exactly like the house to its left and too similar to the house to its right.

And yet the number above the garage marks this house as altogether unique.

I hunch down in the passenger seat of the cruiser, just enough to spy the glow from the second floor through the cold drizzle. A bay window frames the blond woman swaying, the little boy curled within her arms, his cheek resting against her shoulder in a way that suggests he's asleep.

"Where are they going to go?" I ask, eyeing the large "For Sale" sign staked into the front lawn. Just another thing for the neighborhood to look at as they throw sympathetic glances on their way by.

"She can't make the mortgage," Officer Burk confirms through a casual sip of coffee, its pungent aroma filling the car's interior. "Her parents have a farm outside the city. Sounds like that's where they're heading."

"He had *no* life insurance? *Nothing?*"

"She had to take a loan out on the house just to pay for the funeral."

A dull pang throbs in my chest as I watch Betty-Jo Billings

drift over to the window, listless eyes resting on the driveway below, where puddles of water pool in the indents formed by the tires that used to sit there. The exact place where her husband waved to her for the last time before climbing into the passenger side of his cherry-red Ford F-250. The truck he had advertised for sale on Craigslist. The truck he was allowing a prospective buyer to test drive.

Seattle police found Wayne Billings's body fourteen days later in a city dump. The truck hasn't turned up and it probably never will. No witnesses to interrogate, except for Wayne's wife, and all they could get from her was that the driver wore a baseball hat and he was dropped off by someone in a dark sedan. She hadn't been paying any real attention and I understand why. With a two-year-old hanging off her leg and a three-week-old baby in her arms, the poor woman was asleep on her feet, exhausted. When Wayne left, all she was probably thinking about was the family-friendly minivan they would buy with the cash from the truck.

The wipers swish back and forth in a monotonous song and heat blasts out from the dashboard to counter the chill in the damp spring air. I arrived on the West Coast one week ago and, though locals swear it's not usually this bad, it hasn't stopped raining.

I don't mind it at all. I find it soothing, actually.

"It's a real shame. Everyone says he was a decent guy. His kids will never get to find out," Burk murmurs in that wearied voice that tells me that this is just another case to him. He has succumbed to the job. It's not his fault; it's how many cops learn to deal with the kinds of things we see every day.

Detachment.

The case sits open, but the local police force has pretty much written it off. I knew that the second I made the request for the files. Under a generic guise of a Washington, D.C., cop researching similar cases on the East Coast, of course. None of these guys knows why I'm really here.

I peer up at the little boy's angelic face again.

And make a silent promise that Rust Markov—and anyone tied to him—will pay.

Chapter 1

...

LUKE

I drop my glass onto the table with a heavy thud. "Miller can go. I'm ready to run the shop on my own."

Uncle Rust's eyes wander over an attractive woman passing by, on her way to the restrooms of The Cellar, her hips swaying in rhythm with the throbbing bass. "I'll tell you when you're ready."

The mouthful of vodka barely quells the bitterness ready to leap from my tongue. "Seriously? What else do I need to do? Haven't I proven myself yet?" I stare hard at him as he rolls his drink around inside his cheeks. Rust has always shown patience with me, but that's a sign that his tolerance with my drunken persistence is running thin.

"All good things come to those who wait."

"I *have* waited. Hell, I've done more than wait. I've done everything you've asked me to do! Do you think I enjoyed changing tires and going home every night stinking of motor oil?"

He drops a hand down on my shoulder, slightly too hard. "All part of the plan, Luke."

The plan. Rust starting singing "the plan" song to me when I was thirteen. He pulled into our driveway one day, in his latest ride—a silver Cadillac—and dressed in a sharp-looking suit, and I told him I wanted to be just like him. I still remember his words. "Listen to me, kid, and I'll set you up for life."

Eleven years later, I'm beginning to wonder if he really meant it.

"Yeah, well, maybe you can enlighten me on this master plan of yours so I have a better handle on it. Like, why I'm looking at Miller's ugly face across a desk and taking his bullshit. You said the garage would be mine by now." Facing off against the current manager of Rust's Garage—an overweight, under-groomed jerk who barks orders at me like I'm his personal bitch—every day for the past two months since Rust moved me from the mechanics bays to the office as "associate manager" is wearing on my nerves. Miller's no idiot. He expects that at some point his fat ass will be evicted from that squeaky office chair to make room for me, and he's been making me suffer for it since the day my feet hit that dirty concrete floor.

"I need Miller there."

"Until when?"

"Until I say so."

"And then what?" Rust keeps telling me I'm smart, I'm going to go far. I assume "going far" means more than the glory of filing paperwork, ordering parts, and being called "Nurse Boone" by a bunch of greasy mechanics for the rest of my life.

The revenue from the garage isn't bankrolling Rust's high-end lifestyle; that much I know. Neither does RTM International, the online vehicles sales company he co-owns, though that company puts him on the map as a legitimate global businessman.

I have a pretty good idea where his money comes from by now.

But he has yet to admit anything to me and, until he does, I'm nothing more than an errand boy. He can be such a secretive son of a bitch, even when it comes to family.

"I just . . ." I try to bite my tongue, but the dam breaks anyway. "Stop dangling this big plan in front of me like a diamond-encrusted carrot."

I get a sour smirk in response. "How about you stop whining like a pissy brat and spend all this energy establishing yourself as a leader. Run the garage as well as Miller does. *Better* than Miller. Learn how to deal with people. You'll meet all kinds when you're in charge and you've got to be personable and keep them all happy, kid. I didn't build up that place so you can drive it into the ground with your smart mouth."

Same old spiel. "It's hard to believe that's really so important, considering you've got King Kong Grouch dealing with the customers right now." Rust knows he doesn't have to worry about my personality. I'm Prince Charming, for fuck's sake. Just, maybe not after this much vodka . . .

"The customers come back. Plus, he has the guys' respect."

"That's not respect. That's working for a paycheck under constant threat. The dickhead told me he'd cut an hour from my pay today for being late. To my own fucking shop!"

"It's still *my* fucking shop," Rust throws back, his tone warning.

I hold my hands up in surrender. "Fine. But I need to start making real money, Rust. *My* own money."

"You aren't exactly suffering. I've taken good care of you." His manicured fingertip taps the face of my gold Rolex—a hand-me-down from him when he upgraded last year. It's part of the long list of gifts and cash that he's easily doled out and I've gratefully accepted, just as easily as a son would accept something from his father. Because that's the role Rust has played since I was six years old, ever since my dad skipped out on my mom, little sister, and me.

I lean back against my bench, trying to decide if this argument is worth it. I know I can't win. Rust's an unmovable bastard when he wants to be. "I'm just tired of Miller's crap," is all I say. I'm tired of punching in and out every day, of working Saturdays. It's a sucker's life and it's not one I have any interest in living. It's the one Rust promised me I wouldn't have to live.

A harsh chuckle escapes Rust. "You're only twenty-four years old. You've got too many years to go to be tired of people's crap already. Go on . . ." He waves a lazy hand back toward the common area of the club—we're sitting in the VIP section, as usual. It's packed with bodies and thrumming with deep-bass trance music. "It's a busy night here. Why don't you cheer yourself up with a *bliad*."

I roll my eyes. *Go find a whore and get laid.* Classic Rust advice when he's trying to blow me off. Sometimes I listen. It's never hard to find one. Not in this place, not looking the way I do. Like money. That's what these kinds of girls like. And I've never minded playing the part of a guy who has it if the night ends with one of them naked and on her back in front of me.

I down the rest of my drink and flick the empty glass across the table. "I'm going home."

"Probably a good idea. You're obnoxious tonight. Doubt you'd impress anyone in your state."

I have no interest in impressing anyone tonight. Not even Priscilla—a bartender and a sure thing, if she hasn't already dug her claws into a true high roller for the night. "When you hear that I've beaten Miller to death with that fucking stapler of his, don't say I didn't warn you." I slide out of our booth to the sound of Rust's booming laughter. Pushing my way through the crowd, I keep my head down to avoid all conversation.

A sudden splash of cold liquid hits my chest, doing nothing to cool my simmering rage.

Chapter 2

■ ■ ■

CLARA

"I'm *so* sorry!" I peer up through the dim club lighting to take in his face. It's angular and masculine. He's far prettier than the pictures do justice. And, by the deep furrow and the clenched teeth, he's also oh so pissed.

He's too busy glaring at the tumbler's worth of Coke that I just dumped all over his steel-blue shirt to even bother a glance up at me. "Fucking perfect," I hear him mumble.

"Let me get that dry cleaned for you. Please," I offer, my voice a seductive purr, hoping the view down the front of this slutty overpriced dress will finally grab his attention. I place my hand flat against his stomach as I step into his personal space. Physical contact usually works.

Instead, he shoulders past me, pushing through the crowded bar and toward the exit.

Shit. I didn't nurse a drink on this bar stool for the past two hours with the better part of my breasts on display so this asshole could ignore me.

Again.

Tossing a twenty on the counter, which will more than cover my bill, I weave through the other patrons, trying not to be too obvious as I chase after him. He's at least two hundred pounds of muscle and he's carrying himself well, but I watched him chug six glasses of vodka. He's got to be drunk.

By the time I get up the narrow stairs of the underground club to the side street, Luke Boone is in the back of a cab and speeding off, leaving me staring at the taillights as they disappear around a corner, my ever-growing frustration weighing down on my shoulders.

"Strike five for *Rain Martines*," I mutter, picking my way along the sidewalk in my painful stilettos to where my white Audi sits. "'It'll be easy,' they said . . ." I slam the door shut behind me. "'He'll be all over you.'" I start the engine and lean back against the headrest. And sigh. "This isn't going to work."

My phone rings in response.

"Who told you this would be easy?" Warner's heavy Boston accent fills the car's speakers as it kicks into Bluetooth mode. "Don't give up just yet, Clara. What happened tonight?"

I fumble with the gold dragonfly pendant around my neck until I feel the minuscule switch on the back. I flick it, deactivating the listening device. "You heard what happened."

"Walk me through it. Step by step."

I pull out of the parking lot and make the five-minute drive home, filling my handler in on the night's events: how I watched my target stride to the booth—the same booth in the VIP section that he always sits at—as if he were on a mission, pour glass after glass of vodka from the bottle and toss it back, get into what looked like a heated conversation with his uncle, and then suddenly stand up and storm through the crowd.

How I did the first thing I could think of to stop him. "He didn't even look at me," I admit and, after a long pause, add, "I'm not his type, Warner." Despite the posh outfit and the top-to-bottom grooming I've undergone to transform into the prototype of what Luke Boone typically brings home, I have yet to earn so much as a sideways glance from him.

"Yeah, you are. He just hasn't laid eyes on you yet."

"And probably never will, at this rate."

"Impossible."

I shake my head, though he can't see it. "How many nights

can I hang around that club, dressed like an escort, before you guys realize that you've got the wrong undercover on this?" It pains me to admit that.

"Fifteen minutes. Your place." The phone line cuts out, leaving me to brood over my impending failure alone.

Weeks of case preparation, down the drain. I don't know what I was thinking. When my boss called me in to his corner office and introduced me to the man in the suit filling the spare chair, my life changed. Assistant Director Josh Sinclair wanted me. Or, more appropriately, the FBI wanted me—twenty-six-year-old Officer Clara Bertelli from the Washington, D.C., Major Crime Unit. They had a big case, one that stretched internationally, one they've been working for eighteen months.

After two failed attempts to infiltrate the group, they were trying a new strategy and it required a very specific profile. One that they failed to find in their database of FBI agents, so they were reaching beyond their organization, as they sometimes do. They had been searching for a suitable undercover for weeks, and then my file hit their radar and winning bells went off.

My youthful look, my cool demeanor, my impeccable arrest record, my compelling court testimonials, even my diligent case notes . . . Sinclair said I was exactly what they were looking for. Then he asked me if I was interested in being a part of what could be one of the biggest car theft ring busts in U.S. history.

My own set of winning bells went off.

I didn't give it a moment's thought before I answered with an exuberant "Hell, yeah."

But maybe I should have considered it a bit more. Maybe I shouldn't have assumed it'd be as easy as a hooker sweep or busting some idiot john. All I thought about was what this could mean to my career if I succeeded—ideally a job in the Bureau, exactly where I want to be. A bit of my own digging uncovered that Assistant Director Sinclair is the kind of guy that can make that happen.

Maybe I should have considered what it would mean if I

failed, where I could land if I don't pull this off. A very likely possibility, if the past few weeks have been any indication.

I park my Audi in my private garage, appreciating the luxury car's handling ease. Part of my undercover persona and definitely one of the perks, as is everything else that now surrounds me. Back home, my real life consists of a drafty one-bedroom apartment with cracked tiles and a squeaky fridge, a '95 Jeep Wrangler with more miles on it than a retired cargo plane, and chain store clothing bought at 50 percent off. Sixty grand a year with student loan debt hardly buys me more. I'm not complaining—I've always loved my job and my life.

But then I take a smooth ride in this mirrored elevator that will lead me to the top floor with the slip of a key and step into "my" loft-style designer condo—with the computerized control panel for the lighting and sound system to my left, floor-to-ceiling windows to my right, and everything from Miele kitchen appliances to Brazilian walnut floors and travertine tile in between— and I get to experience how the other side lives. A lifestyle I will never afford to have on a regular cop salary.

I have to admit, it'll be hard to leave some of this behind.

Kicking off my shoes, I head over to the wall of windows and take a peek out around the shades that are always drawn. A few condos in the twin boutique loft building next to mine are still lit, but most sit in darkness. There's only one I really care about, though.

The one with my target in it.

Maybe the Feds thought this would be a cute, kismet story for Rust Markov's nephew and me to giggle over when I finally succeeded in winning his attention—the fact that we have a perfect view into each other's lavish homes. I certainly do, anyway. Luke doesn't seem to believe in drawing window covers, regardless of time or state of dress. I haven't yet figured out whether it's due to ignorance or arrogance.

Flashes of light from the TV on the wall fill his living room, each burst highlighting his body, now clad in nothing but boxer briefs and a T-shirt. As with every other night for the past few weeks, I watch him drop down to the white shag rug and begin the nightly regime of crunches and push-ups that give him those hardened muscles. Without fail, drunk or not, he will go through this routine, his bulldog stretched out next to his head, tongue lolling. I've caught my own tongue lolling once or twice, when I had a brief lapse in memory and forgot what Luke Boone really is. For all else that he may be, he has a body and face for magazine covers.

Too bad he's a budding criminal.

At least, that's the assumption. That's why I'm here.

I wonder if the women he brings home know. Or care. I'm guessing not. They're not the type to care about much except what he can buy them. From what I've seen in the reports, the joke's on them because this guy doesn't wine and dine anyone. He's after only one thing and he gets it. Thankfully, on the few nights I've witnessed a "guest" trail him through the door, the women had enough modesty to draw the blinds in his bedroom.

With a heavy sigh of frustration, I head to the pretty water-color painting that hides my safe. I pull the case files for 12—our code name for Luke Boone—out, dropping them on the coffee table, one hand on my zipper as I head to the bedroom to peel off this uncomfortable dress and change into sweats.

I come back to find a six-foot shadow at my window, stealing the same glance across the way at our target that I had not five minutes ago. "Would you stop using your key? I could have been naked."

"I was hoping," Warner throws back over his shoulder.

I offer up a bottle of Chianti. He waves it away, instead helping himself to a can of Harpoon—a Boston I.P.A. beer that he insists on stocking in my fridge—before dropping his big body into my white leather sectional.

I flop into the couch next to him. "I just don't know . . ."

"What don't you know, Bertelli?" Warner stretches long legs out over my coffee table, fanning the thick folder of surveillance notes that I just set down over the glass. "That you're a smart cop? That you were handpicked by the F.B.I. for a reason?"

I smile, giving his knee a friendly pat. "I can always count on you for a motivational pep talk."

"We all knew this wouldn't be a cakewalk."

"No, I know. I just . . ." I yawn, the adrenaline that kept me wired through the night finally seeping from my body, leaving me weary. "We've been pinning all our plans on the expectation that 12's going to fall to his knees at the sight of me. Dog me around and tell me whatever I want to know. That's *clearly* not the case." I won't lie; privately, it's a hit to my ego. I've never had a hard time attracting a target's attention. With my long, wavy chestnut hair, olive skin, and light blue eyes, we all assumed I was Luke Boone's type. On paper, I am. But either something else is at play or I just don't quite fit into the lineup of gold-digging beauties.

Warner sucks back a mouthful of beer, his face pensive. "You said he was fighting with 24 tonight?" The Feds are so clever with their code names.

"Looked that way."

Warner shrugs. "Drunk . . . arguing with the uncle . . . last thing he's in the mood for is putting any work into a woman."

"I guess . . . But what about last time?" He hadn't noticed me last week either, and I had made sure my steps were as slow and purposeful as a peacock's as I strutted past his table on my way to the restroom, my provocative dress clinging to my ass.

"He took the bartender home." Warner stares at me like that answer says it all. Finally, my blank look compels him to elaborate. "Guaranteed lay with no effort and no hassle. He obviously wanted something easy that night."

I roll my eyes. "He definitely had that." And I got an eyeful, making it home just in time to see her do a Full Monty sashay to the bedroom blinds to draw them. Months' worth of surveillance—pictures, written reports, videos—mark Priscilla Grishin as Boone's "go-to girl." Nothing more, nothing less. They're certainly not exclusive. "I'm just not sure this is going to work. I mean . . .

these women . . ." I let my words drift off. These women, they're not common prostitutes working to pay their rent, like the ones I normally deal with. Like the ones I've learned to emulate. These ones stalk through life with their stunning faces and perfect figures—either naturally granted or acquired with the help of a plastic surgeon—with the single goal of climbing the boyfriend ladder until they reach the top and become the wife of a rich husband who will cater to their every high-maintenance need.

They're vapid.

Insecure.

Unkind.

I can't stand their type. And I can't stand the kind of guys who are attracted to them.

"These women ain't got nothin' on you, kid." His eyes dip down to survey my body, which, while well cut from a strict gym regime, can't possibly look appealing right now.

I smack his stomach, a smile creeping out from behind my frustrations. At thirty, FBI Special Agent Warner Briggs is what a lot of women look for in their ideal man. Tall, athletic build, dark hair, square jaw. As charming as a southern boy, though he grew up in South Boston. Extremely successful. The first day he was introduced to me as my handler and lead cover on this case, I'll admit I took a second glance. He certainly did the same of me.

But I won't let my career or my goals get derailed by flings with coworkers and I have no interest in dating another cop. That just has disaster written all over it. Female officers already have it hard enough, without adding on opportunities to be accused of sleeping our way to the top. Besides, Warner has quickly become a friend and sounding board. Something I need far more desperately than a good lay.

"Come on, Warner. Honestly, between you and me . . . what did they think was going to happen if I actually managed to grab 12's attention? Look at his file!" I gesture at it. Three months of gathering intel on Luke Boone. Five one-night stands. Three overnight visits with his bartender. "The guy's not looking for a wife. He's not looking for romance, or even great conversation. He's bringing them home for the one thing *I* won't give him! They would have been better off with an informant for this. At least they're not bound by the same rules."

Warner barks out a laugh. "Come on, Clara! Sinclair's not gonna use an informant for a role like this. They're too unreliable. Winning this case will move him up in rank, and Sinclair's all about rank." He stretches an arm over the back of the couch in a playful way. "Don't worry, you've got this. All you have to do is string twelve along. Let him think that he's got a shot at you. That you're special."

"I *am* special," I mutter, earning his snort. "But this isn't a guy you can string along. He's not into virginal girls and he's not looking to make money off me." In hindsight, how the Feds thought putting an undercover on this target with the hopes of luring him with mere words and seductive gestures is beyond me. Desperation—that's the only explanation I can come up with. They have plenty of evidence at the low level but nothing connecting it all, nothing concrete enough to pull the entire organization down. Not to mention two failed efforts by undercover agents to gain a foothold into the top level, attempting to earn their trust and friendship.

Apparently, neither Rust Markov nor Luke Boone is interested in making new male friends. Female "friends," however . . .

Warner shrugs. "You *say* whatever you need to say to hook him."

I sigh, knowing that Warner's not going to give me the satisfaction of agreeing. He's 100 percent committed to the job. "Well, I can't sit in that bar week after week. People are going to start noticing."

"I'll get the guys to rotate. Make it look like they're hiring you for the night."

I shake my head. "Too risky. None of the girls 12 takes home are escorts. That may turn him off."

"Okay then . . ." He leans forward to scoop up the case files, tossing them onto my lap. "What's gonna work? You're the one with your neck on the line. You're looking to go Fed. This is a big deal for you. So you tell me . . ." He stabs the stack of paper with his index finger. "What's our next move, boss?"

That's one of the things I like most about Warner. He could be an arrogant, condescending dick. The big-show FBI agent versus a mere metro cop pawn. But he's been nothing but a team player from day one. In fact, he reminds me a lot of the guys I work with back home. A tight group who take every opportunity to joke around and let loose, knowing how much we all need the release from what we see in our day-to-day.

Sipping on my wine, I start flipping through the pages of candid shots. Luke Boone is a decidedly handsome target by anyone's standards, with wavy caramel-brown hair that he styles in a sexy mop and clothing that's tailored to a well-honed body, courtesy of daily jogs with his dog and workouts in his building's gym.

Son of Oksana Boone, single mother to him and his younger sister, Ana Boone. Biological father's whereabouts unknown.

Nephew of Rust Markov, who has raised him like a son, footing his tuition for a bachelor's degree in business, followed by two years in a mechanics program. The nephew of a man pegged as the leader behind one of the West Coast's biggest car theft rings by a confidential informant avoiding heroin-dealing charges. The nephew who seems glued to his uncle's side, who is now stepping into a managerial role at one of Rust's legitimate businesses—a car repair garage—and who lives in a million-dollar condo that his uncle gifted to him, either out of the goodness of his heart or to protect his assets.

The nephew who the Feds believe is being groomed to step into a leadership role in the car theft operation.

"Be thankful. *He* could have been your target." Warner taps a shot of Rust Markov leaving his office one afternoon. A man I can't wait to see stripped of his Versace suits and sleeping in a bunk bed behind bars for a very long time.

"Wouldn't be the worst I've had." At forty-five years old, Rust's fit and by no means bad looking. Likes younger women, from what I know. "May have been easier."

"No, it wouldn't. 24's smart. You need the dumb nephew. Kid's too new. Get him comfortable, get him drunk . . . He'll slip and, when he does, we've got him."

"I just don't know what the best way in is with this guy. I don't think it's the bar scene."

Heaving himself off my couch, Warner strolls over to the kitchen to drop his empty on the counter. "We have a few more weeks before the warrant's up. Sleep on it. We'll regroup in the morning."

"'kay. Night," I call out as the condo door shuts. As tired as I am, I know that the stress of looming failure—of being sent back to D.C. to bust pimps and drug addicts—is going to keep me up. I'm half-tempted to drink wine until I pass out, but I'll only feel worse tomorrow. Not that I have anywhere that I need to be.

So I start flipping through the case files, beginning to end, like I've done over a hundred times. Luke Boone's schedule is pretty basic: he's either at the garage, at a club with his uncle, working out, or "entertaining" one female or another. There have been no reports of him disappearing into warehouses or storefronts at erratic hours of the night. The team's never lost track of him in the few hours per day that they're on him. Unlike his Uncle Rust, who continuously slides through their surveillance detail like a bar of wet soap.

Frankly, there's no solid evidence that Luke Boone has any involvement with this ring. Only speculation. Enough to get a sixty-day warrant from the judge. I need to spend time with him to get a better read. Surveillance tapes and reports give me only background. They help me to speculate about what he might respond best to.

So far, all of our speculations have been wrong.

Closing the file, I pack everything back up into the hidden safe and pull out my personal phone, checking it for any messages. My parents are aware that I'll be away for an indefinite amount of time on a case. That's all they know, though, and that's all I can tell them. As far as my mother is concerned, I'm only ever sitting at a desk, working behind-the-scenes detail. If she knew what I was actually doing—the kind of danger I put myself in on a daily basis—she'd beg me to quit with tears in her eyes and Sicilian prayers rolling off her tongue.

If they could see me now . . . This loft is a far cry from the small, semi-detached house they've owned for the past thirty-one years, complete with the original stiff-backed floral couches and the large vegetable garden they tend to in the backyard. It's nothing special, and yet it's their dream come true after immigrating to America from a small town outside Palermo, Sicily, with nothing but one suitcase of clothes and my grandmother's white linen tablecloth. It took almost ten years and at least four honest jobs between the two of them at all times—my mother in bakeries, my father as a janitor—to scrounge up enough money for the down payment.

My brother Dino, older than me by eleven years, remembers those years being tough. Socks with darned toes and jeans with patches in the knees, used toys for Christmas, summer vacations at local parks. Cold winters, to save on electric bills.

By the time I came along—an accident when my parents were in their mid-thirties—they were living in luxury by comparison.

Still, it's nothing like what I'm living right now.

No calls from the family tonight, which doesn't bother me. I talk to them enough. A few texts from my girlfriend Aubrey, telling me about the upcoming girls' weekend that I won't be going to because I'm 2,300 miles away. It bothers me a little bit but I'm used to it. I miss a lot of birthdays and holidays and getaways because of my job.

What I still haven't gotten used to is not seeing a message from David, my latest ex-boyfriend. Nine months of messages all day— every day—until I came home with a black eye and busted lip from a takedown and he decided that he can't handle being with a cop.

I really liked this one, too. I thought he might be different. Stronger.

I thought I'd prove my police college instructor and that author with her PhD label wrong. That keeping a relationship in this field isn't as hard as they made it out to be. I still have that stupid paperback that they handed us in class, about loving a cop. It's at home, collecting dust. At first I thought it was a joke, until I started flipping through the pages and digesting everything I should expect in the years to come. How the long shifts and overtime coupled with the daily hazards earn this field high divorce rates. How the things I see every day make it hard for me to carry on a normal dinner conversation. How I'll have a difficult time meeting men to begin with because of all the trust issues I'll develop, dealing with liars all day long. With a sinking feeling in my stomach, I pushed it off as a stereotype that wouldn't fit me. I hoped that being aware of the challenges would prepare me enough to avoid them.

The dozen or so failed relationships since then have proven that little pocket book not so stupid after all.

My mentor—a staff sergeant in her early forties, who's been divorced twice now—only validated it by warning me to expect a whole lot of heartbreak before I find the right relationship. *If* I ever do. Dating a female cop may be a fantasy involving handcuffs and wild sex, but marrying one isn't a reality most guys can stomach. The day she told me that, three days after David ended things, I went home and cried into a bottle of red wine.

With one last gun check—a habit more than anything else—I lock everything back up into the safe and head for bed. My mind is still spinning, in search of the way into Luke Boone's life. I have only a few shots at this before accidental run-ins become too much of a coincidence.

Another glimpse past my bedroom blinds finds him now stretched out on his back, a flurry of cars racing across his television screen. His arm is wrapped around his dog's body, and he's stroking its belly with slow, affectionate movements.

When I look at him, all I see is just another twenty-four-year-old guy. A guy I might meet at a party or at the club. A guy my friends and I would definitely notice, would probably drool over.

Who I'd gladly give my number to. A guy I'd go home with if I had one too many drinks and needed a release.

A guy I wouldn't believe could be involved in something that left two children without a father.

But that's the thing with so many of the worst kinds of criminals. They don't wear signs, they don't don a uniform. They're hiding in plain sight. It's my job to reveal Luke for what he truly is, which will reveal the man we're really after—his uncle.

But how?

Women. Dogs. Cars. Three things that seem to grab Luke's attention.

I'm an attractive, smart, confident woman—you have to be both smart and confident in a job like mine or you could end up dead—so I have that going for me. You also have to be a little crazy, but I hide that well. Maybe the issue isn't me; maybe it's the surroundings.

I need to find a better place to meet. A place he can't possibly miss me.

Yes.

I hit "one" on my phone's speed dial. Warner picks up almost immediately.

"Hey, I think I have an idea." I smile. "But it involves messing around with that beautiful car of mine."

Chapter 3

. . .

LUKE

"Why the hell did R&S just drop a '78 Corvette in our parking lot?" Miller hollers, bounding through the office door like a grizzly bear about to attack.

"Because I asked them to." R&S, the auto body shop we refer all of our clients to, finished with the car early and offered to bring it here for no charge. I wasn't going to say no to that.

"Last I checked, we don't run a storage lot."

As much as I want to match his angry tone, I temper mine with a smile, knowing my lax attitude will get under Miller's skin more. "I forgot to tell you: I'm expanding our business."

"Oh *really* . . . And does Rust know about this?"

"He knows what he needs to know." I pause. "Relax. I'll have it off the lot by the end of the day."

I get Miller's signature nose flare in return, and then his voice drops to a low hiss. "Rust has been very clear about that coming to this doorstep. This garage runs one hundred and ten percent clean. You need to get it off this property *now* or your uncle will have your head."

Miller seems to have jumped to the conclusion that I'm into something below board. Quite presumptuous of him. I could save him all this stress and just tell him the truth—that the car is a legal side project I've been working on with my friend Jesse for some extra cash.

Cash that I can say *I've* earned.

I'm more curious about what Miller knows of Rust's "other" business. Is it more than I do? I know so little that it wouldn't be hard. But it pisses me off to no end that this fucking asshole might know something that I don't.

I lock my hands behind my head and grin. "Nope. I don't think I will."

Miller doesn't waste another second, charging for the phone. He lifts the old-school receiver up and points it toward me in warning. "Don't make me call Rust down here."

I shrug. "It's almost lunch. I wouldn't mind grabbing a bite with him."

A sneer curls his lips as he punches the keys with his fat index finger. I don't even bother to hide my eye roll as he glares at me, earpiece jammed against the side of his head. "Rust, Miller . . . you need to get down here . . . It's urgent . . . About what?" He shoots another scowl at me. "Your nephew, that's what . . . 'kay." He slams down the receiver.

"Anyone ever tell you that you have anger-management issues?" It thrills me to no end that I can actually say that now. For the year that I was working in the garage, Miller rode my back every day, making my life hell. Now that Rust has moved me inside, making my future position as manager and eventual owner of this garage all the more obvious, Miller can't get away with the same crap. But he still tries.

"I'm actually going to enjoy watching him hand your ass to you."

"What is it exactly that you have against me, Miller? Is it that I'm younger? Better looking? Smarter?"

"Have you ever actually worked a day in your life?" he snaps back.

I pretend I don't notice that the tension in the office has grown to choking proportions as I sort through invoices and answer customer calls, ignoring him. When I spot Rust's navy Porsche Cayenne pull up outside the window twenty minutes later, I throw a lazy salute and stroll past Miller, glad to get away from him.

I find Rust standing with Tabbs and Zeke, two of his longest-standing mechanics here, hovering over the classic, his fingers sliding across the killer paint job that R&S completed for me.

"Hot damn, Nurse Boone!" Tabbs bellows, using the stupid nickname they slapped me with one week into working here. "This for you?"

I fish the keys out of my pocket. "Why? You wanna buy it?" One turn of the key has the engine purring low and steady. Not loud enough to drown out the bell that announces Miller barreling out the door. With groans, Tabbs and Zeke head back to their respective work to avoid his wrath.

"Is this what that loan was for?" Rust slides his sunglasses off to level me with bright blue eyes that match mine.

I nod. "Picked it up for three G's. The widow just wanted it out of her garage. Had it restored to original spec."

"Who did the work?"

"Who do you think?" Rust knows Jesse. He used to work at the garage too.

"He's still around?"

I level a stern glare at my uncle. "Only for these types of projects. And only through me." Rust knows what I'm talking about without me having to say it out loud. Jesse'll never get mixed up with the likes of Rust's "business associates" again. I wouldn't want him to, after what he's been through.

Rust's hand finds his chin, giving it a thoughtful scratch. "You keeping it?"

"Nah . . . though I could definitely use a new car." It'd be an upgrade from the '07 Mustang GT convertible I'm driving now. The first car I ever bought myself, that leaks when it rains. Rust's strange like that; on the one hand, he spoils me with things no twenty-four-year-old could possibly need, like a Rolex watch and gold cufflinks. But the basic necessities, like a roof and transportation? He makes me work for those. Before he handed me keys to the swank condo that I now live in, I was sharing a shitty apartment with Jesse. I think it's a life lesson—to make me see what it's like to struggle like a normal person so I'll work harder to avoid it.

"I talked to Sully already. It's going on the block this Saturday. Should be able to make a solid return on it, given it's an anniversary model and the mileage is low. And I'm lining up two more deals like this as we speak. May need you to front me some cash, though."

Rust's brows spike but he says nothing. Sully is *his* associate, an auctioneer who sometimes helps sell cars for RMT. I don't know if it bothers Rust that I went behind his back, but I've gotten to know Sully pretty well. And, other than his bankrolling the loan for me, I wanted to do this without Rust's involvement.

I stifle my smile as Miller ambles over.

"Miller . . ." Rust gives a single nod.

The big man jerks his chin toward the car. "I warned him to get it out of here."

Rust's lips twist in thought, his eyes shifting between Miller and me. Deciding something. "If Luke says it's fine, then it is. I trust him not to do something stupid." Slapping my shoulder, he adds, "Smart investment. These are the kinds of things I want to see."

Finally. Rust's praise doesn't get thrown around often. I don't miss the grumble of annoyance from Miller. Rust chooses to ignore it, instead turning his attention to the white Audi RS 5 turning into the lot.

"That's an awfully new car to bring here," he muses.

"Probably still under warranty," I add. Why would someone bring a brand-new Audi here and not straight to their dealer? There's one not ten miles away.

The car rolls to a stop and a pair of pink heels appears from the open door.

"Never seen her before," Miller mutters as a young brunette

climbs out. I wonder if she even knows she has a warranty. Miller takes two steps toward her, but Rust's words stall him. "Luke, why don't you find out what she needs."

I smile. There's a rule around here—Miller is the only one who talks to the new customers.

Until now.

"Gladly," I say, heading toward her.

Chapter 4

...

CLARA

I swear, these oversized sunglasses were created for undercover cops.

I watch my target stride toward me, a smug grin on his face. He doesn't have the first clue who I am. I hide the pleasure of knowing that behind a friendly smile.

Whatever they were discussing—something to do with that shiny Corvette, by the way they were hovering over it—must have been resolved, because Rust Markov heads toward his Cayenne with a light bounce in his step. I do my best not to watch him, afraid that anyone will see my disdain for the man radiating.

Just as clearly as I can see the burly shop manager's hatred for Luke. If looks could murder, he would have stabbed Luke ten times over with the glare he's shooting at his back right now.

And I get the impression that Luke couldn't care less.

"Welcome." Luke's bright blue eyes do a quick scan of my black dress pants and low-cut sheer blouse. I fight the urge to cross my arms over my chest, knowing that he can see the lace bra beneath. It's not something I'd normally ever wear, but three of the women he brought home were wearing something similar.

His attention quickly shifts to the Audi, his hand sliding over the roof. "Beautiful."

"I like it." As I suspected, he doesn't seem to recognize me from last week's drink-spill incident at The Cellar.

He dips his head to scan the inside. "Leather interior . . . nav system . . ."

Well, I was right about one thing. Luke Boone loves a nice car. Apparently too much for my purposes. "Would you like some time alone with it?"

He dips his head to the side, giving me another eyeful of that confident smirk. It stills my heart for just a beat. I'm not used to targets looking like this. "How can I help you today?"

"I think something's wrong with my clutch." I *know* something's wrong with my clutch. I know because Warner had one of his guys mess around with it yesterday, giving me an excuse to bring my car here.

Luke watches me closely. "And what did your dealership say?"

Shit. Warner is sitting in the surveillance van right now, listening to the wire, high-fiving the others because he just made fifty bucks off me. When I filled him in on my idea, he argued that it wouldn't work. That someone who drives a brand-new eighty-thousand-dollar car doesn't go anywhere besides their dealer for repairs. I bet him that these guys wouldn't even mention a warranty, that they'd be only too eager to take full advantage of a twenty-something-year-old female.

I guess I was wrong.

I make a point of folding my arms over my chest and assuming an angry stance. "The dealer said that I need my clutch adjusted and that isn't covered after six thousand, two hundred fifty miles."

"And you have . . ."

"Sixty-five hundred miles."

Luke's face twists up. "And they wouldn't let that slide?"

"Nope. So I told them to go to hell and I left."

"Dicks." He shakes his head slowly. "Well, we can take a look at it. It's not covered under warranty here, either, but we'll make sure we're at a discount to what they'd charge you."

"I was told your guys know Audis." From the reports, Rust's Garage has a reputation for being top notch for any and all cars. I wonder if it's because their mechanics are top notch at dismantling any and all cars. Not that we have proof of that.

"My guys know every car. Keys?" He holds a hand out, his

clean, filed fingernails hiding the fact that he has a mechanic's license and was working in the garage up until a few months ago.

"Great." I let my gaze drift over to the bay windows. Beyond them, hoists sit loaded with vehicles. "You guys look busy in there, so I assume it's going to take a while. I can get a ride home from you, right?" I make a point of lifting my sunglasses and locking gazes with him, letting him take in one of my finer qualities, the light blue eyes I inherited from my mom. *Please let this plan keep falling into place . . .*

Twisting his lips in pensive thought that I can't guess at, he first glances over to where the other manager hovers, and then at the large, dark-skinned mechanic who strolls out from an open door. "Zeke!" The man saunters over. "Can you do me a favor and get this car in to check the clutch? Sounds like it just needs an adjustment."

"Miller said—"

"And I'm saying let's not make this lovely lady wait all day for such a minor fix."

He salutes. "Right, Nur— I mean, boss."

"Thanks, man." Luke turns back to me, smiling wide. "Go and grab some lunch. It'll be ready for you when you get back."

He's charming, I'll give him that. And, *dammit,* there goes that plan. I struggle to hide my disappointment. It's one thing when you meet someone and wonder if he's attracted to you. I *need* to attract him, if this is going to work. And, now that I've met him face-to-face, sober, the clock is ticking.

Placing a hand on my hip, I plaster on a playful smile of my own. "And where are you going to take me for lunch?" *Ugh.* I hate girls like this.

He cocks his head to regard me for a moment with curiosity. I wouldn't call it annoyance. It shouldn't be. From everything we've seen, Luke Boone is attracted to women who expect to be kept on ivory pedestals.

He holds out a hand. "Luke."

A small sigh of relief escapes me as I take it, letting my polished fingertips graze his palm as I accept his hand. "Rain."

"Rain," he repeats. "I was actually just about to head out to lunch. Wanna join me?" He glances down at my shoes. "It's a few blocks. Can you handle that?"

Should I play agreeable? Or does he expect complaints? Should Rain Martines expect to be driven? It sounds like such a silly thing to consider, and yet some guys are attracted to bitches and I need him to be attracted to me. There's a fine balance between playing the role I'm supposed to play and being myself, to avoid any bipolar personality changes.

While I spend a few seconds grappling internally with exactly how high maintenance I need to be, Luke begins walking out of the lot. So I grab my purse from the driver's seat and hurry after him, doing my best to avoid the cracks in the sidewalk.

A quick peripheral scan down the side street finds the navy-blue van, where my cover guys watch behind tinted glass. It's both comforting and irritating to have people spying on my every move, listening to my every word. But that's a nonnegotiable part of being undercover. They'll always be within arm's reach when I'm with my target, just in case something should go wrong.

Luke falls into step beside me as we make our way along the sidewalk, his hands hanging from his pockets. "So? What's your story? Where are you from? I'm guessing you're not a Portland native."

"Why do you say that?"

His eyes flicker over my clothes. "You don't look like the type of girl who owns hippie skirts and combat boots."

"And you don't look like the kind of guy who wears skinny jeans and penny loafers."

That's what Portland's all about, after all. Hippies and hipsters. If you don't fit into one of those two groups, then you're stepping off the pages of a Columbia sportswear catalogue. People like Luke and me—or at least Rain—are a minority around here.

"Fair enough. So?"

I'm more than ready for these kinds of questions, though.

"Originally from out east, but I decided to try the West Coast for a while."

"Why not farther south? California's nice."

Valid question. One I can answer with a half-truth. "Would you believe me if I told you I love the rain?"

"You moved across country because you *love* the rain." I glance up in time to see his smirk. "I guess you're well suited to your name then."

That's the reason I chose it, I want to say. As part of the cover design, I get to pick my own name—something that would roll off my tongue, that I'd answer to without hesitation. Normally you go with your real first name and your mother's maiden name, but I've used it so many times, I chose my mother's nickname for me instead. She used to call me Rainy when I was little, because I'd be the kid who threw on her pink rubber boots and grabbed her umbrella at the first sign of showers. I'd spend hours outside, fascinated by the feel of cold drops splattering against my skin as I stomped and splashed through mud, much to my mother's bafflement. It made the hot bath and curling up under a blanket afterward all the more rewarding.

"So you just decided to move across country and try something new because you love the rain, *Rain*."

When he says it like that, in that tone, it sounds suspicious. "And because I needed to get away." I pause before adding, "Bad breakup." *That confirms that I'm single. Check.*

"Hmm," he murmurs, sounding like he understands a bad breakup. I wonder if he does. "How are you liking Portland so far?"

"It's nice, but . . . you know, new city. It's hard to meet people and make friends." Another seed planted. That's the guise. Become "friends" with the target. It's a deceptive term because we all know what that truly means. I'm supposed to entice Luke, make him want more but not give him too much. Therein lies the ethical dilemma that so many undercover operations face. Where do I draw the line? If my target places his hand on my knee, do I let him?

Or do I push his hand away? If he tries to kiss me, how do I refuse him? How many times can I refuse him before he loses interest? How far do I let it go? There was no official rulebook of "can" and "can't" handed to me when I took this case on.

I have only my gut.

And my moral integrity.

And the respect of my colleagues.

And concern for my safety.

And the reputability of my testimony for this case.

"I'm sure it won't take you long. Portland's full of nice people."

"Well, I met one today, didn't I?" It's as close to me handing him a "will you be my friend?" card as I can get without sounding desperate.

Luke merely grins.

We continue on, my heels clicking against the concrete as we weave our way around other pedestrians, most of them also on a lunch-hour mission. A woman ahead juggles a bag of groceries in one hand and a toddler throwing a proper fit in the other, who's kicking and screaming until she loses her grip on her bag and some of its contents spill out the top. People all around pass by without any offers of help. There's no way they missed the debacle.

But Luke doesn't. I watch him as he crouches down and quickly gathers up the contents before offering them to the frazzled mom, who smooths her stray hair behind her ears while blushing. "Stop giving your mom a hard time," he scolds the little boy with a smile, who in turn sticks a thumb in his mouth and tucks himself next to the woman's thigh.

And the entire time, I'm watching Luke from three steps behind, expecting to see his hand slide into her pocket or purse and make off with her valuables. Because that's what thieves do—seize opportunities. Not until he glances over his shoulder at me and then keeps walking do I accept that he was just being a nice guy.

The surveillance reports never mentioned him being a nice guy.

My thoughts are distracted by the scent of deep-fried food as we round the corner. A strip of colorful sheds extends out in front of us, each one covered in menu boards.

"Have you ever eaten here?" Another downward glance tells me he believes what I've led him to believe so far—that I'm too good to patronize a garden shack turned burrito buffet.

"No, can't say I have." The truth is, I've been to these Portland food carts three times already, mainly because *he* comes here for lunch almost every day. More of my failed attempts to grab his attention. Once, I had my camera out and trained on him, waiting for him to look up, to notice me so I'd have an excuse to apologize and assure him that it was just for my latest photography class project—capturing candids of attractive men. Another time, I even sat at the table next to him. But his attention was on his sandwich and his phone screen. He didn't notice me.

Luke juts his chin toward a burgundy cart with a black wrought-iron sign. "They make really good meatball sandwiches."

"No they don't," I throw out before I can stop myself.

Luke's brow spikes.

"No one makes better meatball sandwiches than a born-and-bred Italian. That guy in there, with his Carrot-Top orange hair and freckles, is *not* Italian. So, by default, the sandwiches must be terrible."

An amused smirk settles on his face. "That's a little prejudicial, don't you think?"

"Maybe."

His eyes drift to my mouth, which I've painted with bright red lipstick today. "Let me guess . . ."

"Yes, I'm one of those snobby Italians when it comes to cooking, I'll own that."

"Well, it's the best meatball sandwich I've ever had, but I guess I don't know any better, do I?"

"You do, now that I've told you." I catch the amused twinkle in his eye and I jump for my chance. "Tell you what . . . I'll try this *spectacular* sandwich of yours, and then I'll make you a real one, and you can tell me that you're wrong and I'm right. Deal?" I hold my breath, waiting for him to respond to what some might consider the offer of a date. If he blows me off now, it will be as much of a "thanks, but I'm not interested" as I've ever seen. And I can't tell which way he'll swing. He's harder to read than most. The degenerates I usually deal with wear their intentions like aprons, eyeballing my body, taking any chance to touch me that they can. But Luke isn't a degenerate. At least, not like any I've dealt with before—a twenty-four-year-old guy with perfect nails and a gold Rolex watch and tailored pants, who works behind a desk at a car garage and eats lunches prepared at food carts.

Without a word, he strolls up to the counter, sliding his wallet from his back pocket. Despite all that he is and why I'm here, my eyes can't help lingering on that pleasing view for just a moment, before I force my gaze up.

I mentally pat myself on the back as my self-confidence begins to creep back in. I have his attention and now I'm playing him like he's my own personal marionette. This is what I'm good at.

"I hope you're good with Diet Coke," Luke offers, handing me the foil-wrapped sandwich and my drink.

I hate diet soda. "It'll work. Thanks."

He leads me toward two bar stools at a round-top table. After many failed attempts at garnering his attention, I feel like I've just taken a shot of adrenaline, the thrill of a small victory coursing through my veins.

"Well?" He gestures toward my lunch.

"Don't be offended if I gag," I mutter truthfully, unfolding the wrapper to reveal a mess that I'm liable to slop on this blouse—a blouse that cost more than I'd spend on an entire outfit. The FBI has paid an exorbitant amount of money to make my socialite cover authentic. Right down to the caffè lattes I drink while strolling through the flower markets as I embrace this role. The guys on my crime squad would be pulling aneurisms if they did the math. But that's the FBI for you. Even the embedded listening device in my pendant is custom-designed for this case, the feed bouncing off satellites to reach Warner and my other cover guys. Technology that very few get to tap into. Certainly not an ordinary city cop.

Luke watches me take a bite. While I'll silently admit it's not half-bad—though there's too much salt in the sauce and the meat is a tad dry—I can't give him any excuse to back out of our "date." So I place the sandwich back into its wrapper.

"Don't like it?"

"Were you born without taste buds? Or is it a condition you've come down with?" I tease.

He gives me a lopsided grin; he doesn't seem to care one way or another whether I'm satisfied. I wonder if he's the same with the girls he brings home. And then I push that thought aside, feeling my cheeks heat a little.

I take my time washing the taste out of my mouth with my soda while he starts inhaling his own lunch. The guy must have one heck of an appetite, for the time he spends working out. He always does his grocery shopping on Sunday nights, and that consists of one bag that I watch him unpack through binoculars. He usually eats out or brings home take-out. On the rare occasion that I've seen him in his kitchen, it's been to heat up the contents of a can of Chef Boyardee. A typical twenty-four-year-old bachelor.

My appraisal of him is distracted when he waves to someone behind me. I glance over my shoulder and spot a man in a suit shuffling by, and I'm immediately on edge. It's a natural instinct to assume everyone your target knows is also a criminal and you may be about to witness something illegal.

"Hey, Willie," Luke calls out, wrapping up the other half of his sandwich and thrusting it out.

With a slight frown, I really look at the man—at his gray and wiry beard, at his tattered and stained brown suit, at the '80s-style briefcase clutched tightly within his grip; its seems cracked, the handle broken off.

"Mr. Boone," the man named Willie answers as he accepts the meal with a nod of appreciation, smiling just enough to reveal several missing teeth. "Nice spring day today, isn't it?"

"It is," Luke agrees. "Looking forward to summer."

Muted, sad eyes turn to me. "You take care of him, pretty lady. He's a good man."

I don't even have a chance to answer before he hobbles away. When I look questioningly at Luke, he shrugs, mildly embarrassed. "He comes around on Tuesdays. I usually buy two lunches and give him one." After a pause, he adds, "Reminds me of my grandpa." With a swift movement, he steals the intact sandwich—minus one small bite—sitting in front of me, and begins eating it as if he planned on doing it all along.

My chest swells, just a tiny bit. I shouldn't be surprised by this at all. Even the shadiest of criminals have an ounce of good in them. A soft spot. Luke Boone's soft spot is obviously his grandfather. I make a mental note to get as much information as I can on the man, so I can exploit it.

But I also can't help but look at my sandwich and note that today is Tuesday. I wonder if Luke Boone's the one pulling the marionette strings around here.

■ ■ ■

My car is rolling backward out of the bay door as we approach the garage. A short, stocky mechanic in coveralls yells, "Just like you said, Boone. Small adjustment to the clutch."

"Thanks, Tabbs." To me, he turns and smiles. "See? Told ya."

"Yes, you did." What Luke hasn't told me is whether I'm going to see him again. I trail him into the office. A grouchy Steve Miller sits behind the desk, hammering his meaty fist against a blue stapler. He makes a point of glaring at the clock on the wall. "Didn't think you were coming back."

"I knew you'd miss me too much if I didn't," Luke retorts, stepping around the desk. "You gonna move so I can draw up the invoice?"

"No need. I have it ready here." His tone abruptly switches to something light and airy. "Miss, I pulled most of your information from your ownership papers. If you can just give me your phone number, I'll get this all finished for you in a jiffy."

I recite my new cell phone number and in less than a minute, Miller holds up a printout and thrusts it toward Luke, all pretenses of a man who would use the word "jiffy" gone.

These two don't like each other; that much is obvious. Which means Miller may be a source of information for us down the line. I'll have to flag that to Warner. Until then . . . I fish my credit card out of my wallet and hand it to Luke.

He smirks. "Don't you want to see how much you're being charged first?"

Smooth, Clara. "Of course." I give the invoice the obligatory scan, not really seeing anything, not caring what he's charging me because the Feds are paying. "It's reasonable. Thank you."

My card is processed, and then it's time to leave.

"Let us know if you have any more problems." Luke flashes that wide, charming smile that stalls my feet just a little.

Still no mention of connecting again. In fact, I'd say Luke has gone out of his way to skirt the subject. He's just not interested. That's all there is to it. Or maybe he's waiting for me to bring it up again. But if he's not, then bringing it up will make me look desperate. I'm guessing he doesn't like desperate women.

Luke Boone has me in a tailspin. No target has ever had me second-guessing myself this much, this early. It's just the pressure of the case, I remind myself. "I'm sure I will." I take long, slow steps, ensuring my movements are sleek and appealing, the opposite of my frantic thoughts, and I desperately search for another hook, since nothing I'm casting has caught so far.

"So, when did you say you're cooking dinner for me?"

I fight the urge to groan with relief but I can't keep the smile from exploding across my face. "Whenever you call me." I turn to regard him, to see his smug face—like he knew I was waiting for it all along, like he was toying with me—and nod to the sheet on his desk. "You have my number."

"I do." His eyes twinkle. "I'll call you soon."

Thank fucking God.

I wait until I'm in my car and around the corner before turning off my wire and squealing like a fourteen-year-old who just got asked out to the movies. I dial Warner to debrief, my heart still racing. It's standard protocol to call in after every meeting with my target. Up until now, I've had nothing but failure to report. And, while this may not seem like much . . .

I think I'm finally in.

Chapter 5

...

LUKE

"Screwing the customers . . ." Miller grumbles, pushing the filing cabinet shut with a loud metal bang.

"Only the pretty ones." And she is that. It wasn't until she lifted her sunglasses that she had my undivided attention. Those big, blue eyes up against an olive complexion are striking. I wouldn't have guessed Italian. Mediterranean, definitely.

Exotic, dark-haired, killer body—my type exactly.

"You're going to lose business for the garage."

"Relax. I wasn't the one fishing." And there was definite fishing on her part. For a long while there, I wasn't sure I wanted to take the bait. Everything about her—her upscale style, her expensive car, her cool demeanor—says she's my kind of girl, and therein lies the problem. My kind of girl is good for one thing, and it's not having lunch over at the food carts of Portland. Or conversation, in general.

Give those kinds of girls more and suddenly they become work, and money. Endless streams on both accounts. Rust warned me about them years ago. Thank God I haven't tumbled into any of their traps. Even Priscilla, my fallback lay, who I consider a friend, who knows exactly where we stand in terms of our "relationship" and that I don't have the kind of money she wants—even she will occasionally try her hand at sucking more out of me. A new bracelet, cash for rent, a tank of gas for the BMW that her last sugar daddy handed her . . .

But Rain was cute today, in a feisty way, humoring me by

taking a bite of that sandwich that she was so obviously not going to enjoy. Her nose crinkling up at the sight of it. Her witty little insult. The way she hung back, waiting, hoping for a chance to see me again but not willing to come right out and ask after already being so forward earlier. Girls like Priscilla would have kept pushing. But Rain obviously has some self-respect.

And when she started walking out of the office, I couldn't help myself.

I punch her number into my phone so I can call her after work. If I'm lucky, I'll also have her naked and tangled in my sheets later tonight.

Rust's number flashes across the screen and my stomach tightens. I hope he hasn't had a change of heart about me going behind his back to his auctioneer. If so, I'm about to get my ass handed to me with Miller listening.

"Yeah?"

"You busy?" No anger in Rust's tone.

I glance at the stack of paperwork. "Not really." Miller can do that shit. He likes it.

"Good. Tell Miller you're taking off for the rest of the day. Meet me at Corleone's."

"Corleone's?" My brow spikes. Arguably the nicest restaurant in Portland. A place you don't walk into without a suit and plenty of room on your credit card.

"Yes . . . I think it's time you start meeting some of the people I do *real* business with."

"Is it . . ."

"Just get over here." I hear the smile in his voice.

Finally . . . I bolt out of the office with a grin, stepping over Rain's invoice, which has slipped through my fingertips and now lies on the dirty office floor.

■ ■ ■

If the violin music is supposed to be relaxing . . . it's not. Or maybe it's the pompous company that has me feeling tense.

"Rust speaks highly of you," Andrei says, the glass of brandy resting against his bottom lip, his shrewd gaze scrutinizing me. His harsh accent, his steely demeanor, his cold blue eyes somehow scalding—everything about him—reminds me of Rust's old partner, Viktor Petrova, a successful businessman and by all rights a murderer.

I don't remember Viktor having tattoos on his neck, though. This guy does. A hint of ink stretches out past the collar of his crisp white dress shirt.

I keep my smile muted to match his. "I'm the son he always wanted."

That earns a smirk from him and a chuckle from Rust—because we both know that the last thing Rust has ever wanted is a wife and kids. He's been "dating" the same blond—Ashleigh—for two years now, keeping her around with just enough diamonds and designer gifts in exchange for the occasional home-cooked meal and blow job without any of the commitment. The kind of relationship I should strive for if I want to avoid grief, according to him.

"It's been a while since my last trip to America," Andrei notes, watching the female server set our plates down in front of us. "Service here is as atrocious as usual."

Her hands freeze for just a moment. The beginnings of an apology appear ready to leave her lips when he waves her away with a sneer of disgust.

I catch Rust's eyes. They're unreadable, as always. I can't tell if sitting at this table with this asshole is as uncomfortable for him as it is for me. The service is fine. In fact, it's probably the best damn service I've ever had.

"It will be nice to get home," Andrei adds.

I bite my tongue a second before I ask what brought him here. It's an innocent question—a way to keep the conversation going and distract from the awkwardness I feel—but I know that you don't ask these men any questions. In fact, Rust warned me before we walked into this restaurant that less is more. And not to say anything stupid.

Rust has never needed to come right out and name his Russian mafia ties for me to know that's exactly who his "business associates" are. They're the same type that his father—my grandfather—kept. I've been around these kinds of people all my life. I can't remember exactly when I figured it out but once I did, I've always been equal parts respectful, in awe, and wary of them. There's never been any reason for me to be outright afraid. My grandpa dealt with them, right up until he died of cancer ten years ago. Rust deals with them. While they can be sons of bitches, I've never seen the kind of stuff that the movies make you think when you hear "mafia."

Well, I guess that's not entirely true. But what happened to my friend Jesse's girl wasn't business-related.

"Speaking of sons . . ." Andrei's attention floats to someone behind me.

From my peripherals, a stout guy in a tailored black suit appears and takes the empty seat at our table, muttering a few words in Russian to his father.

Rust leans over and offers his hand, smiling broadly. That's the thing with Uncle Rust; he's a genuinely happy guy unless someone really pisses him off. He always makes people feel welcome. Since he's usually surrounded by dour faces—including these two, right now—people naturally gravitate toward him. "Good to see you, Vlad. This is my nephew, Luke. He'll start managing some things for me soon."

I don't know what "things" he's referring to but I simply nod and stick my hand out. Vlad accepts it and I see that his knuckles are marked by tattoos. More tattoos disappear beneath his cuff and creep out from his shirt collar. I'm guessing the one on his neck matches his father's. A branding, of some sort. From what I've read, all of their markings mean something significant.

Vlad's facial scruff hides his age, but I'm guessing he isn't much older than me. I get the sense that he's had a much different life than I have, though.

He wordlessly analyzes me for a moment with those same

cold blue eyes as his father, and then turns and begins relaying something in Russian to Andrei. I'm pretty sure I hear, "Another dumb American to deal with."

I school my expression. Maybe they don't care, or maybe they assume I don't understand them. But I learned Russian from my grandfather. I might have earned some respect from these guys with that skill, but Rust warned me years ago that it was a good secret to keep under wraps.

I spend the rest of the meal listening quietly while Andrei, Rust, and Vlad pepper casual conversation with hidden messages in both English and Russian. Comments about a contact in Israel. A shipyard, and a person who is willing to help them "cut through the red tape." Someone on the receiving dock that had to be "managed." Nothing that a clueless person would pick up on or become suspicious of.

All things that are making me insanely curious.

Even dressed in an Armani suit and sipping a cognac, I feel like a ten-year-old boy at a table of grown men talking about the stock market right now. Rust should have filled me in before bringing me here. There's no doubt, by the way both Andrei and Vlad watch me, that this meeting is as much about me being weighed and measured as it is a business planning discussion. I can't be sure what they'll decide. Perhaps that I need to be drawn and quartered.

After another hour of witnessing Andrei and Vlad be dicks to the wait staff and toss cutting remarks about Americans as a whole, Vlad drops a pile of cash—just like Viktor, these guys are all about no paper trails—to cover the bill, and Andrei turns to me. "So your uncle says that you're ambitious."

There's no room for doubt. "I am."

A crooked smile touches Andrei's lips, one that doesn't reach his eyes. "I hope so."

Chapter 6

...

CLARA

Bill taps candid shots of two stony faces up on the whiteboard with his chopsticks, the container of pad thai resting in his palm likely cold by now. "Andrei Bragin. Flew in from St. Petersburg two days ago. Staying with his son, Vladimir, who has permanent resident status after marrying his American-born trophy wife. They've just finished eating dinner at Corleone's with 12 and 24. Our informant couldn't catch anything useful. They'd switch to Russian every time she was near, unless they were insulting her." He adds with a smirk, "Douchebag sent his lamb back. Twice."

Everyone shares a collective groan, drowning out the buzz of the sports reel on the TV. It's rather ingenious, having a female C.I. planted in a restaurant that many high-level criminals would frequent. She's worked there for years, feeding random bits of intel whenever the Feds tap her on the shoulder.

My eyes drift over the four guys sitting around the board in our makeshift "safe house"—Bill's garage in a Portland suburb, and by all rights a man cave. I'm used to these kinds of nights back home, getting together with my coworkers for a few drinks and to blow off some steam where we can all be ourselves.

But aside from Warner, I don't know these guys very well. I feel like I need to. They're part of my cover team. The guys who take care of me—who gather information and relay it to Sinclair and me, who make sure my condo's gas and maintenance bills are paid and that I get anything I ask for to help with my case. The guys who are going to keep me alive through all of this.

We don't meet like this often. In fact, we don't ever meet like this, relying mainly on phone calls. But now it seems that our case has found its legs and is about to take off running. We need to be ready to chase after it.

"What do we have on them?" Franky, the lanky agent sitting in the corner of the faded beige couch, asks. He has ten years of experience on a federal auto theft task force, so he's a great addition to the group.

"They're definitely part of an organized family based out of St. Petersburg, with reach across most of the country. Both clean on the books. Off the books, there are some weak links to smuggling gold and diamonds. Nothing solid so far. Vlad's got a mansion out in Burlingame. Nice area."

That name rings a bell from the case files. "Didn't 24's business partner live out that way?" I ask Bill. From what Warner's told me, Bill's been doing cover detail on this case since the beginning.

"Viktor Petrova, yeah. He and Vlad used to golf together occasionally," Bill confirms, his bottle of beer finding a nice resting place on his small, protruding belly. He's got the typical over-forty cop body—still strong but padded.

Viktor. Another Russian mobster. Another dead end in the Fed's attempts to break into this car theft ring, based on what I've read. Originally they tried getting in through Viktor's trophy wife, planting an agent in college to befriend her. Then the wife disappeared without a trace, without a missing person's report, without *anything*. A C.I. confirmed the official rumor was that she abandoned Viktor in the middle of the night. They assume she's in a shallow grave somewhere, but they had no reason to show up at the doorstep asking questions. It was too risky to the investigation. Nothing's been done to locate her since. It's another detail of this case nagging at me.

Then the Feds moved on to a female C.I. who had some pillow-talk connections to Viktor. It may have worked, but he went and got himself killed.

"Alright. While Clara's working over 12, let's see what we can dig up on these guys. Franky, Rix—" Warner looks at the fourth guy, an agent well into his thirties who could pass for a twenty-year-old common thief with his baby face and a pair of worn jeans hanging from his hips. "Keep your ear to the street; look for any orders dropping." Though this network of thieves and wheelmen normally sticks to their group of criminals, Rix has managed to form a friendship with one of them. After four months of throwing darts and drinking beers with the lowlife at a local dive, dropping hints here and there, the guy finally asked Rix to help him on a job. Rix—having all the knowledge and car theft gadgets, courtesy of the FBI—has impressed him with how proficient he is. Now Rix is just biding his time until word spreads and the fence seeks him out for orders. Asking for them would speed things up, but then Rix would get slapped with an entrapment claim and all his intel would be inadmissible. It's a slow process, but it's another way into this ring, and we have to try every possible angle if we're going to get anywhere.

"Bill, where are we at with the safe house? We can't meet here anymore," Warner asks.

"I'm working on getting the one a few blocks down from Bertelli's assigned to us. Looks good for next month as long as the judge extends the warrant."

Warner nods, throwing a wink my way. "Hear that? Go get us something useful."

Chapter 7

...

LUKE

Rust always seems to have one eye on his surroundings. On faces, on storefronts, on nearby cars. I noticed it years ago. It's just something I'm used to. But now, on this hour-long drive along the Oregon/Washington border toward Astoria, I would think his head is on a swivel, the way he scouts his rearview mirror and every side road we pass.

"Expecting someone?" I ask.

"Always. And you need to, too."

I nod, afraid to ask stupid questions that'll make him second-guess his decision to pick me up from the garage, telling Miller that I won't be back today. Rust likes grand reveals. He was always the one insisting on surprise birthday parties and blindfolds when opening presents.

He turns his big black pickup truck—one of six vehicles Rust owns—down a lane gouged by tire tracks and riddled with small stones. Wide enough, though. It looks like it belongs to a logging company, leading into nothing but dense brush and trees. I spot the first camera a half-mile in, strapped to a tree. "Motion-activated," Rust confirms. Another half-mile in, a simple metal gate blocks further passage. More hidden cameras are trained on it. Rust climbs out to unchain the padlock with a key tucked within a lock box. "Don't ever come out here without telling me first," he warns.

I exhale as softly as possible, trying to shake the edginess building in my chest. Wondering what I'm about to see. It can't be too bad, though. This is Rust! The guy who used to let me play hooky from school so we could head up to Seattle for a Mariners game.

When I don't think we can drive any deeper into the woods, we round a bend and a double-story, forest-green metal shed appears, tucked among the trees. It dwarfs the small, dilapidated A-frame cabin set some fifty feet away, overlooking a small lake beyond. Solar panels cover the entire south side of the roof. I'm guessing we're not on any grid out here.

"Who owns this place?"

"Your grandfather. He bought it five years ago."

"The one who died *ten* years ago?" Can't be the other one, seeing as we have no ties to that side of the family. They never approved of my parents getting married in the first place.

Rust smiles. "He has a far reach."

I slide out the passenger side, whistling as my feet hit the ground. Nothing but snapping branches responds. "I never took him for a fan of the outdoors."

Rust throws an arm over my shoulder and tugs me toward the shed, laughing. We're the same height and our builds aren't too far off. Even though Rust has twenty-two years on me, he takes good care of himself, hitting the gym almost as much as I do. That's the freedom of not being tied down with a wife and kids, he has always said. You get to live by your own schedule. You don't have to answer to anyone.

Sometimes I wonder if he's lonely. I wonder, if I follow his advice and keep it shallow, if *I'll* get lonely. I do know that when I'm around Jesse and Alex, seeing my best friend with a woman who he trusts unequivocally, envy spikes inside of me.

Rust unfastens the heavy-duty padlocks, before throwing his body into the metal door. It creaks open, and I sidle in behind him as he hits a switch and fluorescent panels flicker on, illuminating the junkyard within. That's what it looks like at first glance, at least. But closer examination reveals that there's order to the chaos. Closest to me is an assortment of air bags—an expensive car part if you ever have to replace yours. Farther down, catalytic converters sit stacked. Those things are about a grand each. Next to them are the rims of dozens of cars, with what are probably their matching tires beside them. All around the perimeter of this huge, window-less shed are the remains of cars—everything from factory stereo systems to batteries to quarter panels. And in the center of it all sits an array of used vehicles—Hondas, Toyotas, a shiny red Ford truck, even an '87 Oldsmobile Cutlass.

"There's a quarter-million sitting in here." Rust watches my face, looking for a reaction.

An odd sense of satisfaction swirls through me, because I've guessed right all along. I just didn't guess big enough. "So you're chopping cars."

He smiles. "Chopping cars. Selling cars. Andrei has good con-nections across seas . . ." I follow him as he strolls over to pat the hood of the Cutlass. "The foreign market is booming. Eventually you'll be handling exchanges with Vlad. But I want you eased into this, so we'll start you off small. You're going to be handling two of my fences."

Handling fences? What the fuck does that even mean? I'll be Googling that shit the second he turns around. "I'm guessing these cars aren't coming from RTM . . ."

"No, Luke." A wry smile. "They're not."

My uncle is dealing in stolen cars, and not just a few here and there. Stealing isn't a completely shocking revelation for me, given that I grew up with a grandfather who stored cases of name-brand booze under our dining room table and electronics under the basement staircase. All things that "fell off the truck." That's what he'd always tell me when I asked, followed by a wink and a warning to keep it to myself. I'm surprised he didn't use a place like this to store all of that stuff. Then again, Rust always called Deda a "dabbler" and not a true businessman. I'd eavesdropped on enough conversations to know that Rust was pushing him to think bigger scale, to turn the thousands he earned into more. But Deda was happy doling out meat in his friend's downtown Portland butcher shop. It was a good balance, he said.

Rust would argue that he has a good balance too, and his balance earns a helluva lot more.

My mind starts going into business mode, weighing how much Rust nets through the garage and RTM each year—which I'm guessing tips the low seven-figure range—compared to what this must bring in. "What's the risk?" It must be worth it.

He shrugs. Not in an "I don't know" way, but in a "who cares" way. "The cops are too busy chasing the idiots. The gangbangers, the joyriders. I've protected myself. There are enough layers that very few people could ever point out my involvement. The ones who do have as much to lose as I do. I've been running this ring for five years now and I know who to trust and who not to. Besides . . ." His face screws up with doubt. "I have police along the entire Western seaboard in my pocket. They'd tip me off if I were under investigation."

An eerie silence fills the space as I absorb his words, his confidence.

"Isn't it dangerous, though, having all this sitting here? It wouldn't be hard for the cops to figure out who's behind this if they see Deda's name on it."

A finger comes up. Rust's "listen carefully" index finger. "It's not about what they know. It's about what they can prove."

"Deda used to say that."

"And he was right." Another long pause. "So?" His arms stretch out in front him. "You wanted in. Now you're in."

I always knew I'd be doing something involving cars. This? Well, this is definitely . . . something.

My gaze lands on a big Ford F-250. It's probably three years old, but it's been well taken care of. Whoever owns the fuzzy dice hanging from the rearview mirror must have been pissed when their truck disappeared.

The phone in Rust's pocket—I've seen him with various cell

phones enough times to recognize that they're burners—breaks into the eerie silence. No more than five words are exchanged before he hangs up, the air around him humming with energy. He's excited. "You ready?"

I simply nod.

"Good. Because you're about to get your hands dirty."

■ ■ ■

The sky past the mountain range to the east is just beginning to lighten as we pass by the security gates at Pier Two in Astoria, slowing down to take in the black smoke rising from the pillars on the cargo ship about to set sail. The gray-haired guard glances up but then lets his attention fall back to the book he's reading. I wonder how much he's getting out of this.

"His name is Edgar. He has two daughters—one already in college, one about to start," Rust explains as if reading my mind. "Tuition is forty thousand a year. He's willing to look the other way for help in paying that. That's the trick in this business . . . everyone has a weak spot. You just have to find it, and then buy them their peace of mind."

Continuing on down the street about five minutes, Rust pulls into the driveway of a quiet motel, his wheels crackling over the loose gravel of the parking lot. The few spotlights actually working highlight a rental office with blue plastic waiting chairs and those faux wood panel walls that my grandparents had in their basement. Not welcoming, but then again, I'm guessing the people who stay here don't care about being welcomed. Rust continues down to the far end, where the lights are all burned out. I can't even make out the numbers marking the mud-colored doors.

"Tell me we're not going in there," I mutter.

Rust chuckles. "My prissy little nephew." He parks alongside a black SUV. The window rolls down, and Vlad appears, another day's worth of scruff aging him even more. His gaze flickers from Rust to me—my clothes black and ruined from a night of pulling apart cars—and back to Rust. In Russian, he spits out, "Why are you here?" I'm beginning to think he can't manage sounding civil, ever.

Rust answers in English. "Why not?"

Another gaze my way, this one harder. Still in Russian, "Do my father and I need to be worried about the future of our business relationship?"

Rust's lips curl back in a smile that is anything but pleasant. "I trust Luke more than I trust *anyone* else," he says, his voice calm, easygoing . . . full of warning.

I clench my fist and force out a gritted smile, imagining punching that fuck square in the jaw. I'd probably end up knocked out, but at least I'd get the first hit in.

Another second's pause and then Vlad mutters, as if bored, "The crates are all loaded. The ship will be leaving within the hour."

"And the second delivery?"

"*Da.*" Yes. "Already in the containers."

"Good. What's going on over on the other side?"

"Your business is only on this side." He does a cursory glance around before heaving a black duffel bag through the window to Rust.

The weight of it as Rust drops it onto my lap is surprising. He watches me, nodding toward it.

I pull the zipper. My heart rate spikes as stacks of cash appear.

"How do we look?" Rust asks.

How the hell should I know! I want to snap, frustrated with always being in the dark. But I'm guessing that it's not about what I know; it's about how I present myself, with Vlad sitting right here, watching. If they've ripped us off, we're going to find out as soon as we count. And now isn't the time to count.

"We look about right," I answer, keeping my voice as even and steely as possible.

"Talk to you later." Rust pulls away without waiting for a response. It isn't until we're back on the main road that the Russian slurs escape from under his breath. "Count that. Make sure that shithead didn't undercut us."

"You think he would?"

"Vlad was just a pimply-faced little brat when I first met him. Now, look at him. Thinks he's something special."

I guess that means yes. "How much should there—"

"Four hundred K."

I let out a low whistle as I begin thumbing through a stack of hundreds and thousands.

"Andrei gets paid by the buyers on the other side, but Vlad gives me my half up front because my work is done. It's *supposed* to be a partnership. But they've started shortchanging me, claiming an extra five percent for all the red tape. I think they're pocketing it." He scowls. "They'd never try that if Viktor was still in the picture."

"How well do you know Andrei?"

"He's been our overseas contact for five years, but he was always Viktor's contact. A month after Viktor died, he reached out to me, wanting to keep it going."

"Why didn't he go to Albert? Aren't they all—" Do I say it out loud? I settle on, "connected?" Albert was Viktor's right-hand man, after all. The two of them were attached at the hip. I never sat at a table with Viktor without Albert sitting right next to him.

I sense Rust studying me out of the corner of my eye. Did he really think I hadn't figured out who they are? "Because this is *my* network. I've spent years building a smart organization. Besides, Albert has his skills, but dealing on the American side . . . this is what *I'm* good at. All those guys do is bully and threaten, and that doesn't build solid business relationships."

"But Vlad doesn't trust me." It's not a question.

"Vlad doesn't trust anyone." He sighs. "I just surprised him tonight, is all. Normally it's Miller and Vlad who exchange the money."

My jaw drops. "Are you kidding me? Miller's part of this?"

"Has been for a long time. But you don't know that. Understand? Not a word about it."

"You actually trust him to deal with a guy like Vlad? And

with *this* kind of money?" I can't see Miller and Vlad working well together.

"Yeah, I do, actually, and you're going to have to bury whatever beef the two of you have and learn to trust him too. You'll be swapping roles with him when you're ready, taking over the payday with Vlad while Miller handles your fences. Vlad tends to push Miller around, and I know you'll be better at handling him."

I don't see how that's possible, but I don't argue. "How's Miller feel about this?"

"Miller doesn't have a choice if he wants to keep making money." He pauses, as if deciding whether to say more. "He's got some personal stuff going on. Stuff that motivates him to stick with me and make money. You want Miller on your side, trust me. He's a good worker and he's loyal. Another good lesson—keep your doors open but hidden. You never know when someone's going to prove useful in the future."

Jeez. How many hidden doors does Rust have open? Are Tabbs and Zeke in on this? "Look, if I'm in, then you need to fill me in on a few more things. I can't look like the idiot that Vlad already thinks I am."

Rust slouches back into his seat, like he's getting ready for a long drive and a long talk. "What is it that you feel you need to know?"

Where do I start? "How does this all work? How do you get the orders? Who do you phone? What do they do with the cars?"

"Not happy without the whole picture." Rust grins. "Your deda always said that about me, growing up."

Question after question begins spinning into my head. I struggle to ground myself on one, to begin. "What was the other delivery you were talking about?"

"A few Lexuses. An Audi. Some Escalades."

"Chopped?"

Rust's snort fills the interior. "A forty-thousand-dollar Lexus here will go for almost two hundred thousand dollars in Thailand. And Andrei can sell a sixty-thousand-dollar Mercedes in Moscow like *that*." He snaps his fingers.

"Where are you getting them from?"

"Different places."

"Like . . ."

"Insurance scams. People want out of their leases or they need a chunk of cash. But they're mostly coming from parking lots and driveways. I put in an order for what I need and down the chain it goes. Depends on the car, really. Something high-end requires some skill and specialty tools. Old-model Civics and whatnot . . . any eighteen-year-old kid will lift it from a driveway for five hundred cash."

"And the people . . ."

"Bought theft insurance if they're smart," he fires back quickly, seemingly unbothered by the same moral twinge pricking the very back of my conscience. "And if they're driving an eighty-thousand-dollar car and not locking it up in a garage, they're just asking for it."

I guess . . .

"It's the insurance companies that end up paying in the end, and fuck them. I deal with them all the time at RTM. They're already robbing the general public."

But insurance companies just pass on the increased costs to the consumers, so, no matter what, it's the people who pay. I'm sure he must see the hole in his logic. I don't say that out loud, though. There's something more important that I need to clear up. "They're not hurting people to get these cars, are they?" I can't believe that Rust would have anything to do with that, but . . . I pulled a car seat and stuffed bear out of the extended cab in that red Ford truck back at the storage warehouse. It's been bothering me ever since.

I've turned a blind eye to things in the past—like when I knew that Rust's business partner, Viktor Petrova, was abusing his wife—and, though I couldn't do much about it, I've never quite forgiven myself for not trying.

I vowed that wouldn't happen again.

"No, Luke. Gangbangers hijack, and my fences know never to deal with gangs. They're a bunch of crack dealers and meth heads.

They all get picked up eventually and, when they do, they'll squeal to anyone who will listen. There's no need for any of that. There are plenty of ways to get a car without hurting anyone. We're car thieves, not murderers." Rust's mouth sets in a deep frown. "So? You wanted in. Now you've seen it all. Have you changed your mind?"

It's the first time that he's bothered to ask. It's the first time we've stopped to talk in the hours since the others arrived. A man I didn't recognize arrived at the storage spot first, with two younger guys I'd also never seen before, none of whom bothered to introduce themselves. We had every last car torn apart in hours, me following their expert lead. Albert pulled up in a transport truck an hour later. Four goons built for lifting tires hopped out the back and began loading parts into empty crates, then used the forklift to fill the truck, chattering in Russian the entire time.

It was after three in the morning when the truck's taillights disappeared into darkness, leaving the storage shed empty except for a small pool of oil and a few loose screws. No one would ever suspect that only hours earlier it was loaded with stolen car parts.

I look down at myself, covered in dirt, my skin wiped but not clean. "Depends. Are you going to make me pull apart cars, or was that just another 'experience'?"

He laughs. "Everyone should experience a good chop session once. But, no, for now you're going to be lining up the orders with my fences, the guys I have ties to closer to the street. Here . . ." One hand on the steering wheel and eyes still on the road, Rust reaches over and grabs four stacks of cash from the bag. Forty grand, by my calculations. He thrusts them against my chest.

"What's this for?"

"Your cut, which will be much bigger next time." He grins. "Put it in your safe at home."

I let the cash fan through my fingers.

So much cash. There's no way I earned this for what I did tonight.

"Oh, and I have a little surprise for you." He reaches into his pockets and hands me a set of keys. Just like the night he handed me the keys to a new condo.

Only, these are car keys, with a logo that I've drooled over for years.

With waves of excitement and nervousness coursing through my body, I sit back and quietly listen as Uncle Rust walks me through the "how" to this entire operation that he, one day, wants me to run with him.

The giant bag of cash pressing down on my thighs is impossible to ignore.

Chapter 8

. . .

CLARA

"You couldn't get me a real dog, could you?"

Warner's deep laugh vibrates through my phone and into my ear. "What do you mean? He barks."

"I wouldn't qualify it as a bark." I eye the pudgy little thing, which is belly-up and rolling in the grass next to the park bench like his back is itchy, oblivious to my severe judgment. I'm not 100 percent sure that he doesn't have fleas. "Seriously, Warner, why wouldn't you let me pick one out myself?"

Warner's laughter only grows. "What would you have preferred?"

"I don't know. A Great Dane or a pit bull, or something more . . . me?"

"But you're not you," he reminds me. "You're Rain Martines. A little princess who lives in her daddy's condo with her lap dog."

"*That* is not a lap dog. His eyes aren't even in the right place." I've spent days Googling pictures, and based on his smashed-up nose and curly tail and ears like satellites, my best guess is an obese pug–Boston terrier cross, with a little bit of swine mixed in for good measure. But I'm no expert.

"He was the smallest one they had and you need a dog, not a puppy. Come on! He's kind of cute, isn't he?"

I roll my eyes. "I'm changing his name. Who names their dog

'Stanley' anyway?" That's what the tag hanging off his collar read, when Animal Control picked him up. "I'll bet he ran away from his owners because they gave him such a stupid name."

"Whatever he did, I'm glad he was there. You needed a small dog for our case. He needed a home. It's a win-win."

"Yeah, until the case is over. And then what happens?"

"You'll be so in love with Stanley by then, you'll take him back to D.C. with you."

The dog's tongue hangs over his severe under-bite as he pants, staring me down with those bulging, round eyes that belong on a gremlin, waiting for me to toss the tennis ball again. *I doubt that.* I let out a reluctant sigh. Stanley is the least of my problems.

I walked out of Rust's Garage over two weeks ago now, full of confidence and feeling in control. But there's been no call from Luke Boone. He's been at his office and out to The Cellar, based on the surveillance team reports. He's even had that bartender over once. But he hasn't picked up the phone and dialed my number. I've played through a dozen scenarios as to why that might be and what the right next step is without creating suspicion or an air of desperation.

Accidental run-in sounded like the right next move, once enough time passed. What better way to do that than on the park trail he runs every day after work with his bulldog? Fellow dog lovers, unite.

So, Warner took a trip to an animal shelter and picked out Stanley.

"If this doesn't work . . ." I toss the ball across the way. Stanley tears after it like it's a steak, struggling for speed on those stubby legs that are too short for his body.

"Who knows what happened. Remember, we lost him for an entire night. Maybe he's distracted by something."

I remember, all right. While the surveillance team can't be on him twenty-four hours a day, they haven't had a hard time tracking him down whenever they check in. So, when they couldn't find him, we were all on high alert. I held a silent vigil by my window, reporting in when he finally stumbled through the door just after seven a.m., his clothes rumpled and stained.

Very unlike him.

"Maybe." Hopefully not too distracted to notice me out here in my second-skin yoga pants and a low-cut V-neck sweater. I huddle against the chill and glance down at my watch—he's late; he should have been out for his run two hours ago—and then back up at the path to see the sleek body in light gray pants and a navy-blue shirt jogging toward me, his bulldog somehow managing to keep up.

A nervous burn ignites in my stomach. It's the one I always get when I'm about to jump into character. This time it's worse, though, because it's coupled with the fear of another failure. "He's coming. Gotta go." I hang up and drop my phone into my pocket.

And wait, continuing my game with Stanley. He fetches well, at least. I hold back, timing my next throw with Luke's proximity, and then toss the tennis ball along the path. As expected, Stanley goes after it like it's his last meal.

He's going to form an adequate obstacle for Luke, forcing him to turn toward me, see me . . . All's going as planned . . .

And then for some reason, Stanley morphs.

Positioning all four paws squarely, he lets out a howl that only a seal caught in a trap would be capable of making. It works, bringing Luke's feet, pounding against the asphalt, to a halt.

A little too obvious, but . . . good job, Stanley, I silently praise him. *You'll get a bone for—*

Stanley charges toward Luke's dog—easily three times the size of him—and lets out a frenzy of high-pitched barks before he lunges, his little mouth seizing the dog's front leg and attacking it like it's a rag doll.

Crap. I leap off the bench and run forward, intent on getting there before Luke's dog decides to retaliate and maims the little mongrel. Luke's doing his part, shoving against Stanley with his leg, attempting to break up the attack. That's when Stanley releases his grip and latches onto Luke's calf.

Luke hollers in pain.

"Bad Stanley!" I yell, grabbing hold of his stocky body. He relents surprisingly easily, allowing me to scoop him up into my arms. Whatever Jekyll-and-Hyde moment he had instantly vanishes, his little sandpaper tongue darting out to scratch my cheek.

As covertly as possible, I scan our surroundings. Even though I didn't drop my safety word, the commotion that the wire picked up was obviously enough to get them running because Bill is casually leaning up against a lamppost some forty yards away, a smoke in hand.

No doubt his gun is hidden inside the folded magazine under his arm.

"Everything's fine, Stanley," I say slowly and clearly, for the surveillance team's benefit. The last thing I need is them blowing the case by charging in here.

"Jesus! You need to keep that thing on a leash!" Luke snaps, checking his dog's leg.

This can't be good for our relationship. "I'm so sorry. I don't know what happened. He's never done that before." Maybe *this* is why Stanley's owners abandoned him.

Luke looks up. And frowns. "Hey . . . Rain, isn't it?"

At least he remembers that much. I feign surprise to match his. "Yeah. And you're . . . Luke, right?"

He sighs, and it's like all the anger lifts from him in that one act. "Yeah." I can't help my eyes from wandering to his damp shirt. It's clinging to every contour of his chest. Trying to attract a guy like this is an easier pill to swallow than, say, a forty-year-old pimp with plated teeth and extreme body odor. Even drenched in sweat, Luke Boone is easy on the eyes.

He smiles, and I find myself doing the same. Genuinely. "I'm sorry about my dog."

"Yeah . . ." His hand pushes through his soaked hair, the ends curling at the nape of his neck. "So, you named your dog *Stanley*?"

"He's adopted." Like that explains everything. There's a long pause, this one awkward. "We should probably get that bite looked at. Let me take you to the hospital. I'll pay the bill." I wonder if the FBI budget covers being sued by the target.

His easygoing demeanor slides back in with a chuckle. "It's just a scratch. But it's good to see how loyal Licks is." Uncapping his water bottle, he gestures at the panting bulldog sitting next to him, which is sounding ready to keel over from exertion. Taking a long chug of his water bottle, he mutters, "Here you go, traitor," and begins pouring the rest into his dog's mouth. It happily laps it up. "So, you're just hanging out at the park on a Friday night?"

"Stanley loves it here." My gaze drifts past the spot where Bill was standing only a moment ago—now empty—and over the line of cherry trees in full bloom, fallen pink and white petals forming a romantic carpet over the surrounding grass. "It's beautiful."

"It is. I run here every day."

I know.

A small, dark red spot is forming through Luke's light gray sweats. Blood. And an opening. I drop to one knee in front of him, Stanley still tucked under my arm, and curl a finger under the hem of his pant leg to lift it, my fingers sliding up his damp skin. Two puncture wounds and a small trail of blood mar an otherwise flawless, muscular leg. It's more than a scratch but he's right—it's not a big deal. The blood has already begun clotting.

"This looks terrible!" I peer up, catching him getting an eyeful down my sweater before his gaze darts to my face, a few degrees warmer. "Let me clean and bandage that leg up for you. At least. I insist," I push, letting a playful smile emerge.

His lips twist into a matching smile. "Well . . . if you insist."

Another wave of adrenaline hits me, and I'm not really sure if this one is driven by success for the case. "I live just over there." I gesture at the high-rise behind us.

His blue eyes drift to my building, and then to the one right next door. His. A flash of something unreadable passes through his eyes. "Nice and close." Eyeing Stanley, he mutters, "What about Cujo?"

"I'll lock him up." Keeping my terminator within my grip— I've found a new respect for the bug-eyed fur-ball now that he's actually earning his way in this case—I turn down the path that leads to the condo buildings.

He gives the leash a light tug to force Licks into an amble. "So how long have you lived here?"

"I moved in three weeks ago." More like six. "My dad owns the condo. He's letting me stay in it for a while."

"Oh yeah? What does your dad do?"

"Buys and sells property." I shrug. "Lots of it." Rain Martines's daddy has made his riches in real estate and land development. In reality, my dad spends his retired time tending to his tomato plants and making prosciutto in the basement.

"I'm surprised I've never run into you at the park before."

"I'm usually here earlier in the day."

"Right. And what do you spend the rest of your day doing?"

I shrug. "I'm taking a photography class. Sometimes I shop, or go to the gym. I'm figuring out life, basically." As opposed to what my real life in D.C. looks like, which is running out the door with my travel mug of coffee and passing out the second my head hits the pillow well after midnight. To be completely honest, this assignment has felt like one long vacation so far.

"Sounds like fun," he muses. By his lax tone, I can't tell what he really thinks. Is this a deterrent? It shouldn't be. Guys like Luke are attracted to money and a life of leisure. That was part of the cover design. "I bought my condo last summer. I love it here. Great area." He plays it off well, but I know that his uncle bought his condo for him. I wonder if he's embarrassed that Rust funds him for pretty much everything and that's why he's not admitting to it, or if he likes to fool girls into thinking he has money. Or maybe he just doesn't care enough to elaborate.

We turn up the path to my condo building, my eyes focused on keeping my steps in line with his unhurried ones, to appear as relaxed. And I begin playing out scenarios inside my head. Scenarios no normal woman trying to pick up a guy would think of.

I doubt he's armed, given he was out jogging and a gun would weigh him down. Plus, I've never seen any guns lying around on coffee tables in his home. Maybe he's got a knife. It would have to be a small one, though, and I can buy some time if he pulls it on me, until the cover team gets here.

I *should* be able to restrain him with some difficulty, if he tries to force himself on me, for the simple fact that he won't expect that I know how to fight back.

I don't read him as that type of guy, though.

I read him as the type of guy who's going to stroll into my condo, make small talk for ten minutes, ask for a tour, and then strip off his clothes in my bedroom, assuming the leg was just an excuse for my invitation all along.

This is where I have to do things that fit into the "gray area," of my job, to keep my cover, and the case, going.

Like, if he tries to kiss me, I may have to kiss him back.

Sneaking a glance at that mouth right now—curled up at the ends in a perpetual, slight smirk, glossy from a fresh drink of water, and surrounded by the beginnings of a five-o'clock shadow to match the caramel-brown hair on his head—I'll admit it would be far from the worst thing I've ever had to do. Nervous flutters begin to tickle my stomach.

And then his phone rings.

All at once, his demeanor changes. His face turns grim, a glimmer of panic flying through it. Taking backward steps away from me, he reaches into his pocket. "Listen, I have to take this call."

No . . . "Go ahead. I can wait."

"Maybe we can connect some other time?" His steps are hurried as he moves away, a low murmur of "hey" touching my ears. He doesn't look back. Not even once.

I fight to keep the frustration from showing on my face as he disappears down the path to his building.

Stanley lets out a tiny playful noise and then licks my cheek.

I give his head a scratch. "You tried, buddy. We all tried."

I don't know what else to do.

■ ■ ■

"Warner said you were in after the last meet," Sinclair's deep, gruff voice fills my ear. Almost an accusation. "What happened?"

I wasn't expecting a phone call from the assistant director tonight.

"I thought I was. I just need more time. I'm getting somewhere but it's going to take more time." Other cover officers get months—sometimes years!—to form relationships before people begin breathing down their backs. Me? Two freaking months! Less, technically, because the first few weeks were for case prep.

"If we don't have something solid to bring back to the judge, he's not going to extend the warrant. He was already being a tight-ass about granting it the first time around."

"12 took that phone call," I blurt out, desperate to get him off my back so I can think.

"You know better than that," he mutters with irritation.

I do know better than that. I silently chastise myself for saying something so stupid to a high-level FBI superior as I head to the window, Stanley nipping at my heels.

"Your cover?"

"Still intact."

"Good. I'll start looking over the agent files. Maybe I can still salvage this case . . ." Sinclair's words fade out as my eyes land on Luke, walking toward the adjoining bathroom in his bedroom. His bare ass in full view.

"Holy . . ." slips out, heat stirring through me as I admire his sculpted back. *He's a criminal, he's a criminal, he's a—*

"What's wrong?"

I feel my cheeks flush. "Sorry, what were you saying?"

"Special Agent Cortez could pass for your sister. You'll introduce the two of them and then step back. She's a bit older but one hell of an experienced undercover. Never failed."

My full attention snaps back to the phone call. Special Agent Cortez? Who the hell is that? And why is Sinclair using words like "fail" and "step back"? My arrest record is great. And screw experience! My competitive streak comes out in full force. "I'm close. Just another few days. If you bring her in now, it may cause more harm than good."

"How's that?"

"He'll pull back altogether, not wanting to cause friction between sisters." I cringe as the words come out of my mouth. Even I don't believe them.

"Oh, come on, Clara . . ."

"Just give me another week or two." I'm borderline pleading now. Not good. This guy's not going to hire an agent who begs.

"The Bureau's dropped a ton of resources into this operation. I'm battling internal department feuds over my strategy. There's no more room for failure, do you understand?"

"Got it. I'm close. I really am." I press "end" just as my forehead hits the wall, a heavy groan escaping me. "I'm not going to fail," I promise myself, peeking across the way again in time to see Luke disappear to the right. I assume, into the shower.

I dial a new number.

"Yup." That's how Warner answers the phone, whether he's working or not.

"Hey, Warner." There's no missing the defeat in my voice. "Any chance you can swing by?" I hate talking candidly when I know that the call is being monitored for evidence. It'll get erased eventually, but you never know who's listening before it does.

"Doubt it. It's going to be a long one." Voices hum in the background. He's got two other undercover cases going right now, and it seems like he works twenty-nine hours a day, dividing his time among them. "Why? I just talked to you. What's going on?"

"Sinclair called me. He's talking about bringing an agent in and having me pull back."

"Shit."

My panic sparks. "Shit? Shit, why? How bad is that? How often does this happen?"

He heaves a sigh and says with reluctance, "I don't know. It happens, sometimes."

"And what happens to the pulled agents?"

"Sometimes they end up on other cases. Sometimes . . . they don't."

A thought strikes me. "What happened to the other undercovers on this case?" The ones who failed.

There's a pause, and I picture him biting his bottom lip like he always does when he's not sure if he should say something. "Pushing paperwork in Nebraska or Utah or something like that, the last I heard."

Perfect. "This is my one shot at the Bureau, isn't it?" When I applied for the D.C. police force, I didn't have my sights on going Fed. Being *any* type of law enforcement—armed with a gun and the power to change a person's life forever—seemed both daunting and thrilling. But it didn't take long before I started to excel at my job and commanding officers took notice. That's when the career questions began. *How high do you want to go?* they'd all ask. The truth is, I didn't join with aspirations to be the next female chief of police, or run entire units. I just wanted to feel like I was making a difference. A year in, I was already making contacts in the various units, bored with street patrol. Major strings were pulled by high-levels and I was transferred into the MCU. I figured I was in the right place. Doing undercover work came surprisingly easy for me, and I had one of the best arrest and conviction records in the group. But still, I soon found that the cases weren't high-profile enough. I scoured the newspapers, reading about big arrests around the country. Those were the ones I wanted to work on. The kind where a bust shuts down terrorist cells, cripples trafficking rings, saves lives. The kind that the Feds typically spearhead.

So I filled out my application to join the FBI, along with about a hundred thousand other people. Without an "in," I doubt I'll ever hear from them.

Sinclair is my in.

"Listen, I don't know what you want me to tell you. Is this case a big deal? Yes. But I can't say you won't have other shots. I also can't say you will. Sinclair can make anything happen if you impress him. If you don't . . . he can be a real dick. Plus, jobs with the FBI are competitive. The ones who make it are there because they do what they need to do."

I feel even worse now than I did five minutes ago. "'kay. Thanks, Warner. 'Night." I hang up, his words cycling in my head.

They do what they need to do.

A snort by my heels reminds me that Stanley is waiting, staring at me, those giant bat ears perked. "Demanding little brat." I crouch down to scratch his belly, my focus drifting across the way, into the fully lit bedroom, while Luke's in the shower. Searching for an answer.

A part of me simply waiting for him to emerge so I can get another view.

"How do I get through to this guy? Huh, Stanley?"

With an excited butt wiggle, he flips over and pushes his snout past the blinds. When his bulging eyes spy Licks across the way, he throws his head back and begins barking frantically.

"Get back!" I grab him by the belly and drag him away from the window, his claws grating against the hardwood floor. "Our target knows you now. He'll know we live here," I scold.

And then I freeze. Suddenly, I know what I need to do.

Deep into the gray area we go, Clara.

Chapter 9

. . .

LUKE

The hot water sliding over my stiff, tired muscles felt good. The soap seeping into the puncture wounds on my leg did not.

I towel off, thinking about Rain and that fucking little mutt. And Licks, for doing absolutely nothing. I swear someone could be stabbing me to death and that fat bastard would just sit there and drool.

I had the perfect "I'm getting laid" card tonight, after her dog bit me. On her knees in front of me, she looked ready to do just about anything to make up for it, stirring my blood and my cock. And then my burner phone had to ring.

And I panicked.

I seem to panic every time that phone has gone off this past week, since Rust handed it to me, along with the numbers of two fences I'll be funneling his requests through.

It ended up being a short conversation, not that I wanted her overhearing any of it. Rodriguez, one of the fences, saying he picked up a brand-new Jeep Cherokee. I said no, we only buy based on orders coming in from Vlad. Otherwise, we'll be collecting cars, and that's too risky. That's one of Rust's rules and it's a sound one.

So far, I just take requests from Rust and pass them on to Rodriguez, and I'm done. Nothing stressful. Sure as hell nothing that seems worth the kind of money Rust has thrown my way.

Nothing I'm going to complain about to him.

But all the same, I wonder if that nervous bubble that bursts inside my stomach every time the burner phone rings will ever go away. If I'll always be on edge, wondering what people know. Wondering if Rodriguez is a guy I can truly trust.

If this is really what I want to be doing with my life.

Rust promised that Rodriguez is trustworthy, that he'll never name me to the street-level fence he uses. That what I'm experiencing is only virgin jitters and I should always be wary, but soon it'll feel like just another business call. With two layers between us and the thieves, we're protected.

I could have turned around and chased Rain down inside her building, after hanging up with Rodriguez, but I make a point of *not* chasing women.

Maybe it all worked out for the best, anyway. She lives *right next door*. Too fucking close. Start up with her and the next thing I know, she's everywhere. With everything going on right now, I need more space, not less. I can't believe I didn't notice her address on her invoice at the garage.

It sucks, though. I kind of like her. She's gorgeous. She seems smart, and surprisingly nice for a girl who's "figuring out life" on her daddy's dime. I find myself already wondering when I'll run into her again as I step out of the bathroom and into my bedroom . . .

My legs lock up with the view of the lean, practically naked female body across the way.

Rain, standing in the middle of her bedroom.

In next to nothing.

I tighten my grip of the towel wrapped around my waist as I step forward. I've rarely noticed the condo in the twin building across from me. From what I remember, the blinds are always drawn. They're not now, though, and Rain's busy filling her dresser drawers with folded clothes, wearing nothing but a black lace bra and G-string. The woman is no stranger to the gym, her curves sharp, her muscles carved. Does she know that we live parallel to each other? That my bedroom looks right into hers?

I stand there and watch. I watch as she tosses her empty laundry basket to the floor. I watch as she picks up a book from her dresser and sets it on her bed. I watch her lift a glass of red wine to her lips. And I feel myself react. I adjust my towel accordingly, unable to peel my eyes from her as she dives into her bed, stretching out on her back, book in one hand, glass of wine in the other, her legs long and sleek and bent, one folded over the other.

Is she doing this for my benefit? Because . . . *damn* . . . it's working. On impulse, I grab my phone and search out her number, remembering that I had programmed it in there.

I hit "call."

She reaches back over her head to her nightstand to pick up her phone. With a quick scan at the screen—my name likely won't show up because it's blocked—she answers. "Hello?"

"Hey. It's Luke." I step closer to the window, waiting for her to turn her head toward me, to spot me standing here. Basically, to admit to me that she knows I'm here. That she's known all along and that she's putting on this show for me.

She doesn't so much as twitch my way.

"How's your leg?" Her voice has a certain huskiness that I don't remember from earlier. One that stirs the blood flow in my body, especially as I continue watching her lying there, unaware of me.

"Fine." It hurts like hell. The little asshole's teeth sunk into muscle. I wouldn't be surprised if I can't run tomorrow. "How's the mutt?"

A throaty laugh escapes, making me smile. "Resting up for his next attack." She places the book facedown on her bed. Her hand trails up and down her thigh with painstakingly slow passes, stalling on the strap of her panties. Her finger curls under it.

Jesus. I'm not sure that I want her to look over and stop. I'm rather enjoying this show. "Should I be on the lookout tomorrow?"

"I'd highly recommend it."

"What are you doing?" *Besides torturing me.*

She lifts up the book, scanning the cover. I'm impressed that she reads actual books. Priscilla has nothing but stacks of fashion magazines and the gossip rags they sell at the supermarket cash registers. "I was going to read a bit, but . . ." Her mouth moves with the yawn in my ear and then she arches her back in a stretch, pushing a nice pair of tits up into the air. "Think I'm calling it a night. I haven't been sleeping well." Swinging her legs over the side of the bed, her back to me, her waist slender and long, her left shoulder blade decorated in swirls of sexy ink . . .

She reaches back and unclasps her bra with one hand, letting it slip off. And I find myself silently pleading for her to turn around.

She stands up and leans over—giving me a fantastic view of her apple-shaped ass—to hit the wall panel. Her bedroom falls into darkness.

I can't keep my groan from escaping.

"Luke? You okay?"

"Uh, yeah . . ." I clear my throat, realizing that I'm probably breathing into the phone like a psychopathic stalker. She could be watching me right now, my bedroom lit up. I glance down at the formed tent, wondering what she'd think of this scene. I'm going to have to deal with that before I head out. She just gave me plenty to use while I do.

I don't like women knowing how much power they really have over me, that they can turn my brain to mush so easily. I'll lose my upper hand that way. So I punch the light switch on the wall, throwing myself into darkness, too. "What are you doing this weekend?"

"Teaching Stanley not to bite people."

I can't help but chuckle.

"And going out with you." There's a smile in her voice.

I smile right along with her, because that's exactly what I wanted her to say. "That's right. You are."

Chapter 10

. . .

CLARA

One of my strengths—and I don't know if it's a cop thing or just a Clara thing—is my peripheral vision. My brother jokes that I have extra sets of eyes hidden beneath my thick mane of hair.

I had my eye on Luke the entire time—when he stopped in the middle of his bedroom like he'd just walked into a wall, probably still dripping, towel wrapped around his lower half, to watch me. When he wandered over, adjusting his towel around himself repeatedly.

When I used my body to entice him.

My phone rang, and it took everything in my power not to look over when his voice filled my ear, knowing he was standing there. He didn't warn me about the view. Didn't mention it. I'm glad, given my phone is tapped. My surveillance team didn't need to overhear *that* conversation. None of them would believe that I forgot to shut my blinds. I'm not supposed to open them to begin with.

I can't believe I just did that. What would Warner say? What's more, I can't believe I don't feel completely vile right now. I should. If I had done that for any of my past targets . . . My gag reflexes kick in just thinking about the last guy I busted—a beady-eyed pimp with greasy hair and a bad habit of spitting through the gap in his front teeth every few minutes. I quickly push those thoughts away and focus on the room across the way, now dark, wondering if Luke can so easily throw on a pair of pants and go out, or if he's dealing with what I just did to him. I feel a burn course through my thighs at the thought, and admit to myself that I wish he hadn't shut the lights off.

Good undercovers do what they have to do.

I think I've finally caught Luke Boone's interest.

■ ■ ■

"You never call!"

"I called you three days ago, Mom." I roll my eyes, dumping sugar into my coffee. Normally I need two cups in my body before I attempt a conversation with her. But when I pulled my personal phone out of the safe and saw that she had already called four times this morning, I panicked. "Don't do that to me. I thought something happened to Dad." At sixty-one years old, my dad has already been admitted to the hospital twice with chest pains and difficulty breathing. Between a diet of pasta, meat, and cheese and being a heavy smoker for forty-five years, the doctors say he's a solid candidate for a heart attack. Fortunately, he quit smoking a few years ago, and my mom has managed to add one salad a day to his diet. Still . . . he's far from healthy.

She ignores me and scolds in her thick accent, "Isabella calls Josephine every day. Every single day!"

I busy my mouth with a sip of coffee and let her go on about how her neighbors of twenty years—another Italian family who my parents spend half their time praising their rosebushes and the other half lobbing Italian insults at over the fence—have respectful children who call twice a day and visit every Sunday, and have already given Josephine and her husband, Gus, six grandchildren. And how her heart is broken that neither of her children has had babies yet.

I say nothing because I've heard it countless times before. I've given up on promising my mom that I do want children at some point in my life, but that right now my career is more important. She doesn't get it. Her jobs have never been anything more than a means to put food on the table. It's as if she thinks that she can irritate me into getting pregnant.

"How are things at home? How's dad?"

"Oh, you know. Busy fixing the coffeemaker."

I sigh. "Again?" That basic twelve-cup machine has been "fixed" so many times that it only brews three cups of black tar now. I eye the machine on my counter, one of those high-end computerized gadgets that makes everything from espresso to cappuccino with the flick of a button. I considered buying one for them for Christmas but abandoned that idea when I looked up the price. I love my parents, but I'd need to take out a small loan to afford it. "Just go and buy a new one." He's going to lose an entire day, standing around in his garage, tinkering with it.

"And what, just throw this one away?" I can picture her scowl. "Your generation is all about throwing everything away . . ." I tune her out. Another battle not worth having. This is my life, though. These are Clara's real parents. Not the sleek, sophisticated couple that raised Rain.

"How's the weather at home?" I finally manage to squeeze in as I peek past the blinds to see the moisture from a light drizzle cover the glass. And beyond that, Luke, milling around his living room, his coat in one hand, as if he's collecting things before heading out. I wonder where he's going.

My mother's heavy-accented voice pulls me away from him. "What kind of life is this that you can't even tell me where you are? I don't even know where my own daughter is! What if something happens to you?"

"You'll be the first to know if something happens to me," I assure her.

That sets off yet another rant, too fast for me to catch all the words, this one in Italian. She doesn't usually harp on me this much. I know it's because she loves me and I haven't exactly made her life easy. She started sleeping with a Jesus statue by her bed the day I graduated from police college.

Luckily there's a knock on the door. "I've got to go now,

Mom," I interrupt, checking the peephole to see Warner standing on the other side. "It's my boss. I'll call you in a few days." I hang up before I get any more grief. It can be exhausting, talking to that woman. Someday she's going to realize that I'm no longer that little girl who splashes around in puddles in her rubber boots and that I don't make my choices based on her approval. Then maybe we'll have a normal conversation.

"I could kiss you right now." I step back to let Warner in.

"Because of my swarthy accent or because of this?" He drops a paper bag on the counter.

I stick my nose in, inhaling the fresh scent of a buttery choc-olate scone. "Definitely this." Warner learned of my weakness for baked sweets early on. Now he swings by the little shop at the corner anytime he's stopping by my place in the morning. Which is more than I'd ever expect from a handler. Aside from regular check-ins after meets and surveillance from my cover team when-ever I'm with my target, I don't usually see or talk to them. I guess the Feds operate differently than your average city police force. Maybe they pay him to come by and check up on me.

"Bill tells me that 12 called last night?"

"Yup."

"And you have a date tonight?" Warner pushes.

"Yup . . ."

His brow spikes. "That turned around quickly."

"Crazy, right?" I lean over and scratch behind Stanley's ear, avoiding Warner's shrewd gaze. Hoping he doesn't notice the dark bags under my eyes from lack of sleep. I tossed and turned, my body wrapped up in sheets, my mind wrapped up in Luke Boone, all kinds of insane late-night thoughts and hopes fluttering through my mind. Specifically, what could happen if we have it all wrong about him. What if he's an innocent in all this?

"What do you think made him finally call?"

"Besides my beauty and charm?" I glance up to see the smirk. "Who knows? He's a criminal. They run hot and cold, you know that. I can't say what's running through his head." That's a believable answer. We've heard it all before. Interrogate a suspect and you'll get all kinds of skewed logic, crazy explanations for why they do what they do. Like, that murdering a father of two so they can make a grand cash off a stolen truck to pay their rent is completely reasonable.

Wanting the conversation to change course, I ask, "Will you be on tonight?"

"No. I'm heading to San Francisco for a wedding."

"Oh yeah? Who's getting married?"

"My girlfriend's sister."

I stop, mid-chew, unable to hide the shock from my face. "Dude. Girlfriend?" In the time that I've known Warner, he has *never* once mentioned a girlfriend. Then again, he hasn't talked about his personal life at all. If he didn't have such a heavy accent, I wouldn't even know where he was from. "How long has that been going on for?"

He scratches the back of his head and seems uncomfortable. "A year now, I think? I don't know."

"A *year*? Is she on the job?"

"Nope."

"Wow. A year." As much as all the cops I know say they hate dating other cops, dating non-cops—people who will never truly understand why we do what we do—rarely works out. I wonder if it's different for FBI agents. Doubt it. "Why didn't you ever say anything?"

He simply shrugs and then turns on my pricey Canon digital camera that sits on the counter and begins flipping through the pictures. "These aren't bad."

I guess that's all I'm getting out of Warner about his personal life. "You sound surprised."

"What's with all the trees?"

"That's my homework assignment for the week." When we were working on the cover details, I warned them that I couldn't just sit in this condo all day every day. Not only would that look suspicious for a young, wealthy woman; I'd literally go insane. I couldn't get a steady cover job because it would restrict my schedule, so we all agreed that I should tie up some of my time with hobbies that I can easily walk away from. I've always wanted to take a photography class, so two evenings per week, I head down to a camera store to congregate with my "class"—a small group of eight beginners plus an instructor—and learn all about lighting and filters and angles.

"Your homework assignment is trees?"

"Not just trees. 'Trees in different light,'" I mimic my teacher, an eccentric little Asian man with a Mohawk who reminds me of Richard Simmons, minus the spandex jumpers.

"Sounds thrilling." His dry tone tells me he doesn't think so. He sets the camera down on the counter. "Keep out of trouble tonight. You hear?"

"Don't worry. I don't think 12's the kind of guy to put a bullet in a girl's head on their first date."

"Not what I'm worried about," Warner mutters. "Just be ready to tell him anything you have to, to make him back off."

"What, like that he has to wait for my gonorrhea to clear up?" That only works on pimps wanting to sample the goods before they put a girl to work for them. Any other guy will turn and run.

"Just watch yourself, okay?" Warner's eyes skate down over my body. Not in a leery way. In a way I'm used to, being around male cops all day long. I can't fault them. They see it daily—the pimps beating their girls, the husbands killing their wives, the rapists doing unspeakable things to women who dare to go for a run through a wooded area alone. Yes, I'm trained to defend myself, but few women can fight off a two-hundred-pound man with a temper. If Warner's read my case files—which, knowing Warner, he has—he knows that I've been to the ER on five separate occasions. That the three-inch scar across my forearm is courtesy of a gangbanger's knife; that the slight bump on my nose is where a crack whore head-butted me while resisting arrest. It's natural for his kind to want to protect and, whether I like it or not, right now he's seeing a five-foot-five twenty-six-year-old woman standing in front of him, not a trained undercover officer who's quick on her feet and can talk herself out of most situations.

I could get offended, chew him out for treating me like a weak woman, but I know his concern comes from a good place, so I simply smile and nod. And gesture at my baggy gray sweats and ratty Kid Rock T-shirt, a very "Clara at home" ensemble. "I'll go dressed like this. That'll turn him off, right?"

Warner frowns with mock seriousness. "Oh yeah." He grabs my hand and examines my nails, half of my red polish already picked off. "And keep biting these, too. He won't touch you with a ten-foot pole." I've been going for manicures every week to keep up appearances, only to ruin them within a day. I'm just not used to this level of grooming. When I'm playing a hooker, I throw on some press-ons; when I'm a crack whore, the shorter and dirtier and more jagged my nails are, the better. This prissy, put-together image is so much work. I hardly ever wear heels as Clara, and now I have ten pretty pairs lined up in the closet. Dresses are normally reserved for Christmas dinner and weddings, and they all reach my knee. Yet, as Rain, I have a dozen to choose from, all of them selected for one single purpose—to ensnare Luke Boone.

Reaching for the door to the condo, he says, "I'm heading for the airport now. I'll be landing just after two if you—" His words cut off abruptly.

When I glance over, curious, I find Warner standing in front of an open door, face-to-face with my target.

My stomach lurches as Luke's eyes roll over Warner, caught speechless for a moment. As am I. *What is he doing here?*

Warner's skills kick in quickly enough, asking in a dry, almost irritated voice, "Can I help you?"

"Uh, yeah . . ." Luke hangs a thumb off his pocket in a casual way, his gaze darting over to land on me. "I'm here to see Rain."

"Rain? There's *some guy* at the door to see you," Warner calls over his shoulder, playing dumb.

I take easy, slow steps, keeping my face calm as I scramble to come up with a story. This is one of my strengths—lying—and yet right now I'm drawing a blank. We said tonight, didn't we? Why is Luke here now? How'd he get in? And how risky is this that he's meeting my handler? Do I introduce them? Who should Warner be to me? A friend? An ex-boyfriend?

"Hey, Luke," is all I come up with.

Nails hitting hardwood sound behind me. Stanley, jumping off the couch and scrambling for leverage as he scampers toward the door, his curly tail like a screw as it wags. He climbs Luke's legs with his front paws, like a dog missing his owner would.

Luke chuckles and reaches down to scratch his head. "Better greeting than yesterday."

"I guess it's not you that he has a problem with," I murmur, trying for a relaxed tone.

There's another awkward moment, and then Warner sticks his hand out. "Hi, I'm Jack. Rain's brother."

Brother! Good call.

"Luke. I live in the building next door."

I have to pause for a moment as the two of them shake hands. Warner, a guy in a faded Boston Red Sox T-shirt, pretending to be my brother when he's the FBI agent who wants to lock Luke in a small, windowless room and pressure him until he cracks. Luke, in a fitted black golf shirt, pretending to be just a regular neighborhood rich guy, when he's the criminal that the FBI is betting their entire case on.

If this weren't a risky situation, I might laugh.

Was Luke listening at the door? He very well might have been, to figure out if he had the right condo. How much would he have overheard? I quietly play back my conversation with Warner, trying to remember exactly what words were used.

I'm guessing all those same thoughts are going through Warner's head. That's why he's not budging. I need him gone, before Luke decides his surprise visit was a bad idea and hightails it out of here.

"You'd better go, Jack, or you'll miss your plane."

Warner's back stiffens, his entire body unnaturally still. He's weighing his options. If I'm not in danger, then this is a blip but no big deal. If Luke did in fact overhear our conversation, puts two and two together, and something happens to me . . .

But Luke—standing there with his arms now crossed over his chest, that self-assured smirk sitting on his lips—doesn't look like a guy who just figured out that he's under investigation.

Finally, deciding something, Warner stands aside, gesturing for Luke to enter. "Like I said, I'll be landing just after two, okay?" Warner makes a point of tapping his chest as soon as Luke has walked past him. *Get the wire on*, he's saying.

"Yeah, *okay*. And you'll call Dad for me?"

Dad. A.k.a. my surveillance team. They're going to have to scramble to get into place.

"That's the plan."

Warner leaves, and I'm alone with my target in my living room, his eyes casually scanning everything. "Give me a sec?" I don't wait for Luke's answer, heading for my bedroom. I throw on a pair of tight jeans and a fitted sweater—enough to appeal to him—some makeup, and then fasten the necklace and switch on the wire. Everything that could be considered incriminating is locked up in the safe, so I don't rush too much.

Except for my camera, I suddenly realize. It has a candid picture of him that I took one day at the food carts.

Shit.

Panic seizes me. I struggle not to run out of my bedroom, and sigh with relief when I find Luke holding a tennis ball in the air, teasing a now-frantic Stanley, his profile lean and muscular. "He's not so bad." He laughs. "He'll do just about anything for this ball, won't he?"

He'll do what he needs to do. Just like me.

"So . . . this is a surprise."

Luke finally relents, tossing the ball right into Stanley's waiting mouth. "I like surprising people."

"How did you know which condo was mine?"

As soon as I ask the question, I remember that I shouldn't

have. His gaze rolls down, over my chest, my waist, my thighs, and back up. He must be thinking about last night. He's obviously impressed, given he's here now. Maybe a little too much. If he mentions anything about my blinds being opened, Warner's going to know what I did. I don't want him to know.

I reach up, ready to cover my necklace and muffle Luke's answer. "The invoice at the garage. I called Miller and he gave your address to me."

I know that's a big, fat lie. The two-minute read I got off Miller tells me he would tell Luke to fuck off if he called for that.

"You looked pretty shocked when your brother opened the door. I got the impression he wasn't too happy to see a guy there."

"Jack can be a cranky asshole sometimes." That was for Warner's benefit, when he listens to this recording. Then I add, "You know how it is . . . protective brother." Ironically enough, I don't really know how it is. Or at least, I didn't. My brother never stepped into that role until much later in life, when he got his shit together. I didn't need it by then. Before that, he didn't have much time for a kid sister. He was too busy getting mixed up in the wrong crowd, getting arrested for dealing pot. I was only six when our dad kicked him out.

"Yeah, I get it. I have a younger sister."

I know he does. Ana Boone. Twenty-one. Blond hair and blue eyes, looks like a Russian porcelain doll. Drives a Maxima, supplied by her uncle. Enrolled in an esthetician's program.

"You guys don't look at all alike," he muses.

"I know. I'm much prettier."

He smirks. "I take it you didn't grow up together?"

I feel the frown zag cross my forehead. Why is he assuming that? My mind, still in an odd state of slow motion, scrambles to . . . *Right*, Warner's accent. "No, we didn't. He's actually my stepbrother. Related through marriage." We'll need to tweak my official cover story to keep track of these changes. I was supposed to be an only child.

Luke begins nodding to himself, as if that makes sense. "Is he out here on business?"

He's asking way too many questions. This isn't good. A good undercover profile is simple. Not completely boring, but it doesn't spark questions or thoughts or curiosity from the target.

"He lives in Portland now. Thought he'd swing by on his way out of town to check up on me. He brought me scones." I lift the bag for further proof. Needing the subject to change, I ask, "What brings you to my doorstep at . . ." I pick up my phone, " . . . ten a.m.?"

Luke doesn't answer right away, instead simply staring at my face. Like he's deciding what he wants to say. A boyish smile finally curls his lips. "You owe me a meatball sandwich. I've come to collect."

It's so playful, so flirtatious, so genuine, that I can't keep the grin away. "You couldn't wait until tonight?"

"Nope." He pats his stomach. "I'm starving."

"And what if I'm not free?" I fold my arms over my chest, deciding how "hard to get" I should play with my target. With each passing minute, I'm more comfortable with this situation; less inclined to believe that he heard anything at the door, and more on the path that he's simply hoping to put in enough time during the day to get laid tonight.

He grabs Stanley's leash from the bench by the door. "But you are. Come on. Let's go."

I ball my hands into fists, hiding my chipped polish. I guess I'm not getting my nails painted again before tonight's date. Or a blow-out. I've *never* just walked into a salon and asked for someone to blow-dry my hair, unless I was there for a cut and color already. It seems absolutely ludicrous to pay someone fifty dollars when I can do it myself, for free. At least, that's what I told myself before I had it done for this cover.

I've been going twice a week, since.

"And where exactly are you leading me?" That's for the team's benefit. How long will it take to get them in place? Do I go with him? Or should I send him away for an hour, until I get the go-ahead?

"Well . . . I'm assuming you don't have what you need in your fridge." He strolls over to look inside my refrigerator. The cartons of leftover Chinese food and Warner's beer answer for me. "So?" He flashes me a chemically whitened smile, one that I'm betting works well to get him what—and who—he wants.

As if in answer, my phone beeps with an incoming text.

Dad's ready. Go.

I guess that answers that.

"It's your favorite kind of weather outside, too. If you'd open the blinds, you'd know." He hits the button on the wall and the blinds revolve to allow dim daylight into one side of the living room. "That's my condo over there. I live right across from you."

"Seriously?" I plaster on my best mock-surprise face and then focus on sticking my feet into my Hunter rain boots, trying to play it off. "Talk about a small world. That's crazy."

I catch his secretive smile as he passes by me and I follow him out, locking my door behind me. I watch my target's sleek movements and rigid muscles as he moves ahead of me, Stanley trotting beside him. A thrill courses through my limbs. By my turn of luck in this case, I tell myself. Definitely not because of Luke Boone.

■ ■ ■

I've been a cop for over four years now, two of those undercover. I'm used to back alleyways and seedy motel rooms as meet spots for my cases. Pockmarked targets named Jorge and Bruce, who bathe in cheap drugstore cologne and think complimenting a woman's breasts should prompt her to take her shirt off. I'm used to walking through the front door of my small apartment after a day of work and climbing into a long, hot shower, happy that I'm only pretending, that my life's road hasn't led me to such a sad, sordid reality.

Now I'm standing in front of an adorable meat shop in downtown Portland with a gorgeous target to my left, admitting to myself that I've felt nervous flutters like this only once before . . . when I was seventeen and going on a first date with the high school quarterback.

Shaking the stupid out of me, I ask, "What do we do with Stanley? He doesn't take well to being tied to a post." I'm just guessing, seeing as I've known the dog for all of three days. But the last thing I need is him going Jekyll and Hyde again and attacking an unsuspecting passerby.

In answer, Luke scoops up the chubby dog, tucking him under his arm, as if he weighs nothing at all. "No worries. I know the owner, Dmitri. He won't care."

Dmitri. Sounds Russian.

I remember a case that the Washington MCU was overseeing a couple of years back, involving Ukrainian mobsters. They ran a butcher shop in Columbia Heights. It's probably just a coincidence. "Kozlov's Butcher Shop," I read the sign out loud, assuming Bill or one of the other guys on my detail right now will make note. I haven't seen them tailing us. Not that I would. They'd never risk being made by getting close enough to be spotted, not like in the movies, where they make surveillance teams look like complete tools. "I haven't been in here yet."

"I've been coming here since I could barely walk. My grandpa used to work here. He and Dmitri were best friends."

Right. Luke's grandfather. Oskar Markov. Warner gave me the rundown. Luke, his sister, and their mom moved in with Oskar and his wife, Vera, after Luke's father took off. They all lived together until Oskar's death from lung cancer ten years ago, two years after his wife's. Both heavy smokers. Somehow Luke didn't get the message, because he still lights up. I wonder if that has more to do with addiction or the simple fact that Rust still smokes too.

I trail Luke in, inhaling the garlic-permeated aroma. It's obviously an old store and family-run, based on the dated black-and-white checkered linoleum floor and the rows of black-and-white pictures of men in white butcher's aprons covering one side. The owner isn't too concerned about design, and yet there is something decidedly charming about it. Something you'd expect in an ethnic suburb and not in the trendy downtown core.

Jars of pickled herring and borscht line the front of the meat counter, and a wiry gray-haired man with thick-rimmed glasses stands behind it. "Luka!" he exclaims in his thick Russian accent. "I wouldn't recognize you, if not for your deda's eyes."

This must be Dmitri.

Luke dips his head, his usual confident smirk replaced with a sheepish grin. "I'm sorry, I've been busy."

"How is your mother? And Ana?"

"They're good. They send their love."

"And you're taking good care of them?"

"Of course, Dmitri."

"Good boy." Gray eyes flicker to me, prompting Luke to introduce us.

"Dmitri, this is Rain."

Dmitri nods, first at me, and then at Stanley, whose flat nose is twitching from all the various scents. "Yours?" he asks Luke.

"No."

Another glance at me. "I didn't think so." Dmitri wipes his hands on a rag and then grabs a slice of salami and tosses it right into Stanley's waiting mouth. "What can I get for you today?"

Luke taps on the glass in front of the tray of ground meat. "Half a pound each of the beef, veal, and pork. That's what you said, right?" He looks to me for an answer.

"Yeah. I mean, it depends how hungry you are."

Dmitri slaps double that onto a sheet of butcher's paper, wrapping and taping with the expertise of a man who's been doing this for fifty-plus years. He tosses the packages onto the counter without weighing them, with a casual wave. *No charge*, he's saying. "Tell your uncle to swing by, okay? And soon. Nikolai has some business for him."

Luke shares a look with Dmitri and a spike of adrenaline hits me. I'm guessing Nikolai and Rust Markov aren't going to be discussing meat grades.

"Rain, the market right next door should have whatever else you need." Luke pulls his wallet out and begins rifling through an impressive stack of bills. "I'll meet you there in five."

He wants to talk to Dmitri alone. *Crap.* Is it about this thing with Nikolai, or something else? "I'm not sure how Stanley will take to me leaving," I say, looking for a reason to stay.

"Ah, he'll be fine," Dmitri answers, tossing another piece of meat the dog's way. I have a feeling he's right. I could step outside and get hit by a bus right now and it wouldn't faze my guard dog, his eyes glued to the meat counter.

When I still don't move, they both turn to look at me, and I know that I have no choice. Anything else I say will be too suspicious.

"Sure. Don't worry, I've got it." I shake my head at the cash that Luke holds out.

As soon as I see the slight frown zag across his brow, I realize my error. He's not used to seeing girls turn down money. It seems like such a minor thing, and yet it's the seemingly minor things that can be the most explosive when you're undercover.

I walk out, silently chastising myself.

Chapter 11

...

LUKE

The bell over the door rings as Rain disappears around the corner.

"Beautiful girl," Dmitri notes, his brows arching in question.

"She is."

"That thing," he nods at Stanley, still tucked under my arm, his bulging eyes somehow bigger, "is not."

I chuckle, giving Stanley's head a rub and earning a snort in return. "He's not so bad."

"You always were a sucker for the ugly dogs," he murmurs, moving to wash his hands. "Thank God you don't pick your girls like you pick your dogs." A long pause. "She's not our people, Luka."

She's not Russian. My deda always told me to stick with "our people." Old-school thinking. It obviously made an impact on Rust, given the vast majority of people he does business with are Russian. I suspect the people he does the illegal kind with are *all* Russian.

Me . . . I'm much more open-minded. "I just met her, Dmitri."

"And yet you're shopping for meat with her."

I can't help the chuckle. "It's not a ring." Not that Dmitri ever would have bought his wife an engagement ring.

"Well, hopefully you will be settling down with someone and soon. Don't be like that uncle of yours," he mutters. "Sometimes I wonder about him . . ."

All these guys wonder about Rust. Why doesn't he settle down and get himself a wife? They've all got one—women to parade around, cook their meals, and wash their clothes. Basically, to mother them.

"Tell me what this business with Nikolai is about." No more time for relationship talk. It's Saturday. We have a small window of time before the next customer comes in. Perhaps only minutes.

Dmitri pauses, eyeing me. I'm sure he still sees me as the fat little kid who came in here every Saturday, stealing pieces of ham and shoveling them into my cheeks when no one was looking. "We need to sell a car. Stefan . . ." His voice drifts off with a sigh, the displeasure in his face evident.

I don't have to ask what he means. His grandson, Stefan, a fucking pothead and disgrace to Dmitri's family, must have gone out and stolen a car. He's a few years younger than me. I knew early on that he was short half a deck of cards. He has a penchant for theft and has caused Dmitri and his son, Nikolai, problems in the past.

"Hard to sell?"

A severe gaze levels me. "Likely impossible in America. Too risky. I was hoping Rust could help us get rid of it."

I ask what Rust is going to ask. "You can't just wipe it clean and ditch it?"

"What is that saying? When you are given lemons, you make lemonade." Dmitri shrugs. "I could use some lemonade."

"Right." Too much money to just ditch, I gather. The bell announces an elderly couple and the end to our conversation. "I'll talk to Rust. We'll sort this out for you, I promise."

He places his hand over his chest and then holds it outward. A sign of respect and love. Something my deda and he used to do when saying goodbye. My heart instantly warms.

"Talk to you soon." I wave the package of meat at him on my way out the door.

And walk right into Rain.

Chapter 12

...

CLARA

"You used, like, four ingredients. You're telling me that if I do *exactly* what you just did, my sauce still won't taste as good, just because I'm not Italian?"

I lick the tomato sauce off the spoon before dumping it into the sink. "Sounds about right."

He chuckles from his perch beside my kitchen island, elbows resting on the granite, where he's been sitting since we got back. "That's bullshit."

"Fine. Next week we'll do this at your place. I'll sit on my ass and watch you cook for me." The perfect plant for another "date," if all goes well tonight.

His eyes drop down at the mention of my ass, and I feel my cheeks burn under his scrutiny. Turning the sauce down to a low simmer, I move on to the meat mixture, pushing my sleeves up so I can begin rolling the meatballs into perfectly round spheres. Something I could do in my sleep. It used to be one of my Saturday morning chores, helping my mother make this staple in our household. As odd as it may seem, I've always found this process relaxing.

"I guess I should be paying more attention, then, shouldn't I?" Luke slides off his stool and comes around to stand next to me, rolling a sleeve up over a defined forearm with slow, precise skill. He steps in until he's hovering over me, his chest butting against my shoulder.

I pretend not to notice.

Just like I pretended that his hand on the small of my back as we walked home from the store didn't affect me.

He leans toward the simmering pot. "My buddy's girlfriend's sauce smelled as good as this."

"Is she Italian?"

"Russian."

I groan. "Have you listened to nothing I've said today?"

A playful pinch against my ribs has me jumping. "That market has good stuff, from what I've heard."

"Yeah. I'll definitely be going back." I barely noticed what they carried, too busy scrambling through, grabbing what I needed so I could get back to the butcher shop in time to overhear even a word or two of whatever business Dmitri and Rust have together.

Unfortunately, their discussions must have been quick or cut short, because I plowed right into Luke in my rush, already on his way out the door to meet me. We shared a laugh about it, as I hid my disappointment.

And now he's standing so close, and I'm being hit with mental flashes of last night and the body that's against me now heading toward the shower, and I'm needing to remind myself exactly why I'm here in the first place.

To arrest him, and put everyone he works with in cold, dark cells.

I've been in this deceitful place before. And yet this time, it feels completely new and different.

And somehow, more dangerous.

Minty breath grazes my cheek and I can't help but breathe deep. Can't help but turn into it. Can't help but look up into a set of blue eyes that belong to a guy who helps young mothers pick up groceries and feeds homeless old men and doesn't *look* criminal at all.

"You'll have to wash your hands if you want to touch these balls."

He breaks into a broad grin. Replaying the words in my head, I roll my eyes and laugh. "What are you, twelve?"

His gaze drops to my mouth. "I know this may sound chauvinistic, but I love a woman who can cook."

"Why am I not surprised?" I answer, sensing him shifting in slowly. Preparing to let him have a small kiss before I break away with excuses.

But then his phone begins to ring.

The slightest groan escapes him. "Sorry, I've gotta take this."

I swallow the mixture of relief and disappointment rising inside me. "Go ahead."

He makes his way straight for the small patio off the living room, digging into his pocket.

It's obviously a call he doesn't want overheard. I have to give him some credit—he's already smarter than every other scumbag I've busted. They always assume that their code language is ingenious, that no one will understand that when they're talking about types of birds and numbers and what intersection they saw them flying past, they're talking about illegal stuff. Maybe a normal person wouldn't.

From the corner of my eye, I watch Luke take a seat in the wrought-iron chair and light up a cigarette, phone pressed against his ear. He glances over at me a few times but I keep my head down, rolling the meat. Watching the clock. When the first few balls are sizzling in the pan, I grab one of Warner's beers and a glass.

And I push through the patio door, acting like nothing's wrong with stepping out here to offer my guest a drink.

Wary blue eyes flash up to me. *What are you going to do, Luke? Risk looking suspicious by getting up and walking away? Or just stop talking altogether?*

I hold up the can. He nods. So I take my time, placing the empty glass on the table, cracking the can, and slowly pouring its contents in.

"No . . . No . . . He's a dumb ass . . . We have to help . . . You should give him a call . . ." I feel Luke's eyes on me. I turn and offer him my most innocent, oblivious smile and then keep pouring.

While I and the FBI listen in.

"Yeah . . . Can you call Vlad and see what he can . . ."

Vlad. There's that name.

"Really? . . . I don't know . . . Yeah, I guess so. 'kay . . . Thanks, Rust." He hangs up just as I'm holding out the glass for him. "Sorry, that was work."

"No worries. I just thought you might be thirsty."

He pauses for a long moment to consider me, a curious, unreadable look passing over his face. "I am. Thanks." He stands and, instead of taking the drink, he curls a hand around the back of my neck and pulls my mouth into his.

I'm somehow completely unprepared as the taste of mint and just a hint of tobacco fills my mouth, as his other hand slides around my back, as he slips his tongue against mine with the skill of a guy who is confident that it's okay that he's doing this.

And for about three seconds, it *is* okay. As my heart begins racing and I lose my ability to breathe, it's more than okay. As I feel the heat from his hard body press up against me, warming me, this kiss is all-consuming. But then reality comes crashing down and I remember that this is *not* okay. This is my job, and there are several agents sitting in a car right now, listening to every close-range sound coming from us. All of this is being recorded and entered into evidence for people to listen to at a later date.

As gently as I can, I push against his chest until he breaks free. I clear my throat and offer him a genuinely embarrassed smile, though not for the reasons he assumes. "I'm going to burn the meat if I don't get in there."

"So?" He leans in for another kiss, but this time I manage to turn away and his mouth skates across my cheek.

"Listen, Luke . . . That bad breakup I told you about?" I wasn't planning on using this excuse yet, but I guess I don't have a choice. I just hope it doesn't derail everything so soon. "It was *really* bad. Like . . ." I frown for impact. *Lord, forgive me for this lie.* ". . . *abusive* bad. I'm just not ready for this yet." I give his chest a gentle pat to ease the rejection, wishing for the moment that I didn't know exactly what he looked like under this shirt. "I really like hanging out with you, though."

He steps back, his face softening. "Of course. Okay." He has a knowing look in his eyes. Does my little criminal have a sympathetic side when it comes to a woman being hurt? There weren't any records of domestic violence in his family, which is usually what sparks that kind of reaction. But my gut is telling me he knows a thing or two about battered women.

I laugh, an attempt to lighten the mood. "You're just trying to sabotage my cooking. Give yourself a fighting chance for next week when you have to feed me. Nice try." I head for the kitchen, sensing him trailing behind me.

"Listen, I'm sorry I have to do this but I've got to head out. Some work stuff to deal with."

"At the garage?" I don't even need to fake the disappointment in my voice as I start switching out browned meatballs for raw ones. Is this about that phone call? Or is he pulling his chute in this "friendship" of ours already because I just denied him? If so . . . I'm screwed.

"Something for my uncle."

"That's too bad, but I understand. You can come back and eat after, if you want," I offer, nonchalantly. If it really is work, then I can't scare him away with guilt trips and neediness.

"I'll call you." He gives my elbow a light squeeze and then he's on his way out the door.

No mention of going out tonight.

No attempt at another kiss, to my relief.

So why do I also feel a twinge of disappointment?

I lock my front door and, whispering, "Officer Bertelli, out," I switch the listening device off. My phone rings almost immediately.

"You did great."

I frown and glance at the clock. "You're calling me from San Francisco, right?"

"The others were tied up with their kids. They couldn't make it in time."

I shake my head. I should have known that Warner wouldn't leave. "Dammit, Warner. You should have told me. I would have put him off."

"And risk the case? No way."

He's right. But . . . "Does your girlfriend understand that?"

His heavy sigh fills my ear. "She understands that my job comes first."

I roll my eyes. "Good luck with that."

"Whatever. Drop it." The irritation in his voice swells. "How are you feeling after that? Are you okay?"

I know what he's referring to. "I'm fine. Nothing some Scope won't cure." I chuckle, thinking about a story I once heard about a female undercover who was forced into kissing a meth head she was trying to bust, to prove herself and keep from getting shot. She downed half a bottle of mouthwash afterward, trying to rid herself of the vile taste.

There's no vile taste in my mouth, though. In fact, if I concentrate, I can still feel my target's lips—softer than I expected them to be—on mine, and my heart begins to race again.

"Okay, go relax. I'll be on for tonight."

"If there is a tonight," I mutter.

"Don't worry. You've hooked him. He just may not know it yet."

Chapter 13

...

LUKE

"Come on, you can move it, right?" I ask between puffs of my cigarette. With the noise from the city streets and being on the tenth floor, I'm not worried about being overheard.

Vlad's heavy, irritated exhale fills my ear. "Perhaps, but . . ."

Rust warned me that this would be a challenge before he gave me Vlad's number. I insisted on it, though. Because it's Dmitri, and because I want to try to negotiate with the bastard. I like to think I have a knack for negotiations. And because I have to come to some agreement, seeing as I promised we would.

I also want to prove that I'm not the half-wit he seems to think I am. But I really hate talking to this guy. "Dude, come on. They retail for a quarter-million here. What's the problem?" I don't know what the fuck Stefan was thinking, pinching some rich guy's custom-made Ferrari Spider on a weekend trip to Seattle. Then he shows up at his father, Nikolai's, doorstep with it. According to Rust, who talked to Dmitri after my call with him, Nikolai lost his mind. Gave his son two black eyes for being so stupid. At least the idiot was smart enough to jam the tracking system on it.

"I *may* have a buyer. He was talking about wanting to impress a mistress with a new car, recently."

"She'd be impressed, alright." From what Dmitri told us, the owner had every upgrade imaginable put into it. "Look, you can even take an extra five percent off our cut, for your help."

A vacant chuckle answers. "If I do this, the cost is seventy off the top."

"Are you fucking crazy?" Just like Rust warned.

"No, I'm a businessman and this is business. *Dude*."

"There's no way we can give you that big a cut."

"Then I hope you enjoy giving that car back." I hear the click.

"Asshole." I dial Rust to announce, "Seventy percent off the top."

He curses under his breath.

"Do we take the deal?" Rust gave me an earful earlier. I shouldn't have promised to help Dmitri without talking to him first. Now that I have, we have to follow through.

"Let me see if Andrei's still awake. Sit tight. And keep your night open until you hear back from me."

I fall back into my chair and stare at the layers of purple and pink in the sky. I don't want to cancel plans with Rain, but I also don't want to have to ditch her suddenly if Rust calls, like I did this afternoon. After showing up at her house, dragging her out, and demanding she cook for me. She was oddly understanding about it all.

I glance across the way, wondering what she's doing now. Her lights are on but her blinds are closed, unfortunately. Is she sitting by her phone, waiting for my call? I glance at my watch. Eight o'clock. Early by my standards, but she's probably wondering if we're still on. Girls are like that.

Licks groans from his resting spot by my feet and I smile. He hasn't left my side since I came home, after sniffing me up and down, growling a little. I'm pretty sure he's jealous of Stanley. He's going to have to get used to it, because I'm sure I'm going to see Rain—and her dog—again.

She's been in my head all afternoon. The way she hummed when she stirred her sauce, the way she stepped through puddles in her boots, as if she intentionally wanted to make a splash. The way she listened to me when I talked. Really listened. Not like Priscilla, who just goes through the motions.

The way she looked, stretched out in her bed last night.

She's everything I'm used to and yet she's completely new. She's easygoing and witty. She seems smart. She doesn't talk my ear off about the car or the clothes or the jewelry that she wants, subtle hints for things she'd expect me to buy her. She wouldn't even take my money today. That was a refreshing change. Maybe it's because she has enough of her own. But I've never met a woman yet who has enough money. Well, maybe Alexandria Petrova.

Just the thought of that name makes my stomach clench.

When I kissed Rain today and she pushed me back, asking for space because of her past, my blood turned cold. She's been abused. Not nearly as bad as Alex, if the lack of scars indicates anything. But Rain's words brought me back to that scary night over a year ago, to the days after, waiting to hear from Jesse, hoping for good news. Praying that, when all was said and done, my conscience would be cleared for once dismissing what I knew was happening to her.

As soon as Rain broke away and told me about her ex, she became glass to me. Fragile. To be handled with extreme care. The fact that she was so open to begin with was promising, I guess; I think it means that she trusts me.

I'm just not sure how that works in my life. She said she likes "hanging out" with me, but what does that look like? Like Dmitri said, would Rain "fit"? Especially now? Or is this all a waste of time? I hate wasting my time. Maybe I should just stick with Priscilla. There are no pretenses with her. She grew up in the same environment I did; she knows what this world is all about. Her moral compass is as skewed as mine, maybe more.

My burner phone rings. I answer it in time to hear, "Fucking Russians." It makes me smile, despite everything. "I take it the call to Andrei didn't go well?"

Rust heaves a sigh. "No. It didn't. Andrei's siding with Vlad."

"Shit . . . I don't know what to do, here. Do you want me to tell Dmitri or do you?"

"No, we can't back out now." A long pause. And then he says

very precisely, like the idea's coming to him as he speaks, "I want you to go and meet with Aref Hamidi. He handles our shipping, but he expressed interest in becoming involved in more several years ago. He may be able to help us out."

I frown. "Wouldn't it be better for you to go meet with him?"

"You brought this problem to the table, so I think you should be the one to solve it. It's a good little test."

"Yeah, I guess."

"Why? You don't think you can handle this?"

"No, of course I can." I hope I sound more confident than I feel.

"This will be good for building your rapport with him. It's a simple side deal. I'll let Aref know you're coming to discuss some business. Just don't commit to anything until we talk."

"Where?"

"He's hosting a party at his house tonight. Bring a girl with you. It'll look more social."

My gaze drifts over to Rain's window. "I can do that. You don't think this'll cause problems with Vlad?"

He heaves a sigh that tells me that it probably will. "Like he said, this is business. We have our deal with them, and this is outside of that. Plus, I don't like Vlad thinking he has a monopoly. Just . . . we won't mention it to Vlad."

"Got it." I can see Vlad being the kind of guy to fly off the handle. A lot of screaming and shouting. Possibly some threats.

"How's the car?" I hear the smile in Rust's voice, so I know his mood has already shifted. I've never seen him so happy to give me something as he was that day last week, when I drove off the lot in my brand-new shiny black Porsche 911.

I beam, just thinking about it. "Fucking beautiful. Thank you, Rust."

"Well, you make me proud, son."

I hang up wondering if Rust would still say that had I not willingly gone into business with him. Would he still be treating me like the son he never had, or instead like a nephew he checks in on once in a while? Would my name be on the deed to a million-dollar condo? Would I have all that I have?

Dialing Rain's number, a slight bubble of nerves spikes in me as I wait. It's an odd sensation, not one I'm used to. She answers after the third ring. Lick's head pops up as Stanley's yappy bark comes through in the background, making me chuckle and the tension in my back quickly slide away. "Hey. You're still free tonight, right?"

■ ■ ■

She has a nice walk. It's sleek and steady and catlike.

I watch Rain approach my car, her calf muscles tightening with each step, thanks to those wickedly tall red shoes.

The kind I like.

So is the snug black dress she's wearing. Strapless, showing off the curves of her neck and shoulders. One of my favorite parts of a woman.

The entire package is impressive. I suddenly wonder how the hell I could have been distracted enough not to call her the day I met her. How it took getting attacked by her dog to notice her in the park. How I'm going to give her space, when all I want to do right now is touch her.

"Nice car," she murmurs, her crystal-blue eyes sliding over the frame of my Porsche before she slides into the passenger seat. The back of her dress dips down even lower, highlighting her sleek curves and that sexy tattoo. The one I saw last night, when she was in her underwear . . . My heart rate spikes a little.

"New?" She stares at me, waiting for my answer.

Focus, Luke. "Yeah, I just got it last week." I drove it off the lot and around Portland with a massive hard-on for three hours.

Pulling out of the condo parking lot, I let my hand rest on the gear stick. "You look really . . . nice." I steal a glance at her firm thighs and smooth skin. She definitely takes care of herself.

Glass. She's glass, I remind myself.

She dips her head in that almost embarrassed way, the way

she always does when she catches me looking at her, her fingers fumbling with the gold chain of her necklace. She does that quite a bit, I've noticed. Must be a nervous habit. "So, where are you taking me?"

"A business associate's party."

■ ■ ■

"Easily five million. Maybe more," I murmur, taking in the lit-up mansion that sits by Columbia River, handing my keys to the hired valet. Not surprising that Aref would hire someone to manage all the guests filtering through here. Rust said he likes throwing parties and people like coming to them.

I steal a glance Rain's way to see her eyes widen, skittering over all the details, taking it all in. As if she's not used to places and parties like this. Hard to believe, given what she said her father does, what she drives, who she is. The condo she's living in would have cost her dad a million, easy. I know because that's what the one I'm living in cost Rust and they're about equal. An investment, he said.

People don't invest in million-dollar condos unless they've got serious cash available.

Her large eyes catch me studying her. "It reminds me a lot of a place we owned when I was younger. Who did you say this guy was again?"

"His name's Aref." Simple and vague. I don't have much else to go on, except that I'm looking for a tall Iranian man with a slight scar bisecting his upper lip.

She doesn't push. I like that. Maybe it's because of my time with Rust. Maybe it's because there is so much I can't talk about. In any event, too many questions generally irritate me. Sliding her arm through mine, she purrs, "Let's see what kind of wine Aref's serving tonight."

I lead her to the house and into a sea of unfamiliar faces.

Chapter 14

...

CLARA

Who the hell are these people and how do they live like this?

I mean, I know who they are, in general. And I know exactly how they live like this.

Yet, as I stand in the backyard of this palatial home, over-looking the expansive Columbia River beyond, surrounded by landscaping and wealth the likes of which I can't say I've ever seen on the job before, a wave of envy washes over me. These criminals are living in luxury that I'll never experience. Not on a cop's salary. Not even on an FBI agent's salary. I'll be the one trying to bust assholes like this, while they sip their Champagne and rest their feet on the rails of their yachts. And laugh at poor suckers like me.

Of course, I don't have any intel on who Aref is. Yet. The team will be looking into him as we speak, so I'll get a good rundown from Warner later. I'm assuming Aref is a criminal of some sort and in business with Rust, though.

"You like being near the water as much as you like the rain?" Luke holds out a glass of red wine for me, then nods toward the expansive dock below, where two speedboats and a yacht bigger than some homes sit tied up next to a waterfront guesthouse.

"I do."

"So do I. We'll sneak down there later. After I talk to Aref."

My pessimistic side had already written Luke off for our date so when he called, my excitement was genuine, and hard to hide.

He told me we were going to a party but was vague otherwise. I didn't want to press him with questions.

The way Luke's eyes scan over the crowd now, searching, skimming over the attractive female faces without pause, I'm beginning to think this isn't just a casual party. I shouldn't be surprised. A lot of shady business deals don't happen in the back of tinted-window cars and junkyards, like in fiction. They happen out in the open like this, in casual settings like coffee shops and parties and over a nice bowl of pasta.

There's not much I can do here except sip my wine, catalogue as many guests' faces as I can, in case they become important later on, and hope that Luke has the good grace not to simply abandon me.

I nudge him, pulling his attention back to me easily. "Do you know a lot of the people here?"

"No." A pause. "You said your family used to have a place like this?"

"Kind of," I lie. "My dad decided to sell. I wish he had kept it."

"Well, I'm going to have a place like this one day. You can come visit me." He smiles, his eyes dipping to my mouth for a second.

"You're sitting on millions?" I tease.

"Not yet."

"Oh yeah?" I cock my head in a playful, seductive way. "So how are you going to earn all that?" Maybe Luke is the type to brag about his money-making schemes.

"Luke," a deep voice sounds out beside us, interrupting us. I turn to see a man with smooth skin and jet-black wavy hair watching Luke through large, dark chocolate eyes.

"Aref." Luke offers his hand and the man takes it, a smile stretching the scar that cuts into his top lip.

They size each other up, as if they've never met before.

"Welcome. You're enjoying yourselves, I hope?" He has an indeterminate accent—English mixed with something else, and regal-sounding. I shouldn't be surprised. An international operation like the one Rust Markov runs needs affluent ties from all over the world.

"Great place."

Aref's eyes flicker to mine and I respond with a smile and a nod. "I was just admiring your yacht."

"I'm sure my wife wouldn't mind giving you a tour." He reaches behind him and a tiny woman with long, shiny black hair and matching inky eyes materializes, almost magically. Her boyish figure makes her look more like a twelve-year-old girl than someone's wife, though her beautiful, exotic face has an ageless quality to it. "Elmira, would you please show Luke's friend . . ."

"Rain," Luke confirms.

"Would you please show Rain around the yacht?"

She smiles dutifully. Her expression is not altogether unpleasant, but it's not exactly genuine, either.

Luke leans in to place a chaste kiss on my forehead. "I'll come find you." With that, he turns and follows Aref through the crowd and into the house.

Dammit.

"Shall we?" Elmira's voice is soft and soothing, her gaze appraising me as she floats past, her white dress reminding me of Greek mythology. For a moment, I consider dumping my glass of red wine all over it and ending this tour so I can find Luke, but I quickly dismiss the idea. Aref clearly doesn't want an audience for whatever they're discussing. So I follow her down, refocusing my energy for the time being. Wondering how much Elmira might know.

Maybe she's another door into this network.

That's all these people are to me. Doors that I need to figure out how to push open.

Chapter 15

...

LUKE

"I take it you like boats." I scan the framed photos of various ships that fill an entire wall in Aref's office.

"I do. They're all mine. My family owns a shipping company. We have a cruise line, tankers, freight . . ."

I watch him pour a golden drink from a fancy glass bottle into two fat-bottomed glasses. "So, a lot of ships." There must be twenty pictured. And they're all big enough to cross the ocean, no doubt. Rust said that Aref handled the shipping. I didn't think that meant he *owned* the bloody ships.

He flashes a white-toothed smile. "A lot of ships. And some planes, too. And transport trucks." He hands me the glass. "That's how I met your uncle. We were buying trucks through RTM. I liked him the minute I met him. He's a smart businessman."

"He is." My eyes wander over all the custom woodwork and ornate carvings in this expansive office located at the back of the house—past a locked door and down a long hallway, as if designed specifically to avoid prying ears.

"What do you think?" He nods toward my glass.

"Whisky?" Rust took me to a whisky bar and taught me how to drink it. A skill every refined, intelligent man should have, he said. Of course, the night ended with us trying to carry each other home and painting the sidewalk with our puke.

"A Macallan single-malt *scotch*, actually. Special edition, from 1946."

I take a small sip, swirling the pungent flavor around my mouth. It's like nothing I've ever had before.

"I bought it at an auction several years ago for four hundred and sixty thousand dollars."

I struggle not to choke as I swallow. "You're telling me this right here is, like . . ." I do some quick, rough math in my head. "Twenty grand?"

He smiles, clinks my glass in answer, and takes a small sip of his own. Clearly amused. Either he's trying to impress me or show me up. He's succeeded at both.

Aref isn't just rich.

He's filthy rich.

"So tell me more about this opportunity that Rust mentioned to me."

Leave it to Rust to call it an "opportunity" rather than what it is—us needing help to offload this car. I give Aref the rundown. "So, would you know anyone who may want it?"

He stares at his glass, as if in thought. "Yes, I believe that I do."

"It's as custom as custom gets," I warn him.

I get a dismissive wave in response. "That won't mean anything to a buyer in Dubai. When would you need it moved by?"

"As soon as possible." Apparently, Nikolai is a few blood pressure points away from a heart attack with that thing sitting in his garage. Getting caught in possession of a two-hundred-and-fifty-thousand-dollar car at your own home earns instant jail time and a reputation for being an idiot.

Aref pulls a phone out of his desk drawer and punches in a few numbers. Someone answers and he goes off in a language I can't even begin to understand. So I busy myself with savoring the most expensive drink I'll ever have in my life and listening quietly until he drops the phone into his pocket. "I'll have a definite answer shortly, but it shouldn't be a problem."

He seems so relaxed by the entire thing. "You sound like you've done this before."

He shrugs. "I've helped out a few friends."

"And what's this going to cost us?" I hold my breath, waiting for it. The ridiculous terms he's going to lay out to do this favor for us, his "friends." At least maybe *he'll* be willing to negotiate.

Dark, calculating eyes settle on me. "It was Viktor who approached me years ago to see if I'd be interested in shipping merchandise overseas. Cars weren't part of my . . ." He pauses, searching for words. " . . . portfolio. At first I said no, simply because I didn't trust the man. But then I met Rust and I liked Rust. So I agreed to move their cargo for them. They pay me a rate per car and I make sure all the paperwork is legit and no customs officers stick their noses in where they don't belong. It's easy money.

"But I've figured out that there's a lot more money to be had in selling the cars than simply shipping them. And I also know that Rust has a solid organization." He pauses. "I'm a good person to know, Luke. I have buyers in other parts of the world. We could make each other a lot more money if Rust would ever consider selling directly with me."

"What are you suggesting? That we stop doing business with Vlad and Andrei?" I'd be game for that, to be honest.

But Aref's head is already shaking. "No. You keep that arrangement, and I'll keep taking my minuscule fees for shipping. But why not start something new with me in a new market? I can ship and take care of the buyers on the other side."

At what terms? Is he thinking about a partnership? Going halves? Would he try to rip us off like Vlad and his father do? Impossible to say, and I want to talk to Rust before I make myself sound too interested. For now, we have an immediate problem to handle. "How much is *this* deal going to cost us?" I push.

"I'll tell you what—I'll take a cut for red-tape cost and I'll pass on the rest to you. Just this once, though, as a token of my appreciation for your trust, and a gesture of goodwill. If you are happy, then we can talk about a partnership. Fifty/fifty. You and Rust get me the cars and I'll ship and sell them." He's smooth in the way he speaks. Obviously well educated. Definitely more pleasant to deal with than Vlad. "How does that sound?"

Too easy. But if Rust trusts him . . . "I think we can live with those terms." I wasn't supposed to commit to anything, but how can I not commit to that?

His laughter immediately relaxes me. "You remind me of Rust. I'm very glad we met."

So am I. Walking into Aref's office and asking for help face-to-face has been a million times easier than picking up the phone to call Vlad.

"I need to get back to my guests, and I believe you have a lovely lady to entertain out there." He fills my glass with more scotch. That's forty grand, by my calculations. Enough to buy a decent car. I've drunk a car tonight. "I'll find you as soon as I hear something."

"Thanks, Aref."

The second we part ways, I dial Rust. "I'm waiting, but it looks like it's a go. At cost."

I hold my breath and wait for him to berate me, but he only says, "Good." I can hear him sipping a drink on the other end. Likely vodka. He'd bathe in it if he could.

I drop my voice to a hiss. "Fuck Andrei. Why aren't we working with Aref?"

"Come find me at The Cellar when you have an answer." The phone call ends, leaving my frustration skyrocketing. Why the hell is Rust even talking to those other idiots when Aref's sitting here, practically begging?

Chapter 16

. . .

CLARA

"You have a beautiful home." I follow Elmira down the path, lit by flaming torches that dance under the slightest breeze.

She smiles. "Thank you. It's my favorite out of all of them, I think."

She says it casually, but I roll my eyes nonetheless. Maybe it's her prim Londoner accent that makes her sound so snooty. We sweep around a small pocket of guests and reach the dock. She glances down at my shoes. "You should remove those. I've broken plenty of heels over the years."

Over the years? I'm still wondering if she's even considered a legal adult. Regardless, I listen and slip my shoes off to save myself the embarrassment of hobbling home.

Elmira leads me down, down . . . down . . . past the speed-boats, along an impossibly long dock that branches off, and toward the rope and a sign that reads, "Thank you for not boarding."

"I didn't think you could dock a boat like this privately," I murmur, taking in Elmira's name scrolled across the side.

"Enough money buys *anything*." I follow her as she ducks under the rope. "This is Aref's pride and joy. He bought it for me for my eighteenth birthday."

"Nice birthday gift," I offer, silently thinking back to my eighteenth birthday and the six-pack of woolen socks and case of

Budweiser that my boyfriend at the time bought me. I didn't like beer then, either.

"Aref can be a very generous man." Something about the way she says that sounds off. Before I can ponder too much, she leads me through a narrow door and into an interior painted with money, in the form of shiny chrome and crystals and lacquered mahogany walls. The metallic ceiling reflects, and the sleek lighting illuminates, cocooning us in luxury.

It's easy to forget why I'm here as I trail Elmira down marble winding staircases and narrow hallways, weaving in and out of small but lavish cabins, through three floors of sleek living spaces and open decks of white leather banquettes and wet bars.

"Do you spend a lot of time on here?" I ask as we end the tour on the top floor, a deck next to the captain's command room. Elmira punches a code into a panel and the ceiling begins sliding open, revealing the yacht's sunroof, now blanketed by an expanse of stars over the Columbia River.

"We usually spend our winters in the Cayman Islands. It's quite comfortable on here, even though it's a boat."

"That sounds nice." And unfortunate, given that I'd consider squatting if they happened to store this boat in a marina over the winter.

"We also sail along the Pacific seaboard every summer. It's my favorite thing to do." Elmira disappears behind a small bar to produce a bottle of Champagne and another glass. She delivers one to me without asking, even though I'm still nursing the full glass of wine in my hand. Normally I'd just dump a little at a time while no one was looking, but a place like this must be laced with surveillance video. Getting caught doing that would raise questions I don't want asked. "Have you ever been on a cruise?"

I don't even pretend. "No."

"Well, we are here for a few more months. Perhaps we can host you and Luke one day soon."

I'm sure it's an empty offer, but I say, "I would love that." If I can get enough dirt on Luke to convince a judge that this is worthwhile, maybe I'll be around until then. But that's a long time to string him along, hiding behind the guise of a physically abused woman still learning to trust men again.

"How long have you two been dating?"

I open my mouth to object to the term but catch myself. "Not long."

"He's very handsome. And young, too, right?" she says casually, sipping on her drink, curiosity dancing within her eyes, along with other thoughts that I can't get a handle on.

"Yes, he is." It's all superficial conversation but I need to keep it going, regardless. "What about you and Aref?"

"I met Aref when I was sixteen. He was twenty-nine. Our parents arranged our marriage a year later." When she sees my expression, a soft laugh escapes her lips that makes her suddenly sound much older. "He's handsome, and extremely wealthy, so I didn't object. That's the only element of my culture I accepted, though. Otherwise I've fully embraced the Western way of thinking, much to my parents' dismay." She holds up her glass of Champagne, now almost empty, to prove a point, and fills it up again. A tiny body like hers can't possibly handle that much alcohol, that fast.

"And Aref? Has he embraced the Western way of thinking?"

She shrugs noncommittally. "Mostly."

Mostly. As in Elmira's not 100 percent entirely satisfied, perhaps? It's crazy, the things that people will admit to complete strangers when they're unhappy. And drunk. Elmira's shoulders are slouching just enough to tell me she's probably tipsy by now. Plus, she sounds lonely. Lonely people are all too willing to answer questions.

I'd love to come right out and ask her what she means, but if I bide my time, I'll get it out of her. "What do you do when you're not on this yacht?"

She shrugs. "Organize parties. Volunteer at charities. I keep myself busy. Aref wants me to keep busy. He works a lot and I don't know many people in Portland. Those I do know, I don't particularly like. Mostly Aref's business partners and their wives."

Well, that was brutally honest. "So, what does Aref do?" This is beginning to sound like an interrogation—I'm half-expecting my phone to go off and Warner to hiss at me on the other end of the line—but I can't help myself.

She doesn't seem at all bothered, scanning her perfectly manicured nails. "He owns a transportation company."

"Transportation," I repeat.

"Ships. Lots and lots of *big* ships, that bring all kinds of things overseas, like clothing, packaged foods, cars . . ."

Bingo. Excitement bubbles up inside me as the pieces are clicking together. I'm a cat, cornering its mouse. "Cars?"

"There you are . . ."

Luke's voice is like a long, thin needle jabbing into the bubble. It takes all my effort to keep my face neutral as I glance over to see him climbing the steps. His dazzling smile dulls the disappointment quickly, though.

"If you'll excuse me, I should check on my husband. It was lovely talking to you, Rain." Elmira sweeps past me.

"Thanks for the tour. I hope I see you again." I truly do. Unhappy, young wife with loose lips when she's drinking? Definite informant potential.

She pauses and looks over her shoulder, her eyes narrowing slightly at me. Just enough to create a twinge of insecurity on my part. "Yes. I'd like that."

She's cunning, that one. I had better be careful how I handle her.

"This place is ridiculous, huh?" Luke strolls over to the glass panel dividing us from the control room, pulling a cigarette out of his pack.

"You know, they say smoking will kill you."

"Yeah, I think I've heard that." He holds the lighter to the tip, but then pauses. "Does it bother you?"

"No, not really. I guess I'm used to it. My dad was a heavy smoker for years. He just quit a few years back, after my grandfather died of lung cancer." I worry that it wasn't soon enough.

And I just told my target a personal truth about me. Clara, not Rain. I make a mental note to add that to the file, to keep everything in check. But I've coupled it with a strategic lie about my grandfather, who's still alive and well in Palermo, bless his soul.

"Huh . . . Mine died of lung cancer, too. So did my grandmother." When Luke pauses on me for a long moment, then glances down at the cigarette in his hand, as if reconsidering, I know I've struck the chord I was aiming for. Finding a way to relate to your target is critical. "I've been thinking about quitting." With a sigh, he lights up. "Maybe after things calm down."

"Are things stressful for you right now?" I keep my voice airy, curious.

"Just work shit."

"That big, angry guy in your office the other day?"

Luke dips his head to the side to show me his wide, genuine smile, making my stomach flip. "Who, Miller?"

"Is that the one who hates your guts?"

He laughs, taking another drag. "So, you noticed that."

"Kind of hard not to. Why does he hate you so much?"

"Fuck, who knows. Bitter, I think. I was supposed to take over running the garage. But that's been delayed indefinitely, so his job is safe. I thought he'd stop being such an ass."

"Are you going to do something else instead?"

He doesn't answer at first, just smoking his cigarette and peering out at the water through the windows. For a moment, I'm afraid I've gone too far.

"Nah, I'll stay in the garage. Rust is giving it to me eventually. But my uncle's got me doing some other stuff for him. He has a few businesses on the go."

I love how criminals call their illicit activities "business." Like it's a legitimate thing that they get registered and that they pay taxes to the government for income reported. "That sounds . . . exciting?" I'd love to probe more about these "businesses," but I have to slip in my questions strategically.

"Yeah . . . I don't know yet. It's still new."

"You and your uncle seem like you're close."

"We are. He basically raised me. My dickhead dad skipped out on us when I was six. My mom's always been a bit flaky and unstable, and when he left, she went offside. Depression and all that. She lost her job and we moved in with my grandparents." He pauses, as if thinking back to his childhood. "Rust was only twenty-eight years old. The last thing he wanted to do was inherit two little kids, but he really stepped up. He paid for *everything*. Made sure I was signed up for soccer and baseball—all those kid things that my mom was too out of it to pay attention to and my grandparents really didn't understand. They were old-school Russian, you know? Having clothes on your back and food on the table was all they ever focused on." *Yeah, I understand that.* He butts his cigarette into a fancy ashtray stand and strolls over, my nose catching a mixture of cologne and tobacco as he slides into the seat next to me. Normally I can't stand the smell of cigarette smoke, and yet for some reason it doesn't bother me on Luke. "Rust paid for private school, for college, for my mechanic's program. He used to take me to sports games. Spoiled me rotten, basically. Still does." Luke chuckles. "All my friends were jealous. He paid more attention to me than any of their real dads did to them." His voice has grown husky. "I owe Rust everything that I have."

Enough to not give him up if you're looking at jail time? The soft look in Luke's eyes as he talks about his uncle makes me question whether Sinclair's right with this plan. Would our primary target break if a figurative gun were put to his head?

I'm not so sure.

"You seem to be doing well for yourself," I agree. "I mean, your condo, your car . . ." I don't mean to let my eyes rake over him so overtly as I add, " . . . you."

He smirks, his thigh nudging up against mine as he stretches his legs out. No concern for my personal space. And I don't mind at all. Maybe that Champagne put me over the edge. Holding up the glass of golden liquid that he brought onboard, he says, "This is a twenty-thousand-dollar glass of scotch. My second, tonight."

I know my eyebrows are jumping halfway up my forehead but I can't help myself. More than a third of my annual salary about to go down his throat. I hate rich people. "So, what does a twenty-thousand-dollar glass of scotch taste like?"

He offers it to me and I take it, our fingers grazing, the simple touch causing ripples through my body that I wish I didn't feel. I should say no to hard liquor, but when am I ever going to get a chance like this again? "How am I supposed to drink this?"

Shifting even closer to me, until every part of my right side from my shoulder down to my knees is pressed against that hard body of his, he ropes an arm around my shoulders. "First, you let it coat the glass. Like this." Covering my hand with his, I watch the liquid swirl around the glass, his fingers filling the spaces between mine. "Then you inhale." He holds the glass up to my nose.

"Smells . . . smoky?"

With his free hand, he tucks a strand of my hair back behind my ear in a slow, almost cautious movement, before lifting the glass to my mouth. "Just a tiny sip. Just enough to taste it." His eyes drop to my mouth as I follow instruction.

And struggle not to grimace from the potent flavor.

He grins, not offended in the slightest. "Not a fan?"

"Here." I push it forward until it's fully within his grasp and my hand is free. Because I'm enjoying the feel of him too much. "You drink your twenty-thousand-dollar-a-shot manly scotch and I'll stick with this girly Champagne." I mocked it earlier, but it's actually quite good.

He chuckles, falling back into the couch, his eyes roaming over the interior of the yacht. Another sip. Maybe two glasses of that will loosen his tongue enough for me to pry answers from him. "I think I need to start hanging out with Aref more. I could get used to this."

So could I, under different circumstances. "He seems nice. How do you know him?"

"I just met him tonight, actually. But I already like him." A flash of doubt crosses his face.

"What's wrong?"

"Nothing, just . . ." He frowns, pausing as if to decide something. "I work for my uncle and, as much as I love him, he leaves me in the dark a lot of the time. It can get frustrating."

His gaze wanders off over the water, seemingly deep in thought. I nudge his leg with mine. "You know, I've been told I'm a great listener."

"I can believe it." His hand falls to my back and rests there, the heat from it searing my bare flesh above my dress line. And then he heaves a sigh. "It's nothing. Just . . . Aref wants to play a bigger role in Rust's business and I'm trying to figure out why Rust hasn't agreed. He'd be way better to deal with than the assholes we work with right now."

"Assholes?"

"Yeah." He tips his head back and finishes his drink. "Russian assholes."

"Those crazy Russians," I tease, earning Luke's chuckle and a gentle squeeze of my shoulder.

"Hey, bite your tongue, woman. I'm half-Russian. My mom's side."

Come on, Luke . . . give me more. "Well, I'm sure your uncle must have his reasons." I pause. "What kind of business is it?"

"Cars. We sell cars, all over the world."

"Oh yeah? What kind?"

"All kinds. My uncle co-owns RTM International."

Right . . . the legitimate business. The one I highly doubt Luke is talking about right now. But maybe he is, that little hopeful voice in the back of my mind purrs. Maybe this is all just a terrible misunderstanding. After all, why would a man like Aref, who has so much to lose, get involved with a car theft ring?

Tipping back the rest of his drink, Luke slips his hand into mine and pulls me up with him. "Come on. We should go join the party."

I let him lead me down the path lit by flickering torches

and toward the hordes of privileged guests, secretly enjoying the warmth of his hand within mine.

Telling myself this is all good for the case.

Aref meets us at the bottom of the steps up to their two-tier deck. "So Elmira tells me that you enjoyed the tour of our yacht?"

"I did. And your wife is lovely. Thank her again for me."

"Have Luke buy you one for your birthday," Aref jokes, winking.

"Don't be teaching her any bad habits," Luke answers with a laugh, just as easily.

"About that issue . . ." Aref's dark eyes level Luke's. "It's all good."

"Yeah? Great. Thanks, man." He reaches out to shake the tall man's hand.

"You give me a call tomorrow so we can sort out the details. And talk to your uncle for me, okay?"

"I will," Luke promises somberly. "I'm actually heading out to do that right now." I can see the admiration he has for Aref in his eyes. That's a little concerning. Being too trusting, too open with these kinds of people never works out. Guys like Aref get where they are by being as ruthless as they are generous. Whatever Luke may be involved in, I already know that I don't want to find him lying in a gutter.

Someone taps Aref on the shoulder, and with one last salute toward Luke, he gets pulled into another conversation.

"That worked out well . . ." Luke murmurs, his hand settling on the small of my back. "Let's get out of here."

■ ■ ■

Luke's Porsche coasts into my condo entrance with me silently wishing the Feds had gotten me one of these instead of my Audi.

"Thanks for tonight. It was . . . educational, seeing how the disgustingly rich live."

He laughs, revving the engine, his gaze skating over my legs again. I've caught him doing it several times tonight. I need to keep him interested for another date, so I shift in my seat, casually letting my dress slide up just enough, given he seems to respond well to my body. He squeezes his eyes shut in response and begins whispering, "Glass . . . glass . . . glass," under his breath.

"What?"

Heaving a sigh, he reaches over and pulls my hand to his mouth, muttering, "Nothing," as he kisses the backs of my fingers. A gesture I have always written off as completely cheesy and yet somehow sends tingles straight to my thighs. I think Luke is seriously into me, a realization that may be making me excited for the wrong reasons. "I'll give you a call this week. Maybe we can go out again."

"I'd really like that." Letting go of my hand, he leans back in his seat. I take that as my signal to leave, so I do. I can feel his eyes on my back all the way to the condo doors, before he peels out of the driveway.

And I silently accept that I don't want the night with him to end.

Chapter 17

•••

LUKE

The heavy, rhythmic bass at The Cellar is normally a soothing lullaby to me. But tonight it's irritating.

Or maybe it's Rust that's getting under my skin.

"The way I see it, dealing with Aref makes way more business sense than wasting our time with Andrei and Vlad. He has his very own fucking freight system, for Christ's sake!"

"He's young and he's arrogant."

"*I'm* young and arrogant!" I throw back.

"He comes from an endless supply of old money. It's a dangerous combination. Look . . ." Rust leans forward, and his voice drops. "Aref's already shipping *all* of our product. Who's to say he won't try to use that against us in the future? Hold us hostage, claim a bigger share."

"You mean like Vlad?" I pause. "Aref seems trustworthy."

"Don't be naïve. You can't trust anyone but your blood. You and me, that's all." Rust sighs. "Besides, we can't just break ties with a man like Andrei."

"But they're being dickheads. They're ripping us off. You said so yourself—you don't want Vlad to have a monopoly on our business."

"I was pissed off," he mutters through a drink.

"Okay, fine. So we keep getting bent over a table and fucked by Andrei and Vlad, but let's see what Aref can do. It's a big world. Why not have a partnership with him, too?"

"Going into business with anyone else while I'm in business with Andrei is risky."

"What if I ran it? You keep your deal with Andrei and I deal with Aref."

"There's my entrepreneurial nephew . . ." He pats my back. "Let me give it some thought. No more talk of it now, though." His eyes flicker up, past me, and he smiles. "There she is."

The smell of coconut and flowers hits me. "Hey, Luke."

I look over and up to get an eyeful. "Hey, Pris." She likes showing her tits off in tight shirts and I can't help looking at them, even though I've seen them so many times now, they're no longer especially thrilling.

Her sharp blue eyes float over my empty glass. "How about I drive your car home for you?"

I've had too much to drink. That's always her excuse to get into my bed. I guess she didn't ensnare any sugar daddies tonight and her ego's taken a hit. Her confident stride, her nose in the air—it's all an act. I remember when this all started between us, when I first came here with Rust, started meeting his friends, his associates. Started being treated like a man. She was already working behind the bar. I couldn't keep my eyes off of her. I thought I was such a lucky bastard when she started flirting with me. I heeded Rust's warnings, though—he was right about the kind of girl she is—and kept my heart out of it.

And because I did, we've become odd friends. Or at least, we're comfortable together. We've gotten past the acts we put on for others. Neither of us pretends to be something we're not. We've been playing this game for a year and a half now. Long enough that I can tell her to wipe that bright pink lipstick off her lips before they come anywhere near me tonight.

Am I in the mood for this, though? Rain's smart, crystal-blue eyes flicker through my thoughts. I like her. Her and her cute nose as she scrunched it up, hating the scotch. Her, standing next to me, my arm linked with hers.

Maybe I'm starting to like her too much.

It doesn't matter. I'm not wrapping my brand-new Porsche around a light post and, if anyone can handle a stick, I know Priscilla can.

"Yeah, fine. Let's go."

Chapter 18

. . .

CLARA

"Someone's been drinking my beer."

"Said Papa Bear . . ." Warner's blank stare tells me he doesn't catch my Goldilocks reference. "You know I hate beer."

He gestures at the inside of my fridge. "I had six in here. Now I have five."

"Yeah, I gave one to 12."

He scowls, cracking open a fresh one. "My beer is off-limits."

"If he shows up here, I have to offer him something. Which reminds me . . . I thought this place was out-of-bounds for my cover team now that he knows where I live."

"Are you expecting him at . . ." He glances at the clock. ". . . two a.m.?"

"No, but I'm also not expecting my handler, and yet here we are."

"I'm not your handler, I'm your cranky asshole of a brother, remember?"

"Stepbrother," I correct him, rolling my eyes.

"Whatever. Bill's on him. He's out at the club." Clinking his beer against my glass of wine, he announces, "You did great to-night. Sinclair's happy."

"You talked to him?"

"An hour ago. Gave him a rundown. I think there's enough here to keep the investigation going."

Seriously? "There's really not that much."

Warner shakes his head, laughing. "Do you have any idea whose house you were at tonight?"

"I'm guessing the man who ships their stolen cars."

"Well, look at you, Nancy Drew." He chuckles. "Aref Hamidi. Owner of Hamidi Enterprises, one of the wealthiest international freight companies in the world, going back five generations. Also one of the richest families in Iran."

"Impressive fact gathering."

His brow quirks. "Oh, it gets better. He's married to Elmira Zamani, who has ties to the now dethroned Iranian empire. As in, she's distant royalty. As in, almost a real live fucking princess."

"Wow." I think back to her shiny black hair, her exotic features, her regal movements. Doesn't surprise me one bit.

"Yeah. Between the two of them, they have enough money to feed a third-world country."

That doesn't surprise me either. "And their money's dirty?"

"All money is, somewhere along the line," Warner mutters between sips, his cynical side making its appearance. "But, no, not that we've known of, up until now. The Hamidi family has been on our radar for over two decades, given their connections to that part of the world and their business. Right after 9/11, when we were able to get warrants signed with nothing more than a loud sneeze, we used to jam them up bad with searches. They always took it in stride, and they always turned up clean."

"So, what do you think this means?"

He shrugs. "Maybe Aref isn't following the family's legitimate ways."

"Maybe Luke was there on legit business for RTM," I say, playing devil's advocate. Maybe his uncle isn't dragging him down with him.

"Maybe. All I know is Sinclair was like a fat kid in a candy store tonight. We thought Rust's network was strictly with the Russian mob, but this is even bigger."

"I guess he'll get an extra-big shiny medal then, won't he?" I mutter, wryly.

Warner chuckles, perching on the arm of the couch. "Something like that."

I suck back my wine, considering the expanding landscape of this criminal enterprise. "I don't get it. I mean, you have that much money and yet you go and do something stupid and illegal to get more?" My words are rhetorical, of course. Everyone has their motivations—even criminals. Usually it's pure, blind greed.

A phone starts ringing. I eye Warner's pocket, where I know his personal iPhone is tucked away. "Are you going to answer that? She's called three times."

"Yeah, to yell at me for missing the wedding. I don't need that right now," he mutters through another mouthful of beer. It's going down fast tonight.

I chew the inside of my cheek, deciding if I should say what I want to. "You should call her. Smooth things over."

"Why do you care?"

"Because I need to know that there's hope for a normal relationship in this job."

He laughs, sliding from the arm to fill the couch seat next to me. "Sorry to burst your bubble, but there's no such thing as normal for us. What we see, what we have to do, the way we learn to think . . . no one but us will understand that. You're doomed the second you start having feelings for someone."

"Jeez, Warner! Then why are you even bothering with this poor woman?"

He shrugs, twisting and turning the tag on his beer can for a long moment before dark eyes lift to meet mine. "I guess I'm just biding my time until I find the perfect non-normal partner for me."

He's waiting for another agent, or cop, or . . . the way he's looking at my mouth right now, I'm afraid to think that he's waiting for me. When did *that* happen?

Thank God his work phone pings, ending the awkwardness.

"Okay . . . 12 should be entering his condo any minute," he confirms, reading his screen.

All thoughts of anyone else disappear as I find my way over to my window. "Did he meet with 24?" I ask, peeking past the edge of the blinds.

In time to get a clear shot of that dark-haired bartender stepping into Luke's bedroom before the blinds shut.

It feels like a punch to my stomach.

"Bill said he's not alone."

"Yeah, I see that." I hear the strain in my own voice. And *Luke* closed his blinds this time. He's never bothered to before. He's hiding her from me. He took me out tonight, kissed my hand goodbye in such a sweet, genuine gesture, and then went to the bar to pick his bartender up.

I'm so stupid.

"Clara?"

I turn back to see Warner watching, a stern expression on his face. "You okay?"

"Of course." I glance back, taking in the glow of the light within his room.

A mental picture of what's going on behind it hitting me like a wave of sickness. This is what he does. I knew this. It shouldn't bother me, and yet it does.

"Clara." Warner's voice is right behind mine now, the warning in it.

"What?" I step away from the window, around him, and head back to the couch, downing half my glass of wine. Suddenly, I want my guest gone. I want to be alone.

But I get the sense he's not going anywhere. "You're not falling for 12, are you?"

"Jesus, Warner! What do you think I am, an idiot?" I burst out laughing, releasing some of the tension in my body. "I'm not going to fall for my target. What's wrong with you? He's a fucking criminal! You think I'm going to just throw my entire life away for some guy?"

"Is that why you're yelling at me now?"

"I'm not . . ." I temper my tone. I *am* yelling. "I'm not yelling at you."

"It wouldn't be the first time it's happened," he offers, all traces of his usual smile gone.

"What do you mean? What does that mean?"

He sighs, shaking his head to himself, like he'd rather not tell me. "I was handling a human trafficking case two years ago, with a female undercover agent," he begins. "She was good. Smart. Our target was this young Turkish guy. We were making great headway in the case. Until she fell in love with him."

"Oh, please, Warner. I—"

He holds his hands up. "All I'm saying is that I've seen it happen. Woman sees the good side in the guy, wants to change him, thinks she can . . ."

"So you think I'm an idiot."

"Special Agent Mason wasn't an idiot."

"She fell in love with a guy who *traffics humans*, Warner."

"She wasn't an idiot," he reiterates, his words slow, his voice loud and hoarse, full of emotion. "Actually, she reminds me a lot of you. Young, like you. Still not completely jaded by the job." His eyes drift down to my mouth.

The silence in my condo is deafening. Even Stanley's normally heavy breathing seems to have stalled. I check my tone, sensing an explosion if I don't tread lightly. "She got fired?"

"I wish." His faint head shake answers me. "Found her in her cover house with a bullet in her head."

A shiver slips through my body. I've heard of undercovers having death threats shouted at them at trials and I myself have had the shit kicked out of me once while trying to buy heroin, but actually getting killed on the job is rare. "Jesus."

"Yeah." Warner bows his head for a moment in silence, and I can see that it's still heavily under his skin. "Not sure how he found out, but knowing how hard she was falling, I'd bet she told him. So . . . don't do anything stupid, like fall for your target. I don't want to bury another agent." He studies me with big hazel eyes, giving me a brief glimpse of the sadness behind them.

I give his shoulder a friendly rub. "Don't worry about me, Warner."

He shrugs. "He's a good-looking guy. Sounds nice enough. Could trip up anyone."

"You want me to set you two up, don't you? Forget me. Maybe my big brother can get in close with him and crack this case."

"Alright . . ." The tension in the room vanishes instantly as he tosses his empty can into the kitchen sink. "Get some sleep, wiseass." He ducks out of my condo, a little more quickly than usual.

Warner's words of warning linger in the back of my mind long after I crawl into bed, Stanley snoring by my side. My bedroom blinds are drawn open, eyes locked on the condo directly across from me.

My heart rate spikes when Luke strolls out of the bedroom and into the kitchen, his sweatpants hanging dangerously low on his waist, the ridges in his stomach hard and defined, even from this distance. Grabbing a glass from the cupboard, he fills it with water from the fridge tap. I guess he worked up a thirst.

My thoughts are laced with bitterness, but that doesn't stop me from moving. Before I realize it, I'm out of bed and standing a few feet away from the glass, admiring him as he sucks back a glass, and then another. Setting the glass down on the counter, he stares at it for a long moment. And then his attention suddenly shifts out the window.

To me.

Can he see me? No, there's no way—my room is in complete darkness, my pajamas are black. He doesn't wave, he doesn't smile, he does nothing but stare, his hands dangling beside his hips, a look of disquiet on his face.

He's riveted.

Then his head snaps toward the bedroom, as if someone has called him. I'll bet she did.

On his way back, he hits the wall panel, casting the space into darkness, closing the remaining blinds. And an unpleasant feeling begins coursing through my body, keeping me company until I finally drift off.

■ ■ ■

Licks wants to know if you'd like to go to the park.

Well, my target's up early today. He's normally not up until noon on Sundays. Maybe she made him breakfast. Maybe they did it again *before* she made him breakfast. Does that kind of girl even know how to fry an egg?

I toss my phone onto the counter and rifle through my thoughts, searching for my rational ones, as I down my orange juice. A night of sleep always clears my head. Helps me think more logically. I'm a logical thinker. No room for emotions in this job.

So, I'll admit that I'm attracted to my target. He's a nice guy. He's good-looking, he's charming, and I'm playing a role where I need to attract him. It only makes sense that my human instincts will get a little scrambled. As long as I keep my head, I'll be fine.

It's actually a good thing that he brought that whore over. If she's giving him what I can't, then maybe he'll be more apt to play the waiting game with me. All I have to do is act normal and keep charming him. No problem.

A second beep.

Licks wants you to bring Stanley, too.

Not a bad idea. Maybe Stanley will do me a favor and bite Luke again.

I take another minute to chew my thumbnail nervously, and then I punch out a return message.

Stanley will oblige. Meet us at his favorite park bench in an hour and bring your throwing arm.

See you then.

An hour. That barely gives my cover team time to get in place. I'm definitely keeping Warner and the boys busy lately, after weeks of nothing. It's silly, really, that they have to be there during even the most minor of meetings.

Warner answers the phone with a groan.

"Ready for another glamorous day sitting in your car and making sure I don't fall in love with my target?"

He swears under his breath.

Chapter 19

. . .

LUKE

I slow to a stop, my heart rate pounding as hard and fast as my feet just were against the pavement.

And I admire Rain, sitting on the bench with the row of cherry trees blooming behind her. Teasing Stanley, who paws the air in front of her, begging for the ball with those bulging eyes of his. It's a rare sunny day, the rays making her chestnut hair look almost red. Even though her exterior appearance—her expensive clothes, the perfect makeup—matches that of Priscilla, Rain is beautiful in a more confident and sophisticated way than Priscilla, or any other woman I've ever been with.

I realized that last night, with Priscilla splayed out on my bed, waiting for me to climb on top of her. When I first met that woman, she was only telling me what she thought I wanted to hear. Once I got to know her and she opened up, I knew that she would never be someone who would truly care about me beyond our superficial friendship. But I didn't care, either. We both got what we wanted out of each other without a headache or guilt.

Until now.

Today, I woke up—way too early—with a weight settled on my chest. One that wouldn't let me fall back asleep. One that I needed to resolve right away.

I don't do well with guilt.

My moment to admire Rain doesn't last. The second Stanley

spots me, he abandons his owner, tearing down the path, those offset eyes on Licks. I'm ready for him this time, though, grabbing his stout little body before he goes for Licks's legs.

I laugh as he squirms. "Why so angry, buddy?" He answers with a round of snorts as he playfully nips at my hand. Crouching down, I hold him at nose level with Licks, who just sits there, looking apathetic. "You guys need to learn how to be friends. You'll be seeing more of each other." *I hope.*

The sound of slow, even heels pulls my attention up. Rain is taking her time coming over, tucking her hair behind her ear. Her skintight jeans only accentuate the fact that she has perfectly toned thighs. A cropped black leather jacket hugs her upper body, the gold from her dragonfly necklace jumping out against it. *Hell,* she's fucking hot.

And I'm dripping in sweat from my run.

A cool smile touches her lips. One that doesn't reach her eyes. "He obviously doesn't like sharing your affections," she says with an unusual hardness in her voice.

Shit.

I knew it.

She saw Priscilla come in.

I didn't even think about the possibility until I stepped into my bedroom last night and spotted the faint glow burning beyond Rain's blinds. I made a move to shut my own blinds right away, but I could have sworn I saw a face peering out from the edge of her living room window. And her bedroom curtains were open later. They're never open. I know because ever since that night I saw her lying on her bed, I've been checking every night.

So, if she saw me bring a woman home last night, just hours after dropping her off, why the hell is she here now? Why did she even answer my text?

She tosses a tennis ball first in the air and then across the path, into a clearing on the other side. Stanley leaps from my arms with surprising agility, taking off for it.

"He has a lot of energy."

"Too much, most days," she agrees. "What are you up to today?" Her eyes drop over my shirt, clinging to my body. "Besides showering."

"I have some things to do." I need to sort out the Ferrari stuff with Aref later. But not before I sort this out. "You?"

"Same." She smiles at me but it's off. Forced.

Stanley, oblivious to the growing tension, bounds back with the ball in his mouth, dropping it in front of me with a bark. I toss it across the way, freeing my hand to reach for hers. After a second of hesitation, she gives it to me, her long, delicate fingers slipping into mine, the contact spiking my already racing heartbeat.

I lead her over to the park bench, leaving Licks stretched out in a patch of grass. I never have to worry about him running away. How do I bring this up? *Do* I bring this up? In reality, I just met Rain; we're not exclusive, we're not even really dating. We're "hanging out," as she calls it. But something tells me that how I deal with this now is going to dictate what happens tomorrow.

I don't know a lot about what's going on in my life right now, but I know that I want there to be a tomorrow with Rain.

So I decide on blunt honesty. Rust has always schooled me on being straight up and dealing with things head on. Not to dance around issues, because it's a waste of time and breath and patience.

Locking eyes with her, I say, "You saw me come home last night, didn't you?"

Surprise flashes across her face before she smothers it. Her mouth opens and closes several times. I can almost see the various answers churning, as she decides whether she should lie or not. "Yes," she finally says, breaking our gaze to watch Stanley roll in the grass like he's got a terrible itch on his back.

"I went out to meet my uncle after I dropped you off and had too much to drink. My friend Priscilla gave me a ride home."

"Is that what you call it? A *friend* giving you a *ride* home?" Her voice is low, unreadable, and yet telling me everything I need to know. Yes, seeing me with another woman bothered her.

I sigh. "No, that was a friend driving my car home and then coming up to spend the night with me."

She winces but then smooths her expression yet again. "Look, we just met. We're just friends, right? So I get it. You don't have to explain anything to me."

"That's the thing. I feel like I do because . . . nothing happened." When she rolls her eyes, I quickly continue. "I'm not lying. Look at me." I gently grab her chin, directing her gaze to mine, hoping she sees the truth for what it is. "I wasn't into it." Sure, watching Priscilla pull her clothes off made me hard and when I stripped down, I was physically ready. And then I thought of Rain—of her smile, of her laugh, of how she's a breath of fresh air in this world that I'm finding myself in, a world in which, when I'm lying in the quiet dark and taking longer than usual to fall asleep, doesn't feel quite right. And I thought of how she would feel if she knew what I was doing.

The fact that I cared what Rain might think was jarring. Even my best friend, Jesse, says I'm a selfish bastard.

Suddenly I didn't want Priscilla anymore.

I told her I was too tired, too drunk. She just shrugged and climbed into the shower to wash a night's worth of club work off. Another sign that she doesn't really give a shit about me. I pulled my sweatpants on and grabbed a drink of water from the kitchen. That's when I saw Rain's bedroom blinds open. That's when I knew, without a doubt, who I wanted to be with last night.

"Why are you telling me this?" she asks quietly, her focus seemingly fixated on the pebble she's shifting around with the toe of really sexy black boots.

I slide my hand over hers, pulling her eyes back to mine. "Because I want to be honest with you."

She stares at me through shrewd eyes for the longest time, likely measuring my words. I hold her gaze. Stanley's incessant barking is what finally breaks the spell, forcing her to turn away long enough to toss the ball extra far. "Are you going to have more friends driving you home?"

I push the strands of hair that always seem to fall across her face back. "Do you want me to?"

After a pause, she shakes her head. "But . . . I can't give you *that* right now. I don't know how long it'll be before I can. I just . . ."

"I get it." I don't, really. I need to talk to Jesse about this, about how to handle this. About what *not* to do, about how to resist the urge to push. Because right now all I want to do is drag her back to my condo and into my shower.

The first genuine smile of the day stretches across her face.

"There it is again," I tease, cupping her jaw as gently as possible, my thumb running the length of her lips. They're just so tempting. I can't help myself; I lean in and kiss her as softly as I can. Not like I did on her balcony.

She hesitates for only a second before responding, her lips tasting so sweet next to the salt that's coating mine.

Two howls of complaint sound beside us.

"Are you fucking serious?"

Rain's head falls back with laughter. Licks, previously in a borderline coma, now stands next to Stanley, in front of us. Protesting. "I guess they've found common ground."

"Yeah, well, they'd better get used to this and a lot of it," I mutter, flashing a sly grin Rain's way to catch the flush in her cheeks. I wish I could spend the rest of the day with her. I'm considering how to shirk all responsibility and do just that when my phone starts vibrating in my pocket. I know it's Rust without looking. "Shit, I'm sorry. I've gotta get going."

"Yeah, you do." She drops her gaze down again. "Go shower."

"Join me?"

She only smiles, snapping her fingers at Stanley. He trots over obediently. "Here." She stands and tosses me a paper bag that was sitting beside her on the bench. "Your lunch for today, and tomorrow, and the next day . . . so you don't have to eat that awful street meat."

I let my phone ring as I watch her walk down the path, those slow, sleek movements stirring my blood.

Chapter 20

...

CLARA

"Good save on that, Bertelli," Warner's voice fills my ear as I walk along the path, not ready to go back to my condo yet.

"Thanks." I toss the ball for Stanley. For the hundredth time today. Somehow he still hasn't lost weight.

"I can't believe he came right out and admitted to the bartender. Surprised me."

"Yeah, me too." More like flabbergasted, actually. Criminals don't admit to doing jerky things because criminals don't realize that they're in the wrong. Hell, almost any other regular guy would consider that a pass, seeing as we barely know each other. And yet Luke came right out with it, those beautiful baby-blue eyes staring at me in earnest.

"What a fucking lie, though, that he didn't bang that broad."

"Yeah." But Luke was telling me the truth. I know it was the truth.

What I can't believe is that he could read me in the first place. That I walked in prepared to act like nothing was wrong, like I didn't want to punch him in the face for the not-small twinge of disappointment stirring in my gut. That I couldn't hide my true feelings. That I even have true feelings.

"You played it up perfectly. Not too upset but just enough."

Played it up, that's exactly what I did.

And the massive relief I felt when he said he didn't screw that whore? Also not real. Not at all.

Chapter 21

. . .

LUKE

A Jaguar sits to my left and a high-end Volvo sits to my right.

I'm not out of place here, I think to myself, smiling as I hit the "arm" button. My Porsche chirps. My fucking beautiful Porsche.

Man, I'm so lucky to have Rust in my life.

I stroll through the downtown parking lot, my keys swinging casually by my finger, a cover for the nervous knots twisting in my stomach as I head toward the building Aref instructed me to go to. I've talked to him several times since Sunday. Sometimes about business, other times just to shoot the shit. I can see why Rust likes him. *I* like him. For all the money he's got and as arrogant as he is, he's still a cool guy. And making the arrangements for this Ferrari? Piece of cake. I've done nothing besides make a few phone calls to Dmitri and Nikolai. There's been virtually no risk to me.

Not until now.

"Gold Bonds," I say to the security guard behind the desk, and he waves me through, directing me to the fourth floor without another look.

I've never stepped inside a jewelry wholesaler business, so I don't know if the security level is normal. All I know is that it's tight. Four cameras, two armed guards, three bulletproof security doors, and one metal detector later, I'm heading down a narrow, sterile hallway to the office of Jerry Rosenthal.

Anyone paying Aref, anyone taking money from Aref, gets

it through this guy. He doesn't do dark motel parking lot drops. He's too classy—and too smart—for that. Apparently that's been a bone of contention with the Russians, but the simple fact is they need Aref's ships. He doesn't need them for anything.

"Sit." Rosenthal waves his stubby hand toward to the chair across from him before dialing his phone. "He's here," he mutters into the phone. "Yes . . . okay." Shrewd gray eyes glare at me. "Address?"

I dig the folded sheet of paper out of my pocket and slide it across the desk. The one with detailed instructions to the garage where the Ferrari's sitting, waiting to be driven into a moving truck trailer and taken away by Aref's guys. They're already in the general neighborhood, but Rust told me not to hand over the address until I was sitting in front of Rosenthal. Just in case. This is our first deal like this with Aref and, while I don't think he's going to screw us over . . . I'm going to trust Rust.

Rosenthal reads the address and then throws the page in the shredder and hangs up.

"What now?"

"Now . . ." He strums his fingers, each one decorated in a gaudy gold ring, an unfriendly look on his face. ". . . we wait for the phone call."

I let my eyes wander over his desk, which is clear except for one neat stack of papers in the top-right corner and a strange metal contraption with various metal rings hanging off it. I can't help but eye it, thoughts of mobsters and cigar cutters and missing fingers flashing through my mind.

"Give me your hand," he demands abruptly.

As much as I don't want to, I don't know what else to do, so I humor him. He picks up that weird metal thing and slips one ring over my fourth ringer. "You're a size eleven. Would you like to see the latest wedding bands that just arrived?"

"Only if they come with a noose."

Finally . . . his face breaks out in a wide smile, displaying a gap between his middle front teeth. "Okay, okay." Rolling over to a wall panel, he punches in a few buttons and a lock pop sounds. Pushing open a hidden display case full of gold and diamonds, he says, "How about a piece of jewelry for a lovely woman? You must have one. Or two."

This guy is unreal. Is *this* what he does while waiting for drops to take place? I open my mouth to decline his offer when a particular piece catches my eyes.

"Ahh . . . of course." How he knows exactly what I'm eyeing I have no idea, but the little man stands—and he truly is little; I'm guessing five-foot-two—and seizes the necklace from its hook. "One flawless carat in each. White gold, rhodium-plated."

The mention of rhodium reminds me of the pile of catalytic converters back at the warehouse. I know it's worth a lot. Rosenthal dangles the necklace in front of me, letting it sway back and forth, the sparkling raindrops almost hypnotic.

I'm picturing it around Rain's slender neck. "How much?"

"Ten."

I laugh. "What's that, a five hundred percent markup?" Rust filled me in on this guy before I got here. While he runs a legit wholesaler's business, that doesn't mean he buys completely legit. A good chunk of his stock is coming from smuggled inventory at 50 percent less than what's considered market standard.

"What are you saying? That I'm trying to rip you off?" That sour look has returned.

Trying to rip me off is exactly what he's doing, but I need to be careful. He's still holding our money. "No, I'm saying that I didn't come in here to spend ten grand for a necklace."

He hangs the necklace back up, but I know he's going to come back with a lower offer. This is all negotiation 101. Before he does, we're interrupted with ringing. He's on the phone for all of three seconds, long enough to say, "Hello . . . Okay." Punching a code into a safe behind his desk, he pulls out an overstuffed manila envelope and drops it on the desk, sliding it across. Stacks of money sit inside. Stacks that will earn Dmitri's wide grin, no doubt.

Hell, I'm grinning because some of this is mine. Handler's fee,

Rust calls it. I glance at the necklace again, hung so intentionally front and center. I wonder how Rain would react to that? She'd probably tell me I'm fucking crazy. I've known her for only a few weeks. We've barely kissed. But it'd be a good gift down the road, maybe. "How much are you *really* going to sell that to me for?"

He twists his mouth tight. And then smirks. "Only because you're a good friend of Aref . . . two."

I dig the cash out and slap it on the table. "Now that's more reasonable."

He has the jewelry wrapped and packaged in under a minute, certificate of authenticity and everything. When I walk out of there, it's with a smile and a handshake and an "until next time." I make it all the way past the last security door before my smile falls off abruptly.

Vlad is here.

His eyes widen in surprise, and then narrow as they drop to the messenger bag hanging over my hip, where I've tucked away a shitload of cash. "What are you doing here?"

I should probably bite my tongue, but I don't like the way he's talking to me. It makes my brass balls come out. "None of your fucking business." What am I doing here? What is *he* doing here!

He takes a step closer, the smell of black coffee and salmon assaulting my nose. "Why are you here?"

I decide that starting a pissing contest with this guy isn't the best idea. "Buying my girlfriend a necklace." I pull the long, slender box out of my jacket pocket and hold it up as proof.

The way he pushes his tongue over his teeth, he doesn't seem too impressed with my explanation. "How's the Ferrari?"

Shit. Has he truly figured out that we went through Aref to move it? "Don't know what Ferrari you're talking about. I have a Porsche. And it's awesome." I stroll past him, out the door.

Feeling his eyes on my back the entire time.

I don't trust that guy at all.

Chapter 22

· · ·

CLARA

An incoming text message wakes me up. I paw at my nightstand, squinting to read my screen through one eye.

What are you doing today?

It's Luke. Suddenly I'm wide awake and sitting up.

Gym. Shopping. No big plans. Why?

Road trip?

I smile.

Where?

Into the mountains.

My glee gives way to wariness. Into the mountains? Kind of random. Unless . . . Knots begin to form in my stomach. Has someone tipped him off? Will this end with a bullet in my head? Things a normal person doesn't have to worry about, but I have to make sure that I don't ever forget. Not for a minute.

I'll need some more information about these mountains of yours.

I have to check out a car.

To buy?

To sell.

My sheets fall away from my body as I crawl out of bed, frowning at my phone. To make sure I'm reading it right. What? Does he mean . . . Could he be *this* stupid? *This* trusting of me? A slow, sinking burn ignites in my chest. It's not curiosity or excitement, like what I normally feel when I'm about to nail someone to the wall.

It's disappointment. He's about to prove the Feds right. He's about to prove to me that he's a criminal. But that's what I'm here for, I remind myself. He is what he is. It doesn't matter how nice he is, or how attractive, or how he makes me feel.

I quickly punch out:

I like road trips.

Great. Pick you up in an hour.

Where EXACTLY are we going?

This podunk town in the interior. Called Sisters.

I immediately dial Warner's number, my resignation already taking over whatever stupid fantasies my subconscious may have spun about all this being a big mistake. There's no thrill in my voice. "Get dressed. You won't fucking believe it."

■ ■ ■

"I just had it washed, too," Luke grumbles, deftly steering his Porsche around the potholes as we crawl up the old dirt driveway. "They need to pave this, or some shit."

"I can't imagine what that would cost," I say, not really listening. Too busy taking in the line of trees ahead on this mile-long drive to somewhere unseen. High mountain peaks create a striking background for the vast acreage of fields and trees surrounding us. "Stop for a sec?" I ask, rolling down my window.

He does, and I aim my lens out to capture the view. My instincts tell me that, no matter how this all ends, this picture—full of beauty and tranquility and peace—is one I'll pull out many years from now, with fond memories. "Who did you say lives out here?"

"A good friend of mine named Jesse. He used to be my roommate." Rounding the bend, we stop in front of a farmhouse with a big front porch and an old swing that sits empty, save for a colorful quilt stretched across the back. A dog lies at the top of the stairs, his chin resting on the wood as he takes us in, whiskers twitching but otherwise unmoving. "They've done some work around here." Luke's eyes graze the matching red roofs over the house, garage, and barn.

A row of cars sits in front of the large barn, the shiny black muscle car and dingy yellow farm truck so odd next to each other. Corrals and fence lines stretch out behind as far as the eye can see.

The sound of horses pounding against dirt pulls my attention to our right. "Do they live here?" I point out the two little girls on the backs of galloping thoroughbreds. Several other horses nibble peacefully on the fresh spring grass.

"No. They board horses here."

I trail Luke to a garage, inhaling the fresh air, absorbing the tranquility. The peace I don't often find in my life. "It's beautiful out here."

Luke's eyes are hidden behind a pricey pair of sunglasses, but I feel them studying me all the same. "If you like this sort of thing."

Does he not? Does he want a city girl whose nose twitches at the sight of a horse? Not sure what to say, I finally go with, "You have to admit, it's nice to visit, at least."

Slowing his footsteps, he reaches back long enough to give my hand a squeeze. "It is really nice to visit." Letting go, he cups his hands around his mouth and booms, "Welles!"

A clang sounds, followed by a few curses, and then a moment later, a young guy with a red-and-black checkered shirt and worn jeans streaked with black emerges.

"Boone." He sticks a dirty hand out.

Luke laughs. "Get the fuck away from me before you wreck my clothes, you gearhead." Reaching under the back of his shirt to produce a thick envelope that I didn't know was there, he slaps it in the guy's palm.

My stomach tightens. I know an envelope of cash when I see it. And lots of it. Now that I've seen it, it's evidence. It'll hold up in court. But what has Jesse done to earn that?

"Never could stand getting dirty, could you?" Eyes so dark they look black settle on me, catching my breath for just a moment.

"Rain, Jesse. Jesse, Rain," Luke says by way of a quick introduction.

"Nice to meet you. I'd shake your hand, but . . ." Jesse holds his up in a blank-faced apology. I get the impression he doesn't smile a lot. I've met guys like him before. They're smart, hard to read. That tends to make them more dangerous for undercovers.

And then his gaze drifts behind me and he lets out a loud whistle. "Uncle Rust finally gave in to your whining, did he?"

"I earned it," Luke corrects with a smirk.

Exactly how, I'd love to ask, but I bite my tongue. He's never said much about the recent "gift," but by the way he gently shuts his doors and generally babies it, I can tell it's a source of great pride on his part.

"We can race," Jesse suggests. So, I'm guessing the black Barracuda is his.

"On these roads? Hell no. But I'll let you play with it later. So?" He nods toward the garage.

"Come see for yourself." Jesse leads us in, a slight swagger in his step, suggesting he doesn't have a care in the world. Or that he has everything he wants. Another glance around this ranch would make me believe it.

At the far end of the spacious garage is an old pea-green Mustang, its engine out and in pieces beside it. Jesse and Luke stop in front of a Corvette with faded red paint and rust panels, its hood up, an array of tools lying all around.

Are these stolen cars? Are they fixing up stolen cars? What exactly is going on? A horse ranch with boarders and children coming in and out, and a small car theft ring in operation right here, out in the open with the doors rolled up? That doesn't make any sense.

Jesse leans in and cranks the engine. It comes to life in a loud purr.

"Wow. Sounds a helluva lot better than before," Luke exclaims, his face lighting up with childish excitement.

"I'll need another week, probably," Jesse answers, offering the tiniest smile of pride. Even covered in black grease, he's an attractive guy. And perhaps another criminal.

"That's fine." Turning to me, Luke says, "Jesse's somewhat of a god when it comes to engines."

"Is that who I think it is?" a female voice calls out. A few seconds later, a pretty blond rounds the corner and heads straight for Luke, throwing her arms around his neck in a friendly embrace.

"Oh, man. Are you two dressing the same now?" Luke jokes, peering down at her red-and-black checkered jacket, that typical cockiness suddenly edged out and replaced with something soft. "This is what happens when you move out to the mountains, isn't it?"

"She keeps stealing my clothes," Jesse mutters, but his eyes are twinkling as he takes her in, all pretenses of being aloof vanishing.

Luke gestures to me. "Rain, this is . . ." He holds his hands out, palms up, in question. "How should I introduce you?"

What?

"Hi, Rain, I'm Alex." She smiles and turns to face me, giving me full view of the thin scar that runs down the right side of her face, from temple to jaw. It's a clean line, like that from a blade or a sharp piece of glass. Something she was slashed with. I avoid gawking openly at it by focusing on her eyes instead, the color a mesmerizing reddish-brown, reminding me of rich terra-cotta tiles.

"Hi. It's nice to meet you."

Alex stands behind Jesse, wrapping her slender arms around his waist, resting her head against his back. Jesse may be complicit in something illegal, but they make a really cute couple. "What color are you going to paint this one?"

Luke kicks the tire gently. "Red. Should get a good return on it."

"Well, we appreciate it. It gives Jesse and Sheriff Gabe something to do."

Sheriff Gabe?

A scuff of boots against the gravel announces someone new a

second before I hear, "When is she going to stop calling me that?"

"Never. You'll always be the sheriff to me," Alex answers, smiling at an older version of Jesse.

There's a sheriff involved in whatever scam this is? I shouldn't be surprised. Small-town law, keeping the peace, no one the wiser. Still, this is getting more interesting by the minute.

"I wish he was still sheriff. Then he wouldn't be in here, fucking up my engines," Jesse says, turning to lay a tender kiss on Alex's cheek. If her scar bothers him, he doesn't let on.

Maybe he's the one who gave it to her?

Jesse heads for a rustic sink beside the wood table that runs along the entire back length of the garage, neatly lined with tools and jars of small bits.

"So you finally got rid of the Mustang, did you?" Gabe reaches, patting Luke on the shoulder with a "nice car," before sticking his hand out in front of me. "I'm Gabe. And you are . . ."

Screwed, if this guy has radar for fellow law enforcement. My biggest selling point is that there's absolutely *nothing* about me that hints "cop," and yet all I can think about right now is a story about this one guy on the D.C. force who had the uncanny ability to peg every last undercover he ever met.

I hope to God Sheriff Gabe isn't that talented.

I smooth away my internal struggle with a smile as I return the handshake. "I'm Rain. Nice to meet you."

As he walks past Luke, I hear him throw a low mutter of, "Well, it's about time."

Luke smirks. "How's your restoration going?"

"It's coming. I'd be driving it by fall, if you'd stop giving Jesse all these cars to fix up."

"Better money than what I'll make in town," Jesse throws back.

Luke pats the back of the Corvette like a proud parent. "This one will go up for auction in a month if it's ready."

Gabe knocks the side panel with his knuckle. "And it came from . . ."

"I already told you, Dad," Jesse protests but Gabe ignores him, black eyes just like his son's leveled on Luke. His voice overly calm.

And I realize what this is. An impromptu interrogation. Gabe wants to see if Luke's story matches his son's. He's asking the questions that I want to, but can't. Which begs the question: how much does the retired sheriff know about what Luke and his son are involved in?

Luke smiles easily. A smile that says he knows exactly what Gabe's getting at and it doesn't faze him. "For three grand, off some old guy in Boise who bought it thinking he could fix it up before he realized that not everyone is meant to rebuild cars."

"Hey! Just like you!" Jesse chirps with mock surprise, smirking at his father.

A long pause, a shrewd look, and then Gabe relents with a slight smile and a nod, satisfied with his answer.

And giving me mine. There's nothing shady happening here. Luke and his friend are flipping cars honestly. I release the breath I held trapped in my lungs, relaxing with each second that passes, swimming in relief. Relief that I haven't witnessed anything damning to Luke yet, that I can hold onto this fantasy that Luke hasn't been pulled into the theft ring for just a while longer. Because the sooner I'm proven wrong, the sooner this case will be over, and the sooner I'll have to look into those big blue eyes and condemn him.

But today . . . I can relax.

"Come and show me your new ride," Jesse says, wiping his somewhat clean hands on a rag. But I don't miss the low murmur to his dad as he passes. "I already told you, none of that shit will come here."

None of that shit. So both of them know something about Luke's involvement with Rust and it seems that neither approves. I wonder how much they know. I wonder what it would take to make them talk.

Too many questions I can't answer, but I do know that Jesse's another door. So is the sheriff. More mental notes, more potential informants.

"You interested in looking at car engines?" Alex asks me as the three men wander toward the Porsche.

I should really stick with Luke in case something important is mentioned. I should.

But my gut tells me that what's happening over there is just three guys with a love for cars getting hard-ons for Luke's latest toy. Nothing the FBI needs to invade. I'm more curious about this girl and what happened to her face. There's *definitely* a story there.

"Not particularly . . ." I laugh.

She waves me toward the barn and I follow. "Do you all live here?"

"Just Jesse and I. His mom and dad and sister live next door, over there." She gestures to the ranch-style house hidden behind a line of trees.

"You must get along well," I muse. As much as I love my parents, the idea of buying the house right next to them brings a dull ache to my head.

"We've been through a lot together," she says absently, draping her arms over a newly mended fence, her gaze locked on the two horses drinking from a stream not far from us. "They're such beautiful animals, aren't they?" A slight frown zags across her forehead. "I used to be afraid of horses growing up. Can you believe that?"

"I can, actually. They're big animals. Have you lived here long?"

"About a year."

I glance around at the place. "It's a really nice ranch."

She smiles, the movement pulling at the scar. It must bother her, because she adjusts her hair to cover it. "It is. I'm very lucky to own it."

So *she* owns this ranch? A girl with a giant scar on her cheek, who can't be more than in her mid-twenties, *owns* a place like this? I sense a much deeper story behind her words, but she only leans forward to scratch the head of the old dog that sauntered up so quietly. "Hey, Felix." Its nose twitches as it grazes my jeans. Smelling Stanley, no doubt.

The tranquil countryside is disrupted, the horses' ears twitching as the Porsche's engine suddenly comes to life. Jesse and Luke stand at the back, their arms folded as they study the exposed engine; Gabe's sitting in the driver's seat. "Boys and their toys . . ." Alex murmurs.

"I think Luke would marry that thing if he could. I was afraid to get in it; I may dirty it." The surveillance team has tailed him to the car wash three times this week already.

She laughs. "Yeah, I remember his room at their old apartment being really neat. I'm sure the new place is pristine."

"I know, right? What twenty-four-year-old guy has a cleaning lady come every week?" I've watched the plump blond lady scrub his floors and dust his furniture every Sunday afternoon like clockwork.

And then I bite my tongue, because I've admitted to something that Luke hasn't told me. That I wouldn't know unless I've been, say, scoping out his place. It's so minor, it'll probably never come up, and I shouldn't give it another thought . . . but those are the kinds of insignificant bits that can create colossal fuck-ups in a case a year from now. I'm not normally so careless. It's just that I keep forgetting why I'm with Luke in the first place.

"How did you two meet?" Alex asks.

"I brought my Audi into his garage."

She nods, gazing over at him. A sad smile takes over her face. "He's a really good guy." Her hand wanders to touch her chin, her finger grazing over the thin white line that I'm sure she never forgets is there. "So, tell me . . ." She suddenly turns and catches me staring at her scar. "Have you ever ridden a horse before?"

Chapter 23

. . .

LUKE

"You pick her up at The Cellar?" Jesse asks, taking a sip of his beer as he watches Alex help Rain climb into a saddle of the tall black and white horse. By her hesitation and stilted movements, I'm guessing she's a first-timer.

"Nah. She came in once to get her car fixed, started flirting with me. One thing led to another."

"I'll bet Miller loved that." Jesse's dealt with him before; he's seen firsthand the hate-on that he has for me.

"Miller can suck my balls," I mutter. "Actually, she has a condo right across from me."

"Ahh . . ." He nods and smiles, as if I've said something important.

"Ahh, what?"

"One of those million-dollar condos?"

Now I know what he's getting at. He's also met the kind of women I normally go after, and he's had plenty of comments to make about them. "Yeah, her family has money. So?"

"I'm just messing with you, man. She seems different. Nice."

"She is," I argue. "Both."

"Is Priscilla willing to share?"

Mention of Priscilla brings me back to thoughts of last week, to how relieved I was that Rain believed me, and forgave me. "I think I'm done with Pris."

Jesse smiles at me. A big, non-Jesse smile.

And I wait for it. I know it's coming. "So, Luke Boone is finally hooked."

"It's only been a few weeks, if that."

He shrugs. "Sometimes it only takes a few seconds."

"We're taking it slow."

"And yet you brought her all the way out here, to meet us? To meet Alex?" He folds his arms across his chest, turning to face me. Of all the guys I've ever met, Jesse's never been afraid to call me on my shit, to chew me out for being an idiot.

"It's a long drive out to the middle of fucking nowhere. I needed the company." To tell the truth, the long car ride flew by, and we talked about nothing.

"Isn't that why you always bring Licks with you?"

"Yeah, well, Rain drools less than Licks does."

Jesse bursts out laughing, something he never did when we lived together. Pre-Alex.

"You sound happy, man." I slap his shoulder. "I'm glad."

"And you? Everything's good?" A shadow passes across his face. "How's Rust?"

I shrug. "He's fine. It's all fine. You know." He doesn't know. He suspects, just like I once suspected before being brought into the fold. But I'll never come out and tell him. That'll just drag him into the mix and I won't do that to him.

Never again.

"Boone . . . Fuck. Why are you even hanging around those people? Didn't we go through enough last year?"

"This isn't tied to that. Viktor's gone, out of the picture."

He shakes his head. "I keep hoping that you're going to get your wake-up call, like I did. You'll be scared out of your mind, and you'll regret even thinking that life was appealing, and you're going to just get the hell away from it." He looks ready to continue his tirade, but he finally relents with, "Alex doesn't want to be sending birthday cards to the state pen." He pauses, his jaw clenching. "Or a graveyard."

"Don't worry. Rust has it covered. He's smart. And a grave-yard? Seriously? These guys aren't like that. They're assholes, but they don't just off people for the hell of it. Come on." Alex and Rain trot past side-by-side, Rain letting out a giddy burst of laughter now that she's gotten the hang of it. "How's Alex doing?"

At the mention of Alex, Jesse's eyes locate her and soften. I've never seen a guy so balls-in-a-purse whipped by a woman. "She's great. I mean, she's remembering things, here and there, but she's handling it all really well."

I hesitate before I ask what I've been waiting to talk to Jesse about for days now. "So, how hard was it to be with her after what he did to her? I mean, did it take a while for her to let you . . .?"

Jesse gives me a "what the fuck are you asking and why?" scowl, forcing me to elaborate. "Rain's ex . . . I don't know what *exactly* he did to her but, he did something. We're taking it slow." Excruciatingly slow. A-long-shower-a-day-keeps-blue-balls-away slow.

Instant understanding passes over Jesse's face, and a mutter of "shit" slips out. "Well, it was a bit different with Alex, you know that. With her memory and all."

"Right." I guess their situation is too unusual. That's not going to help. I heave a sigh. "I just don't want to make any asshole moves and scare her off."

"Well then don't be yourself." I raise my eyebrows. "Okay, okay. I'm kidding. You *should* actually be yourself. The version who isn't so wrapped up with all this shit." He flicks my watch to make a point. "She doesn't really seem like the type. And . . ." He watches the two women for a moment, in deep thought. "Just follow her lead. She'll let you know when she's ready."

"And what if her lead is holding hands and watching reruns of *Friends* for the next year?"

"Then your hand's finally going to be useful for more than one thing." He gives me a swift but soft punch to my stomach as he stands.

"You're a really shitty friend, you know that?"

"And yet you won't go away and leave me in peace," he says, chuckling as he lowers the hood on my engine.

Rain's laughter fills the quiet again, followed by the sound of water splashing. We're drawn to the fence line to watch the horse she's riding pick up speed and tear through the stream, sending water spraying everywhere. She seems to have figured out the right posture and stance quickly, her thigh muscles tensed as she holds herself just shy of the saddle, moving up and down with the rhythm. Giving me a fantastic view of her ass.

"I think I've found my new hobby," she shouts my way, adding, "Am I any good?"

"Yeah, not bad," I mutter, adjusting myself before everyone here knows exactly how good I think she is.

Jesse's chuckle carries through the air.

Chapter 24

...

CLARA

The sky is beginning to change color by the time we're saying our goodbyes, following an afternoon of riding and leisurely grooming the horses, which Alex informed me are both named Felix.

"That was fun. I hope we see you back here again," Alex says to me, before shooting a pointed look at Luke.

He laughs, reaching around her neck to give her a warm hug. "Next time we'll bring Licks and her mutant with us." He moves away to say his goodbyes to Jesse and Gabe, leaving the two of us together, me securing the camera I've had out a few times this afternoon, sneaking candid photos of the farm and of Luke. For the case, I tell myself.

"Keep him out of trouble for us, will you?" Her worried eyes settle on Luke's back.

So, Alex obviously knows *something,* too. "What kind of trouble can Luke possibly get into at the garage?" I ask as casually as possible.

"I'm not worried about that place. He just . . ." She purses her lips. "He just hasn't had the best role models in his life. He's been misguided."

"By who?"

"By people who love him. I think they do want him to be happy, but the way they're going about it is wrong."

"He's a grown man now. I'm sure he'll do the right thing. Right?"

"Yes, he will do the right thing. Eventually." She smiles sadly. Her fingers graze the side of her face again. Almost absently, she whispers, "I wouldn't be here right now, if it hadn't been for him."

I fight the urge to go into cop mode and coax answers out of her, knowing that if Gabe heard me, he'd see right through me. And, if he wants to protect his son by association—as any father would—he'll warn them that there's an undercover on Luke and this case will be over.

Alex's words could mean many things—*she wouldn't be here, at this farm; she wouldn't be here, with Jesse*—but the fact that she touched that horrific scar tells me that it's more than that.

"Just take care of him for me," she says with a reluctant smile. "I worry about him. He's a good guy, with a kind heart."

A lump forms in my throat. A person needs to be a solid judge of character in my job. I'm an excellent judge of character. I sense that Alex is a genuine person, and that my target did something monumental for her.

"Sure, okay," I lie. I'm not here to ease her conscience or to take care of Luke.

I'm here to do the exact opposite.

And for the first time, that makes me feel ill.

Which tells me that I've broken one of the most basic rules of undercover work: don't get emotionally attached to your targets. That's never been an issue for me. I've never cared about what I'm setting them up for or what's going to happen to them once I've done my job. They're all grown-ups, making their own decisions. No one's forcing their hand.

"Thanks for the cash, man," I hear Jesse say to Luke, slapping his hand. "It'll come in handy. We still have a lot of work to do around here."

"Yeah, like paving your driveway so I don't kill my car on it."

"Okay, Princess."

Luke gives him the finger. "I'll call you in a week to see how it's going. Maybe you can drive it in?"

"Drive to Portland?" Jesse's face screws up. "Fuck that."

"How are we even friends?" Luke blurts out.

"Because you're desperate and lonely?"

Luke laughs, reaching forward to give Jesse a guy hug. I hear him murmur, "Miss you, man," before he climbs into the driver's seat.

Both Gabe and Jesse smile at me. "Good to meet you, Rain." Gabe jabs his thumb toward the driver's side. "Keep that one honest, will you?"

"I'll try my best," I say with as much conviction as possible. They all care about him; that much is obvious. Maybe they'll succeed in convincing him to follow a different way of life. I haven't proven anything about his current way of life conclusively yet, but it's looking more and more grim by the day.

Luke's car kicks up a cloud of dust as he heads down the driveway, honking his horn in farewell.

"So, you and Jesse are flipping cars?"

His smile tells me he's proud to talk about this. "I take care of the business side of things. You know, finding the right car, talking to the owner and negotiating the price, dealing with the auctioneer. And Jesse . . . well, he's a whiz in the garage. He can make any car run like new in a quarter of the time it takes most mechanics." He shrugs. "We each walk away with a good chunk of change and we both love doing it."

"How many have you sold?"

"Four. I figure one a month is a good side business for now."

"How entrepreneurial of you," I tease, but inside I'm beaming that he's not above earning a legitimate income. "It's too bad Jesse and you live so far apart."

"Yeah . . ." Luke slides on his sunglasses and settles back into his seat now that the road has smoothed out a bit. "I don't really have a lot of friends like Jesse. I mean, I've got plenty of people I talk to, but he and I are different. I trust him."

"You're so easygoing. I figured you didn't have trust issues," I say casually.

He smiles. "I do. Not sure why."

I'm pretty sure I know why. "I get it. I have my group of girlfriends back home and I kind of stick with them."

"You must miss them right now. That's a big move, coming all the way out here."

"We still text a lot, so it's not so bad. And everyone's busy. But, yeah. I do really miss them," I answer truthfully. "They're all at our annual girl's weekend in Loudoun right now. It's a wine region in D.C." I missed the last trip too. Sometimes I'm afraid they're going to blacklist me. "We're a special group."

"Nice. And what makes them so special? Tell me about them."

I can't tell if he's truly interested, but we do have a long drive— and while I should be using it to gather information, opening up myself is how I'm going to get him to do the same eventually. Plus, being able to talk about my real friends—Clara's friends— relaxes me.

So I start listing the ways that we're all so different and yet our personalities seem to mesh perfectly. How we can be our true selves around each other—strengths, flaws, and all—without fear. We just "get" each other. We praise each other's successes and call each other on our bullshit. We're laughing from the moment we say hello until we're forced to say goodbye.

I finish with, "I don't know what I'd do without them in my life."

"You haven't stopped smiling the entire time that you've talked about them. They sound like a lot of fun." He grins. "Do you have a picture?"

"Not on this phone." I freeze. Normal people don't have two phones unless they work, and he knows that Rain doesn't work. I quickly improvise. "I just got this iPhone a few weeks ago after my last one broke. I need to get it fixed so I can upload everything to Cloud."

He nods, buying my answer.

Wanting to steer the conversation away from my accidental slip and knowing that I need to be focusing on Luke and not myself, I say, "Speaking of friends—thank you for bringing me out today. They're all nice people. I really like them."

"Well, they loved you." He turns to flash me a smile. Like us approving of each other is a big deal for him. The funny thing is, hearing that makes me happy. I care that they approve of me.

"Have you known them long?"

"Nah, a few years. We've just been through a lot together."

"Alex said sort of the same thing earlier." I'm not sure how to broach the subject, but I decide morbid curiosity is fair reasoning for anyone. "So . . . that's a terrible scar on her face."

He nods in agreement.

"What caused it?"

Luke's jaw visibly tightens. "It's a really long story."

I wait another second before pushing. "It's a really long drive."

I know the signs of indecisiveness. Shifty eyes, multiple swallows, licking lips. He's considering how much he should divulge, if anything. How awkward this three-hour drive will be if he blows me off.

His thumb drums against the gear stick, but otherwise he says nothing. So, I tentatively rest my hand on top of his. With just a moment's hesitation, his fingers shift and entwine with mine, until my hand is encapsulated and we're shifting together.

And I tell myself that this doesn't cross any moral lines. That I'm doing what I need to do to make him talk. That also enjoying the feel of his warmth is no big deal.

"She was married before hooking up with Jesse." I feel his eyes flash to my face. "The guy was a possessive asshole. Used to slap her around, hurt her. Treat her like shit, generally."

"She obviously left him."

"I guess you could call it that. She definitely got away," he says cryptically.

I think I know where this is heading. "Before or after she hooked up with Jesse?"

"The guy fucking deserved it. It's not like he was faithful to her. Hell, Pris was screwing him regularly! Jesse risked everything for her. His whole family has. He treats her like a queen."

I reach for my bottle of water, hoping such a casual act will lessen the tension suddenly growing in the car. "She seems to think you played a big role in her getting away. That she wouldn't be here if it weren't for you."

"Uhh . . ." He lets go of the steering wheel to scratch the back of his neck—an embarrassed gesture. "I was just at the right place at the right time." He pauses, then adds, "And I did the right thing. For once."

"Did you know her husband?"

"Yeah. My uncle's business partner. I met him two years ago, when I started hanging out with my uncle more. Thought he was so cool back then, all rich and Daniel Craig–like. He had this really controlled, suave way about him. A Russian James Bond. He'd bring Alex around sometimes. She looked really different back then." He snorts. "Never in a million years would I have pictured her with a guy like Jesse, shoveling shit and picking hay out of her hair."

"She seems really happy." The frequent glances toward Jesse, the small smiles. I don't think I've ever seen two people so in love.

"She is. She got pushed into that other life too young, surrounded by the wrong people. Got trapped."

Some could say the same is true of Luke, I guess. Not that he's been forced into this life. Courted into it, perhaps. Shown the glamorous side, the benefits. And frankly, if I step back and let go of my moral compass and my profession, I can see how someone could be blinded by the shiny parts of this life. Especially when it's someone you trust and feel indebted to leading you down this path. Someone who's basically your father.

Because even knowing what I know, how many times have I wished that I had the condo, the yacht, the car, for keeps?

"So you knew he was abusive?"

There's a long pause, where he opens and closes his mouth

a few times, but not saying anything. Choosing his words. "I'd see a slap, a harsh word. Figured she was just like the young, rich wives—putting up with it because of the money." His hand squeezes mine tightly. "But, yeah, I knew." His voice grows thick with remorse. "And I did nothing. None of us did, except for Jesse. I regret it every day."

There is no room in my job for emotion. And yet abuse cases are my weak spot. I've seen plenty of them and, while I've heard all the sound reasoning, I struggle to understand the women who stay, and I abhor the family and friends who suspect abuse but do nothing.

There's no room for that now, though. I need to coax more out of Luke, not condemn him. "Well, it must have been hard, with him being your uncle's business partner, right?"

"Yeah," he agrees. "But it wasn't just that. Viktor Petrova was not a guy you wanted to cross."

Suddenly, a mess of puzzle pieces snaps together.

Chapter 25

...

LUKE

The drive went by too fast. I'm not ready to drop her off yet. That's probably why I blurt out, "So you're coming to my place tonight, right?" the second I pull my car into her condo building driveway.

"I am?" A smile of surprise touches her lips. Not an "I can't." That's good. I guess that means she's not sick of me yet, and she doesn't hate me for what I admitted to her about Alex and ignoring what I knew was happening.

I shrug. "That was the deal we made last week, right? I cook dinner for you?"

Her head falls back with a smile as realization strikes her. "That's right. I was hoping you forgot."

I chuckle. "Not a chance. I'm gonna prove you wrong." Those sandwiches she packed for me were like nothing I've ever had. I was half-tempted to walk down to the food cart and force the guy behind the counter to take a bite and admit that his version is shit.

"Okay." She grins at me. I'd kill to know what's going on inside her head right now. I'm just seconds away from leaning over to kiss her when she says, "Let me just grab a shower," and jumps out of the car. I watch her walk through her doors. So beautiful, so graceful, so . . . *glass*. I have an hour. Enough time to go deal with this raging hard-on she's giving me. "Follow her lead, my ass," I mutter, repeating Jesse's words. "She's going to lead me into some serious pain."

Chapter 26

. . .

CLARA

"Well, you're definitely making up for the slow start," Warner mocks by way of greeting.

"That was Viktor Petrova's fucking wife!" I exclaim, the phone tucked under my chin as I turn the shower on. "The one Sinclair had an informant on before she went missing."

"Yeah, I caught that."

"You should see the scar on her face, Warner. It's *bad*."

"Knife?"

"Hard to say, but I'm guessing yeah. How she ended up on a ranch in Sisters, Oregon, though . . ." Running from her ex, likely.

"We're doing background checks on all of them. Alex, the sheriff, Jesse Welles. I take it the car detail is a bust?"

"Yeah, looks like it's all legit. I took some pics of the cars. I'll send them your way to add to the files. I've got to get ready for tonight."

" 'kay. Bob and Franky are on. Watch yourself. And can you try to get something useful for once?"

"Shut up." I smile as I hang up, strip, and climb into the shower, washing the day's sweat and dirt from horseback riding from my body. Thinking about Luke. About his smile, his laugh, his piercing eyes, his full, plump lips . . .

My phone starts ringing, pulling me from the shower.

"Warner says you're with the target again tonight?"

"Uh, yeah . . ." I fumble with the tap and grab a towel, caught off guard by Sinclair and his abruptness. Not even a hello. "Heading over there soon."

"Good. I want you to push hard on the Petrova angle."

"You think she has intel on the ring?" I know she does, but I'm not admitting to it out loud.

"Maybe. But I'm looking for solid leverage that we can use to make 12 flip on 24."

"It's an abuse case where a dickhead got what he deserved," I blurt out.

"And more, I'm guessing. The property's listed under a 'Water Fitzergald.' Willed to her a year ago."

Huh. "So, she's using a fake name." I guess that explains Luke's confusion when he was introducing us.

"That or the real Water Fitzergald is buried in a deep hole on that massive, valuable plot of land."

I frown. "I don't see it." That would mean I read her wrong. I'm never *that* wrong about someone.

Sinclair chuckles and it's not at all warm. "Well, excuse me if I've seen a lot more in my twenty-plus years in the Bureau than you've seen in your two minutes of handcuffing local crackheads," he snaps. "Stop questioning me and start digging. I'm guessing that sheriff is culpable, too. For all we know, 12 and his friend tampered with Petrova's car and they're the reason he's dead. Both of them have the know-how. If we can get 12 on a murder rap, he'll be singing Markov's name from the holding cell within a day."

Even as Sinclair talks, my head's shaking, Alex's words, the look in her eyes as they passed over Luke, cycling through my mind. He saved her life. In the short time that I spent with her today, my gut says she was telling the truth—that she needed to be saved.

But, at what cost?

Oh God, what if Sinclair's right? Am I going to help hang a murder around Luke's neck? No . . . I've met murderers. Even without proof, someone like me can see it in their eyes—the instability, the danger. There's none of that in Luke's eyes. I don't believe he's capable.

I grit my teeth. There's no point arguing. This call is all about posturing and personal agendas. I'm nothing but a soldier, expected to do as I'm told. This is the part about my job that I despise.

"Okay, I'll do what I can."

"No, you'll do what you *have* to," Sinclair corrects, his tone slow and clear and screaming "read between the lines." "We've poured too much money and time into this case to lose it."

"Got it."

■ ■ ■

It's foreign, experiencing Luke's home as an invited guest walking through his door, instead of a lurker hiding behind a curtain. From my condo, it's just surveillance detail on another target.

But the moment I step through the solid wood door—my nose hit with the scent of sandalwood, my eyes admiring the mixed patterns and fabrics and perfectly positioned artwork that screams "decorator," my ears lulled by the surround-sound rhythmic music—I feel like a switch goes off.

The switch that says I'm on the job.

"I hope you don't mind that I brought him." The second I release Stanley from his leash, his snout hits the ground and he takes off like a hound. "I felt guilty leaving him all evening after being cooped up all day."

"Nope. Maybe that'll keep Licks busy."

I peer up to meet Luke's eyes and boyish grin as he takes in the sheer black blouse and simple miniskirt I chose for tonight. I need to dress to keep his attention, after all. "You look nice," he offers, his voice low and gravelly. He steps in close and I hold my breath, expecting him to lean in and kiss me.

Hoping he does.

But instead, he slides his hands into mine and pulls me into the kitchen, walking backward, his bare feet padding softly against the hard wood. He somehow makes a pair of dark blue jeans and plain gray T-shirt look expensive. He smells expensive, too. And irresistible, I admit, inhaling deeply.

"So . . . what's for dinner?" I warily eye the collection of opened cans and torn packages set out over the kitchen island. An iPad sits in its holder next to it all, open to what looks like a recipe page.

He seizes the sides of my waist and hoists me onto a bar stool, his arm flexing beautifully. "Doesn't matter. Tonight's my turn to cook, so you're going to eat whatever I make."

"I thought the deal was meatball sandwiches?"

"I can't win that, so I've revised our deal."

"With Chef Boyardee?"

"With Chef Boyardee," he repeats with a smirk. "Don't worry, I'm classing it up."

"Yeah, I can see that," I mutter dryly, holding up the jar of pickles and ketchup.

He ignores me, handing me a glass of red wine. "Here. Drink this and shut up while I make my specialty Italian meal."

"I can do that." At twenty-six, I probably drink a tad more than I should. That's another one of those stereotypes that no cop wants to admit to but is unfortunately a real side effect of the job for many of us. "Though I may need a lot more to stomach what you're about to serve me."

"Are you kidding? This is the best. I should really bottle it and sell it by the case." I watch his back with admiration as he passes the wooden spoon through the skillet over the stove. Every appliance in here appears pristine and brand new, never used.

"I wasn't allowed to eat it growing up."

That stops him dead. "What kind of horrible parents would do that to a kid?"

"Ones who believe in only homemade." I chuckle. "They grew up in Italy, so that's what they know. Old school."

"So . . . what, that means—"

"No Chef Boyardee, no Kraft dinner, no Campbell's chicken noodle soup."

The honest, shocked look splayed across his face makes me laugh. "I didn't think there were people like that in this country."

"There are. I was a child deprived of fattening, crappy food. Such a sad life."

"Wow." He shakes his head absently, checking the recipe several times and then, with the awkward movements of a person who has no clue what he's doing in the kitchen, begins measuring out the shredded cheese and mustard. "I'm surprised, given what you said your dad does, that they wouldn't be more progressive."

What my dad does.

He means what Rain's parents are like, and here I've been talking about what Clara's parents are like.

Shit. My heart rate spikes. Warner's going to grill me for risking my cover when he listens to this later.

Thankfully I'm saved from an answer. "There was this week that Alex stayed with Jesse and me after Viktor bashed her up good. We came home to dinner every night. I thought I had died, I was so happy. She's a dynamite cook."

Alex. Sinclair's words jump out at me. Begrudgingly, I ask, "So, how did she end up all the way out there?"

"Sheer luck." Luke licks a dab of sauce off his fingers as he stirs the pan, the simple action stirring flutters in my lower belly. Or maybe it's him in the kitchen, in general. He said he hates cooking and yet he's going to all this effort for me. Even my ex-boyfriend, David, who told me he loved me after a month of dating, never cooked for me. Not once.

I take another long sip of my wine. My body is already warming with the effects of the alcohol. It's too easy to forget myself, to relax and enjoy my company. I need to watch myself. While getting drunk isn't a career ender, it's definitely frowned upon when it comes time for the court case. Any evidence that I gather outside of what's recorded on the wire will be riddled with holes by the time a defense lawyer's done with me.

Knowing this, I still can't seem to control myself. Perhaps it's my subconscious, sabotaging my ability to gather hard evidence against Luke.

"She said she owned the ranch?"

"Yup." He throws some buns on a plate.

"Did she buy it after she divorced her ex?"

"She didn't divorce him. He died." He frowns. "Why so many questions about Alex?"

Shit. "Sorry, I'm being nosy. I'm just really curious. She seems like such a strong girl, after everything she's been through. And she's so happy. I just hope that I can be like her, too, one day." I keep rambling until I sense him relax. That's what a good undercover does—talks herself out of corners.

"Because of what your ex did to you," he says softly, delivering a plate full of some strange concoction in front of me, and topping my wine up. "You'll get there. I'll help you in any way I can." Sincere blue eyes gaze into mine.

I can tell that he means what he says.

A ring from his pocket breaks the spell. He quickly scans it and then drops it back in his pocket without answering. "Rain, meet Cheeseburger-roni."

Knowing that the soft interrogation has to be dropped for now, I focus on my meal, poking it with a fork. "How am I supposed to eat this?"

"Shit," Luke mumbles through a mouthful as a gob hits the floor. He snaps his fingers. Stanley, the faster and arguably smarter, beats the bulldog, cleaning the hardwood with his tongue.

"Like that, I guess," I say, laughing. "Well, you have Stanley's approval."

"Do I have yours?" He watches me take a bite using my fork.

"Not bad," I admit, washing it down with more wine, flashing him a smile. "I still win, though."

"Oh yeah? And what do you win?" His eyes dip down to my mouth, stealing a heartbeat. I like having Luke's attention, his interest. His affections. Too much.

When I don't answer, he merely smiles, taking a drink.

"Water?" I glance at the clear liquid.

"Rust got me on vodka. It's pretty much all I drink now. When I'm not drinking twenty-thousand-dollar-a-shot scotch, that is."

"Vodka and Chef Boyardee." I make a gagging sound, earning his roar of laughter.

We finish dinner in comfortable silence, sharing frequent glances and smiles, both dogs waiting patiently by our legs for another accident. I'm sliding the piece of soggy bun into my mouth when his phone rings yet again.

He offers me an apology and answers. "Yeah?" A pause and then his eyes flicker to me.

I'm immediately off the stool, collecting plates and heading for the sink, using it as an excuse to stay within earshot while looking preoccupied.

Luke grabs onto my forearm with a frown. "No, don't worry about it," he says to me, nodding toward the living room. "Go and relax." Then into the phone, "No one. Just . . . a friend."

I earn another twenty seconds of hovering time by pouring another glass. It's the Bureau's fault if I get drunk tonight.

"No . . . I can't . . . not tonight. I'm busy . . . No!" Aside from when Stanley bit him, I don't think I've heard him snap. "Tomorrow . . . Yeah. No . . . *Tomorrow*."

Still within earshot, I float over toward a wall of pictures with mismatched frames that match in that perfectly eclectic way. The faces that stare back at me are all ones that I've seen before, that sit within the safe in my condo. His sister, both as a bright-eyed, plump-lipped little girl who you want to put on a shelf and simply stare at, and as the curvy blond who garners plenty of attention; his mother, both as the knockout that ensnared Luke's father and as the sallow-faced, haggard-looking woman she has become.

My eyes are transfixed on Luke, though, through many stages of his life. The little boy in pajamas who sits in his grandpa's lap, skinny legs dangling over the side of the burgundy armchair, a swirl of cigarette smoke creating a grainy haze above their heads. The gangly preteen boy sitting in the bleachers at a baseball game, his uncle's arm thrown over his shoulder, that wide, innocent grin stretching across his face. The tall, lean young man in a blue graduation cap and gown, flanked by his mom and sister on one side, his uncle on the other.

Basically, all the versions of Luke that aren't within my case files. The human side of him, which always gets lost in the ugly.

A small lump forms in my throat as I step away from the pictures and shift toward the windows in Luke's cozy, dimly lit living room.

I'd hate to see what prison does to him.

The call doesn't last much longer, though, and I've gotten nothing out of it, other than that someone's trying to get Luke to go somewhere or do something, and he's refusing. I assume, to be with me. I wonder who the someone is.

That small voice in the back of my mind whispers female names. I shush them away, because there's no room for jealousy here. "So that's what my condo looks like from your angle," I call out over my shoulder.

Dishes clatter into the sink. "Shielded and uninviting? Yeah."

"Some of us aren't exhibitionists . . ."

A pause. "Are you admitting to watching me?"

"No."

The floor creaks with his approach but I don't turn around. "So what have you seen?" There's no suspicion in his voice. Only playfulness.

I relax. "Besides a certain black-haired *friend*?"

He groans. "I knew that'd come up again. Yeah. Besides that?"

I hesitate, but then can't help myself. I've never been shy. I can't be in my job. "You should probably not shower after dark." Flashes of the night I caught him bare-assed and heading into his shower hit me, and my cheeks flush. While I'll admit that I've seen that, there's no way I'll admit to camping out every night since, hoping to catch another glimpse.

"Why? I've got nothing to hide."

"Yeah, *clearly*." *But don't you, Luke?*

Heat from his chest radiates off of him, warming my back as he leans in, his breath rolling over my ear. "I don't think you minded."

My entire face burns up, not because we're talking about it, not because he's right, but because Franky and Bill are listening to this. I've had wires on me while I've flirted before. Heck, I had a case only eight months ago where I had to entice this sixty-year-old guy in the lobby lounge of the D.C. Ritz into selling me some cocaine. He was obese, sweating profusely, and reeked of cigars and beer, and for two hours my cover team listened to him tell me all the dirty things he wanted to do to my body up in his hotel room. I had to play along, encouraging it, getting him so worked up in his seat that he willingly pulled his stash out of his pocket and said all the magical words I needed to hear to nail him with a Class A felony. He was looking at twenty years in jail and at his age, that's a death sentence. It took all of twenty minutes to get him to plea bargain with the name of his supplier.

The guys teased me about some of the dirty shit I said for months after, taping newspaper clippings of sex phone operator jobs that I'd be great at to my Jeep's windshield. I never cared because I didn't mean a word of it.

But now with Luke pressing against me, I'd do anything not to have a wire on.

Luke settles his hands onto my shoulders, and his fingertips begin tracing the outline of my collarbone in a slow, seductive rhythm. "I remember this one night when your bedroom blinds were open . . ."

Shit. Of course he's going to bring that up. "That must have been another condo."

His chuckle tickles my ear, sending shivers down my spine. "No, it was definitely yours. I remem—"

Deny! Deny! Deny! I spin around. My one hand covertly smothers my pendant, my other flies up to cover his mouth, stifling his words and the proof of what I had to do to capture my target's attention.

Even in the darkness, his eyes glisten with a mischievous glint, his breathing coming in quick, heavy pulls. Because he knows that I'm well aware of what he's referring to.

And, by the recognition flashing across his face, he's figured out that that was no accident.

Roping strong arms around my body until I can feel every contour, every ridge, every hard part of him, he leans down and settles his mouth on mine, my fingers the only thing separating our lips.

If I could think straight, I'd come up with an excuse to stop this. My thumb wouldn't be hovering over the tiny switch on the backside of my pendant.

But all I'm thinking about is how good Luke feels, and how much I'm starting to like him. And how much I want this to happen.

I switch the wire off and slip my fingers free.

Luke's large frame swallows me up as soft, full lips land on mine, with an odd mix of tenderness and need that wasn't there the first two times he kissed me now radiating off him. It's intoxicating enough to dissolve the last of my focus, as I let myself be consumed by all of him. Until I'm no longer a cop and Luke isn't who he is. I'm just a twenty-six-year-old girl with feelings and needs who's attracted to this beautiful man.

For the first time, I let my hands wander shamelessly over his body—over cut arms, and a solid chest, and strong shoulders. My fingers coil through the curls at the nape of his neck; his hair is even softer than I imagined, and I've imagined it a lot.

His arms tighten, pulling me in even closer against him, until his groin is digging into me. I can feel how much he wants me, and it only turns me on more. A smooth hand slips under the back of my shirt, grazing the small of my back, just the slight touch of his fingertips on my bare skin sending shivers through every sensitive spot on my body.

I know I don't have long. The little voice in the back of my head screams that I have to restrain myself. I can't let this go too far, too fast, or it'll up the stakes for the next time. But on the other hand, I want to make the most of these moments with him because I won't get them again. That's why I don't stop him when he shifts back toward the window, until I feel the cool glass against my skin. Shifting his feet in between mine, my legs naturally move to accommodate his body as it presses up against me.

It isn't until his hand slides up the length of my thigh, under my skirt, that reality sinks in.

I break away from his mouth to whisper, "Slow down."

His mouth finds my neck, his body pressing up harder, his fingers curling around the side of my panties. This has gone too far. "Luke!"

A sudden bang sounds at the door. Stanley and Licks bolt up and run over to dance in front of it, howling at the top of their lungs in a horrendous choir.

It finally grabs Luke's attention, though, a wild, confused look clearing the heady haze from his eyes. "What the hell?" He checks the clock on the TV on his way to the door. He leans up to the peephole. "Seriously?" Luke throws open the door to find Franky standing there in a pair of jeans and a bomber jacket, a pizza box balanced in his hand.

"That'll be twenty-two forty," he says, his eyes surveying the condo with lightning-quick speed, zeroing in on me.

"We didn't order pizza."

"Yeah you did," Franky argues, matter-of-factly.

"No." Luke pauses. "Well, *I* didn't. Unless . . ." He glances back. "Was dinner really that bad?"

I smile and shake my head. "Don't get me started on shitty fast-food pizza."

Franky holds up a piece of paper and scrunches his face up. Glancing at the door, and then back at the paper, he begins apologizing. "Aw, man. I'm so sorry. This dyslexia, you know? It makes me fuck numbers up sometimes. Between that and the sporadic hearing loss . . ." His eyes dart to me, and I hear the message loud and clear.

Feigning shock by opening my eyes wide, I quickly switch my wire back on, Luke's attention still on Franky.

"No worries," Luke says.

"Sorry about that. Good evening, miss." He salutes and leaves. I wonder which condo isn't getting their pizza tonight.

Luke throws his door shut and pauses to rub the back of his head, a look of bewilderment on his face. He shakes it off with a laugh. "Well, that was weird."

Now that the haze has dispelled from around my head, I'm able to see more clearly. "Listen, I should probably get going."

"Wait." Luke levels me with a pleading look that I can't peel my eyes from. "I'm really sorry about that. I shouldn't have let it go that far. You're just so . . . *Shit*." He hangs his head and closes his eyes, guilt radiating off him.

"It's okay. Really." I close the distance and collect his hand in mine, lifting his knuckles to my lips in the lightest kiss, one that hopefully no one can hear.

"I won't let that happen again, I promise. Just stay. Watch a movie with me . . ." He begins leading me backward, away from the front door. He nods toward Stanley, sitting beside Licks on a giant denim dog bed again, now that the excitement is over. "Come on. Stanley really wants to stay, see?"

"Stanley's licking his own junk."

"Well, you definitely don't want to interrupt him while he's doing that."

"Fine. A movie and nothing else." I drop into the couch.

"Finish this off." I quietly watch him empty the last of the wine into my glass, my gaze wandering as he turns his focus to the plasma on the wall. The surprise guest didn't completely kill it for him, based on the prominent bulge in his jeans. Is that why he wants me to stay? If so, he's persistent, I'll give him that much.

"What kind of movie do you want?" I look up to find him smirking, full well knowing where my attention just was.

My cheeks burn. "Whatever you want."

Diving into the couch beside me, he hooks an arm around my shoulders and scrolls through a list of shows he's recorded on the DVR, finally landing on one.

"No."

"What? Why not? Don't you think it's a brilliant concept?"

"Filming people while they wander around the jungle naked is not brilliant. It's the dumbest thing I've ever heard of."

"Fine." He keeps scrolling until he reaches a string of *American Idol* episodes.

"Chef Boyardee and reality TV? Seriously, are you twelve? Give me that!" I yank the remote from his hand and begin scanning the movie channels, looking for something that's at least vaguely stimulating to my brain. Wondering how the hell anyone could be grooming this guy to run an international car theft ring.

He's nothing but amused, easily relinquishing control, seemingly happy to twirl the ends of my hair and let me choose some action adventure with robots and dinosaurs and a hot male actor.

Luke keeps his word, pulling me against his side and holding me through the movie. Trying for nothing more than an occasional kiss against my temple. Just like I'd expect from any decent, loving boyfriend.

■ ■ ■

"What the hell happened in there?"

I brace myself against Warner's harsh tone. "He pulled me in for a kiss and I guess the wire switched off when our chests rubbed together."

"What was he doing, lying *on top* of you?"

"No! And stop yelling at me!"

"I'm going to call Sinclair and pull you off."

"Go ahead and try!" I catch a reflection of my face in my bedroom mirror; I'm wearing a hideous sneer. "Because I can guarantee you Sinclair won't take issue with *anything* that happens, as long as he gets what he wants."

There's a moment's pause, and when Warner speaks again, he's unnaturally calm. "Why do you say that? Did he tell you that?"

"Basically. He called me before I went over."

Warner's heavy sigh swirls into my ear. "I almost walked out of another case tonight when Bill called me."

"Look, I'm fine. The case is fine. We're all fine."

"Are you sure? He didn't . . ."

"No. I didn't let it go too far." I totally let it go too far. "You need to relax a bit. Go get some sleep. You sound exhausted." The guy never stops working.

I hang up with Warner and head straight for my window, opening a section of the blinds. Just like I promised Luke I'd do. He wanted to walk me home but I made him stay, on the condition that I'd wave to him from my room so he'd know I was safe.

Sure enough, there he is, waiting. Lights on. Changed into a pair of track pants, I assume for his daily obsessive workout.

Shirtless.

My heart rate jumps. I simply stand there with my arms over my chest, admiring the view. Glad that there's a street and two flights of stairs between me and that right now.

What? he mouths, corded arms stretched out to either side of him, a smirk curling his lips. Knowing exactly how attractive he is.

I can play this game.

It's a dangerous game.

The adrenaline junkie in me—it's in all undercovers—likes dangerous games.

My fingers move quickly as I unbutton my blouse and let it drop to my feet. A quick glance to the condo beside Luke—the only one that might have an awkwardly angled view into my bedroom to see what I'm doing right now—confirms that no one else is watching. Taking a deep breath, I reach one arm behind me to unclasp my bra while my other hand hits the button for the blinds. They revolve shut just as I let the lace fall.

I dare peek around the edge. And giggle. Luke's head is bowed and pressed up against the glass. Track pants don't hide much.

I switch off the lights and spend the next hour spying on Luke, as he attempts to get his usual crunches and push-ups in and ends up heading into the shower.

I probably shouldn't have done that.

Chapter 27

...

LUKE

"Fucking Russians!" Rust slams the office door behind him as he storms in. "Where's Miller?"

"Said he had to go on a parts run. Didn't want to wait for the delivery guy anymore. Why? What's up?" Rust sounds more agitated than he was when he called last night, trying to drag me out to The Cellar to talk.

Rust shakes his head. "Just got off the phone with Andrei about the Ferrari."

Shit. So they did figure it out. "I knew that was going to come back and bite us. What'd you say?"

"The truth. That they didn't want to do business with us so we were forced to go elsewhere."

"And?"

"And now they're claiming *another* five percent upcharge for handling fees for the next shipment. Something about needing to bribe more officials. Plus he said the orders will be light for the next round."

"You told them to go to hell, right?"

Miller's chair protests with a loud creak as Rust drops into it, his forehead in his hands. "Not yet. I've got to figure out the right way to handle them."

"Fuck 'em! We're taking all the risk and they're undercutting us. We've already got another pipeline, remember?"

"And I've already told you, it's not that easy. If I just stop doing business with them, this could get ugly, Luke."

"What does that mean, exactly?"

Rust sighs, his hard gaze locked on the gray-tiled floor. "I'm not sure yet, to be honest. They need us if they want this organization working for them, and it's a smooth-running operation. I just can't figure out why they're dicking me around so much." He groans loudly, and then slaps the desk, which I know means he's switching gears to something else. That's Rust. He doesn't get too bogged down with one problem. He keeps his focus and things move at a fast pace. That's why he's so successful. "So you're going up to the Astoria warehouse this week?"

"Yeah. Rodriguez has a few chopped cars to unload." The second part of my role—driving to the warehouse to accept an order and pay Rodriguez—makes the phone calls seem like a piece of cake. I've only had to do it once so far. My hands were cramped by the time I got home, from gripping the steering wheel so tight. I've never felt relief like I did after parking Rust's truck and getting back into my car. Done with it.

"Okay. I'll send you the code to the gate. Let me know what time you're going up."

My phone begins ringing. Aref's name flashes across the screen. "Speak of the devil." Aref's obviously not using a burner phone, so it must not be about the Ferrari. "Just give me the word, Rust."

He hesitates and then nods. "Talk to him. See exactly what he's looking for. In person." He holds a finger of warning up. "But don't commit to anything."

I nod my understanding to Rust, the receiver to my ear already. "Hey, buddy. How's the pretentious scotch?"

"Still pretentious," Aref's smooth English-laced accent answers with a laugh.

"Were your ears burning? Rust and I were just talking about you." I give my uncle a salute as he leaves.

"Only good things, I hope."

"Always. What can I do for you?"

"Elmira and I are hosting a few friends on our yacht this weekend. We were hoping you and your woman could attend."

My woman. I smile. Is she mine? Does she want to be?

"It'll be an overnight sail along the Columbia River. We'll stay in the mouth, given the water's too choppy beyond that at this time of year. What do you say?"

"Sounds perfect." For more than one reason.

Chapter 28

...

CLARA

I've never seen Warner's brow quite so furrowed. "Anything closer than that and we risk being spotted."

"I'll be fine."

"They likely wouldn't do anything until you're in deeper waters. It'll be twenty minutes to reach you, if we gun it."

I laugh it off to alleviate my handler's worries, even as mine linger. "Relax. If so much as a hair on the back of my neck spikes, I'll fake a stomach bug and grab one of the Jet Skis. It's that simple." Luke's too genuine to be able to hide his suspicions of me, I remind myself. He has no clue.

But what about Aref?

Luke said that the billionaire businessman, who *must* be a part of this ring, specifically asked that he bring me. Has Aref discovered who I really am? He'd have to have a ton of money and powerful connections to crack through the agency's undercover operations files. But, based on what I saw of him, if anyone could pull it off, it would be Aref.

"Relax, Warner. This is a great opportunity to get intel. Drinking, intimate setting. Seriously, I'll be okay." After a pause, I add, "Sinclair seems to think so." I've already had a call from the big boss telling me as much.

Warner folds his arms over his chest, his jaw tense. "He called you again?"

"Like you said, he wants to win this case."

Warner answers with a head shake, clearly unimpressed. His eyes drift down to the plunging neckline of my red silk dress. Luke warned me beforehand that the invitation calls for formal attire; that Elmira likes to go all out when she throws these "little gatherings." I feel ridiculous, leaving the condo dressed like this mid-afternoon. "Did you get your own cabin, at least?"

I wonder if Warner's like this with all his female undercovers. My gut is beginning to tell me that he isn't. That the extra attention, the way he drops everything for me—including his girl-friend's sister's wedding—may have less to do with his devotion to the job and more about an interest in me. It's too bad I just don't feel the same way about him. Maybe I would, if I weren't on this case. Maybe when I'm done with it, things will change.

"I don't know, big brother. I'll figure it out. That's the least of my worries." A conflicting storm of trepidation and excitement brews inside me. Luke's words from the other night rang true—I know he meant what he said about not pushing me—but will it be the same when I'm lying next to him in a bed?

And how exactly will *I* feel?

I stoop down to scratch Stanley's ears. "You be good for Uncle Jack, you hear?" Stanley responds with a yelp and a few licks of my hand. "See? He's okay with me going. Be like Stanley."

"You want me to lick you?"

I smack his stomach. "And if I don't come back with the yacht, Stanley's all yours."

Warner glowers at me.

■ ■ ■

"We're so happy you could join us, Rain." Elmira somehow manages to make her London accent sound seductive. She's in another long, flowing dress, this one as black as her hair. A plunging neckline and smattering of diamonds hanging from a gold chain diminish the fact that she has next to no curves.

She certainly has the princess genes in her.

"Thank you for inviting us," I offer as a man in an all-white suit swoops in to collect my overnight bag wordlessly.

"Cabin Five, please, Gabriel," Elmira directs him with a graceful wave of her delicately toned arm. "And our other guest will be in Cabin Six, right across the hall."

I glance back to watch Gabriel slip Luke's bag from his hand, admiring the tailored silver-gray suit he arrived in at my condo.

"Luke said you may be more comfortable with your own room," Elmira explains, a curious flicker in her obsidian eyes.

"If it's not putting anyone out."

"We have just enough room." She pauses. "You look surprised about these arrangements."

The truth is, I'm floored. This guy is given the perfect excuse to get into bed with me for a night, use the old "Oops. Sorry, I was asleep," cop-a-feel move, and he's not using it? In fact, I'm sure he's setting himself up for a lot of inappropriate questions and obnoxious comments, if these men are an eighth of what the guys I work with are like.

"Come." She turns up the stairs to the second deck, giving me the view of her bare, slender back. It's way too cold to be dressed like that. "We'll be setting off shortly. Let me introduce you to everyone."

I follow her, pausing to glance back once. To find Luke's eyes on me.

■ ■ ■

"She couldn't decide between the Tuscan villa or a cottage in Provence, so I just bought her both," the blond drones, taking an extra-long sip of her Champagne, perched on the edge of the couch.

"Your mom's lucky to have such a generous daughter," the red-head next to her says, eyeing her freshly painted blood-red lipstick in her compact.

Half an hour sitting on this couch and all I've heard about is how much money these people have and how much they spend, how frivolously. Maybe that's why I've somehow managed to pour three glasses of Champagne down my throat, despite being mindful. In fact, I'm in need of a refill. It's going to be a long night, and I should be more careful.

At least I've had no indication—no odd looks, no whispers, no anything—to suggest I should be worried about a late-night dive with an anchor tied to me. Yet.

I haven't learned one valuable piece of information, relegated to the wives' circle while the men congregate on the upper deck. Is this how it always is with these guys? Wives dependent on their husbands for their money, sipping on Cristal while the men make their covert deals. At least, I assume that's what they're doing up there. Successful criminals are successful because they're *always* looking for the next opportunity. If they'd put that kind of dedication toward a legitimate life, most would still do quite well.

I want to slap each and every one of these women's faces. Even Elmira sits with them, quiet but smiling, her attention seemingly riveted to the vapid circle of chatter.

"Excuse me." I wave my empty glass in the air as I make my way over to the server. There are several staff onboard, graceful ghosts who appear with food and drink at the right moment before disappearing into the background once again.

I can't go back to that pit of shallow minds, but simply storming in on Luke may not be the smoothest option. So I instead wander over to the rail and admire the coastline in twilight, my last chance before everything is shrouded in darkness. Astoria's city lights line the water's edge in the distance, and beyond them is the jagged border of the mountains.

A gentle rocking and cool breeze makes me pull my jacket tight to my body. The entire afternoon traveling up the Columbia River from Aref and Elmira's palatial North Portland home has been . . . enchanting. Hours of nothing but scenic views—valleys and forestry and inlets—has made me struggle at times to remember why I'm here to begin with. And that there is a cover team following along the coastline in a car, worried about getting to me before my body is tossed overboard.

Even with my heightened senses, the exponential increase in danger, I'll miss this when I'm back in Washington, D.C., knocking on cheap motel doors again.

"Have you ever driven along it?" Elmira sidles up to me, her gaze settling on the Astoria–Megler Bridge ahead, a four-mile-long architectural masterpiece highlighted by the purple sky. A full drink in her hand, a slight swagger in her movements. She's drunk. I may be slightly tipsy too, but I can handle myself better than most.

"Not yet."

"You should have Luke take you. Great views. There are plenty of beautiful pictures to take from up there." She pauses. "You're not from around here, are you?"

"No." I give her the thirty-second cover story spiel. It comes so naturally to me that I almost believe it myself now.

"I've never been to Washington, D.C. I hear it's nice."

"It's nothing like this."

"Will you be staying long, then?"

"Not sure." *Depends how secretive your husband and Luke are.*

She nods slowly. "I'm heading back to London in July."

"With Aref?"

She sighs. "Depends on what kind of business he stirs up here. His family's company is well run and he gets bored easily. He's been *very* bored as of late."

Bored. A great excuse for risking felony charges. *Idiot.* I should never be surprised and yet I always am.

"You've thrown a nice party," I offer genuinely.

"That's what I do. Throw parties," she murmurs dryly, sipping from her glass.

A loud, unattractive howl sounds behind us and we both glance at the three overdone women laughing on the couch.

"They certainly like everyone to know how much money they have, don't they?" Elmira muses, a derisive smirk touching her lips.

"I've noticed."

"People who grow up with nothing and suddenly have everything don't know how to behave around it. They end up looking like cheap reproductions and sounding like tacky fools. I wish they were forced into charm school before being handed any checks."

Interesting thing to say about the guests at her party. "So they're really not your friends?"

"I tolerate them. They're certainly not like me. Or you."

I fight the urge to laugh, and give myself a pat on the back for fooling even the born-and-bred wealthy likes of Elmira.

She glances up to the third deck, to the male-dominated party. "Aref does business with these people, so I play nice and don't let them see me cringe at every asinine comment that comes out of their mouths."

I smile. "I have a few relationships like that." That basically sums up my life, listening to and laughing at what scumbags have to say while I set them up for a takedown. Luke is the first target that doesn't make me cringe. That I actually look forward to seeing.

With a sly grin, she turns her back to the water to face the group, dropping her voice. "The blond in the blue dress? The one chattering on about buying houses for her mom? That's Laurel. She was an escort. That's how she met Philip. He paid her to suck his cock and I guess it was true love."

I choke on a mouthful of Champagne, hearing such a crass word come from such seemingly refined lips. "Really . . ."

A wicked giggle escapes her. "And Celia? The redhead? She was the nanny, hired by the wife. Broke the marriage up when the baby was just five months old. Her real name is Peggy-Sue but she changed it about a year ago. Said Celia sounds more distinguished."

I meet her impish grin with one of my own. "I like this game. What else you got?" This may be easier than I thought.

Her face twists. "The big bald man standing on the other side of Luke? He spends one night a week at the RiverPlace hotel with his boyfriend. His wife, Carla—the curvy one in the black lace dress—has no clue, but that could be because she's too busy fucking the seventeen-year-old pool boy, so . . ."

"So cliché," I joke, an edge of unease sliding its way in. This is the kind of stuff surveillance teams pick up. "You seem to know an awful lot about everyone."

"Aref makes it his job to know who he's going into business with."

And the people around them, obviously. I feel her dark eyes on me as I take a calm sip, training my focus on Luke while my senses go into overdrive. What exactly is Elmira telling me right now? Has Aref been looking into me? What could he possibly find out? Not much. I've stayed in role. But I think back to that comment earlier, about taking photos on the bridge . . . It could have been coincidence, or it could be a hint that they know about my classes.

That they've been following me.

Suddenly I'm gauging the depth of the water and distance to the shore, wondering if I could actually make it down to the Jet Skis in time, wishing I were a stronger swimmer. But I can't think like that. I have to assume nothing. Playing the curious new girlfriend is the only direction I can take. "Any juicy info on Luke that I should know about?"

The breeze carries her low, throaty chuckle as we both turn back to face the dark waters. "Well, you definitely don't have to worry about where his preferences lay."

"That's good. What else?"

She sips her drink slowly, her words deliberate. "He's too trusting, wouldn't you say?"

I struggle to keep my face stoic, even as I feel the blood drain from it. "I don't know about that. I do know that he really likes your husband."

"Aref can charm anyone he needs to in order to get what he wants. He is, first and foremost, a businessman. There's a reason he and his family are so wealthy." She pauses. "Luke likes Aref because Aref wants to be liked."

I frown at her warning tone. Or maybe I'm just paranoid. "Are you saying he shouldn't trust Aref?"

Dark eyes flicker to me. "I'm saying that Luke may be getting in over his head, and that is not a good place to be with these people."

A sinking feeling hits the pit of my stomach. Is Luke in danger? "Why are you—"

I gasp as strong arms suddenly wrap around my body.

Chapter 29

...

LUKE

Two hours of listening to these guys talk world politics and business is about all I can take. Partly because I'm not interested, but mostly because I have no fucking clue what these guys are talking about. Islamic rule? A Scottish referendum? North Korean missile launches?

I guess I should add CNN to my lineup of reality TV and sports. Too bad I hate watching the news. I can't talk about business with Aref around these guys. So when I saw Rain leaning against the rail, her sexy, sleek curves calling to me, I had my excuse to detach.

"You two enjoy yourselves. Take a tour, if you'd like. There will be another course of appetizers circulating soon," Elmira says, shooting a hard look at Rain before drifting away.

Rain's body is rigid beneath my fingers. "What was that about?"

"I just don't know how to read her." With a deep sigh, she shakes her head. "It was nothing. How's your night?"

Standing behind Rain, holding her like this, gives me easy access to her slender neck. I dip my nose into it, inhaling the scent of her—rose petals—my eyes stealing a glance at the swell of her breasts.

Remembering the night she gave me a millisecond's worth glance at them at the window last week. It seems she's more comfortable getting undressed for me from thirty feet and two glass panels away. If that's what she needs to do for now, I'll grin and bear it. From what I've already seen, it will be well worth the wait.

"Much better now."

Her body finally relaxes into mine as my arms tighten around her waist, her ass pressing into my hips, about the exact time that my dick begins to harden. *Perfect*. Well, at least she knows she has my full attention.

When I asked Aref for two cabins, he laughed at me. Part of me wanted to take advantage of this situation, even if just to lie next to her. But, after last Saturday, I know that the likelihood of me controlling myself is near zero, so I figured I'd heed Jesse's advice. "Follow her lead." She has an out. If she decides she wants to climb into my bed, it'll be 100 percent her choice.

And I'm 1,000 percent ready.

Sure enough, another waiter circulates with a tray of shrimp in minutes.

Rain groans. "I think I'm going to explode if I keep eating." Her hand moves to her lower belly. Without hesitation, I cover it with mine, the width expanse of my fingers splaying over hers, feeling the seam of her panties through her dress with the tip of my pinky. She tenses for just a moment but, after taking a deep breath, she falls farther into me.

"How are the wives?"

She rolls her head until her cheek leans against my chest, and in a low voice, she admits, "Arrogant and boring. Listening to them makes me want to gouge my eyes out with a spoon."

"So . . . good?" I chuckle.

She flashes a grimace at me. "Sorry. They're just not my type. You know, the kind you can never fully trust."

I smile. I want her to enjoy this night, but I'm happy she's not *that* type. More and more, these women aren't my type either. My type is quickly becoming Rain, and only Rain.

I can't keep my mouth from grazing that soft curve at the base of her neck.

She stiffens momentarily before her head falls back, giving me easier access. "You were up there for a while. Anything interesting?"

"No. They were talking politics, mainly. I could have used that spoon on my own eyes after you did, actually." I let my words drag over her silky skin with my lips. "Hopefully I can get Aref by himself later."

Her chest heaves with a quick breath and my arm automatically tightens, fighting the urge to curl my hand up and around one of those perfect tits. "You have business to talk about tonight?"

"Yeah, but only a bit, I promise."

"That's okay, I understand." She turns into me just slightly. "How well do you know him, anyway? You said you just met?"

"Aref wants a partnership with us and I need to test the waters to find out exactly what his terms are." I'm probably saying more than I should but, I swear, her body is yanking the words out of me.

"Do whatever you have to do. We're here all night." There's a pause, and then, "What kind of partnership? With the garage?" Her hips grind back into me and my mind goes blank, momentarily.

"Uh . . . no. But it has something to do with cars."

Her free hand rises to slide over my cheek, her trim nails scraping against my light stubble. "We should spend some time with Aref and Elmira tonight. Get to know them better."

"Sure. We can do that." *Or we can spend the rest of the night in your cabin; to hell with Aref and Elmira, and Rust, too.*

Taking her hand in mine, I lead her around the corner, out of prime view. I spin her around in my arms and press her up against the railing, my hand behind her to soften the impact of the metal bar against her back.

The burn in her eyes, the sharp peaks at the front of her dress where her nipples have pebbled, the way her hand settles on my chest, sliding over the contours, makes me think she feels the same way that I do.

But I wait. Something I don't ever remember doing. I wait

for her to make the first move. I begin to think it's not going to happen, and then I see the decision flicker across her face. She nods at me, like she can read my mind. That's all I need before my hand's weaving through her long hair at the base of her neck and I'm crashing into her mouth, tasting the sweet Champagne she just finished on her tongue.

If this were any other girl that I've ever been with, we'd be halfway down the stairs to my cabin by now. As it is, I don't know how I'm going to actually get any sleep with her across the way. "Stay with me tonight?" slips out before I can help myself. I quickly follow it up with, "Just to sleep, that's all. I promise."

She doesn't answer, closing her mouth over mine again, her palms sliding flush up the length of my stomach and chest, one chilly tip finding its way between the buttons of my shirt to slip under, grazing my skin.

I can't help myself anymore, my hand groping her ass through the smooth silk, ready to lift her onto the ledge and press myself in between her thighs.

A horn blasts nearby.

"Coast Guard!" someone hollers in the background. It takes Rain's palms pushing against my chest to catch my attention.

"Hey." She giggles, her cheeks red.

I lost control with her again. It's too easy. "I'm so sorry."

"It's okay." Her nervous fumbles with that dragonfly necklace make me wonder if it really is okay, but then she gives me a quick pat on the chest and a kiss on the lips before slinking away and rounding the corner.

At some point while we were distracted, a few guests decided it would be a good idea to break out the coke. Rain and I watch as they scramble to snort every last line already laid out on the table before the Coast Guard boards.

Aref marches over to us, his strides much quicker than normal. "If you have anything that you don't want them to find, I suggest you deal with it quickly. We won't be allowed in our rooms while they search."

"Does this happen a lot?" I ask.

"It's happened once or twice to me since I bought this yacht," he admits. "What can I say? It attracts a lot of attention."

"But how can they just do that? Don't they need a warrant or something?" Luke asks.

"Not on a boat. They have full jurisdiction on U.S.-sanctioned open waters," Rain says and then presses her lips together.

"She's right. They can jump onboard and tear this place apart." He winks at Rain. "But, please, continue enjoying yourself. We'll be rid of them soon." As he's turning, I catch the easygoing smile slide off his face, replaced with a frown.

He marches away, shifting over to another couple, I assume to warn them of the same. "I hope this night doesn't end up in handcuffs," I mutter quietly, as the lit-up Coast Guard boat—dwarfed by the size of Aref's yacht but looking threatening all the same—speeds toward us.

"Why would it? Do you have something to hide?" Rain asks.

I smile down at her, roping my arms around her waist. "Nope. Not a thing."

Chapter 30

...

CLARA

Bill looks good in a Coast Guard's vest, I'll give him that.

But what the hell is he doing here and how on earth did he finagle a spot on the Coast Guard ship? This has Warner written all over it. He's worried about me; I get it. Fine. But at the risk of blowing my cover? *Jesus.*

"What's wrong?" Luke asks, worried eyes on me.

I take a deep breath as I watch the small army of men and two women climb onboard, armed with assault rifles and emotionless faces, and I expel my frustration and anger—because there's no reason for Rain Martines to be experiencing either—and give him the broadest smile. "I hate interruptions."

And, deep down, I do hate that we were interrupted. Because in that hazy moment, I was fully Rain and there was no taint of right or wrong, no little Sinclair and Warner sitting on my shoulder whispering orders and warnings.

Luke's blue eyes sparkle, dropping down to my mouth at the same time that his hand grips my side, squeezing gently. An edge of guilt washes over me. Not because I didn't enjoy every touch, every kiss, every feel of him against me.

Because I did.

"Sir, Ma'am . . . any contraband onboard that you would like us to be made aware of? Telling us now will lessen repercussions when we find something in your belongings."

Oh hell. He said "when." Now I know what's going on. I bet a million bucks that Bill's got an eight-ball of cocaine or something else that gives him the excuse to pull me off this yacht. To "rescue" me out of a situation he doesn't want me to be in.

He can't do this to me. Not now.

Not after I just told Aref that I'm clean. That'll give him—and Luke—a reason to cut me off completely.

"No, we're just here to enjoy a night with our friends, and we'd like to get back to that as quickly as possible," I say slowly, clearly, shooting a very brief but cutting glare of warning.

Bill turns on his heels and heads toward the stairs that lead into the cabins. *Please don't do this.*

Luke rubs my back. "Don't worry, it'll be over soon. Can I get you a drink?"

"Yes!" I answer, a tad too eager. "Another glass of Cristal."

He smiles and strolls toward a waiter. Quickly glancing around to make sure everyone's distracted, I spin to face the sea, my hiss low but enunciated. "Don't do it, guys. If I get busted on here, I'll never get invited back. I'll be the idiot who didn't ditch her stash and lied to Aref. You can kiss this cover goodbye." That's all I can manage before Luke returns, handing me a drink. I suck it back quickly.

And I watch.

For almost an hour, the guards tear around the yacht in search of some reason to end this party. I grit my teeth, preparing myself for the inevitability that I will be that reason.

One . . . two . . . three . . . one after another, the guards appear from decks below, unsuccessful in their treasure hunt.

Bill is the last to come out.

His hands empty.

"Thank you for your cooperation," one guy offers to Aref, and then hops off.

I fall into Luke's shoulder with relief while the other guests rush down to their rooms to check the upheaval. The wait staff sweep in to collect empty glasses and plates, and I get the impression that the party is coming to a close.

"See?" Aref's hands spread out, visibly more relaxed himself. "No worries."

"I'd be pissed if I were you," Luke mutters.

Aref waves a hand, acting like he doesn't care. "Fuck them. It's over. Come on." He nods his head toward the stairs. "We should talk."

I don't get more than two steps in before Elmira appears. "Rain. Let me show you to your room." Her lithe arm stretches out, beckoning.

"I'm sure I can find my way." I glance over at Luke, hoping he'll ask me to stay.

He leans in and kisses me quickly. "I'll come find you when we're done."

With a forced smile, I follow Elmira down the winding staircase to the first floor where the cabins are. "You are worried about him, aren't you?" she says softly, stopping in front of a door.

"What makes you say that?"

She peers up at me with knowing eyes. Her diminutive, childlike appearance is a good cover for a very smart, very manipulative woman. "Because of what I said. Because you like him and . . ." She leans casually against the lacquered wall. " . . . because you are smart enough to understand what kind of business our men are involved in."

I mimic her stance, though inside warning flares are going off. What does she know? "He doesn't talk to me about that stuff."

"Aref was like that with me for a long time. It's normal." She sighs, glancing between the cabin doors. I'm assuming the one across from me is Luke's. "But eventually his walls started coming down. Don't underestimate the power of sharing a bed, if you really want him to trust you. To treat you like a partner." Her dark red lips curl into a sly smile. "Have a good night."

I wander into my room—a small but elegant cabin with

just enough space for a bed and nightstand on either side—and find my overnight bag ransacked by the Coast Guard. At least, I assume it was by the Coast Guard. I don't really care. There was nothing of value in there, and nothing that could identify me for what I am. I focus on folding my clothes up and pulling out my night things, while replaying all of Elmira's words.

Her warning about Luke. Is she working *with* Aref by telling me this, or against him? Is it a test? Are they seeing if he has the guts to stick around? If *I* do? A glance down at the four-inch scar along the inside of my elbow reminds me of the last time I dealt with a husband and wife. I was still in uniform and answering a domestic abuse call. While my partner was handcuffing the drunk husband for punching out his wife, she had a change of heart and took a swipe at me with a paring knife.

Aref and Elmira don't seem like the drunken knife-wielding type. They're more calculating than that. Perhaps they're the type to pay a late-night visit to my room. Or pay Luke a visit to his room. Is *that* what Elmira was warning me about?

I can't even call Warner to see what he thinks because, for all I know, this room is bugged.

I know I can't just sit here and wait. So I venture out of my room, more intent on keeping Luke out of trouble than catching him as he gets himself deeper into it.

Chapter 31

...

LUKE

"You deal with Vlad. You know what he's like."

Aref puffs on his Cohiba, a model of sophistication as he leans back on the couch in a plum-colored pinstripe suit. If he spends four hundred grand on a bottle of scotch, I'm afraid to guess what his clothes cost. "Yes, I do. Difficult at the best of times. Someone I'd like to feed to a pit of crocodiles most other times. With Viktor gone, it's increasingly been the latter." He shrugs in an "I don't really give a fuck" way. "But I'm fortunate. If he tries to dick me around, then he gets to find another reputable source for shipping." His smirk suggests that would be pretty damn hard. "I imagine they're going to take issue with you making deals directly with me."

"Or anyone else, besides them." I lick the spicy taste of my own cigar from my lips as I let my head fall back and take in the million stars above. I could definitely get used to this life.

Aref seems to ponder this while ashing his cigar in a tall planter next to us. The others have vanished into their cabins; otherwise we wouldn't be able to talk so openly. My own eyes keep drifting to the set of stairs that will lead down into my cabin and, more importantly, Rain's.

"There's no reason that you and I can't establish a business for different parts of the world," he finally says.

"That's exactly what I told Rust." I have no fucking clue where

Vlad's delivering all the chopped cars, other than the few countries Rust mentioned earlier. Thailand, China, I assume Russia. "Where are you proposing?"

Aref doesn't miss a beat. "Africa. There's a big demand for SUVs by government and military. I've had someone reach out to me, to see if I could help."

"And they don't believe in paying the manufacturers?"

Aref chuckles. "Not these people. They don't believe in paying, period, if they can get something for free. This would not be free, but it would be discounted by their standards."

I weigh my words carefully before I speak again. "Vlad and Andrei have been making business less profitable for us. If you were to present us with a fair arrangement, I'd say Rust would have a hard time saying no to you. But it's got to be a long-term plan, not something to pull us in before you start adding upcharges at every delivery."

Aref holds his hands up. "That is not how I do business."

I'd like to believe that. He seems like a stand-up guy. "Let me ask you something, though . . . you have all this." I wave a hand around. "So why get involved? You could lose everything. I don't get it."

He draws another puff of his cigar. "'Why, customs officer, I had no idea what was in those crates. Prove that I did before you can charge me with anything.'" His smile is foxlike, his eyes darting behind me, as Elmira sweeps past me with an ashtray for our table. "My wife doesn't like that I smoke cigars."

"That's not true. I simply don't enjoy finding filth polluting the soil for my cannas," she murmurs, her eyebrow raised toward the evidence beside him.

He laughs and reaches up to grip the back of her slender thigh through her dress. "To answer your question, Luke, I'm in a risky business but I don't take stupid risks. I'm careful about who I do business with and who I trust. And I *always* go with the winning horse. This woman here?" He peers up at her, his dark eyes glassy with booze and lust and adoration. "She's the only one I trust completely. We have no secrets between us, and she has an un-canny radar for bad business propositions. Spots them within five minutes." His hand shifts up to her ass, giving it a good squeeze, showing me a hint of an aggressive side that I wasn't quite sure existed.

Bending down to plant a kiss on his lips, she slips away qui-etly, Aref's eyes trailing her swaying hips until they disappear. "I never thought I'd find a woman who understands me completely, who feels like my equal. When that woman doesn't like someone, I don't like someone. And I don't do business with them. Those other men here tonight married foolish cows, and they spend entirely too much effort keeping them happy and quiet. Elmira doesn't feel they are good partners for us, and that's why my busi-ness with them is limited and will never expand beyond what it is. Of course, they have no clue how much more money they could be making. They think they're on top of the world."

Why is he saying all this? Is he about to tell me that she doesn't approve of Rain? I'm not sure how I'm going to handle that. Rain is the first woman I might actually have feelings for.

His eyes flash to mine and I see the recognition there. "She likes your woman."

I feel my shoulders sag with relief.

"Elmira thinks she's very smart. She could be a good partner for you. But do you trust her?"

I can't help but chuckle. "It's only been a few weeks, Aref."

"And yet you've spent more time with her than you do with most women, right?"

I pause before answering. How the hell does he know? Has he had me followed? Before I have a chance to ask, he goes on. "What kind of woman do you think she is? Is she one of those . . ." He gestures absently toward the couch down below, where the women sat earlier. " . . . who you buy with diamonds and houses, or is she a true partner, like Elmira?"

The mention of diamonds reminds me of the necklace I bought her, that I've tucked away for a later date. Because I've already assumed there will be a point in our relationship when I can give it to her without it feeling weird. "I honestly don't know, Aref."

That's exactly why Rust has never settled down. He's always said he doesn't trust a woman not to sell him out for the right price. I'm the only one he trusts. He knows I'd never sell him out.

Would Rain balk at the very idea of dating a guy involved with a car theft ring? What would she say if she met Vlad? She already met Aref, and said she liked him, but those two are day and night. Would she want anything to do with a guy like me if she knew what I'm getting into? Does she have a right to know?

Leaning forward, Aref butts his cigar out in the ashtray, half of it left. "Fair enough." He smiles. "One of the best things I ever did was marry Elmira."

"Oh, man," I say, chuckling. "I never took you for a romantic."

"It's not romance, it's survival. You'll learn. You fall in love with a woman and then she takes her clothes off for you and suddenly your tongue is flapping, revealing all your secrets. Marrying a woman keeps the courts out of your bedroom."

And out of *his* bedroom, I assume he's saying. He's afraid I'm going to talk. "Duly noted. But I think I'm okay for now." Aref is fully aware of our cabin arrangements tonight. He even made fun of me for it.

"You know I was only a few years older than you when we married? It didn't take long for her to ply the truth out of me." He shakes his head, chuckling. "Just be careful what you tell her. Rust says you're new to this business. It can be overwhelming. Maybe it's not a good time to get into a relationship."

I'm searching for the right answer—the one where I say that there's no way in hell I'm ditching Rain because Aref suggested it—when his long finger points to something behind me.

Red silk catches the corner of my eye as I turn.

"I forgot my toothpaste, of all things. I was hoping I could borrow yours." Flashing a sheepish look toward Aref, Rain adds, "I'm sorry, I didn't mean to interrupt you."

He waves it away, as he waves everything away. Nothing seems to bother him. "I should retire. Elmira's waiting for me."

Rain's eyes trail Aref down the steps as she makes her way to me. "I'm really sorry."

Can I trust you? I pull her down onto my lap. The deck is empty except for a late-night staff member, clearing the last of the empty glasses, and of course the captain, in his control room. I wonder if he stays awake all night. "How are you feeling?"

She giggles. "Drunk? And exhausted." She yawns.

"Right, toothpaste." I can't tell if that was an excuse to bring me downstairs or not. I'm hoping it is. Rain yelps as I lift her into my arms and carry her right back the way she came, setting her on her feet when we reach the steps. I do so while stealing a kiss, replaying Aref's words yet again.

Everything about Rain so far does fit into my life. Her patience, her acceptance. She definitely enjoys having money. How long before she doesn't want to live on her daddy's dime? How long before she's looking for someone else to provide for her? I assume that's what she'll expect at some point, seeing as she seems to be floating through life right now.

I trail after her down the steps, so preoccupied with all these thoughts and questions that I end up bumping into her when she stops.

"This is your room." She points to a door, and then the one right across. "And this is mine."

My eyes get caught in the dip of her dress, that dragonfly necklace nestled perfectly in between her breasts, her nipples pressing through the silk. Is that a reaction to me or the cool night air we just escaped?

I'm gawking at her when I hear, "Toothpaste?" She's staring at me with a raised brow and an amused smirk.

"Right . . ." I stifle my groan as I head into my room—ransacked by those asshole Coast Guards—and come back with a tube. She's already moved inside her room, half-barricading the door with her body, holding her toothbrush out to steal a strip.

Not inviting me in.

"Good night, Luke," she says, lifting onto her toes to lay a light kiss on my lips. "See you in the morning." The door shuts and, a moment later, I hear the interior latch.

Dammit. It's going to be a long night. "Follow her lead . . . follow her lead . . ." I mutter, ducking back into my room. I toss my suit jacket toward a small table. Missing it completely. My fingers fumble with the buttons on my shirt. Stripping off my pants and shirt, I throw them on top of my jacket and then drop down to begin my obsessive nightly regime. Because, *fuck*, maybe that'll keep me from heading back out and knocking on her door.

It's not helping. The push-ups are damn painful, actually. I'm halfway through my reps, lying flat on my stomach, and ready to give my hand a workout so I can finish, when I hear the lightest knock on the door. So quiet that I may be imagining it.

Still, I bolt for the door.

Rain stands there, tucking strands of hair behind her ear in that nervous way. She lifts her fingers to my mouth and steps into me, forcing me backward. Pressing the door shut with her body—in a worn Washington Capitals T-shirt that is so threadbare I can see the curves of her body and a hint of skin underneath—she reaches back to latch the door.

Chapter 32

...

CLARA

"Do you always answer the door in your underwear?" I can't help but marvel at the ridges in his stomach, a perfectly formed eight-pack of muscle. By the light sheen over his chest and the tension in his muscles, I know he was doing his nightly workout.

And I'm assuming the prominent erection is the same one from hours ago.

Luke's eyes are taking all of me in. I purposely wore this T-shirt. It may not be sexy black lace, but that would be too overt an attempt at seducing him. It just grazes the tops of my thighs. It's soft and paper thin and so worn that it's borderline see-through. And there's nothing underneath it to obscure his view of me, one he seems to be appreciating.

He must know why I'm here. I made a point of locking the door and all.

But am I doing the right thing? Too many thoughts are swirling inside my head right now. My worry for him after Elmira's subtle warning, her not-so-subtle push for intimacy as a way to get the information that I want, the pressure of the case and the need to get something valuable out of this trip. The fact that I *want* to get closer to Luke, for reasons other than the case.

When I snuck upstairs and overheard Aref suggest to Luke that he shouldn't be in a relationship right now, I panicked and committed to this plan. Above all else, I can't risk my connection with him.

Because maybe I can help him. Maybe he doesn't have to go down in this mess, once everything is exposed.

I spy his suit in a rumpled mess on the floor beside me. "You really shouldn't leave this lying here like this. You'll ruin it." Leaning over to pick it up, I hear his sharp inhale as the back of my shirt rides up to far beyond inappropriate.

I take my time, draping his jacket and pants over the chair before turning back to find his piercing blue eyes blazing. And I know I've gone past the point where I could just turn around and walk out. So I close the distance, until I'm a mere foot away. I reach up and begin tracing the slick ripples in his stomach with my fingertips, something I've longed to do for weeks. "You're somewhat fanatical about your body, aren't you?"

The smile has fallen off, replaced with an almost pained expression, his fingers balled into fists at his sides.

He's waiting for me, just like he said he would.

Pressing my palm against his chest, I step in until I'm close enough that his breath tickles my cheek. I let my mouth graze his neck, my own breath skating across it until goose bumps erupt on him.

That must be his breaking point because his hands are on me in the next instant—one grasping the back of my neck and the other one roped around my back to pull me tight. My T-shirt bunched in his fist, the cool air cascading over my bare skin.

"Lights?" I catch a glimpse out through one of the two large oval windows to the sea beyond. Anyone out there can see in. And, by anyone, I mean my surveillance team. I'm not risking them watching me do this.

Luke obliges, pulling me backward with him to the bed, fumbling with the switch without ever leaving my lips. The cabin is thrown into darkness, save for the natural moonlight streaming in through the panoramic windows. Streaming in such a perfect way that I can still see him clearly beneath me as he sits down, pulling me on top to straddle his lap. He has my T-shirt up and over my head in seconds.

"Well, that was fast," he smirks, breaking free long enough to let his gaze travel down over my breasts, my stomach, and farther down, to where nothing but a thin layer of his cotton separates us.

"I guess I should have made it a little more difficult," I tease, reveling in the heat radiating off him.

"No, I think I prefer easy." He chuckles at his own joke, leaning down and taking one of my nipples into his mouth, his large hands a warm expanse over my hips as he pulls me hard against him. It's impossible for me not to grind myself against him.

And tell myself over and over again that this is okay because it's for the job, even though my conscience isn't buying it anymore.

Luke flips me over and rests me on the bed as if I weigh nothing, his tall frame looming over me for several long moments, his gaze shifting from one body part to the next.

I'm fairly confident about my body—I work hard enough to maintain it—but being under such intense scrutiny by someone so beautiful, so sculpted, starts to make me feel self-conscious.

"No, don't," he warns, his hands gently touching my knees, stopping them from closing completely. "You're perfect. Almost too perfect." He pushes his boxer briefs down and climbs onto the bed to fit himself in between my legs, forcing my thighs apart. "Sometimes I wonder if you're even real."

I close my eyes with his words, as his mouth finds my collarbone. I *am* real. At least, parts of who he's seen are. And *this* is real, what's happening between us right now.

I feel like the Velveteen Rabbit.

Right now, part of me wishes I had a fairy godmother to wave a wand and make Rain Martines come alive. But if she did, then I couldn't help Luke. And, more and more, I want to help him.

I feel the tip of him rubbing against my thigh, and my body instinctively lifts and moves toward it, beckoning him in. I'm standing on the edge of a cliff right now, and I have no choice. I have to jump, even though the landing is going to hurt.

But I know the fall will be pure ecstasy.

He groans and I expect him to fish out a condom. But his hands and mouth begin wandering instead. Strong hands that make me feel dainty and cherished, the way they squeeze my hips and caress my breasts and slide inside me. I remember wondering if he was a selfish guy, focused more on his own needs.

I couldn't have been more wrong, I realize, as he seems to worship every part of my body with his fingers and mouth, until my thighs are clenching around his head and my fingers are weaving through his hair, yanking on the soft strands.

Begging him.

I'm so riled up by the time I finally hear the condom wrapper tear open that he slides right into me with a moan and a muttered curse.

Guilt and happiness go to war inside of me as I fall.

I wonder which one will win.

■ ■ ■

With my head against his chest and his fingers drawing circles on my back and his heartbeat lulling me into sleep, my body jerks with his sudden words. "Hey Rain, can I ask you something?"

"Sure." That's about all I can manage, I'm so content right now.

His fingers continue their dance along my back in the silence of the cabin. "Have you ever done anything illegal?"

Hearing his tone switch to something more serious is like being thrown into a bath of ice water, my postcoital bliss effectively ruined, reminding me that I have a purpose here. I take a deep breath and relax my body. "You mean like smoke pot?"

His low chuckle tickles my eardrum. "Yeah, sure."

I decide to be honest with him. "A few times. And when I was fourteen, I stole makeup from the local CVS, too."

"Did you get caught?"

"Yup. Turns out I'm a shitty thief. I didn't even see the camera pointed on the makeup aisle as I stuffed my pockets."

"What happened?"

"Well, thankfully my mom knew the owner well so he agreed not to press charges. But, man, did my dad ever make me remember not to do it again." I groan, thinking back to the aftermath. "It was September and we were in the middle of a heat wave. I couldn't wear shorts for a week, because of the welts across the backs of my legs."

There's a pause and then Luke's body tenses. "Seriously?"

"Yeah." I turn my head until my chin is resting on Luke's chest and I can see him staring down at me, his hair mussed but still sexy as hell. "I told you my dad was old-school Italian, right? Well, he grew up with the belt. So my brother and I grew up with the belt, too."

Luke seems speechless for a moment. "And you still talk to him?"

"I've forgiven him, yeah. I mean, that's what his dad taught him and that's all he knew. For years, I didn't even realize how wrong it was." I've never talked openly about this with anyone before. I can't believe I'm doing it now, with my target. Then again, maybe he understands, in a way. He was raised by people who obviously love him, but who also haven't grasped how wrong what they're doing is. They don't live their days flogging themselves with guilt. They've long since convinced themselves that it's okay.

It becomes ingrained in them, and in each new generation following. Somehow, Rust convinced his nephew that this life he's leading him into is something to strive for.

"Has *he* realized how wrong that is?"

"Yeah. We had our differences growing up. I moved out when I was seventeen, and lived with friends. I was still in high school. We didn't talk for a few years."

Luke doesn't say anything for a long moment. I'm not surprised. Most people who don't deal with that sort of thing don't know how to reconcile the fact that I still talk to my dad, that I love him, that I'll do anything for him. That tells me that, for the other ways that Rust has corrupted his nephew, he never raised a hand to him, which is more than I can say about the criminals

I've busted in the past. They usually have a handful of kids with different baby mamas. *If* they acknowledge them, it's usually with abusive words and backhands and general neglect. Stereotypical, yes. But also real. I remember this one drug dealer who had his scrawny thirteen-year-old son, whose voice hadn't even dropped yet, muling cocaine and pot around school. Of course the kid got roughed up and robbed. When he went home with a bloody lip and told his father what happened, his father beat the shit out of him for letting them take the drugs.

I'm guessing the Markov/Boone household was a semi-normal family home to any bystander—the smell of eggs and bacon wafting from the kitchen on Saturdays, church on Sundays, a perpetual pile of muddy kids' shoes at the doorstep every other day.

Finally, Luke sighs. "That's just . . . kinda crazy, Rain. But you're fine now? I mean, it seems like you're fine, with you living in his condo and everything."

"Yeah, we're good. He finally realized how wrong it all was. We understand each other better now. I think he respects me."

"What made the difference?"

"It was around the time I—" I rest my head against his chest again, fighting the shot of panic that rips through my body. I almost slipped. I was so close to admitting that it was around the time I became a cop. *Jesus.* I need to stop talking.

"Around the time . . ." Luke prompts.

"Around the time . . ." My mind spins, searching for a lie. ". . . that my grandfather died. My dad didn't have a good relationship with him and he regretted it. He didn't want the same to happen with me, so he apologized." *Man,* I'm good at lying. I scare myself sometimes.

He pulls me into him, laying a kiss on my forehead. "I'm glad it all worked out." Both of us sigh. I imagine for very different reasons.

"Why did you ask if I've done something illegal?" I prop my head up on my elbow to see his face.

His eyes are on the ceiling, his Adam's apple bobbing up and down with his swallow. "What would you say if I told you that I've done some illegal stuff? That I'm involved with some illegal stuff now. With my uncle." Finally, his eyes shift to meet mine. I see a hint of something like fear in them.

I'd say don't tell me, dammit! Don't admit it. Don't crush the tiny, stupid hope burning bright in my chest that everything is just one big misunderstanding.

This is it, though. This is what the Feds have been waiting for. This is what *I* have been waiting for.

I hope he can't read my inner turmoil in my face. "I'd ask if you were hurting people."

"No! I mean . . ." He releases a deep breath, like he's been holding it, and then chuckles, "I'm sure there are people cursing us seven ways to Sunday, but . . . no one gets hurt." Strands of my hair have fallen forward, covering part of my face. He tucks them back behind my ear to give me an unobstructed look at his eyes. I study them. So open, so honest, staring wide at me. Almost pleading with me to trust him.

Either he really believes that no one is getting hurt or I'm the biggest sucker undercover officer on earth. "What are you two doing?" My tongue feels leaden with the question.

"It's not just us. There's a whole network of people. It's all still new to me, though. Rust just pulled me in a few weeks ago." Luke's fingertip traces my bottom lip. "He wants me to run it with him one day."

The Feds were right.

My stomach is churning and my heart feels heavy. I've never wanted to be wrong on a case before. "Is Aref a part of it, too?"

He nods.

"Were you guys discussing it tonight?"

He nods again. "And you."

"What? Me?"

He chuckles. "Yeah . . . He warned me to be careful about what I say because the second you take your clothes off, I'll start spilling my guts like a sorry sucker. I think he's just watching his own back."

That's exactly what he's doing. Both Aref and Elmira are up to something, I'm fairly certain. The question is what, exactly? Is it simply testing anyone new, protecting their empire? Is this cabin bugged as well?

I push that fear away. If it is, I need to use it to my advantage, feeding them what they want to hear. "Do you feel guilty about what you do?"

He hesitates, as if considering that. "Honestly? I'm not sure yet. I think part of me does, but then Rust throws me a pile of cash and a Porsche and I kind of forget." He lets go of my face and focuses his gaze on the ceiling, his voice cracking with his admission. "That sounds shitty. I guess I'm greedy."

"A lot of people would have a hard time turning that down," I concede, as hope sparks inside me. A shred of guilt means a *chance* to turn away. Unless he's lying to me about everything. Only time will tell, I guess. I plant a kiss against his neck, decidedly my favorite body part on him. It allows me to whisper, so quietly that no room bug will pick it up. "And no one's getting hurt?"

His jaw bumps against my cheek as he shakes his head. Pushing my chin up with his hand, he locks eyes with me again. "I don't hurt people."

Oh, Luke. My heart begins to hurt for this guy, in some ways still such an impressionable boy. He's going to have a rude awakening when Sinclair gets ahold of him. When he drops those evidence photos in front of him, like I expect him to, of Wayne Billings's dead body, and the other victims. And he proves to him that while not directly . . . Luke *does* hurt people, by helping his uncle keep the vicious cycle alive.

His thumb drags along my bottom lip. "You don't have to be afraid of me. I could never hurt you. I can't stand the idea of anyone hurting you."

I believe him.

I wonder what Luke would say if I came home with my eyes blackened and my lip split open up after a bad day at work. Would he accept it as part of my profession? Or would he give me the same ultimatum that David did: it's either my job or him. I resented David for forcing me to make the decision, even though it was an easy one. Of course my career would come first, before any guy. That's been my philosophy since the day I joined the police force and I've never questioned it.

Until now, it would seem. I guess maybe my feelings for David were never really that strong. Or, maybe my feelings for Luke are growing much too strong.

I inhale deeply and dare ask, "What are you doing with your uncle, Luke?"

He cups my jaw gently, pulling my face into his in a kiss much sweeter than before, his forehead pressed against mine as he whispers, "Would you leave me if I told you?"

"Maybe I'm greedy too." I force a smile. *No, I won't leave you until I have to arrest you.*

He suddenly flips me over onto my stomach and reaches for another condom on the nightstand, his tongue following the swirls of the tattoo on my shoulder.

I give in. He's not ready to divulge everything to me. This is just the beginning.

The beginning of a true "us" in his eyes.

And the beginning of the end for Luke Boone.

■ ■ ■

I lie for hours in Luke's arms, watching him snore softly, his face more boyish and angelic than it deserves to be. Replaying his words—his admission.

And with the eastern sky beginning to lighten beyond the window, I don't care about any of it. All I want to do is lean forward and kiss him. Steal him away from the bad stuff, convince him to start over because I believe he isn't beyond saving yet.

I'm so fucked.

It doesn't take a genius to see that we've just reached a new level in our "relationship." One with a steady climb of constant texting and spending time together. And sex. There's no way I can maintain this. Not as an undercover with a federal surveillance team on me.

I need to distance myself.

Luke doesn't stir as I pry myself from his arms and dress. I duck out of his cabin and tiptoe into mine, being sure not to make even the slightest sound as I slide into my bed. When I fake a few morning coughs, I make sure I aim them directly at the dragonfly necklace that sits exactly where I left it on the nightstand.

Chapter 33

. . .

LUKE

"Shit . . ." The second I crack my eyes to find the other side of my bed empty, panic takes over. I went too far. I told her too much.

Scrambling out of bed to pull a pair of pants on, I throw my door open, intent on begging, apologizing, denying . . . anything.

Rain, who must have been just leaving her cabin, lets out a small yelp as I surprise her in the hallway. After a delayed second, she smiles. "Hey." Her eyes trailing over my hair remind me that it's probably on end. I self-consciously reach up to begin taming it.

"Don't." She laughs and curls her hand over my bicep to stop me. "It looks good like that. How did you sleep?"

She's impossible to read. I can't even guess at what's going on inside that pretty head of hers, about what I told her last night. "Never better." My gaze drops before I can help myself, taking in the long, tight sweater and leggings that hug every curve I had my hands and mouth on last night.

She smiles secretively, her hand falling to squeeze mine. "Must have been all that fresh air."

I pull her toward my door, ready to peel off every stitch of her clothes to prove to her that I'm not a bad guy, that I would never hurt her. "Rain, I—"

She gives me a soft, tentative kiss. "They're serving breakfast on the top deck and I'm starving. I'll see you up there?"

She's halfway up the stairs before I can manage, "Yeah."

She's fine. Everything's fine.

Everything's amazing.

Chapter 34

...

CLARA

The sail down the Columbia River, with the sun's rays kissing my skin and a gourmet breakfast fit for the Queen and the nattering, annoying voices of the former nanny and escort were easy. Pleasant even.

It wasn't until I climbed into Luke's car that the first beads of sweat began running down my back. Now, twenty-five minutes later and in front of my condo, my clothes are drenched and I'm in desperate need of a shower.

"Is everything okay?"

"Yeah, why?"

Luke's brow is furrowed a bit. "Well, not that I minded it at all, believe me, but . . . I've never heard you talk so much. You seem nervous. I just hope . . ." He stalls. "You're not uncomfortable around me now, are you?"

Uncomfortable. That's a good word for my agonizing.

What I did last night was *so* wrong, on so many levels. My wire is on again, as it has to be. I'm terrified that Luke's going to say something that will reveal to my cover team that I wasn't in my room last night. Because if they find out, I'm gone. On a plane back to D.C., off the case. Blacklisted in the big book of undercover officers. Probably blacklisted, period.

So, to reduce the risk of that happening, I brought up everything I could during the drive home to keep Luke's words from wandering in that direction. Anything that came to mind—my pet rabbit when I was five; the time I broke my leg playing soccer, age seven; my first trip to Italy when I was nine; a terrible case of food poisoning when I went to Jamaica at nineteen.

It worked. Up until now.

"I'm not uncomfortable at all. But I meant it when I said I need to take things slow." I take his hand with a smile. And I give him the excuse I mentally prepared earlier this morning, laden with lies and laced with regret. "I went on one date with my ex and then, suddenly, all of my time and focus was consumed by him, almost overnight. I don't even know how it happened, but I stopped doing what I love to do. Being who I am."

Luke frowns. "Like how, exactly?"

"Oh . . ." I begin spouting off the common dating atrocities all girls have committed at one point or another. "I cancelled out on a trip with my girlfriends because he was afraid I'd meet someone else. I started working out for him instead of for myself. I ignored my family, stopped responding to my friends' messages, and when I was with them, I was glued to my phone, waiting for his texts. He liked to play golf, so I'd spend my Saturdays driving him around in the cart. I'd sit around at these pretentious lounges with his loser friends, and listen to them discuss Socrates and Confucius like the pompous, self-indulgent asses they were." Somehow, fragments of my real dating history—Clara's string of failed relationships—are now leaking in, creating a Frankenstein of a boyfriend. "He wouldn't let me wear heels because I'd be looking down on him and he had a major height complex. He wouldn't let me wear leather because of the oppression of the 'bovine population.'" I cut myself off abruptly when I notice that Luke's lips are pressed together tightly.

"He sounds like a real winner," he says with mock sincerity. "I can see why you fell for him."

I can't believe I dated *any* of them. It's embarrassing, admitting it now. "I don't think you're like him at all, *believe* me. But I just need to make sure that I don't get caught up in *this*," I gesture back and forth between us, "and forget who I am again."

The undercover cop who just slept with her target.

Oh, hell. I'm sweating again. I need to get out of here.

He reaches up to cup my jaw, his smile brightening his eyes. "You can wear leather and heels and I don't really golf. We can take it slow. Whatever you need." His eyes dart to my mouth and he leans in to kiss me. I have to kiss him. There's no excuse for not kissing him, I tell myself.

His lips just graze mine when his phone rings. Again. It's been ringing and vibrating for the entire drive home but he hasn't answered it, even though I've told him he could, every time. He lets his forehead fall against mine gently, groaning. "Sorry, that's probably Rust. I've ignored him enough. He's going to lose his mind if I don't answer."

"That's okay."

He smiles. "God . . . how are you so understanding?" I just smile until he plants a quick kiss on my lips. "I'll give you a call later? Or you can call me?"

I force myself to pull away from him and step out of the car, hearing him say "yup" just as I shut the door.

■ ■ ■

"What the fuck was that? You could have blown the entire case!"

"Don't be so dramatic. That woman was making me nervous, so I sent Bill in. I thought you were made for a minute there." Warner heads straight for my fridge as Stanley trots over to greet me. They were waiting in the stairwell for me when I came up the elevator.

"You caught on to that too, huh?"

"Yup. I've been on pins and needles all night long." He slams the door shut, beer in hand. "How was your game of tonsil hockey?"

Didn't waste any time bringing that up. "I had no choice. You know that. I have to give him *something* or this cover will be dead in the water." I lean over to give Stanley's belly a scratch. He responds with several hoggish snorts. "I can't believe I've missed you," I mutter.

"You didn't have to—"Warner stops mid-sentence with a deep inhale. Pinching the bridge of his nose, he finally heaves a sigh. "Whatever. I'm not arguing with you about this. You're the one on the front line. I trust you." He cracks a can.

"It's beer o'clock already?" I check my watch. Noon. Warner looks like he hasn't slept at all.

He ignores my jab. "There were a lot of veiled comments but nothing incriminating on the wire. Did you witness anything useful?"

"Besides some lines of coke?" I hope he can't hear the lie in my voice, when I say, "Just a lot of rich assholes wining and dining and passing out on a giant yacht." And a conversation that could arm the Feds with everything they need to get the noose ready for Luke's neck. I'm not ready to divulge that yet. I *can't* divulge it, now. I can only set Luke up for future admissions. When I'm ready.

He nods, more to himself. "Yeah, rough life. Sounds like 12's walls are starting to come down for you, though. That's good."

"Yeah. Slowly." I hate that Warner trusts me so much. All my cover guys do, because they need to in order for us to win this case. Still, it makes this deception that much more painful.

"Why'd you tell him all that stuff about an ex, before he dropped you off? Sinclair's going to grill me on that if he listens to it."

"Because I have to keep playing hard-to-get. Otherwise I'm going to run out of excuses for keeping him out of my pants."

He grumbles in response. "And what the hell was all that other rambling? You had a pet rabbit?"

"Yeah, until the crazy old man next door shot it and ate it for dinner."

He pauses, mid-sip. "What the fuck, Bertelli."

I shrug. "I had an interesting childhood."

Pouring the rest of his beer back in record time, he crushes the can and tosses it to the counter. "Yeah, I think I'll need sleep to hear about that. I'm going to crash. It's been a long night for all of us." At the door, he throws back, "And, by the way, you sleep like the dead."

"So I've been told." I release a breath of relief as the door clicks. And make room for more guilt to slide in as I pull my window blinds open. Luke's pacing back and forth with a phone pressed to his ear, already changed into sweats. I'm sure he'll be going for a run.

My heart begins beating frantically, and I can't tell if it's fear of getting caught or excitement over him in general. Or worry for Luke and what may happen to him. Probably all three. But I do recognize the ache growing inside me. It's there because I already want to see him again.

"This is so bad," I whisper as Luke tosses his phone on the couch and leans over to give Licks a good head scratch.

Stanley throws his head back and begins barking, hopping around like a bucking bull as he watches Licks. Maybe he catches the motion, or maybe it's just a fluke, but Luke suddenly looks up. He begins laughing.

I can't help but laugh too. "Can't you learn how to play a little hard-to-get, Stanley?"

Luke holds up a leash to the window and nods toward the park behind our buildings. He wants to see me again? Already? He starts doing the running man in the window, looking absurd. And adorable.

Dammit . . . So much for distancing myself a bit. Plus, I hate running. I don't run for anyone. David was a runner and I refused to go with him.

Now, all I want to do is see Luke.

Throwing Stanley's leash on him, I change and head out the door.

No wire.

No cover team.

Pushing aside my guilt.

Chapter 35

. . .

LUKE

I hate being woken up by the phone.

"You need to open the garage today," Rust tells me, his own voice rough after a late night at The Cellar, where I debriefed him on my meeting with Aref.

"Fuuuuuck," I moan, rubbing my eyes as I read my clock. "It's seven a.m.!"

"Marie just called. Miller won't be in today."

"Who's Marie?" Then it dawns on me. "Miller's married?" I can't imagine what kind of woman would put up with him.

Rust sighs. "Miller went to the hospital last night."

"Shit . . ." I mumble, sliding my legs out of bed. "Is he okay?"

"They thought it was a heart attack at first but there haven't been any signs. They think it's severe stress, coupled with high blood pressure."

"Stress? What the hell does he have to be stressed about?" I chuckle. And then stop, because the guy's in the hospital and I'm being a douche.

"He'll be out for a few days, so you need to keep things running smoothly. Come on, Luke. This is why I put you in the office."

Miller has never missed a day of work. It's something of a joke around the garage. "Yeah, no problem. I'm on my way." Tossing my phone onto my bed, I stretch my tired body and wander forward to my window to stare out at the wall of closed blinds across the way.

Rain met me on the path behind our condo in tight pants and a fitted sweatshirt. After keeping up with me for an hour—I had to carry Stanley for most of that, ready to collapse—I asked her back to my place, hoping to drag her into my shower with me so I could lick the clean coat of sweat off that perfect body of hers.

She smiled, lifting to her tiptoes to kiss me with salty lips. And then turned me down for a photography assignment.

It damn near crushed me.

But, at the same time, it makes me respect her more. The girl she was describing yesterday, when I dropped her off? The one who ditched her life to cater to some guy who sounds like someone I'd punch if I had the chance? That girl sounded needy and weak, and that's not what I want if I'm going to have a woman in my life for more than the occasional night.

I've always been attracted to confidence, and I saw Priscilla and those other women as being just that—strutting in, grabbing attention, getting what they want. But now that Rain's in my life, I realize how stupid that is. Pris is drowning in insecurity. She needs beauty and money and a man to attach herself to in order to feel self-worth. She chooses her friends based on their looks and their lifestyle and what they can do for her. She chooses men who attract her with their money. I know because she's admitted as much to me.

Priscilla lives with a ticking clock hanging over her head, because when her looks start to fade, all that she'll have left is a vapid group of girlfriends who trash-talk each other behind their backs and a rich husband who relies on her to wash and fold his socks while he dips into the next generation of insecure, beautiful gold-diggers for his dick fix.

But Rain knows who she is. She's gorgeous, but she doesn't wear her beauty like it's all she has going for her. She can be forward—in a cute, sexy way, like the first day we met at the garage—but she's strong enough to tell me to back off, to slow down, without fear. That's confidence and self-respect. That's telling me that she won't hesitate to go after what she wants, but she won't just give herself away. I have to earn my place in her life.

And she's obviously independent. As in, she doesn't need a man. Yeah, okay . . . She may still be relying on her father to bankroll that independence. But in a sense, so am I, right now. I get the impression that she has a plan and goals for the rest of her life. I haven't pushed her on it so far, because I have to be ready to share the same information if she asks me, and I'm still not sure how she'll take my answer. But Saturday night changed things for us. I felt the distinct shift.

Rain is someone I can trust.

Looking down at my morning wood, coming alive with thoughts of the night in my cabin on the yacht, I consider that maybe I should throw some boxers on if I'm going to stand this close to my window in daylight, like I'm begging to see her. Especially if she happens to peek out from around her blinds. It wouldn't be the first time she's done that.

Fuck it, I don't care if she knows how much I like her.

Chapter 36

...

CLARA

An engine roars on the other side of Luke's office wall, rattling the hanging picture frames. "I hate it when they do that," Luke mutters, digging the key out of his pocket. "Thanks so much for walking Licks. Poor guy's probably dying right now."

"Of course. It's no big deal." I look over at the empty chair. "How is Miller doing?"

"He's back home now, but he'll be out for most of the week." Luke slips my key ring from my hand and begins fiddling with it.

Hooking a spare key to his condo onto the ring.

My target is giving me unsupervised access to his personal space.

"You really think this is smart?" I tease, holding it up.

He laughs and grabs my waist, pulling me into him. "I've already called security to let them know you'll be there. They'll be on the lookout for the gorgeous brunette with the ugly little dog. They shouldn't give you any problems."

"Licks isn't exactly a looker either—you do realize that, right?"

He doesn't answer, stealing a slow, deep kiss that makes my knees buckle and me forget where I am for a moment.

This can't happen. I push against his chest. "I'd better head over there now. It's almost seven. He's probably about to burst."

"You know, if I came home tonight and found that same gorgeous brunette lying naked in my bed, I wouldn't complain."

Luke's arms curl around my back. He pulls me into him again, until I can feel the bulge in his pants.

My cheeks flush, knowing Warner is listening to every single word right now. Knowing what it feels like to be with Luke, free of a wire and observation, makes the time that I am on the clock with him all the more unpleasant. "What time do you think you'll be home?"

He sighs. "Fuck, I don't know. The way things are going, I'd say around ten. This week is really busy and I don't know how to do half of what needs to be done around here."

I peck his cheek with a kiss and pull away. "Then you'd better get back to it. I'll talk to you later."

■ ■ ■

"We're not staying long," I warn Stanley as the two dogs race for the giant dog bed by the window.

I should just turn around and head home right now. But I can't help myself from wandering through Luke's home. I've been inside only once, and he was here. Now, I'm free to inspect. For a few hours, if I want. Bill's watching the garage, in case Luke leaves work early.

What will I find here? Something to incriminate him? Because he handed over his keys to me trustingly, anything I find is admissible. Warner giggled like a schoolgirl when he found out I had access. I'm sure Sinclair's going to be happy. But I'm not really looking for things pertaining to the case.

I just want to explore Luke's personal space.

I make my way through his kitchen, opening drawers and cupboards to find neatly piled pots and polished silverware, small appliances still in original packages. The only cupboard that looks well stocked and frequented is the one full of hard liquor.

He is twenty-four, after all.

After sweeping through bare closets and a spare bedroom with nothing but a bed to fill it, I move on to his bedroom with hesitant steps.

Because any curious female would do the same of the guy she was dating. And sleeping with.

Turning his lamp on, I find his sheets in a rumpled mess. He normally makes his bed in the morning, based on what I've seen. But he did say he basically ran out today. So, I do him a favor and take the time to make it for him, stealing a quick inhale of his sheets as I smooth out the creases.

And then the hairs on the back of my neck prickle because I feel like I'm being watched. Or I'm simply afraid that I'm being watched.

Glancing out across the way, I see my apartment, blinds closed and dark. I stroll over to the panel and hit the switch, closing his blinds.

Just in case.

Luke's words earlier replay in my ear and my heart begins to race. I stretch out on his bed, burying my face in his pillow, as I briefly allow myself the luxury of imagining myself granting his request.

Wishing I could.

Just the thought has my thighs burning.

With a groan of frustration, I roll off and gingerly open his nightstand. It's bare, save for multiple boxes and brands of condoms—some opened and half-empty—and a long, slender black jewelry box. I pull it out and flip it open, catching my breath as sparkling diamonds wink back at me. I finger the delicate chain, instantly mesmerized by the beauty of the stones, each encased with a setting in the shape of a drop.

A raindrop.

"Holy shit," I mumble, pulling out a folded sheet of yellow paper tucked into the inside of the lid. It's an appraisal certificate from a jewelry wholesaler here in Portland. A row of digits—the necklace's value, for insurance purposes—glares up at me.

I snap the case shut and slide it back into the drawer quickly, knowing that I probably wasn't supposed to see that.

But I'm positive that the necklace is for me, and it's real. When did he buy that? And why? I don't have to ask with what money because I know. I also know that when he does give it to me, I'll have to smile and gush over it. But that won't be hard. What'll suck is handing it in to evidence after the case is over, because I can't keep it.

I should be disgusted with him for giving me gifts bought with dirty money.

But, if I'm completely honest, all I can think about right now is how beautiful that piece of jewelry is and how thoughtful he is and how I can't wait to feel him slipping it around my neck.

This is exactly what Luke meant when he said that he's been blinded by wads of cash and a Porsche.

My stomach begins churning with self-loathing.

After searching his bedroom closet and finding nothing but a well-hung, neat wardrobe of dress clothes and more shoes than any man should own, I make a quick stop in Luke's bathroom, stepping over the towel he left on the floor. I don't pick it up, not wanting him to know I was in here, too. Scanning his medicine cabinet, closet, and vanity drawers, I find only cold medication and basic hygiene supplies, albeit a lot more of the latter than I'd expect the normal guy to use. Luke is meticulous with his appearance, though, so I'm not surprised.

There are no prescriptions of any kind, no embarrassing rash creams, nothing that tells me I should be heading to the doctor for tests. That's a relief.

As is the fact that I've uncovered nothing to use against him in our case.

So, I grab Stanley and head out.

Chapter 37

...

LUKE

"I can't believe you're making me watch this," I hiss into the dark theater.

She gives me a look of shock. "You're kidding me, right? There's blood, carnage. And aliens. What kind of guy doesn't like aliens?" Her tone is almost accusatory.

I hold my hand up. "I've never dated a girl who likes this stuff."

A sly smile forms on her face. "Are you afraid of scary movies?"

I throw my best "seriously?" game face on. "Me? Come on." I slept with my light on until I was ten because monsters lived under my bed, waiting for a chance to kill me. The hell if I'm admitting that to Rain, though.

The way she throws buttery popcorn into her wide-grinning mouth tells me she sees right through my lie.

"Shut up." I lean in to steal the piece from her fingertips about to go into her mouth, licking the salt and butter off her lips on my way. We're sitting in the back row of a half-empty theater because I insisted and she didn't complain, and dammit, she's wearing a short skirt. When I saw which movie she chose, I decided I'd rather be touching her for the next ninety minutes than watching the screen. It's been four days since the overnight cruise, since I felt the inside of her.

Just thinking about it now—about the feel and smell and taste of her—I'm getting hard.

While a red-eyed alien gnaws on some guy's face on the giant screen in front of us.

I don't really care. I'm just happy to be out with her. Turns out that running the garage on my own is exhausting. Miller's been doing a heck of a lot of work that I don't know about, while I make my own hours and fuck off at odd hours of the day. I haven't left the place before nine any night this week. No wonder the guy hates me so much.

Couple that with the added anxiety of relaying orders to fences for the next shipment, and I can barely get a workout in every night, I'm so tired.

I throw my arm over her shoulder and rest my other hand on the inside of her bare thigh, letting my fingers run along silky soft skin. She smiles, plants a kiss on my lips, and mouths, "Watch the movie." Then her hand drops to hold mine in place, like she knows exactly what I'm intending on doing.

Great.

Forty-five minutes of gore over a deafening sound system later—when I've jumped out of my seat at least five times, earning laughs from Rain each time—I finally lean in to admit, "Fine, I'm terrified of aliens. I'm probably going to have nightmares tonight. Are you really going to make me watch the rest of this?"

She rolls her eyes but then smiles. "Alright . . . let's go." She reaches over to collect her jacket and purse. I use the opportunity to slide my hand farther up.

It's so loud in here that I can't hear her small gasp as my fingers weave under her damp panties, as one finger slips into her, but by the sudden tension in her body and hard swallow in her neck, she wasn't expecting that.

Though it sure as hell feels like she wants it.

She hasn't pushed me away yet. She's too busy scanning the other rows, the corners, and the ceilings for cameras. There are none on us. It's all safe. Only when she seems to accept that does she ease back into her seat. Her eyes land on mine. Thanks to random flashes from the screen, I can just make out the fire in them.

Finally, she gives me a tiny smile as her thighs fall apart. She lifts her hips up just slightly. I take the access greedily, yanking her panties all the way down until they hit the dirty theater floor. I push her thighs farther apart as I begin working her with more fingers and my thumb, her skirt riding up higher. *Fuck,* I wish it weren't so dark in here.

Her jaw's clenched tight, like she's trying not to make a sound, not that anyone would hear anything in here. Maybe that's what spurs me forward, makes my fingers move faster, a little more aggressively, wanting her to lose control. "Come on, Rain . . ." I mumble into her ear, grabbing hold of her lobe with my teeth. "Let me hear you—"

Her hand slaps over my mouth, smothering the rest of my words, a glare of warning in her eyes. Maybe dirty talk embarrasses her? I keep going with a smile, my own blood flowing south. Watching her lips part and her eyes close as she gets more and more wet, as she starts squirming against my hand, until she grabs hold of the back of my head and smashes her lips into mine, smothering any moans that might have erupted as her body spasms around my fingers.

I have no fucking clue what's happening in the movie anymore, thank God. Right now I'm ready to unzip my fly. I'm hoping Rain will return the favor, but I won't ask. She seems to read my mind because her hand wanders over my lap, gripping me through my jeans, her thumb flicking the zipper pull.

And then her hand is suddenly gone. She collects her purse and panties from the seat next to her and whispers, "I need to use the restroom. Will you be okay here for five minutes? You know . . . with the scary aliens?" She points up at the screen.

I slap her ass in answer.

My head falling back in complete and utter frustration.

Chapter 38

...

CLARA

I stare at my flushed face in the restroom mirror, my hands shaking as I process what just happened. What I just *let* happen.

When he called me to go out tonight, I immediately suggested the movies, knowing it was a way to be with him without deceiving my cover team or worrying about what might be said. I figured it'd be a good way to slow things down a bit, too, while still gaining his trust, keeping his attention. We could hold hands, steal a kiss or two without Warner or Bill hearing anything over the blasts of the speakers.

Of course I picked a gory movie, something to steer my mind and body away from the fact that I don't want to just hold hands and kiss. That the devil on my shoulder convinced me to wear a short skirt, and that I was wet the second my ass hit the leather seat of his car.

I can't believe I just allowed that to happen.

While wearing a wire!

With my cover team listening!

I'm sure that's not the first time this back row has served a tawdry purpose. It happens often enough. Two years ago, I got called to the local AMC to bust two sixteen-year-olds for indecent exposure after they got a little carried away. There have been plenty of "incidents" of guys going in alone and coming out in handcuffs because they felt compelled to jerk off. So where the hell do I fit in, exactly? The horny teenager or the pervert?

Desperate for Luke. That's what I am.

I was keeping an eye on the entrance from the second we sat down, watching for someone from my cover team. I didn't notice any lanky male forms slipping into the shadows. Even if someone did, he wouldn't be able to see what was happening.

Still!

What if I'm wrong and the Feds now have the sounds of me getting off recorded, for all to hear?

Needing some reassurance, I pull out my phone. "Oh my god," I groan, clutching my stomach, as I see the four missed calls from Warner. My phone was on vibrate, but I can normally feel it through my purse. If I hadn't been . . . distracted, I would have noticed it going off.

It starts vibrating again.

I manage a weak and croaky, "Hello?"

"Where are you?"

"Restroom. Why?" I close my eyes. Here it is. It's coming. I'm so screwed.

"12's car just got jacked."

It takes a moment for his words to register. "What!"

"Yup. Right out of the parking lot." Warner starts laughing. "Serves him fucking right."

"Who the hell—" I dive down to check the stalls for feet. It's empty, fortunately, but I lower my voice anyway. "Who would take *his* car?"

"Whoever it is, I'm about to give them a medal." I roll my eyes as Warner continues. "One guy, definitely a professional. Punched in the driver's-side window and reprogrammed the keyless entry. Forty-five seconds, in and out. I timed it! Got it all on video, too."

"You sure sound impressed," I mutter, groaning.

"Oh, come on! You've gotta admit this is pretty damn funny."

I purse my lips together. "Yeah. The jackass does deserve it." But, *oh, man,* is Luke ever going to freak out. He loves that car. I look at my watch. There's still about thirty minutes left in the movie. "Did you put a tail on it?"

"I called Franky. He caught up pretty easily and is following him right now."

"'kay. What do you want to do, boss?"

"We can't give the locals a heads-up until 12 reports it stolen. I'm hoping he's got a high-end tracking system on it that this guy doesn't get to first."

I stuff my panties into my purse. As short as my skirt is, there's no way I'm putting them back on after they've been on that floor. "Got it. I'll get him out of here."

I duck back into the theater in a completely different frame of mind than when I left five minutes earlier. Luke's leaning back in his seat, legs spread casually, a smug smirk on his face.

"Hey, you wanted to leave, right?"

He reaches up to take my hand and pull me down. "No, we can stay. I know you really wanted to watch this."

I shrug. "I've kind of lost track of things. I can always rent it another time. I figured we could head back to your place . . ." I let my words drift off as my hand wanders over his lap again. *Yup,* still rock hard.

Too bad that's going to shrivel in about four minutes.

■ ■ ■

"It was right *here,* right? I'm not crazy, am I?" Wild eyes scan the parking lot as he hits the alarm button on his key fob for the tenth time. As if the car is magically going to appear.

"No, you're not crazy, Luke. I'm sorry." I stroke his arm soothingly. "You really should call the police now, before they get too far away. Maybe they can still find it."

His hands push through his mane of hair, sending it into disarray as he comes to terms with the fact that his car was stolen. He pulls his phone out from his pocket, frantically dialing, his jaw set. "Yes, my car was stolen and you have a tracking system on it . . . Yup."

"I hope whoever did this hasn't found it yet," I mutter, holding out no hope. Proficient thieves—and, by the sounds of it, this guy is—will find and disable one of those within minutes of pulling away from the steal site.

"They'd have to find all three," Luke answers, a hint of his calm, confident demeanor returning.

Of course Luke would have not one, but three tracking devices on his car. I can guess who suggested that.

I wait quietly as Luke calls all three agencies. Sure enough, one has already been deactivated. But two are still intact, and the police are dispatched quickly. With those calls done, he dials someone else. "Hey, Rust? . . . You won't fucking believe what just happened." And then Luke just starts laughing.

Because even he must see the irony in this.

■ ■ ■

"Do you realize how lucky you are?" the officer muses as he takes down Luke's driver's license, comparing it against the paperwork found in the glove compartment. "Most of these cars end up across the ocean."

"It's not luck," Luke murmurs, that cocky smile back. His arm curls around my waist, pulling me against him with a relieved sigh. I fall into him because it's three in the morning and I just really want to sleep.

"Still . . . Could have ended up driven into a wall in a high-speed chase instead of parked in a storage locker."

"He's right," I say. "That would have really sucked, hey? You love this car."

He peers down at me, a deep furrow in his brow. "Yeah, that would have." I search his eyes for any recognition that he helps screw people over in the exact same way.

I'm sure I see it there.

"Do you have any idea who stole it?" Luke asks the officer.

"We'll be collecting evidence on the site and car. You'll get a call when you can come and pick it up," the guy drones on. He obviously hates his job. I wonder if he signed up for this or if he did something stupid in a previous assignment to relegate him to police impound detail.

If I keep my own stupidity up, I might be taking over for him some day.

"Alright. Let's grab a cab back to my place." Luke pulls out his phone.

"Sure, but I'm going to head home. I have to get up early."

He frowns. "For what?"

"I volunteer . . . at a soup kitchen once a week. Tomorrow's my day." *Mental note—find a soup kitchen and start volunteering there once a week.*

Nodding to himself, he admits, "Yeah, I guess it's pretty late. I need to be at the garage in a few hours, in case Miller's still out." He leans in to kiss me softly. "Soon?"

I force a smile, hoping the casualness of his invitation doesn't tip the team off that there has already been a first time. "Sure."

Chapter 39

■ ■ ■

LUKE

"Did they tell you when they'll be finished with the car?" Rust's voice is groggy, like he just woke up, even though it's after ten and he's showered and shaved for the day and is standing in the garage's office.

"A few days. I just ordered a replacement window. They said that'll take a week to come in."

He tosses the keys to his Cayenne to me. "Take mine until it's back."

"You sure? I can rent a car."

He waves my concern away with a dismissive hand, his eyes roaming the white walls of the tiny space, where we've managed to cram two desks into enough space for one.

"Listen, if anyone asks, tell them your engine was giving you problems and you sent it to the dealer for repair."

I frown. "Why?"

"Because some jackass stole my nephew's car and I want to find out who! I'm going to make a few very discreet calls to see if this is a local crew or something bigger. We don't want anyone moving in on us. It puts more heat on the area."

"Alright. Where are you going to be today? RTM?"

"No, I need to sort out a hiccup." I stare at him, waiting for him to elaborate. "Some deliveries that haven't made it to the warehouse yet. Not sure what the delays are."

It's almost funny: in one breath he's condemning the people who stole my car; in the next, it's business as usual. Am I the only one who's been feeling more than an ounce of empathy for these people who we royally fuck over? I wonder, if Rust had been the one to walk out of a movie theater and see his car missing, whether he'd have second thoughts about what we're involved in.

"How are you handling things around here?"

I nod slowly, looking over the neat piles of color-coordinated folders in front of me. Four days ago, facing the organized chaos that is Miller's desk—a two-foot-tall stack of paperwork that combined invoices, customer orders, and a half dozen other forms that I have no clue what to do with—I would have answered Rust with a lot of bitching and moaning.

But I slowly figured my way through things, sorting paperwork, making calls. I actually feel like I have a handle on running this place. Of course, there's still plenty I don't know, but the place hasn't come to a halt without Miller.

"It's going pretty good, actually." I get to talk to people, and I actually feel useful because I can usually diagnose what's wrong with their car based on their complaints. Plus, the guys around here seem to like me more than Miller. That's not to say I'd ever get rid of Miller, but still, I like feeling like I'm managing something.

Most of all, though, there isn't that same anxiety I feel when I'm on the phone with Rodriguez or the other fence, Cage. The tension that stiffens my back every time I pass on another message for another car they need to steal. Another person I'm about to screw over.

Here, I'm actually solving people's problems, not creating them.

He starts rubbing his chin in that very "I have an idea" Rust-like way. "I feel like I haven't seen you in weeks."

I laugh. "I saw you last Sunday night. It's been stupid busy in here, with Miller gone and me figuring things out. I've been working late every night. Hell, last night was the first time I saw Rain since the weekend."

"Rain?"

"That girl I took with me to Aref's party."

"Right. You never gave me her name before. How'd you meet this girl, again?"

"She's the one who brought her Audi in that day, remember?"

"Ah . . . yes. Pretty girl." He nods slowly, smiling. The smile is quickly wiped away with a frown. "You're spending a lot of time with her."

"Not really." Not nearly as much as I want to. Every night when I get home, my eyes wander to my window and across the way, looking for her. She said she'd be busy with some assignments that she's been slacking on this week. I don't know what kind of photography course this is, but she seems to be taking it fairly seriously. That, or this is all part of that speech she gave me about "not losing herself to another guy."

"More than your usual girls."

"So?"

He shrugs. "So, you should bring her around one night. I'd like to meet her."

"I don't know if we're quite there yet." Introducing her to Rust is basically introducing her to a parent. Worse, I'd actually care if Rust didn't approve of her. It would crush me.

"Fine. Then at least meet me at The Cellar tonight and pretend that you remember who I am."

I start laughing, earning his smile.

The door squeaks open and a haggard Miller walks in.

"Hey! Look who made it back! You feeling better?" Rust exclaims, watching his diligent manager amble toward his desk.

"I'm fine. Marie's just overreacting," Miller grumbles in response.

"Hey, I had no idea you were married," I say.

Rust chuckles. "Maybe you two should actually talk once in a while. Who knows? You may learn to like each other. Miller, take it easy. Let Luke handle more. I need you firing on all cylinders, right?" I'm guessing the high-browed look Rust shoots Miller has nothing to do with operating the garage. The big shipment night is coming up and Miller will be the one picking up the payout from Vlad in the dark motel parking lot.

"I'll be fine." Miller clears his throat, bringing up all kinds of phlegm that contradicts his words.

Rust knocks against my desk. "Tonight. We have some things to talk about. And . . . I'll have some paperwork for you to sign." There's that smile again. The one I always see when he's about to surprise me. "I wouldn't recommend changing the name, though." He winks. "'Rust's Garage' is kind of known around these parts."

My jaw drops. Out of the corner of my eye, I see that Miller's is hanging low too. "Seriously?" Rust is keeping his word and signing over the garage to me?

"And set something up with Aref at Corleone's for later this week." He levels me with a stare on his way out the door, and I know I had better get my ass in gear and not get distracted by his latest display of generosity.

I look up to see Miller watching me quietly. I wonder what he's thinking. Probably that my first order of business is to fire him. Truth is, if this week taught me anything, it's that Miller is a really good manager and this place needs him. "I took care of most of the invoicing and orders. Payroll's done. There's just that yellow folder left that I had no idea what to do with."

"Maybe you're not completely useless, after all," he grumbles as he begins rifling through the unfinished work.

"Relax. Your job is safe," I chuckle. "You run this place better than I ever could."

That seems to soften him a bit. "No car today?"

I wait until he lifts his oversized mug of coffee to his mouth before I say, "It's with the cops, being processed for evidence after some asshole jacked it last night."

Coffee sprays out of Miller's mouth and all over his monitor, over his desk. "Son of a bitch," he growls, grabbing a wad of napkins nearby, only to knock the mug over with his elbow, spilling the rest of the coffee onto paperwork.

I know Rust said to keep it on the down-low, but this is Miller. I'm over the initial shock. Now I'm equal parts annoyed and amused by the irony. The part of my conscience that keeps chanting, "You fucking deserve it," keeps me from getting too angry.

"Here." I toss a roll of paper towels his way.

He grabs it with one meaty hand. "Joyrider?"

"No way. Had to be a professional hit. They found it in a storage locker in NoPo, just off Highway 5, waiting to be moved no doubt." It's shocking how quickly I've come to understand this whole operation. "They're processing the car right now. I'd love to see who they were planning on selling it to." Saying that is as close to admitting that I know all about the ring and what Miller does for Rust. A part of me wants to talk to Miller openly about the entire thing, to see what he thinks, to ask him if he ever wishes he were *just* the garage manager.

"I wonder," he mutters, clearing his throat several times. He looks about ready to collapse, his face red and swollen, swiping at a bead of sweat running down his brow.

"Are you sure you're okay? You can go home if you need to. I can manage for the rest of the week. I don't want you dying on me."

"It's nothing. Just this damn cold that Paige gave me. It's more annoying than anything."

"Paige?"

"My daughter."

"You have a daughter?" I don't mean for it to sound as incredulous as it comes out.

"I have three." He falls back into his chair. "All teenagers now."

Miller's gene pool is walking around Portland right now. With breasts. I'm trying to picture that but, taking in the deep cleft in Miller's chin and his trunk-like limbs, I'm struggling. I hope they got their looks from their mother. I have no idea what she looks like, but I'm guessing anything would be an improvement.

By the glare Miller shoots my way, I'm guessing he can read my mind and he's about ready to punch me. I deserve it. I'm being an asshole. "Probably why you're so stressed out," I offer.

"Yeah, probably," he mutters, hanging his head a little as he tries to salvage an invoice.

Chapter 40

...

CLARA

"Do you think we'll get anything useful out of this?" I ask through a yawn, waiting for the caffeine in my coffee to kick in as I watch Warner toss the ball across the park for Stanley.

He huddles into his rain jacket. "Not sure yet. We'll see if this plays out like we hope it does."

The tracking companies worked fast, dispatching police to storage lockers in North Portland, where the thief left Luke's Porsche and took off on foot to a parked car three streets away, Franky waiting in the wings for him. Franky tailed him for a few blocks before calling a friend of his, a local cop on duty. As soon as the thief saw the cruiser, he sped up and began weaving in and out of traffic. It was dangerous enough to bring him in on suspicion of intoxication.

Of course the guy had a bag of speed in his pocket.

Sometimes these idiots make it too easy.

By the time Warner got there and played him the video of him stealing Luke's car, the thief was ready to turn in everyone he knew to avoid charges. It's always the same. They're so predictable. There is no honor in keeping quiet with these guys.

Apparently he was hired by someone with a "thick, mean accent, like the bad guys from Bond movies" who promised that he'd get eight grand cash if he lifted the car and left it in that particular storage locker. "He was paid for 12's car, specifically?"

"Specifically. From the sounds of it, anyway. He was given the plate number and the address of the garage to scope it out ahead of time."

That means someone was following us to the movie theater? Shivers run down my spine but I push them aside. "So how is this all going down?"

"We're working with the local office on this. We need to," he rushes to say, when I glare at him. "Don't worry, your cover is intact and it'll stay intact. But there will be a point where we need to bring in more people. We've got a local undercover who fits the profile ready to head to the jewelry wholesaler downtown with a phone number. I'm assuming the wholesaler is acting as the middleman with the money. He'll have a mild description of who's coming to collect. As soon as the person on the other end of the line confirms that they've got the car, they'll hand the money over. That's how it usually works."

"Who runs the jewelry store?"

"A guy by the name of Jerry Rosenthal. We're looking into him and Gold Bonds right now. Not sure if we have anything on them."

I frown. That name . . . That name was on the certificate for the necklace at Luke's place. Is that mere coincidence? Or does Rust's organization also use this Rosenthal guy for their money exchanges? How many car theft rings would be operating through the same middleman? There can't be many. Maybe only one. But, if that's the case . . . No, I was with Luke. I saw his face. It wasn't the face of a guy staging a theft of his own car as part of an insurance scam. He was genuinely shocked and upset. And relieved, too, when they found it. Plus, he put three tracking systems on it.

"What are you thinking?" Warner asks.

That something just doesn't add up here. I'm used to sifting through thousands of seemingly useless pieces of information that make no sense until we have the entire picture. We spend most of our time speculating, downright guessing, and not being able to act without concrete evidence. This is definitely a case that's testing my skills at deduction.

I shake it off. "So we're going to go through with the money drop and arrest the person who shows up at the storage locker?"

"Nope. The person who shows up at the storage locker is going to find a black Porsche 911 with a matching license plate loaded with bugs." Warner smiles as I start to understand the plan.

"You're going to try and get through the fences." I toss the ball for Stanley again. This still isn't sitting right. "But this was an intentional hit. What happens when they see 12 driving around in his car again? They're going to know that the one they've got is staged."

"He won't be driving that car around anytime soon. I'm impounding that car for as long as we need to."

"How are you going—"

"The magic of being a Fed, darling."

I smile as he scratches behind an impatient Stanley's ear. Warner's not usually so overtly cocky about the power he wields with his badge.

"And what if 12 tells everyone that his car was lifted but the cops found it, and the person who did this hears about it?"

"It's a risk. But if I were running a gig like 12 and 24 are and someone stole my car, I'd keep it quiet while I was looking for the thief, because I'd be pissed."

"It's a big risk," I emphasize.

"And we need a big break in this case."

I nod slowly. "What's your take on the thick, mean Bond accent? Russian?"

"Sounds like it but it doesn't make sense. Why would 24's associates steal his nephew's car?"

I shake my head, wondering the same thing. "Luke did say that the Russians he was working with were assholes. Maybe he did something to piss them off? Or . . . do you think they were fishing to see if Luke has a tail on him?"

"If so, then we need to be extra careful."

"Yeah. That means no more face-to-face visits, big brother. Not even pop-ins to my condo. It's too dangerous. There's nothing stopping someone from tailing me. And you, too."

I feel Warner's eyes on my face but I keep my eyes on Stanley. "Yeah, you're right." I don't miss the disappointment in his sigh.

Chapter 41

. . .

LUKE

"Dinner was magnificent. Please tell the chef," Aref announces as the waitress sets our drinks down in front of us. She's the same one that served us last time. What a difference between the two nights, for both her and me.

She smiles. "He'll be happy to hear that." Her eyes drift over both Rust and me as she collects the last of our dishes.

"What can I say, Rust, except that I'm very pleased," Aref offers.

"So am I," I throw in, the burn of the scotch not nearly enough to quell the relief I feel. Maybe working with a guy like Aref will help erase the hint of distaste and guilt I feel being involved in this racket.

"I'm glad Luke connected us for this. I have my network onboard for one order, to start. And . . ." Rust pauses to place his napkin on the dishes that the server carries, on her way past. ". . . I think Luke's already made it clear that this does not involve our other partners. That shipment will go through as planned. If all goes well here, it'll be the last one."

Aref waves away any concerns. "You know I prefer business with you. And I already have a buyer who will make it well worth our while. He needs delivery in two weeks."

Rust begins chuckling, but I see the tension in his jaw. "Sorry,

Aref, but that's not doable. It's too risky, especially with what we're looking for."

"I'm afraid he'll go to another buyer if I don't produce."

"They all say that. Buy us five weeks and we can deliver. That I will guarantee."

Aref's lips purse tightly, but then he seems to relent with a nod and a smile. "I'll see what I can do."

Chapter 42

...

CLARA

"They took the bait." I can almost see Warner's big, goofy smile through the phone as I pace around the island in my kitchen. "It's sitting in a commercial warehouse right now. The bugs picked up a couple of names that mean nothing so far, but we're working on it. Also, our C.I. at Corleone's just confirmed that 12, 24, and 36 were at dinner two nights ago."

36. New code name for Aref.

"I'm working on a warrant for the restaurant's surveillance videos, but her descriptions of the three of them match. She recognized 12 from the last time they were there."

I'll bet she did, my jealous streak snarls. "Did she overhear anything valuable?"

"That both 36 and 12 are very pleased about something."

I used to like getting calls from Warner. Now I dread them. Maybe because I see the walls closing in on Luke. And fast. "Hey, I was thinking of swinging by and dropping lunch off for him. When's the next surveillance detail?"

"Ah, shit. I just pulled Bill and Franky off him. My agent has a huge rip planned in NoPo that I need all the guys on. Two kilos' worth of coke."

"Okay. I need to touch base with him at some point soon though."

"I'm sure he's busy setting up cars to steal."

I roll my eyes. "Yeah, probably."

"Did Sinclair call you again?"

"No." Thank God, Sinclair's eased off me a bit, letting the proper channels work. "Why?"

"Just . . . if he does, just say yes to whatever he tells you to do and then ignore him and keep doing what you're doing, at your own pace. No one can expect 12 to spill his guts after a few meets."

Alarm bells go off inside my head. "Is he talking about pulling me off this case again?"

"Don't worry about that. You're in too deep for him to pull you out."

You have no idea.

"How about I put the guys on you tomorrow. Does that work?"

I lick a gob of tomato sauce off my thumb. "Yeah, I guess. I'll just go . . . kill time somewhere."

"Don't you have pictures to take and homeless to feed?"

"I suppose."

"It's a rough life you lead, Bertelli."

"Yeah, yeah." I set my phone down and go about wrapping some sandwiches in foil, then packing them into my oversized purse, along with my camera.

Stanley paces at the door, like he knows who I'm going to see. "Sorry, not this time."

■ ■ ■

Luke's eyes light up the second I step into the office, and my insides tighten. I knew this would be the right move.

"Can we help you, miss?" Miller asks gruffly.

"*You* can't." Luke is on his feet, coming around his desk within seconds to plant a kiss on my lips. "This is a nice surprise. You want to go and grab lunch?"

"Actually, I was in the mood to cook this morning, so . . ." I hold open my purse and he peers in. And groans. "Damn, is that what I think it is?"

"Can you take off for an hour?"

He pulls his wallet and keys from his desk in answer.

"Actually, why don't you let me drive. I can't surprise you if you're driving." And, if for some reason someone comes to check up on 12's whereabouts, they'll see his uncle's Cayenne that he borrowed and assume he hasn't gone anywhere.

■ ■ ■

"I've never actually been here," Luke says as we step through the entranceway of the Japanese Garden, one of Portland's highlights and a place I've visited at least once a week since I began this case, both for the serenity and the chance to experiment with my camera. Enough that the lady charging admission at the front waves at me.

"Why doesn't that surprise me?" I smile back at him. "I'd love to see it in the fall, when the leaves begin to change."

"Then we'll come here in the fall and you can see it all." There's a pause. "Right?"

"Right." I smother any doubt in that one word with a broad smile and then focus on the oddly shaped trees and exotic pagodas ahead. Inside, sadness is quickly building. I have no idea where this case will be by then, if this thing with the Porsche is going to pan out. Luke may very well be behind bars by the fall.

He could hate my guts.

"What's wrong?"

He's frowning at me, and I realize that I'm not hiding my feelings very well after all.

"Nothing. Come on." I grab his hand and lead him down my favorite path. Acres of beautifully cultivated land are divided into five themed gardens. Stone pathways weave throughout, climbing hills, edged with exotically shaped bushes and rich green moss, connecting bridges over ponds and streams. Each plant, each tree, each man-made structure was placed with such intent, creating an enchanting serenity that I've come to love.

"How easy is it to get lost in here?" he murmurs as we wind along the path, through a denser section. We haven't crossed paths with a single person yet, which is kind of nice.

"Not easy enough. See that waterfall over here?" I point out the gentle cascade, and then hold my camera up to show him a shot I took of it when I was fooling around here a few weeks ago. It was a rare sunny day, the rays hitting the rocks in such a way that the water sprays sparkle.

"This is amazing, Rain." He takes the camera from me and begins flipping through the images, a serious frown drawing his brow together. "Why haven't you ever shown me any of these?"

"I don't really know what I'm doing yet."

"Sure looks like you do," he murmurs, and my ego swells.

"Besides, I didn't think you'd be into that sort of thing."

"I'm into anything you're into." A smile curls over his lips. "Have any pictures of me?"

"Not yet," I lie. That memory card is hidden away, for just me.

"Hmm . . . we'll have to change that." He hands my camera back to me with an arrogant smirk. "So, where are the picnic tables? Because I'm starving."

I burst out with laughter. "That's the thing . . ." I loop my arm through his and pull him off the main path, to head up a set of perfectly staggered stone steps. "We're technically not allowed to eat in here, so we'll have to do it where it's not so obvious."

"Are you suggesting we break the garden's law?" His eyes widen with mock seriousness.

"Because you have a problem with that, right?"

"That's right, I do. You're leading me astray with your wicked ways."

"I've been known to do that." I chuckle. "Relax. It's a Wednesday and they're calling for heavy rain this afternoon, so no one's going to bother us." I know because I tend to come here on those days and stand on the Moon Bridge, letting the drops soak through my hair, my clothes, and my skin as I capture the downpour using the waterproof casing that I bought.

He smiles. "Don't worry about me. I think my conscience can handle breaking the garden's law."

I hesitate. "Your conscience is already handling quite a bit, though, isn't it?" We haven't so much as hinted at Luke's work with his uncle since the night on the yacht. Either Elmira was right and pillow talk does loosen these guys' lips substantially or he regrets ever telling me.

By the look on his face, I'm afraid it may be the latter, and I need to be careful. To be honest, I'm not sure I want to know. It will only add to the guilt. I brought him here because it's private enough to enjoy our time together but public enough that it can't get out of hand again, like it did at the movies.

"It's getting a little bit harder lately, but nothing I can't deal with," he finally admits.

"Do you plan on doing it forever?"

"I dunno . . ." He kicks a loose stone off the path and follows it as it skitters away. "I've just always figured I'd spend my life working for and with Rust. I don't know what else I'd do."

"Well, you could just work in the garage, right? And you like fixing and reselling those cars with Jesse."

His jaw tightens. "It bothers you, doesn't it?"

I sense the first bricks of a wall being laid between us, and that's something I absolutely can't have. Slipping my arm around his waist, I step in front of him, my body intentionally pressed against his, as I look up into bright blue eyes that I've begun to see in my sleep. "I just don't want you to get into trouble, or get hurt."

"I'll be fine." He pushes my hair back from my face and smiles. So confident.

So very wrong.

"And what are *you* planning on doing, anyway, 'Miss Figuring Out Life'?"

So he remembers that ambiguous answer. He really was listening to me that first day. "I'm not sure yet. It's hard to know which path to take when you're so young, when you have so much to experience."

His stomach grumbles between us, making us both laugh and his cheeks turn just a touch pink. It's the first time I've ever seen him at all embarrassed. We step into a small, leafy alcove with a simple wooden bench and I hand Luke his sandwich. He has it unwrapped and in his mouth before I even sit down.

"You're the fastest eater I've ever met in my life," I muse.

"So, seriously . . ." He balls the foil up in his fist, his tone growing somber. "You're not planning on going back to D.C., are you? I mean, I know you have your friends and family there, but . . ." His words trail off.

I'm a natural liar. I tell lies all day long. So why is it becoming harder to lie to Luke with each passing day that we spend together? I feel the urge to get up, to step farther away, as if that will somehow make this easier. I wander over to a nearby lattice structure. "I don't know. Maybe one day." I hesitate, knowing I shouldn't make this harder on myself by asking. "Do you want me to stay?"

"Maybe." Sincere eyes meet mine. "Honestly, I don't really know what I'm doing with my life or how things are going to play out here. But I do know that, if I looked out my window tomorrow and knew that you didn't live across from me anymore . . ." He clears his throat and ends with a soft, "I wouldn't like it. At all."

"I know what you mean." I turn away from him so he can't read the fear on my face. More and more, I catch myself trying to imagine a permanent life here. A *real* life. With Luke. It always ends with the same damning question: how could that ever work, with him being who he is and me being who I am?

It can't.

That reality weighs more heavily on me, but I have to push my growing disappointment down and keep pretending for Luke's benefit. For the success of the case.

"I do love Oregon." My gaze wanders over the quiet, natural beauty surrounding us, which isn't limited to just this garden. "Being near the river, and the ocean, and the rocky mountains, and all this nature . . . the weather."

He chuckles. "I've never met anyone who actually loves rain. It's kind of weird. But cool, too," he adds quickly, as if afraid to offend me. "I just don't get it."

I shrug. "It's not so much that I *love* rain. I just have a healthy respect for what it does. People hate it, but the world needs rain. It washes away dirt, dilutes the toxins in the air, feeds drought. It keeps everything around us alive."

"Well, I have a healthy respect for what the sun does," he counters with a smile.

"I'd rather have the sun *after* a good, hard rainfall."

He just shakes his head at me but he's smiling. "The good with the bad?"

"Isn't that life?"

He frowns. "Why do I sense a metaphor behind that?"

"Maybe there *is* a metaphor behind that." One I can't very well explain to him without describing the kinds of things I see every day in my life. The underbelly of society—where twisted morals reign and predators lurk, preying on the lost, the broken, the weak, the innocent. Where a thirteen-year-old sells her body rather than live under the same roof as her abusive parents, where punks gangrape a drunk girl and then post pictures of it all over the internet so the world can relive it with her. Where a junkie mom's drug addiction is readily fed while her children sit back and watch.

Where a father is murdered because he made the mistake of wanting a van for his family.

In that world, it seems like it's raining all the time. A cold, hard rain that seeps into clothes, chills bones, and makes people feel utterly wretched.

Many times, I see people on the worst day of their lives, when they feel like they're drowning. I don't enjoy seeing people suffer. I just know that if they make good choices, and accept the right help, they'll come out of it all the stronger for it.

What I do enjoy comes after. Three months later, when I see that thirteen-year-old former prostitute pushing a mower across the front lawn of her foster home, a quiet smile on her face. Eight months later, when I see the girl who was raped walking home from school with a guy who wants nothing from her but to make

her laugh. Two years later, when I see the junkie mom clean and
sober and loading a shopping cart for the kids that the State finally
gave back to her.

Those people have seen the sun again after the harshest rain,
and they appreciate it so much more.

Luke has seen only the gold watches and fancy cars, luxurious
apartments and beautiful women, promises of endless money and
opportunities. But sooner or later, he is going to face the storm
that comes from the choices he has made. It's going to pummel
him where he stands, drown him in regret, punish him for his
ignorance and greed.

I can only hope it's harsh enough to make him leave this life
behind for a new one. An honest one that he can be happy with.

I focus on the moss growing between the stones by my feet,
unsure of what else to say except, "The world needs rain."

"Well, I have you. Does that count?" When I dare raise my
head, I find that his eyes aren't on the trees or the pagodas. They're
on me. On me leaning against the arbor, on my long pencil skirt,
on the low-cut tank top peeking out beneath my jean jacket, on
my neck. "You're not wearing your necklace today. You always wear
that."

My hand goes to my chest as I feign shock. "Oh, wow, I can't
believe I forgot that. I never do."

"You almost done that with sandwich?" Luke peers up at the
sky, squinting slightly as several drops land in quick succession on
his forehead. "I think that downpour is coming sooner than we
thought."

"You afraid of getting a little wet?" I tease, wrapping half of my
lunch back up and zipping it into my purse. I know he'll eat it later.

"Are you?" I see the gleam in his eyes as he stands and my
stomach explodes in a ball of flutters. Suddenly I feel like prey
that's about to be stalked, though I'm guessing Luke's intentions
are very different from that of, say, a lion stalking a gazelle.

Like a giddy teenager, I take off around the corner, weaving
through the bushes and trees that I'm quite sure visitors are not

allowed to touch, let alone run through. I make it all of fifteen feet before strong arms rope around my body and pull me down. Luke's body breaks our fall.

"Well, this is kind of nice." He peers up at the low-hanging bush that forms a thick canopy over us with a smirk. "Look at that. We're totally hidden." And then suddenly he has me on my back, pinning my arms down above my head with one hand. He's right—we're in a low-ceilinged lair, layers of broad-leaved branches cocooning us in a long, long tunnel.

Invisible to the unsuspecting eye.

The rain intensifies, and even under this protection, more and more droplets find their way between the overhang to land on us. Thank God I was smart enough to bring a nylon purse here and close it before I dropped it and took off. "Wow, it's really coming down now. And it's a cold rain. That can't be good for your—"

Luke shuts me up with his mouth, shifting my thighs apart to fit against my body just right. I'm vaguely aware of the wet chill against my bare legs as Luke hikes my skirt up, until it's pooling around my waist.

This is exactly what wasn't supposed to happen today. But now that it's started, I can't stop it.

I don't want to stop it.

"You good with this?" he whispers as he unbuckles his belt and unzips his jeans. I answer by intentionally stretching my thighs apart. The move makes him groan into our kiss, breaking free just long enough to tear the foil off a condom wrapper that he smoothly dug out from somewhere while I was writhing wantonly beneath him.

I hold my breath as fingers push my panties aside and I feel him lining himself up to slide inside me. There's no foreplay this time and I'm okay with that. Just looking at him is foreplay right now. I haven't stopped thinking about being with him again since—

"Hello?" a reedy female voice calls out.

Our mouths break free, and we lock wide eyes. From this vantage point, all I can spot are a pair of black-and-white polka-dot rain boots. I'm guessing the woman can't see us. I'm hoping she couldn't hear us. We both press our lips together and keep quiet and still as she calls out, "Hello?" again.

A long moment later, the rain boots begin shuffling down the path at an easy pace. I see my navy purse dangling next to them. "Shit, she has my camera and my phone and—" My words are cut off with a gasp as Luke pushes into me, his mouth against my ear. "Don't worry, we'll go get it back in a minute."

"Only a minute?" I tease between ragged breaths. My eyes close as he fills me completely, until the raindrops don't graze my face anymore, and the branches don't scratch at my legs, and the cold, wet ground doesn't touch my skin.

Until I'm consumed by the feel of Luke.

■ ■ ■

"Thank you so much. I must have set it on the bench and somehow forgot it when it started raining." I check inside to find everything there, including half a sandwich.

"Eating is expressly forbidden in the gardens, you know." Black-and-white polka-dot rain boots woman—the same woman who smiles and waves when I come here—now peers over her glasses at me, her tight bun making her look all the more severe.

"Oh, I know. That's just there for later."

"Right." A sniff of disapproval escapes her as her eyes trail down my clothes—soaking wet. That's fine. I was in the rain, without a proper rain jacket or umbrella. That's what happens.

"Well, thank you for keeping it safe." I don't look back once as Luke and I walk hand-in-hand back to the parking lot. That's when Luke bursts out laughing.

"It's not *that* funny." But I can't keep the smile off my face.

"Actually it is. You should see yourself."

"Yeah, well, you're not looking so spectacular right now, either." That's a flat-out lie. Even with his hair plastered against his forehead and neck in wisps, and his shirt clinging to his body, blood still races through my limbs every time I think about touching him.

"But at least I'm not covered in dirt." Reaching behind me, he begins picking off leaves and grass. Some twigs. "I guess rain doesn't make everything clean, does it."

"Shit." I peer down at the back of my skirt. It looks like I was rolling around in mud, which is basically what I was doing. "Do you think she knew?"

He laughs. "I'm guessing she has a pretty good idea."

"Awesome." I shake my head but smile. "I guess I won't be doing my next photography assignment here."

Chapter 43

. . .

LUKE

I interlace my fingers through Rain's as we weave through a thick crowd at The Cellar, the deep bass vibrating through my chest as usual. Though I've taken plenty of women out, I've never brought one in.

But Rain's different.

"Trust me, there's no need to be nervous. You're gonna love Rust."

Her broad smile sprouts those sexy dimples. "If he's anything like you then I don't doubt it. I just hope he likes *me*. I mean, he's basically your dad."

"He'd have to be insane not to love you." She's wearing dark red lipstick tonight. I can't wait to take her home and let her cover my body with it, something I normally never like.

Passing the bar, I catch Priscilla watching us from behind a wall of customers. I'm sure she's figured out by now that it's over between us. I'd be surprised if she cares. A quick glance down sees Rain's big blue eyes in that general direction. I wonder if she's put two-and-two together.

I speed up, passing by the stocky bouncer watching over the VIP section to land in our typical booth. "Rust!"

"Well . . . well . . ." As usual, Rust's on his feet immediately, patting my back as he always does, before turning his attention to Rain. "So you are the lady stealing all of my nephew's time lately."

I don't blame him for doing a lightning-speed appraisal of her. I did too, when she stepped out of her condo in this creamy, tight lace dress, the sleeves long but the dress short enough to give me an instant hard-on the minute she climbed into my SUV.

She dips her head, smiling. "Not all of it." Eyes dart to me, twinkling. "Some."

"Please." He holds an arm out toward the booth. Rain slides in, spiking my adrenaline yet again as I see those mile-high legs in full view. "Drinks?" Rust snaps his fingers at a nearby waitress while pouring a glass of vodka from the bottle he never sits down without.

As Rain gives her order, Rust is busy flashing approving eyebrows my way. That's a good start. "So, Rain, Luke tells me you moved here from D.C. not long ago?"

They go back and forth for the next fifteen minutes, Rust asking her questions about her life, her family, her plans. She answers him with the grace and ease of someone who's practiced the words, no signs of the nerves she told me about earlier.

Suddenly, Rust squints as if thinking hard. "You know, you look familiar. I can't quite figure it out."

"Do I?" She frowns at me. "I don't know why I would. I just moved to Portland."

"You saw her that day at the garage."

His forehead furrows deeper. "Yeah, but . . . have you been here, to this club?"

"Uh . . ." She glances around the space. "Yeah, actually. I think I may have come here once."

"Really? Hell, we could have been here at the same time," I say.

She shrugs. "Maybe? I don't know. My brother recommended a couple of places and I checked them out. Didn't really stay long. You know, on account of not knowing anyone."

Rust is watching her over his drink in that way he has, when I know he's weighing someone. And I'm watching him watch her, not liking it.

Which is probably why none of us notice the irate Russian suddenly hovering at our table. No warning. No hello. Just his beady, calculating eyes leveling Rust with a glare that makes me nervous. I instinctively rope an arm around Rain's shoulders and pull her into me.

"What are you doing here?"

It takes me a moment to realize he's talking to me, the question so absurd it's almost laughable. When I don't answer, he clarifies with, "I didn't see your *Porsche* parked outside."

He's still bitter at me for shutting him down at Gold Bonds after the Ferrari deal. "No, you didn't." A small part of me has wondered if Vlad had something to do with the jacking, just to be a dick. Rust told me not to say anything, but I can't help myself. "It's actually in the police impound, being processed for evidence after some asshole stole it. Would you know anything about that?"

Vlad's eyes bulge momentarily before he composes himself.

Rust sighs. "Vlad, what brings you here?" By Rust's expression, he's not surprised by the visit in the least. He waves for another glass and then slides in, making room for the asshole.

Vlad answers Rust in Russian, his tone cold and cutting. "I heard about the SUVs."

Shit. The deal with Aref. This clearly isn't a social call.

Rain's fingers dig into my leg, looking up at me questioningly. She must sense the tone. Russian doesn't sound poetic at the best of times. Angry Russian sounds downright scary.

Rust takes his time, sucking back a swig of his vodka. "And?"

"And you are using our connections to do it." More Russian. Vlad refuses to speak in anything but.

Rust now switches from English to answer him in Russian, his tone snappish. "*My* channels, my connections. *I* built those. I don't get involved in your side. Stay the hell out of mine."

"You don't get involved? You've been asking a lot of questions about our side lately."

"Yeah, because you're gouging me with each new shipment."

"Do you want out?"

Rust shrugs in a way that tells me he's getting a bit drunk and therefore bullish. "Maybe."

"Because the next shipment is expected on time."

Rust dips his head, taking several deep breaths. Finally, "Relax, Vlad. I'm just diversifying is all. All the orders are out and plans are set. You'll still get your cars next week and none of this other stuff hits your soil, so there's no competition with your current buyers."

"Was this *his* idea?" I keep my eyes on the crowd, knowing that the asshole is referring to me.

"Luke only does what I ask him to. This lands on me." A pause. "Got it?"

Vlad's lips curl back like a feral animal's. Finally, he says, "Got it." He downs his drink. Standing up, he leans over just far enough to spit on the floor beside us before marching off.

Rust shoots me a "told you" glare before smiling at Rain. "I'm so sorry about that. Some of my business partners are prickly."

"I can't say I'd want to work with him," she offers, and then leans into me with a smile, seemingly unbothered by the exchange. We stay for another hour or so, Rust telling stories about me as a little kid that make Rain laugh gleefully, and it's like the whole Vlad thing never happened. Even I start to believe it's not a big deal.

Until Rain slides past me to hit the restroom and the cheerful mood Rust forced for her benefit vanishes. "This isn't good, Luke."

"How did Vlad hear about the deal with Aref?"

He sucks in a breath in thought. "I don't know. Aref isn't stupid enough to tell him and he's never met any of the fences. I keep all the layers away from each other. Helps avoid issues in case someone gets nabbed. Only you and Miller ever talk to Rodriguez and that group, and I know neither of you have said anything." He pinches the bridge of the nose. "I should have let this partnership die with Viktor. I knew better."

"So, what now?"

"Now . . . we make sure that the shipment for Vlad and Andrei goes out next week." His fingers strum against the table as he eyes the people nearby. "Listen . . . how well do you know this girl?"

"Pretty well, why?"

"Something about her rubs me the wrong way."

"You've got to be fucking kidding me!" I slam my glass down, glancing over my shoulder to make sure she's not coming up on me. "She's perfect, Rust."

"Too perfect." He shakes his head. "I don't know . . . She didn't tell you that she's been here before?"

"I never asked!" I can't remember half the places I've been to. They all start to look the same after a while. "She's not like the women you normally see me with. That's the problem."

"Maybe." A smile. "You really like this one, don't you?"

"Yeah. I do."

He dumps his drink back. "Maybe that's why she raises the hairs on my neck."

Chapter 44

...

CLARA

"So, what were your uncle and that guy arguing about? Because he sounded pissed."

"It's just the language." Luke chuckles, turning into the underground garage in his building. "Russians always sound angry to people who don't understand them."

"Did you understand them?"

"I can't believe you were at The Cellar when I was, and we never met."

I know a brush-off, and Luke's trying to brush me off. "I know, crazy, right?"

"But Rust noticed you." Luke glances down at my bare legs. This dress doesn't allow for much coverage and, by the way he's been eyeing me all night, that's a good thing. He veers the SUV into his private garage with ease.

"So, did he give his blessing?"

Slipping his hand around the back of my head, he pulls me into a long, hard kiss. The kind that I give him when I'm not wearing my wire. The kind I can't enjoy right now.

"He loved you. He can't wait to see you again."

No small relief fills me. There's a reason no one's been able to get close to Rust so far. He doesn't trust easily, or completely.

But he trusts his nephew.

"You, in this dress, have killed me tonight." Luke's hand lands on my thigh and slips upward as he adds, "You're coming up for the night, right?"

I grab hold of his hand just as his fingers begin curling under the lace of my panties. "I can't."

His forehead drops against mine. "Are you sure? It's been too long since that day at the garden . . . I need you again."

Fuck, shit, fuckity shit. My stomach leaps up in my chest and I have to look away from him before he reads the panic that I'm sure is written all over my face. How the hell am I going to explain that one to Warner? I'm *so* screwed. There's not much I can do about it right now, except not make this worse. "I know. But I *can't* right now. You know . . . female issues."

His head falls back with a big groan. "Ohhhh."

Thank God he's not smart enough to question why on earth I'd wear a cream-colored dress that barely covers my ass when I'm on my period.

"You could still come up, though . . . right?" The way he looks at me—hopeful, almost pleading—well, apparently he's plenty smart enough to understand that there's nothing stopping at least one of us from getting off tonight.

I'm sure as hell not having the sounds of *that* recorded, even if Sinclair condones it.

I pat my abdomen. "I've got bad cramps. I could use the sleep."

He nods and offers me a reluctant smile. "I could take care of you? You know, get some Tylenol or . . ." He laughs awkwardly. "I don't know what. I'm new to all this."

"You're sweet, thank you. But I just need some sleep. And Stanley serves as a good heating pad." The fur-ball creates a rather inconvenient obstacle in the center of my bed.

Luke meets me at the back of the car and walks me out hand-in-hand, stopping to punch in the code for the garage door that will hopefully keep this one from being stolen. That's when I spot Warner behind a pillar, baseball cap pulled down over his brow.

Gun drawn.

My mouth drops open. What the hell is he doing? Luke has met him! He thinks he's my brother!

We make eye contact, and Warner retreats a few steps, the relief visible across his face. Any second now, though, Luke is going to look up and spot him. So I do the only thing I can think of. I slip my hand around Luke's neck and pull him down into my mouth in one of those kisses made for movies, which buys Warner enough time to dart behind a large truck.

"I thought you needed to go home?" His blue eyes dance as they take me in.

I smile, my hands rubbing the contours of his chest that I so desperately want to spend the night with. "I just wanted to make sure you knew how I felt about you."

He leans down and matches my kiss. Somewhere behind us, I assume Warner is watching.

■ ■ ■

"Are you insane?" I yell into my phone, kicking my heels off. I figure if my handler's about to tear me a new asshole and get me kicked off the case, I should go down swinging.

"What the hell was I supposed to do? The last thing I heard was that 24 made you in the club. Then nothing. Fucking static!"

I frown. "What? You mean you couldn't hear us after we parked?" I quickly play the damning conversation back in my head, trying to remember what was said and when.

"I don't know if it was because of the underground vents, but I couldn't hear a thing. I thought . . ." Warner's words trail off.

"You thought my cover was blown." It all makes sense now.

"Yeah. That's the only reason I would risk the case. You know that."

I flop into my couch, feeling the lead weight float away. They didn't catch Luke's comment about the gardens. "I get it. Sorry for yelling at you."

"Did he say anything important?"

"Nope." I kick off my heels. "Just small talk. Sorry."

"You kidding me? We got some good intel tonight. I called one of our translators and had him listen to the recording right away. Basically, 24 is going into business with someone else and it involves SUVs. The Russians are pissed."

"A deal with 36, maybe?" *Shit,* I'm not supposed to know that. Luke only told me about that possibility on the yacht that night. I quickly add, "They've been spending a lot of time together, so that would make sense."

"They didn't say. But 24 *did* say, and I quote, 'Luke only does what I ask him to.'"

I squeeze my eyes shut. Every day, the evidence against Luke dribbles in. Soon, it's not going to matter whether he incriminates himself through me. We're going to catch him, regardless. Maybe that's for the best. This is going to end anyway. Maybe Luke never has to know who I am, what I've done. He will go to jail and I'll go back to Washington, D.C., and that'll be the end of this. That would certainly be the best outcome for *me* after the hole I've dug for myself.

But the possibility of this doesn't bring me any relief.

"It'd be great if you could find out exactly what 24 asked 12 to do."

I push the ever-present tension away so I can get through this call. "Sure. I'll just pull my wand out and get Luke to speak."

There's a pause. "Luke?"

"I meant 12. Look, I spend so much time with him. What do you expect?"

"I expect you to keep your head on straight."

I roll my eyes, silently chastising myself. "Anything else?"

"Yeah, they talked about a deal going down next week. Try to find out when and where."

"I'll just pull my wand out and—"

"Alright, smart-ass."

"You've been in my shoes before, Warner. You know when a target is ready to trust you. 12 isn't ready yet. I asked him if he understood what they were saying and he immediately brushed me off. You heard it."

"Yeah, I did. But you need to start getting deeper. Don't get me wrong—you're doing great. We're getting somewhere, inch by inch. But we need to move this along now."

"Why?" Warner's never pushed me before. That's his boss's role. "Is Sinclair worried about getting an extension on the warrant?"

"We've got plenty to keep this going. I'm more worried about 12 keeping his damn hands off you for too much longer. I'll give him some credit, given his previous routines, but I don't see how much longer he's going to buy the whole abused girl story."

I'd say we're far past that. "I can handle 12."

"Like you did tonight?" There's that edge in his voice again. It's almost an accusation. Or maybe my guilt is starting to affect my hearing.

I ignore it. "Hey, did you catch the exchange about Luke's car being stolen? Vlad seemed genuinely surprised. I don't think he was the one who had it stolen."

He sighs. "Well, we'll find out within the hour, no doubt. If it was him, he's going to ditch the one he has like a ticking time bomb. And then that angle is fucked." Warner swears under his breath.

"Okay. Listen, I'll set up dinner for tomorrow night. You guys should get some sleep."

"Yeah. Bill just left and I'm heading out too."

"'kay. Good night, Warner. And thanks for looking out for me." I hear his hesitation. "We're all just doing our jobs."

Some much better than others.

■ ■ ■

I down the glass of water by my bedside, diluting the salty aftertaste in my mouth.

"I'm so glad you're feeling better," Luke murmurs, eyes closed, his perfect, naked form stretched out across my bed. Sated. "I wish I could return the favor."

I nuzzle up against his side in nothing but panties, my face burrowed in his neck. "Another time." I'd love that time to be right now, but I can't very well all of a sudden not be on my period. Even Luke would find that odd, I'm sure.

Fortunately he doesn't find my method of communication tonight—opening my bedroom blinds, turning my lamp on, and standing in front of the window, waiting for him to notice me—odd. In fact, he says he loved our game of semi-charades. Me, beckoning him with my hand and then patting my bed. Him, holding up a leash and ten fingers, for ten minutes. Me, watching him purposely peel off his dress shirt and pants in front of me and replace them with his track pants and T-shirt.

Me, unzipping my dress and letting it drop to pool at my ankles.

Him, running out the door and making it here in five minutes, his breathing ragged, Licks on his heels.

Us, free of any federal wires.

Unfortunately, I'm now left with an ache in my lower belly that has nothing to do with my period, squeezing my thighs together in frustration as I drape myself over him and inhale his delicious scent.

"Any big plans for tomorrow?" he asks.

"Well, I was thinking that I should maybe call Elmira. Go shopping or something with her." And see what I can get out of that woman about this deal her husband made with Luke. I slowly circle his nipples with my index finger as I casually ask, "Do you think you could call Aref and get her number for me?"

He paws for his phone on the nightstand, making me laugh.

"I didn't mean right this instant. It's two a.m."

A lazy, satisfied smile touches his lips, making him look all kinds of adorable. "I need to call him anyway. He's probably up. And if he's not, I'll leave a message." A second later, "Aref, hey . . . Vlad paid us a visit tonight . . . Somehow he found out . . . Yeah . . . Don't know . . . Nope, pretty pissed off actually. You may hear from him." I hear a low murmur coming from the phone but

I can't make out any of the words. "Okay . . . Listen, Rain wants to meet up with Elmira. Send her number to me so I can pass it along? . . . Cool. Later."

His hand flops down with his groan.

"What's wrong?"

"Nah . . . Nothing."

"Doesn't sound like nothing." I can feel the thread of tension begin to course through his body again, the one that vanished with his release. So I reach down and wrap my hand around his semi-hard cock. He exhales and his stomach muscles spasm as I begin stroking slowly. But finally, with a light sigh, I feel him relaxing again. "It's just that thing earlier, at the bar."

"The angry Russian?"

"Yeah. Remember how I told you that Aref wanted to do more business with Rust? Well, Rust agreed to a deal and somehow Vlad found out. That's why he was pissed."

"Why would he be pissed about that?"

"Because he's an asshole? Don't really know. He's still getting what he wants, so it shouldn't fucking matter."

"Should you be worried? Will he stop doing business with you?" Selfish hope swells inside me.

"I'd actually be happy if we were done with him. I don't like him. But, I doubt I'll be that lucky. He just wants to be a dick about it, I guess."

I open my mouth, about to ask him the million-dollar question—what is his uncle in business with Aref and Vlad for—when his phone chirps. He holds it up for me. "One sultry Iranian wife's number, as requested."

"Sultry, hey?" I peel myself away from him so I can save Elmira's number into my phone. "Thank you. I appreciate it."

"Anything for you." His eyes drift over my near-naked body. "How are you feeling? Can I do anything for you?"

Yeah. Walk away from these people before it's too late.

I force the sadness down with a smile. "Lying next to you feels good. You're like a giant heating pad."

"Well, in that case . . ." He yanks me back to him and, taking my hand in his, he guides it back to his now full erection with a playful grin. "I swear, I'll make it up to you."

■ ■ ■

"Come over tonight. I'll pick up dinner. Some lasagna or something." I hear the smile in Luke's voice.

"Is that your way of telling me you want me to make *real* lasagna tonight?" That's a whole day's production, if I want to make fresh noodles and everything.

And yet I know that I'll do it if Luke asks me to.

"I'm just kidding. We can have whatever you want. There's a great Thai place nearby."

"Let me grab it. Say, seven?"

"Just text me when you're on your way."

"I'll call. I like hearing your voice." Texting has become too dangerous now. I can steer a live conversation, cut off words before they implicate anyone. But a message from Luke saying "Thanks for last night. You give amazing head" is pretty black-and-white in the transcripts.

My relief escapes in a sigh when I hear the line go dead. I have survived another recorded conversation without getting burned by Luke revealing what we've been doing. How I've broken my team's trust and jeopardized my career, because of feelings I have for my target. Because this isn't just about the case for me anymore.

I'm able to reconcile my guilt somewhat, telling myself that everything Luke has revealed to me, he's revealed only because I've crossed the line with him. That rationale doesn't come without side effects, though. Namely, the little voice in the back of my head that's not so little anymore. That screams and yells at me. That tells me I'm an idiot. That Luke isn't going to change, that he's lying to me because that's what he is—a liar and a thief. That I've dug myself into a hole that I need to start trying to get myself out of.

That I'm not really helping Luke by hiding all of this from my team. Maybe slapping handcuffs on his wrists and hauling him into the station, bursting his bubble about the fictional Rain, and making him admit everything that he's admitted to me is the only way to *help* him.

Maybe . . .

My next call is to Warner, to set up cover. "I'm going over to 12's place tonight, for dinner."

" 'kay."

There's a long pause of dead air, something I'm not used to with my handler. "Warner? You okay?"

Another long pause. "The Porsche was moved again three hours ago."

"So, I was right. Vlad didn't have it stolen."

"Doesn't look like it."

I frown. Who else would want to steal Luke's car, specifically?

"I'm assuming we've passed to a second fence. A two-deep fence line is what we've seen in the past for these big rings, so hopefully the next stop is the cargo container."

The next stop. How much closer will that be to the person who can finger Luke in a lineup? "That's good."

"Yup." Again, that tightness in his voice.

"Are you sure you're okay?"

"Yeah, just . . . Rebecca and I decided to take some time apart."

So the girlfriend finally has a name. "I'm sorry, Warner."

"It is what it is." So matter-of-fact. "What do you have planned for today?"

"Uh . . . just some grocery shopping and stuff. I'll talk to you later?"

"Sure." The phone clicks awfully fast. He's obviously more upset about his breakup than he'll ever let on.

Maybe I'll buy him a case of beer and invite him over later this week.

But today . . . today, I have something more urgent to do. Searching out Elmira's phone number, I head over to the safe behind the painting and dig out my personal phone to make the call.

Chapter 45

...

LUKE

"Fuck!" I slam my phone down, earning Miller's glare. "Sorry. The cops are still dicking me around." My car was supposed to be released last week, but apparently they have a backlog in their investigations unit. They said I'd get it back next week. Maybe.

Miller grunts as he eases his body out of his chair and drops several checks on my desk. "Here. I guess you're supposed to sign these now, right?"

"What is this for?" I eye all the digits staring back at me.

"Tax man."

"Already? I thought all that got squared away with the lawyers when we changed ownership over."

Miller laughs, an odd and grating sound. "You're never squared away with paying taxes. These are the next installment. Don't worry, the money's already sitting in the account to cover it. You just have to sign it over."

I scrawl my name across the line and hand it back. "Don't ever leave me, Miller."

He responds with another grunt as he ambles back to his corner. I pick up the plaque that showed up mysteriously on my desk this morning, tracing the engraved letters that spell out "Nurse Boss Boone." And I smile. Tabbs and Zeke are obviously behind it. It's their way of congratulating me, while still getting their digs in. I don't mind so much anymore.

I can't believe this garage is mine. Not bad for a twenty-four-year-old guy. Based on the numbers I just handed over to the government, and the earnings statements I saw while signing ownership papers, I could make a good, solid living off this place if I keep it up.

A good, solid *clean* living, running this place and flipping cars, just like Rain suggested.

I eye my burner phone sitting next to my personal phone. Quiet and unassuming. I haven't gotten used to it. Do I really want to spend the rest of my life carrying one of those around? Wondering who's listening on the other end?

Do I really want to sit at a bar with my girlfriend and my uncle and worry about an angry Russian showing up to yell and spit at us?

I lay in Rain's bed last night for hours, listening to her breathe against my chest, thinking about everything. Wondering if, when she actually finds out what I've been doing with Rust, she'll change her mind and leave me.

Stupid, really. If I should be worried about anything, it's jail time, not losing my girlfriend. Yet Rain, and what she'll think of me, is the one constant worry that keeps popping into my head. Lately, it's even louder than my worry about disappointing Rust if I tell him that I think I want out.

What will he say?

Chapter 46

...

CLARA

"Did they give you any trouble?" Elmira closes in for a double air kiss on either side of my face.

"Not at all." Aside from the registration lady's once-over of my jeans and black boots. By the time I made it through the security gate, a valet, and a front desk, I knew this was the most exclusive of exclusive clubs.

"Good. We pay enough in membership fees that they shouldn't." She offers me her trademark smile—small, slightly standoffish—before gliding down a long hall with signs pointing toward the swimming pool. Other signs point toward the squash and tennis courts, a curling rink, and a golf store. Double-glazed doors with iron inserts hide a spa. I'm guessing the soothing smell of essential oils in the air is coming from there.

"Thanks for meeting me today." Honestly, when I called Elmira this morning, I expected to get her voice mail, but she answered. I held my breath when I suggested lunch and I deflated with disappointment when she declined, saying her day was full. Then she suggested I meet her here, as she was on her way for her morning swim.

"Of course. You sounded like you wanted to talk." She leads me into the spacious change room. "These are all visitor lockers." She points to a row of cream-colored metal. "It's quite secure, so you're fine to leave your purse, your jewelry . . ." Dark, youthful eyes—free of all traces of makeup except some mascara—flicker to my chest, where my dragonfly pendant normally hangs. "I'll meet you out there in five?" She doesn't even wait before she disappears around the corner.

My wariness grows. She makes me uncomfortable. If it weren't for this case, and for Luke, I'd go out of my way to avoid her.

But she may know something that can help me, I remind myself, as I peel off my clothes, slide on the bathing suit that I stopped and bought on the way here, and head out to the pool. Elmira's already there, her shiny black hair tucked into a cap, making her look more like a little girl than ever before. We're the only two in the pool area. I do a quick scan of my surroundings, as I always do. No lifeguard, no cameras. No other swimmers.

That's a little surprising, given the people milling about the rest of the clubhouse. But this isn't a bathhouse with hidden, steamy alcoves, I remind myself. This is safe, neutral country club territory.

Still, the hairs on the back of my neck rise. If not for the wall of windows opposite me, overlooking the green, I'd be more than a little concerned.

Elmira dives off the edge with the sleek movements of a well-trained athlete and swims the length of the pool before pausing, her eyes trailing over my one-piece. "It's warm enough."

Okay.

Inhaling a lung's worth of chlorine-scented air, I dive off the side and into the deep end, reveling in the feel of the tepid water. When I emerge, I find Elmira waiting for me, treading water in the center of the expansive pool. "So, how have you and Luke been, Rain?"

It could be my paranoia, but the way she says my name . . . "Uh . . . we're good. Great, actually." What is it exactly about this woman that puts me on edge like this?

"Yes, Aref says that you and Luke are growing much closer." She adds, almost as an afterthought, "Luke told him, at dinner the other night."

I highly doubt that Aref and Luke were talking about our relationship, but I play along. "At Corleone's?"

"Yes. That's right." She says nothing else, waiting. She's fishing. She wants to know what I know, what Luke has told me. Maybe she's here at her husband's bidding. The deal's in motion and he wants to know who can identify him, should things go sideways.

I'm not giving her anything. "I'm glad Luke feels that way."

"Did he tell you that he and Aref struck a deal recently?" She mentions it so casually, as if we were drinking cappuccinos at a café patio and talking about our husbands' legitimate jobs.

I was counting on her knowing. The question is, what can I get out of her? "He mentioned it, yeah. I didn't get many details, though. Luke's still pretty tight-lipped."

A small, amused smirk touches her lips. "I took you for a woman who would do whatever she needs to get what she wants."

It's an art, speaking as Elmira does. The average person would miss it. Or, if they were already paranoid, they'd stumble and stutter over their words, giving her the answers she's looking for without uttering a word.

But I know how to search for the crack in her armor. "Like you?" I volley back. Elmira is clearly more than just arm candy. Does she actually help *run* their empire?

She smiles. There's something that looks like respect. Does she realize that she's finally met her match?

That's why her next words are so jarring. "You need to get him to back away from the deal."

I swallow my shock. "Why?"

"There are things in play now. Plans that began some time ago, before Luke ever became involved, and when they come to fruition, there will be no room for Luke in them. The less involved he is, the better."

My heart is pounding against my chest as I digest what I begin to realize is more warning than threat. "What things?"

The creak of a door introduces several ladies, chattering and laughing as they enter the pool area in their bathing suits. When

I turn back, Elmira has begun her laps again. I guess our conversation is over, for now. I trail her in the next lane, using this time to process.

There are things in play? What plan? And who does it involve? Obviously Aref, but who else? Have Aref and Elmira figured out that there's a full FBI investigation underway? Aref sure as hell isn't playing on our side or *I'd* know. And she can't know who I am, or he wouldn't have gone through with this deal to begin with.

I almost wish I had worn a wire today, so that I could talk through this with Warner. Then again, nothing would have been captured while in the pool.

It finally dawns on me.

This meeting spot was a very intentional choice on her part.

I eye her black-capped head as she glides over the water with a smooth breaststroke. Elmira suspects that I'm wired. Or she's at least afraid of it.

We continue our laps for a good twenty minutes, until my arms are sore and my breath is ragged, and I still haven't figured out what angle she's playing here, what benefit there is for her in warning me.

"Hey," I call out as she pulls her lithe body out of the water and grabs her towel. The only sign that she's tired is a slight pant. She peels off the cap to let her long black hair cascade over her shoulders, and then crouches down beside me as I hold myself over the side of the pool with folded arms.

"If you care about Luke, get him to back away from this deal. It won't end well for him otherwise," she says, her words hard and slow and unmistakable. "Aref likes Luke. But he loves money, and he's a businessman who keeps all of his doors open."

My mind begins spinning with possibilities. "Is one of those doors Vlad?"

"Enjoy the pool." She stands. "And trust that I'm saying this for your benefit. And Luke's." I watch her stroll toward the change rooms.

Trusting that woman is the last thing I see myself doing.

I wait five minutes before ducking out, hoping that I might tail her.

She's already gone.

■ ■ ■

"Come on, just one episode!"

"Why do you like this show so much? You don't even get to see anything. They blur all the good stuff out!"

Luke's brow spikes. "The good stuff?"

I roll my eyes. "You know what I mean."

"I don't." His fingertip tugs at the V at my T-shirt, exposing the lace on my bra. "Why don't you show me."

I smack his hand away with a smile and point at the screen.

"Fine . . . Maybe there's a good movie on. One *without* aliens." He scrolls through the pay-per-view channels, taking a second to check his phone screen. He frowns.

"What's wrong?"

"Nothing, just . . ." His frown deepens, and he moves to set his phone back down on the end table. "Nothing. I was just expecting a call."

"Oh yeah? A work call?" The dragonfly pendant hanging around my neck weighs ten pounds tonight.

Elmira's words weigh ten times that.

I've replayed them all afternoon, twisting and turning them, trying to read between them. Unable to figure out her motives. Aref's wife wants Luke and Rust to back out of the deal. She can't know I'm investigating him; otherwise she'd never bother trying to get me to steer Luke away from business with Aref.

Unless she knows that I've already been sabotaging the case so far.

I'm torn between doing my job—or at least, making it appear like I am—and relaying Elmira's warning, something I can't do with ears on me.

"I'm just waiting for Rust to call me, to sort something out."

Perfect intro. "How is he after last night? Did he and that Vlad guy work things out?"

He snorts. "I doubt it. That guy's an asshole."

"I'm sure your uncle wouldn't want to lose his business, though, right?" I choose my words carefully so as not to repeat anything we've shared in our private moments, going off only what's been captured on the wire. But it's getting harder to distinguish the conversations; there have been so many private moments now.

"No, not yet anyway. Not until he has things up and running with Aref."

I curl up into his chest. Hating myself for setting him up like this. "How long will that take?"

"Well, we've got a deal with Vlad next week and one with Aref in about a month, so we'll see how that goes."

I close my eyes against the sound of that "we." "Big ones?" I hear myself ask.

He sighs. "Yeah. One of them's worth—" A phone rings and Luke's hand jumps, his words dropping off. But it's not his phone ringing. It's mine. There are only two people who have that number besides Luke: Sinclair and Warner. But neither would be calling me while I'm meeting with my target.

Unless it's serious.

"Sorry, I need to grab this. I was waiting for my mom to call." I step over Licks and Stanley, curled up on what I'd now call the communal bed, and move to where Luke won't hear the male voice on the line.

"Hi."

"Can you talk?" Warner's gruff tone fills my ear.

"Yeah."

"We've got a big problem." He sighs. "24's body was found this morning."

I turn toward the kitchen, away from Luke, so he can't see the color drain from my face. "Why am I just hearing about this *now*?"

"Because *I* just found out an hour ago. I was waiting for Sinclair to make a call on our next move."

Shit . . . "How bad?"

"Bad. Execution-style, in a black SUV. But he was obviously roughed up beforehand. The kind of roughed up when someone's trying to get answers. I think this may have something to do with the Russians and this other deal."

"No shit."

Luke snorts in the background. I glance over my shoulder at him to find him staring at me in disbelief. "You talk like that to your mother?"

I turn away, feeling like I'm about to vomit. Luke's listening to my conversation. I need to be careful what I say. "So what happens next?"

"Well, at first Sinclair was ready to bring 12 in and give him the hot-lamp treatment."

"No!"

"He changed his mind. We don't have 12 on anything solid. It's better to see where his head's at after he finds out. He may sing like a little choirboy. I just called Franky and Rix so they know. They're listening in on this all right now. I've got more reinforcements coming. We need around-the-clock surveillance."

"Is that the best choice?" I'm struggling to make my answers ambiguous to Luke but clear to Warner. "Is that the safest option?"

"It's the only option right now because it's what Sinclair has ordered. You need to stay on 12. Have your gun on you at all times."

"*How?*"

"I don't care how. Figure it out. If we lose 12 too, this case is dead."

Lose Luke. I can't even think about that without feeling a sharp pain piercing my heart. "Okay. Yeah, definitely. How long before . . ." Before Luke's happy, oblivious bubble is crushed.

"Uniforms just pulled into his building. 12's marked as his next-of-kin."

Of course he is. And that's why Warner called now. He had no other choice.

"Keep them from asking too many questions. We can't let the locals fuck up this case for us."

"Got it."

"You can do this."

"I'll talk to you later, Mom." I force myself to take a few breaths before I turn around. "Hey, sorry about that." I can't keep the shake from my voice.

Luke stands, frowning. "Are you okay?"

"Yeah, it's just . . . just some procedure my dad's having done next week."

"Is it serious?"

I swallow against the bitter taste of my lies. "As any surgery is."

Luke pulls me into his side and kisses the tip of my nose. "He'll be fine. Don't worry."

"Thanks."

Leading me back to the couch, he waves the remote toward the screen. "I'll even watch this if it'll make you feel better." He has a sappy Nicholas Sparks movie highlighted.

I manage a laugh, which quickly morphs into tears. Why the hell am I crying? I'm an undercover cop and a criminal got himself killed doing illegal shit! I don't care about Rust!

But I do care for Luke.

This is going to crush him.

Knowing that breaks the last of my defenses and suddenly the tears are flowing down my cheeks. For Luke, for what he's about to go through. For the anguish of replaying what his uncle's final minutes might have been like. Not the uncle who led a car theft ring. The one who raised him the way a loving father raises a son.

Wiping them away with the back of my hand, I manage to get out, "Nicholas Sparks movies don't make me feel better."

"Okay, I'm sorry." Luke takes turns brushing and kissing away the steady stream. "What else do you want to do?" He glances out the window. "It's raining outside. We could go run around in the park?" He pauses. "Naked?"

I burrow my face in the crook of his neck and he wraps his arms around me, his chuckles soothing.

That's what makes the severe knock on the door that much worse.

"Million-dollar condos and security doesn't screen anyone, do they? I'm sorry."

I trail him over, nearly stepping on his heels. He checks the peephole and his face pales.

"Who is it?"

A momentary flash of him opening the door and Vlad being there with guns aimed hits me. With Rix and Franky watching, I know that's not likely. Still . . .

He looks at me, worry etched over his face. "It's the cops."

Another second and another knock on the door.

Finally, he opens it. And steps back. I know what he's thinking. That they're here to take him in. I almost wonder if that would be better.

"Are you Luka Xavier Boone?"

He folds his arms across his chest. "Yeah."

I stand three feet away and watch as the storm—the rain I've been trying to save him from—hits Luke.

And I don't feel an ounce of satisfaction.

Chapter 47

■ ■ ■

LUKE

"Hey." A hand softly squeezes mine. I peer up into Rain's eyes, brimming with tenderness.

Where am I? Still sitting on my couch, with a bowling ball weighing my chest down. Where I've been since the police told me that Rust is dead. They wouldn't give me any details, other than that he had been identified by their forensics team and that the death was under investigation. And then they grilled me for ten minutes, asking me if Rust had enemies, if I was aware of any altercations that Rust had been in lately.

One name came to mind immediately.

But, to name him would mean opening up a giant can that I don't know how to handle yet.

Rain told them in a polite but firm way that they needed to leave and we'd get back to them soon.

"Is Bridgette okay with watching the dogs?" My next-door neighbor, a thirty-eight-year-old wealthy divorcée with two boys in private school, has always been willing to dog-sit Licks when I'm in a jam.

"Yup. For as long as we need." Rain holds up her keys. "Let's go."

She insisted on running back to her condo to pick up her car keys. I don't know how long she was gone. I don't know why she insisted on driving her own car. I don't know how I'm going to get to the front door.

But I manage, with Rain holding my hand the entire way.

■ ■ ■

"This one, right?" Rain asks, pulling her car into the driveway of the tidy white bungalow where I grew up. It was my grandparents' home, and when my grandpa died, Rust not only let my mom have it free and clear, he also sunk money into it, replacing the roof, the furnace, and the flooring, and bringing the '60s-style kitchen and bathrooms into the twenty-first century.

Rust has always been there to take care of us.

And now he's dead.

Bile rises up my throat for the hundredth time in the last hour. I'm about to ask Rain to stop the car so I can hop out and puke. Thankfully, the driveway's short and I'm out of the car within seconds.

"It's a nice, old neighborhood," she murmurs, her eyes roaming over the giant oak trees that Ana and I used to climb. Clutching her purse tight to her side, she takes my hand. "Come on, let's get inside."

Even in this perpetual state of shock that I've fallen into, I can't help but notice the edge in Rain's movements. Maybe she's wondering the same thing I am—does this have anything to do with the angry Russian from last night?

And am I next?

I don't see any benefit to killing me. But, without Rust, the entire organization falls apart, so killing Rust wouldn't be smart on Vlad's end either.

Which leaves me wondering . . . who the hell did it?

She leads me up the front steps to the covered porch that my mom used to sit on, waiting for Ana and me to come home from playing with the neighborhood kids. They don't creak like they used to, thanks to Rust, who had the entire thing replaced after Ana, at eight years old, fell through a rotten floorboard. I remember that day well. Rust and Deda went head-to-head, my old-school Russian grandpa's philosophy of hiding imperfections behind a fresh coat of paint every year the cause for Ana's broken leg.

It was the first time I ever saw my grandpa, a stubborn man by his own admission, relinquish power to Rust.

My mom answers the door in a red robe, the light from the porch highlighting the near black roots of her platinum-blond hair. For a woman who works as a hairstylist, I'd think she would stay on top of that more. I asked her about it once; she said she liked the look.

"Luke, what are you doing here so late?" Her worried eyes dart between me and Rain. "Is something wrong?"

That painful ball forms in my throat again. I don't know how to tell her. She and Rust have always been close. The only reason she wasn't listed as next-of-kin instead is because Rust knew how fragile she was. God knows what this will do to her.

Ana appears in the doorway behind her, the same confused look on her pretty face.

Rain gives my hand a squeeze. Somehow it helps. "Yeah." I clear the rasp out of my throat. "Something's definitely wrong."

Chapter 48

. . .

CLARA

The elevator doors open to allow residents off, freshly showered, dressed, and ready for a day of work. We're the exact opposite, in rumpled clothes and with red, tired eyes, which watched wave after wave of emotion grip Luke's mom and sister, their tears coming from a seemingly never-ending tap of grief. What Luke didn't shed in tears he made up for in cigarettes, burning through one after another, he and his mom emptying three packs while sitting on the steps of the front porch.

Like sitting ducks.

Only a dozen cars traveled down the quiet side street all night, but each one had me ready to pull the gun tucked inside my purse—that I grabbed from my safe before we left, using the excuse of forgotten car keys.

"Hey." Luke sticks his hand out to hold the elevator door. "Don't take this the wrong way, because you've been amazing, but . . . I need to be alone for a bit." I've seen the look that now sits in Luke's eyes many times—the vacant stare of a person who doesn't know what to do next.

But it's against my direct orders. And I'm not letting him walk into his condo without making sure no one's waiting there for him.

"Sure, okay. Do you mind if I just go up to grab Stanley?"

He shakes his head quickly, like he forgot about the dogs. "Yeah, of course."

The elevator ride up is silent, Luke leaning back against the wall, his eyes closed. No doubt exhausted. I'm exhausted, and I'm used to going a full day without sleep. Still, my mind frantically works to find a way into his condo without sounding forceful. "Hey, with everything going on, I couldn't find where I put Stanley's leash last night. Let me go grab it? Stanley's less obedient in the morning for some reason. I'll bring Licks home, too."

"Yeah, sure," Luke says absently, his keys dangling from his fingers. I pull them from him with a smile, unlocking the door, giving me the advantage of walking into his condo first. Everything looks the exact same, right down to half a glass of red wine sitting on the kitchen counter and the brown Thai food take-out bag.

I move through quickly, pretending to search for the leash— that I didn't forget to give to Bridgette when I dropped off the dogs—with my gun hidden between my purse and my rib cage. If my behavior seems erratic, Luke doesn't seem to notice, dropping down into his couch, his head hung, his elbows resting on his knees.

My heart aches for him, in a way that it isn't supposed to, in a way that isn't allowed. I force it down to focus on the more critical matters at hand.

"Weird. Can't find it," I call out when I've checked the last closet and can clear Luke's condo from any crazy Russians wanting to exact more punishment. Slipping my gun back in my purse, I squeeze Luke's shoulder. "Let me go grab the boys. I'll be back."

I duck out and run down the hall, cutting chitchat with Bridgette short and forcing Licks to gallop behind me. Luke has moved into his bedroom and shut the door behind him. I can hear the shower running.

So I quickly update Warner.

"Sinclair made some calls. We've got jurisdiction on the murder now. We're running a couple of partials from the SUV. See if that gives us anything we can use. Anything on that end? Phone calls? Visitors?" he asks.

"Nope. Nothing."

"That'll change soon. The media's all over this now."

Shit. We haven't so much as glanced at the TV since last night. Reporters can be insensitive assholes, creating ugly headlines to hype a story with little consideration for the people it impacts.

My body is starting to ache. "Okay. I'm going to grab a bit of sleep, before I accidently shoot someone."

"Keep your phone by your ear. I've got eyes on the outside." There's a pause and then he asks, "What does your gut say? Do you think he's going to spill?"

"Too soon to tell. Right now he needs some space." I make sure my tone leaves no room for persuasion.

"Okay. Be ready. Once the shock wears off, these guys tend to do stupid things, and fast."

Not Luke. That's just not him. But I don't say that to Warner because he wouldn't understand.

I make sure every deadbolt is latched in place and then, drawing the blinds, I set my purse on the ground for easy access to my gun. Just in case. Peeling back layers until I'm left in nothing but my tank top and panties, my fingers graze the dragonfly pendant. Desperate for the day I no longer need to wear it. I know that day is coming soon. I just hope I'm strong enough to handle the aftermath.

I set it on the coffee table and stretch out on the couch, trying to catch an hour or two of sleep.

Sleep doesn't come to me, though.

My eyes are fixed to that closed door, and the eerie silence behind it. The shower stopped running long ago.

And then I hear it. The first sob.

It seizes my heart in an instant. I don't know if the microphone will pick that up. It's pretty far away. But I grab the remote and throw on one of the music channels, just loud enough to kill any possibility. He has the right to suffer in private. I think Warner would understand that, and if he doesn't . . . fuck all of them.

What none of them would understand is me tiptoeing from the living room to the closed door. Trying the handle, I find it unlocked. I slink in quickly, making sure not to make a sound as I shut it behind me. Daylight squeezes through the edges of the closed blinds in slits. Between that and the muted TV flashing in the corner, there's enough light for me to see Luke's towel-clad body lying on his bed, his back to me, one arm curled under his pillow.

Without a word, I crawl into bed, until my chest is pressed against his back and my arm is wrapped around his waist and my hand is curled within his. And I listen to him cry softly, his tears rolling down his cheeks to slide over my fingers.

Not until he quiets do I offer, "I'm so sorry, Luke. Really, I am."

A deep, ragged breath lifts and drops his chest. "Vlad killed him. Or someone for Vlad."

"How do you know?"

"It's all over the news. They found him in a stolen black Mercedes SUV. That's what we were lifting for Aref to ship overseas. He has a buyer in Africa who specifically wants black SUVs."

"That's what this illegal thing that you're into is? Stolen cars?" It's the first time he's ever said it so blatantly.

"Yeah. Mainly chopped cars, but some high end. Rust has an organization through Portland, Seattle, San Francisco . . . basically the Western seaboard. He rounds them up on this side and Vlad sells them to buyers overseas. We ship them in Aref's cargo ships and we split the profits. But Vlad started dicking Rust around, claiming higher payoffs to get people to look the other way. Rust was sure he was ripping him off. Then Aref stepped in, wanting to get in on some of the money. He had a buyer lined up in Africa. So, I convinced Rust to do a separate deal with him. That's what that was about the other night. Vlad was pissed."

"At you?"

"Rust told him that the deal was all on him and that I had nothing to do with making it. To protect me, I think."

This, in a nutshell, is everything that we've been waiting to hear Luke admit.

I hold his body tighter.

"But what good would killing Rust do for Vlad? Don't they need Rust for this deal you were talking about?" I have to remember to choose my words carefully, so I don't sound like I actually know what I'm talking about.

He rolls onto his back, and I get my first look at his tear-stained face. "That's what I can't figure out. Rust was the only one who knew all the levels and players and how everything worked—all the fences and wheelmen, who was lifting the cars, who was chopping them, how they were moving from location to location. I don't see how either delivery is going to happen now that Rust is gone."

"Unless Vlad figured things out on his own . . ." I say, more to myself, as the mess of clues starts to make sense. A plan was in place, Elmira had said. Was that the plan? Was Vlad honing in on Rust's protected network? Based on what Luke just told me, they were splitting half the profits. But if they removed Rust . . . "Vlad could take over and not split profits, right?" But how does Aref fit into all of this?

I can see the wheels churning inside his head. "Yeah . . . I guess. But I don't know how they'd figure that out. I mean, I know two of the fences, and Miller knows two, but aside from dropping an order that Rust gives us and paying the fences for delivery to the warehouse, we don't see anything but a wad of money at the end of it."

My ears perk up. That big, burly garage manager is a part of this too?

"It's not that easy to figure out. I mean, if the cops can't do it . . ."

Unless someone's been doing their own surveillance on Rust. One that doesn't require following laws and respecting privacy. I can only imagine how much easier it would be to get things done when we aren't held back by warrants and civil rights. I mean, look at the kind of information I've gathered through dishonest means!

He wipes away a stray tear still sitting on his cheek, vacant eyes locked on the ceiling above. "This just doesn't feel real. I can't believe he's gone." He shifts until an arm ropes around my shoulders and he curls into me, our noses grazing. I automatically inhale the scent of him, freshly showered and smelling of soap, his skin soft and warm against my body.

Feeling the walls tighten around us, as Elmira's warning screams inside my head. I'll never forgive myself if I don't try to stop this.

"Luke?"

Red-rimmed eyes open to meet mine.

"Whatever you have going on with Vlad and with Aref . . . it's over. Forget about it. Please, just walk away. I can't lose you." I can't keep my own tears from unleashing, because I know that I'm going to lose him regardless. "Please. Just promise me it's over."

He blinks back a fresh wave of tears. And nods, pulling me into his bare chest.

I don't mean to drift off in Luke's bed.

■ ■ ■

"Hey." I feel someone shaking me awake.

"Hmm?"

A gentle kiss touches my temple. "Your phone's been ringing nonstop. Do you think it's important?"

My phone.

Warner.

I bolt up in bed and sprint out of the room.

"I've been trying you for an hour," Warner says, his tone thick with accusation.

I dart toward the small mudroom on the opposite side of the condo. "Sorry, I didn't hear it."

"Really? Because I've been listening to it ring on the wire. It was pretty damn loud."

"I fell asleep," I hiss, checking around the corner to make sure Luke hasn't appeared yet. I doubt he's in any rush to move.

Dead silence answers me. Infuriating me. "Any reason you're calling?"

"Just checking in."

"I have to take the dogs out and grab a change of clothes. Watch that he doesn't leave." I hang up before Warner can argue with me.

■ ■ ■

Licks trots through my condo, his nose to the ground, oblivious to his master's devastation. I gave Luke one of the Ambien pills that his mom slipped into my hand as we were leaving her house, a full container from her own medicine cabinet. Hopefully it knocked him out by now.

I didn't like leaving him but I couldn't risk making this call from his place, on my phone. It's just a hunch, one that's been bugging me, one that may sabotage this case, but it will give me the answer I need.

"Hello."

The sound of that woman's crisp London accent triggers my unease. I get the distinct impression that she knows who's calling, even though the number is blocked on my personal phone. "Hi, Elmira."

"We've been watching the news. How is Luke doing?" Calm, cool, collected. Not the reaction I would expect after a business partner of her husband's was found murdered.

"As well as to be expected."

"Please send our condolences. Rust was a good man."

"I didn't know him well, but I know he was well liked."

"How is Luke taking it?"

"Not well. I feel so sorry for him. He's had such a rough couple of weeks. First, with his car being stolen, and now this." The two don't even begin to compare but it doesn't really matter, for my purposes.

"Oh? I didn't know that happened. I'll bet he loved that car."

"Yes, he does." I hesitate for just a moment, but then commit fully. "Luckily the cops found it in a storage locker right away."

There's a short pause. "Well, that's *lucky*." Is it just me or has her voice risen an octave? I'm sure she's weighing my words. Wondering if I have my own hidden purpose for telling her.

But I can play the same game that she does. "Yeah. I just wish they'd release it. I don't know why they're not. Being assholes, I guess."

"Local police are lazy."

"Must be it."

There's another long pause. "If there's anything at all that we can do to help Luke during this time, please let us know. We'll see you at the funeral."

"Thanks, Elmira." Now that my small trap is laid, I toss the phone back into the safe, leash the dogs up, and head back to Luke's.

But not before I find myself standing in the rain, waiting for it to wash away the filthy feeling of my betrayal to my team.

Chapter 49

. . .

LUKE

Rain squeezes my hand.

It's a warning squeeze, signaling that I'm getting too worked up.

I take a deep breath to calm myself. When Rust told me he was making me executor to his estate a few years ago, I didn't spend too much time thinking about it. I definitely didn't think that, at twenty-four years old, I'd be planning a closed-casket funeral for him. But now that the police have finished gathering evidence off of him—there's no need for an extensive autopsy; it's pretty clear that the bullet through the brain is what killed him—that's exactly what I'm sitting here doing, with a very calm and collected Rain on my right side and the emotionally unstable duo—Mom and Ana—on my left, fighting me tooth-and-nail for a traditional Eastern Orthodox service.

"Rust didn't want a service of any kind, or a wake. He made that very clear in his will. Which I spent all morning going through with the lawyer," I say, tempering my tone. Rust never had much patience for the funeral process and he sure didn't believe in God.

"But what about what *we* want? What his mother and father would want?" my mom cries, rubbing away the fresh tears streaming down her cheeks. "If we go by those stupid papers, well . . . why don't we just toss his body into the family vault!"

Reading between the lines, he's basically asking for just that. But I don't say that now.

"Are you going to keep fighting me on this? Or can we just move on with the arrangements?" Because I just want this to be over with.

"We can arrange for a lovely—and quick—service at the burial site for you that may help serve everyone's needs while respecting Mr. Markov's wishes," the funeral director offers with a sympathetic smile. It's the same smile she's worn for the past hour, relieving it only with well-timed frowns or closed-eye nods to convey her deepest understanding. I wonder if these people are born with funeral worker genes or if they take extensive schooling for it, because everyone we've walked past on our way into this office is the exact same.

Rain's ringer is off but I can hear her phone vibrating in her pocket. It's been vibrating nonstop since we sat down in here but she hasn't so much as pulled it out. I lean over. "You can take that if you need to. It could be about your dad." With everything else going on, I haven't even asked her what's happening with him and she hasn't mentioned it.

She frowns. "Yeah, I probably should. If you're okay here?"

"What else do we need to do?" I ask the funeral director.

She lays a catalogue out in front of us with utmost care. "Well, there is the matter of choosing a casket, writing the obituary . . ."

Her words drift off as I turn back to Rain. "We can handle this."

She pats my leg and then stands. "Okay, I'll just be outside."

I watch her walk out, feeling immediately lonely. She's been by my side—watching reruns of my stupid favorite shows, feeding me, walking the dogs with me, lying next to me while I fall asleep—since the cops first showed up at my door. I don't know what I'd do without her.

Chapter 50

...

CLARA

"This is creepy. And disrespectful," I mutter, glancing over my shoulder at the casket on the other side of the room, an elderly man lying peacefully within.

"Why? He doesn't care. His visitation doesn't start until tonight." Warner holds a finger to his lip, checking for blood. I was halfway down the hall, passing a row of viewing rooms, when an arm shot out and grabbed me. I threw a fist out and connected with flesh before I realized it was my handler who was abducting me.

"You're insane. Have you been waiting here all this time? I was just about to call you. Way safer than this."

"Relax. I can explain my way out of anything," he mutters. "And I honestly don't know what's safe anymore. I feel like there are more eyes on us than we know about."

"Why do you say that?"

Warner reaches up, his hand grazing my chest as he grasps my necklace, switching the wire off. "Our decoy Porsche got dropped off on the side of the road last night. Wiped clean and abandoned."

Last night. Only hours after my phone call with Elmira. A mix of satisfaction and guilt stir inside me with the proof that my hunch paid off. Aref set that car theft up and staged it to look like Vlad was behind it, should the thief get busted and questioned. I have my guesses as to why.

Maybe I'll still have my chance to ask him myself.

But for now, I have to look disappointed for Warner's sake. "Do you think someone tipped them off? Or did they find the bugs?"

Warner shrugs. "Hard to say. We knew it was risky to begin with. But it means we've lost that lead. At least we got a few names and locations out of it, though." He clamps up as low voices pass by in the hall. "There's more." Turning, he levels me with a hard stare.

It makes me uncomfortable. Like I've done something wrong and am about to get called on it. "What?"

"A G-Class Benz and a Lexus LX were hijacked last night."

"Hijacked?"

"Yeah. One of the drivers has a few scrapes. The other one's in the hospital for gunshot wounds. Both SUVs are black."

Black SUVs. Exactly what Aref's African buyer wants.

"Rix's guy called him this morning, asking him to help out with a couple of rush orders that just came down the pipes. They need the SUVs within the next forty-eight hours. We're thinking that someone's pushing up the date for a shipment and bringing in guys from around the street to fill the order fast. 24's usual crew isn't normally sloppy, but someone is definitely still running the show. Too coincidental to be anything else."

"It's not Luke. I mean 12. He's too preoccupied. His phone hasn't even left his nightstand in the last two days."

"Well, it's sure someone."

"Vlad." I say it with certainty, though I can't be 100 percent sure that it's not Aref. "I'm betting one of those two cut Rust out of the mix and took over."

"Maybe. All I know is that we're about to lose whatever edge we had on this investigation."

I hold my breath as I ask my next question. "Is Sinclair about to haul Luke in?" I'm not ready to say goodbye yet.

"Not yet. He's still hoping for a break."

"Was there anything coming out of the investigation on 24?"

"Some grainy video from a business that we're analyzing, and a ton of fingerprints on the SUV that are probably the registered owners'." Warner peers at me through hard eyes. "Stay on him. Don't let him out of your sight, and . . ." He heaves a sigh. ". . . do whatever you have to do to get him talking. Sinclair's orders."

Suddenly Warner's risky in-person visit and shutting off the wire makes sense. This is off the record. I don't back down as he looms over me. "What exactly does that mean?"

"It means keep doing what you've been doing." His jaw clenches. "Like that night after you met 24 at the club . . ." He leans in farther, until he's so close his spearmint-scented breath tickles my nostrils. ". . . when I watched 12 show up at your building and not leave until the next morning."

Warner was spying on me? "You said you—" I bite back the accusation because I have no right, after everything I've done. Swallowing against the bubble of hysteria rising, all I dare ask is, "Does Sinclair know?"

A wicked smirk answers me. "Sinclair doesn't give a shit as long as he gets what he wants and our hands stay clean in the courts. And you've worked hard to make sure everything on the wire keeps us looking good, haven't you?" His eyes drift to my mouth. "You even had me fooled for a while there."

"Warner, I . . ." I can't seem to find the right words. There are no right words for this kind of betrayal.

"Just keep the case conversations on the wire and everything else . . . off." His iciness melts slightly. "And promise me you won't blow your cover."

I swallow. "I promise."

He looks about ready to say something else but then presses his lips firmly shut. Cracking the door open, he checks the hall, and then disappears.

Leaving me shaking with guilt.

Chapter 51

...

LUKE

I hang up as I pull into the lot at the garage. "Rust's partners at RTM, offering their condolences."

"That's . . . nice of them?" Rain offers hesitantly.

"Yeah . . . I give them two weeks before they start talking about buying me out of Rust's share."

"Is RTM . . ." she pauses, "part of that business you mentioned you had with Aref and Vlad?"

"No. This is completely separate. A hundred percent legit. Just like this garage. Rust kept that other stuff away from here."

"And it's all yours now?"

"Yeah. Or it will be, once it goes through probate. He already signed the garage over a few weeks ago." All kinds of thoughts have been crawling into my head these past few days. Namely, did he have an idea that this might happen? And if he did, why the hell didn't he do more to protect himself? Why didn't he tell me to fuck off when I pushed him on the Aref deal?

"So, what are you going to do?" Her eyes land on the garage sign hanging above us.

"I don't know. There's definitely more than enough here to keep me busy and comfortable." I take her hand. She's been more quiet than usual since leaving the funeral home. This must be a lot for her to deal with. It's one helluva way to meet my mom and sister.

"It'll take months to sort out all the legal stuff, so I have time to decide if I want to step into Rust's place or—"

"Take his place where?" Her pleading eyes rise to take me in.

"At RMT. Doing something that's not going to put a bullet in my head. That's all, I promise." I'm still upright and breathing, with no sign of Vlad, so I have to think he's not too worried about what I could possibly say. But what kind of future is this? If Rust's death did anything, it served as a wake-up call. Maybe Vlad is right—I am an idiot, because I got myself involved in a multi-million-dollar car theft ring with the fucking Russian mob and I didn't see this coming.

I don't want to live the rest of my days worrying that I may piss someone off and end up dead. What kind of life is that? A hundred Porsches don't make it worthwhile.

"That, or you could just take the money and start over. Clean," Rain suggests.

"Yeah." Whatever it is, it won't be anything to do with stealing cars. "Let's do this." I nod toward the garage and then slide out of the car. It's the first time I've been here since Rust died.

Was murdered.

"Luke." Tabbs is the first to walk up to me, offering a clean hand and a rare, somber expression. "If there's anything we can do, please let us know."

I nod, afraid my voice will give away my grief. "Is Miller inside?"

"Yup. He's been pretty much holed up in there."

I find Miller sitting behind his desk, staring at his lap. When he finally looks up and notices us standing there, he's on his feet instantly, coming around the desk to offer me his hand.

"Luke, I . . ." He clears his throat. He looks even worse now than he did after his short hospital stay a few weeks ago. He may even have lost weight. His face looks gaunt. "I'm sorry about Rust. He . . ." He bows his head. "He was always good to me."

"For what it's worth, he always spoke highly of you. He trusted you unequivocally."

"I'll . . . uh . . . I'll take care of things around here. Don't worry about any of that."

There's just no way I'm ready to come back here. "Thank you. I just . . ." I exhale heavily, sliding my hands into my pockets. Looking at the wall across from me, where an array of recognitions and business awards for the garage hang, including one of a smiling Rust shaking hands with the mayor of Portland after winning an area consumer award, a lump fills my throat. He was so proud of this business. He took pride in all his ventures, legal and otherwise. Everything he touched was successful. Until now.

"It's hard, Miller. I'm still waiting for it to really hit me. But don't worry. You'll always have a job here while I own this place."

He clears his throat again, his voice turning rough. "You can count on me." Then he storms past us, out the door and down the hall, rubbing at his cheek as he disappears into the restroom.

I feel Rain sidle up to my back, her arms roping around my waist to give me a hug. "Were they close?"

"Yeah, you could say that. Miller's been running this place since it opened." My phone's ringing, pulling me away from thoughts of Miller.

It's the police. My car is *finally* being released.

I'd let them keep it if only I could have Rust back.

Chapter 52

···

CLARA

"Security just let through a delivery guy with more flowers," Luke says, dropping his house phone on the counter, taking in the floral jungle that's sprouted in here. Bouquets from Luke's business partners, Dmitri, other family friends.

Nothing from Vlad or Andrei. Not a word. That both comforts and worries me.

Luke rubs his eyes, tired from a day of running around and drug-induced sleep.

I rub his back affectionately. "I'll take care of it. Why don't you go and jump in the shower? It'll make you feel better."

"Yeah . . ." His gaze drifts over my body, and I see a sudden spark of interest. It's the first one I've seen in days, which, up until this morning, was a saving grace.

Back when I thought that this little affair of ours was a secret.

I can't believe Warner knows. And Sinclair. And maybe the rest of my cover team. Here I was, thinking I've been careful and covert all this time.

He reaches up to tug at the hem of my shirt. Tugging me toward the bedroom.

Keep doing what you're doing, Warner told me. Orders from the top. I wonder if I'm going to get burned for it at the end. Will this be the last case I ever work on? Has Sinclair written me off?

I can't think about that right now, though. I need to focus on keeping Luke safe.

"Go ahead." I nod toward his bedroom. "I'll wait for them to bring the flowers up."

I listen for the sound of the running water, and then I quickly text Warner to confirm that there is in fact a real delivery truck outside.

There's been no indication that Vlad is looking to get rid of Luke too, and pulling my gun out to receive flowers is probably an overreaction on my part. But I get it out anyway, tucking it into the back of my pants as I wait by the door.

The knock comes within minutes.

I open the door to a young, brunette woman with a clipboard for me to sign. I do a quick appraisal and decide she's simply here to deliver flowers. "Here you go," she says, handing me an exotic arrangement of black orchids.

I don't have to read the card to know who these flowers are from. They have Elmira written all over them. And, because they do, I start picking through the leaves and stems, searching the entire bouquet for anything suspicious.

"Who sent those?" Luke's sudden voice behind me makes me jump. I spin around, hoping he was too distracted by the flowers to notice the bulge of my gun on my back.

I hand him the card.

"You should probably call and thank them," I suggest, looking down at the towel wrapped around his waist. "Maybe after your shower."

"No point wasting time," he mutters, grabbing his phone and punching out a number he's memorized. "Rust always used to say that." I step in closer, both so I can touch his bare skin and so he doesn't step out of earshot.

"Hey . . . I did. Thank you. They're really nice . . . Of course, thank her for me . . . Yeah, I know . . ."

I lean in and press my lips against Luke's arms. And plead with my eyes. He looks down at me and sees the silent words. I know he does. *You promised me to walk away,* I remind him.

He brushes the hair off my face. "Listen, with Rust gone, any deals he made—" Aref has obviously cut him off and is controlling the conversation now. I wish I could hear him. "Right . . . I couldn't even help if I wanted to. He's the only one who knew the business. I don't see how this shipment for Vlad is going to go through, and yours . . . Okay . . . Thanks." He frowns slightly as he hangs up.

"What's wrong?"

Luke stares at the flowers, through them, for a long moment. "Aref took it surprisingly well."

"Are you happy about that?"

"Yeah. But . . ." Concern clouds Luke's eyes. "That's a lot of money for Aref to just walk away from."

Unless he's not walking away from anything at all.

"Aref already has a lot of money," I offer.

"Yeah." Pulling me close to him, he leans down and kisses me. "I don't want to think about any of it anymore."

"Good plan. I'll meet you in there in a minute." I seize his hands before they wander far enough to discover my gun.

"Okay, but hurry up. I need you." He pulls me flush with him, proving exactly how much.

Once he's safely out of view again, I hide my gun in my purse and unfasten my necklace, leaving it on the counter.

Chapter 53

...

LUKE

The family limousine takes the winding road toward our family vault, located in one of the older sections of River View.

"This cemetery is beautiful," Rain murmurs from beside me, her hand tucked within mine, where it has been for the morning, her thumb rubbing soothingly against mine.

I glance out to see the crop of Japanese maples, their trunks gnarly, twisted forms, covered in moss. "Those trees used to freak me out," I admit, realizing just how long it's been since I've been here to visit my grandpa's grave.

"Remember Deda used to tell us that faeries danced in those woods at night for Baba?" Ana pipes up with a sad smile, adjusting one of her big curls. She's back to her normal, perfectly packaged self. My mother, on the other hand, hasn't done as well, the heavy black makeup only highlighting the puffiness around her eyes. She hasn't been back to work since Rust's death and I doubt she has plans to go back anytime soon. I'm sure I'll be covering her bills for a while.

So many cars line the road near the plot site. For a guy who didn't want a service or a wake, there are a ton of people lingering in the light drizzle for him. The guys from the garage all stand in a quiet row, waiting to help carry the casket to the gravesite. They're hardly recognizable in their suits.

The black Barracuda tells me that Jesse's here. I wonder if

Alex came with him. I don't think anyone would care, one way or another, if they recognized her. Viktor's long gone.

Even Priscilla's here, struggling to make her way through the grass in spikey heels, her arm linked with a guy I've seen at The Cellar. Plenty of other familiar faces from the club are also here. Rust was a permanent fixture there, after all.

There are also plenty of people I don't know, and don't care to know. I keep my head down and hold Rain's hand as we make our way to the giant oak tree where I've stood twice before, overlooking the snow-capped mountains in the far distance.

Rust always said they had prime real estate around here.

My arm wrapped around Rain's body on one side and my mom's on the other, we stand in a quiet row under black umbrellas as a solemn man in a suit reads scriptures in Russian. My mom's addition. I didn't fight her on it because I know Rust wouldn't have wanted me to.

The entire thing lasts no more than fifteen minutes. Then the sea of black umbrellas begins to disperse, and I finally bother to take in faces. I see Miller standing next to a short, round woman. On her side are three girls in simple dark dresses, I assume his daughters.

One sits in a wheelchair, her frail legs dangling, the muscles in her face slackened.

I realize how little I know about a guy my uncle trusted to run his business for the last decade. I'm guessing he hasn't had it easy. Nor has his kid. And here I've had everything handed to me on a platter.

But now it makes more sense why he's been helping Rust with the "other" business.

I'm considering walking over there and introducing myself to them when Rain's body tenses beneath my touch. "What's wrong?" I follow her stare to a line of hard-faced men in black suits standing on the far side. Vlad, like a statue next to his father.

Adrenaline and shock shoots through my limbs.

"No, Luke." Rain yanks on my arm, keeping me close, a split

second before I charge over there and punch him square in his misshapen nose.

I bow my head and hiss, "He kills Rust and then shows up at his funeral!"

Her cool fingers touch my cheek, pulling my face to hers. Her eyes pleading. "Don't do anything. Don't say anything."

"How can I do that?"

"You *have* to," she urges, roping her arm around my back. "The less he thinks you suspect, the safer it is for you and your family, right?" She grits her teeth. "If he comes over to offer his condolences, you take it. You hear me? You know nothing. You suspect nothing. No one knows anything. Okay?"

"*Jesus.*" How the hell can I do that? I inhale deeply. If I was on edge before, now I'm hanging by a branch over a cliff.

Chapter 54

...

CLARA

Sinclair was right. Like a group of sadists, the Russians swept in quietly to admire their work. While I can identify only Vlad and his father, the team of undercover agents weaving themselves into this impressive crowd have no doubt taken candid snaps and will have every last one of them identified shortly.

Even Warner is here, in his role as Jack. Just a sympathetic brother who heard what happened and wanted to lend his support to his sister, should Luke notice. He hasn't, now too occupied with staring at his feet and taking deep breaths. Basically doing everything he can to heed my advice, because he knows I'm right.

"Luke." That odd accent fills my ear as Aref appears behind us, dressed as sharply as always, clasping his hand. "Do not hesitate to call if you need anything at all. From either Elmira or me." Like a black shadow, the tiny woman appears from behind him to stretch onto her tiptoes and plant a kiss on Luke's cheek. "We'll keep your family and Rust in our prayers," she coos. And then obsidian eyes shift to meet mine. She closes in for a hug. "Luke will not forget all that you've done for him."

I want to pin this little woman down, slap handcuffs on her, and drag her into a room where I can pull the answers out of her silver-tongued mouth.

But I smile instead. I'll have my chance.

Wave after wave of people pass by, paying their respects to the nephew of a "kind and generous man." Luke does well, nodding and offering tight-lipped smiles to them all. But the way he's leaning into me and the pallor of his skin tells me he's overwhelmed.

And finally, it happens. The tattooed knuckles of Vlad Bragin reach out. "I'm sorry that my last words with your uncle were ones of anger," he says. Nothing about him—his stance, his expression, the way he locks eyes with Luke and holds it for five long seconds—says that he's sorry at all.

Luke's jaw tightens, his hand around my waist squeezes, and I'm afraid he's going to start uttering threats and accusations. But then he simply nods.

The rest of the line passes, and I keep my vigil next to him, the stoic girlfriend, while my eyes trail Vlad weaving around the various intimate groups. The rain has stopped and people are already lowering their umbrellas, making it easier to read all the faces.

Certainly easier for the various FBI agents scrambling to salvage a case that may have been buried with the body of Rust Markov.

Or perhaps wasn't.

Vlad passes Aref and slows, exchanging a few brief words and a handshake, before moving on. I expect him to rejoin his father and duck into his car now, but he doesn't. He veers off slightly, stopping in front of a burly garage manager whose face is tightening with anxiety with each passing second.

Miller takes two steps away from the girl in the wheelchair to receive whatever Vlad leans in to say in his ear. It's quick, but it's clearly impactful, because Miller's face pales. He nods as Vlad walks away, staring vacantly at the casket that waits to be lowered for a few long minutes before stepping back to his family.

Smiling down at them as worry and fear and guilt fills his face and his shoulders seem to sink. Smiling like a father who loves his family, who will do anything for them.

And it clicks.

A quick glance up at Luke tells me he didn't see it, too busy trying to get through the last of the Russian mafia. A glance over at Warner tells me he did. He's already moving away from the crowd, punching numbers into his phone.

"Rain?"

I peel my hyperalert focus away from him and give it back to Luke. "Sorry, yeah?"

"We're going to order some dinner back at my mom's." He nods over to his mom and Ana, standing next to Jesse. Alex didn't come. I wonder if it's because she'd rather remain hidden. "Do you want to come?" His eyes beg me.

"Yeah. Of course."

He sighs, relieved, leaning in to kiss me softly. "I don't know how to thank you for everything you've done for me, for us. Honestly. I . . ." He stalls, faltering over the next word, his mouth poised to utter words that I fear will both swell and break my heart.

"Rain?" Warner interrupts the disastrous situation.

Luke looks past me, his brow furrowing.

"Not sure if you remember me. Jack, Rain's brother." Warner sticks his hand out. "Rain told me what happened. I'm sorry for your loss." Eyes back on me. "And I'm sorry to do this but we've got to go. *Dad*'s surgery was this morning." His eyebrow spikes in that knowing way.

I feel sick to my stomach. Because I know what that look means.

Sinclair's made the call.

He thinks he's found his break.

"Oh . . . right." Luke gives his head a slight shake. "I'm so sorry. With everything else going on, I completely forgot. I hope everything's okay?" Just like that, he believes me. He trusts me.

No . . . Not yet. I close my eyes as the moment I've been dreading is finally here. This is it for Luke and me. In a few hours, he's going to know everything. He thought this was bad? Everything is about to get a whole lot worse.

"You'll call me? Let me know how things are?" he asks, cupping my cheek with all the affection of a boy in love.

A lump forms in my throat. "Give us a minute, Jack?"

The hardness in Warner's eyes fades for a fleeting second. He nods once and moves away. On his phone again. Making plans for the systematic destruction of Luke's entire life.

This is my job . . . this is why I'm here.

And Luke does deserve this for his part in crimes that hurt others.

I wish I believed that. Maybe then I wouldn't feel like I've led a young lamb into a mountain lion's den.

I started out wanting to bury every last person who was involved with Wayne Billings's murder in the name of a red Ford truck. I still feel that way. But at some point, I allowed myself to care.

Maybe even to fall in love.

Maybe that's why I can't resist this overwhelming urge to stop Sinclair from stretching Luke's neck out on a chopping block.

"It'll be fine. Your dad will be fine. Okay?" He wraps his arms around my body, cradling me in warmth. I absorb the last small amount of comfort I'm ever going to feel from them while I curl my arms up in between us, sliding over his chest, taking in those curves.

My fingers reach for my pendant and switch the wire off. "Luke, I need you to listen to me carefully. Everything you've ever told me about Rust, the car stuff, *everything*, stays between you and me, okay?"

A frown flickers across his forehead. "Yeah, of course."

"No . . . no matter *who* asks you. You don't know *anything*, got it?"

I spot Warner's head pop up in my peripheral vision, aimed my way, a deep frown marring his face. Surveillance has let him know that the wire is off. I squeeze tight against Luke's body and whisper, "You'll get through this, I promise."

"Ready to go?" Warner made quick time back.

"Yeah." I pull away from Luke and smile. "I'll call you later."

I feel Luke's eyes on us as we make our way to Warner's undercover car.

"Surveillance lost you for a second," Warner states, matter-of-factly.

"I guess it must have gone off when he hugged me." I hear the bitterness in my voice, and pull out my sunglasses to cover the tears forming in my eyes.

Chapter 55

∎ ∎ ∎

LUKE

"I'll pick something up on the way. Just heading home to have a shower and grab Licks." I need my dog with me. "I'll see you in a few hours."

"You know what you should get? A giant bucket of fried chicken. Uncle Rust would love that." Ana's laughter carries over my car's speaker.

"One bucket, coming up." I smile, thinking about how Rust would show up to our house with a bucket on Sundays and the four of us would play Monopoly. He'd never let anyone win. Said that wouldn't help us in the long run. It's been a long time since I've spent any real time with Ana, or my mom. I think I need to change that. They seemed to really like Rain, but I wonder if that was just circumstance. Rust had warned me that my mom would be a hard one to win over for any woman.

My mind is so wrapped up in thoughts of Rain and my family that I don't notice the black sedan pulling up next to my private garage. Time seems to just hang in the moments that I stare at my reflection in the tinted windows. Waiting.

When the sound of an automatic window opening hits my ear, my heart slows, each hard beat bringing with it increasing dread. Expecting to see the nozzle of a gun pointed at me. Maybe the same one that killed Rust.

In those few seconds, I see Rain's face flash before my eyes.

But the person behind the glass isn't Vlad or Andrei or anyone with a semiautomatic. It's a salt-and-pepper-haired guy with silver streaks along his temples and a sharp black suit.

Holding up an FBI badge. "Get in."

I assume there's protocol for what the FBI is supposed to say—introductions, at least. But I get the impression this guy doesn't give a shit about any of that.

"But my dog—"

He cuts me off. "We'll make sure Licks is fine."

A sinking feeling hits my stomach. The FBI knows the name of my damn dog.

This can't be good.

■ ■ ■

"So you're telling me you have no idea who this guy is?" demands Special Agent Joshua Sinclair, jabbing at the black-and-white picture taken at the funeral today.

The fucking Feds were at Rust's funeral.

"His name is Vlad," I say calmly.

"Yes, we've already established that. Now I want you to tell me how he knew Rust."

I shrug. "He did business with him."

"What kind of business?"

"You'll have to ask Vlad that."

Air hisses through Sinclair's gritted teeth as he inhales sharply. We've been playing this game—where he lays out pictures of every Russian mobster who shook my hand only hours earlier and asks me about them—for nearly an hour, three times over. The two hours before that they left me sitting in this FBI interrogation room to stew in my own terror, a giant wall-to-wall mirror across from me and countless faces hidden behind it.

And they still won't tell me what this is about.

The three times I've asked if I need a lawyer, Sinclair's asked me if I've done something that deserves a lawyer. I think I've held up well, given I'm ready to piss my pants.

"Don't you want to help us find your uncle's killers? The people who did this to him?" A new set of pictures is tossed down in front of me. Of Rust, hunched over the steering wheel of a black SUV, wearing the exact same burgundy shirt he was wearing the night Rain and I met him at The Cellar. No wonder he wasn't answering any of my calls the next day. They must have got to him on his way home.

I look away from the image, but not before it is firmly emblazoned in my mind, tears stinging the back of my eyes, threatening to spill. This guy's a fucking dick.

Tap, tap, tap over Vlad's face again. "What do you know about him?"

Rain's words of warning echoing in my ears. "I've already told you everything that I know."

"What about him?" A glossy shot of Aref lands in front of me.

And that confirms that this is about more than catching Rust's murderer. I shut right down. "A friend of Rust's. That's all I know."

"I think you're lying." He sits back, folding his arms over his chest. He's a big guy, probably about my size, and yet I feel small in this room with him. "I think you know exactly who Vladimir and Andrei Bragin are. I think you know that your uncle's been selling stolen cars to them to be exported overseas, by Aref Hamidi." He leans in. "And I think you've been helping him do it."

I focus on my gold watch, trying to hide the panic. How the hell do they know all of this? "I own Rust's Garage, and I work in the office. That's all I do." I hope he can't hear the shakiness in my voice.

"Oh, I think you do plenty more. Helping us now will make things easier for you later. The way I see it, there are all kinds of things we could pin on you. You could see ten . . . fifteen years locked up. I think they'd like a guy like you in there. And I'm guessing your friends won't be helping you out."

If he's trying to scare me, it's working.

Suddenly, he switches directions. "What do you know about Alexandria Petrova's disappearance?"

I hear her name and my head snaps up before I can control

myself. He lays down an older picture of Alex, back when she was still driving a Z8 and wearing Versace.

"Nothing."

"You sure?"

I shrug. "I used to see her around."

He nods slowly. "I've launched an official investigation into her disappearance."

"She's been missing for over a year and *now* you're investigating?"

"So you know she's missing?"

I clench my jaw and he smiles. Sneaky bastard.

"So you don't know anything about where she is or what may have happened to her?"

Where the hell is this coming from? "No." I pause, feeling like this asshole just slipped an invisible noose around my neck and it's tightening with each word out of my mouth. "I think I need a lawyer." The firm Rust retained for his estate stuff also has a criminal law division.

Sinclair stands, leaving all the pictures on the table. "For the record, I believe Vlad killed your uncle and we have evidence that may help us prove it."

Hope sparks inside my chest.

"But I'm less inclined to pursue that while a car theft ring that's hurting innocent people is still in operation. One that I think Vlad killed your uncle in order to take over. Chew on that while we get you a phone to call your lawyer from." He takes a few steps but then stops, waving at someone behind the glass to come through. "But first, I'd like to introduce you to someone."

The hairs on the back of my neck stand, his tone suddenly lighter than the one he's used for the last hour.

The wait for the door to open feels like forever, and when it does—when I see the face that appears, her light blue eyes zeroing in on mine to hold them—I feel like someone's punched me square in the chest.

"Luke, this is Officer Clara Bertelli."

Chapter 56

. . .

CLARA

I've always enjoyed that moment when the target realizes who I really am. The predictable emotions that cycle across people's faces—recognition, understanding, shock. Sometimes it stops short at anger; other times it finishes with resignation, because they know they fell for the ruse and they're done for.

But I've never seen a target's face filled with such hurt.

Not until today.

Doors close somewhere outside the observation room. Warner and I watch an officer stroll in and drop a brown bag and a Coke on the table next to Luke. I know that it's from a certain food cart vendor without asking. Just another way for Sinclair to send a message to Luke.

We know everything there is to know about you.

The lump in my throat is making it difficult to talk, to swallow . . . even to breathe. I'm not sure who got kicked harder in the chest when I stepped into that interrogation room. Luke certainly looked like he had taken a swift boot.

For a moment, I thought I was going to leave a pile of vomit on the floor.

There was no time to utter a single word, or apology. Sinclair did it for impact, quickly ushering me back out and leaving Luke in the room by himself. To stew over every intimate moment we shared, every dangerous word he ever spoke to me, every way that

I could nail him to the wall with what I know, while waiting for his lawyer.

He looked worried before. Now, he looks terrified.

All I can do is hold out hope that it didn't work to scare him enough to talk, that he'll remember my words, that the lawyer who shows up is good. Because I know they don't have enough for a conviction and the second the lawyer pushes to see the charges laid and the evidence, they're going to realize that too.

I feel Warner's eyes on me. They've been on me a lot since we arrived at the station.

"What's with the Alexandria Petrova angle?" I ask. "Why does Sinclair care about a late mobster's wife?" Sinclair hasn't mentioned digging up information on her since the night he called me on it. I figured that with all the other evidence trickling in, he had forgotten about it. Stupid of me.

"He doesn't. But he's going to try and use it to keep Luke on obstruction, leveraging what we got from your detail."

"Will that even work?"

He shrugs.

"So, what's going to happen then? Are they going to just show up to her ranch and interrogate her?" An image of police cruisers rolling up the driveway to dig up painful truths the poor girl has put past her hits me. I close my eyes.

"You look sick."

"I feel sick."

"Luke Boone is not an innocent, misunderstood guy, Bertelli." He holds up a stack of case files. "Look at the shit he's mixed up in. Did you forget that while you were sneaking around with him? *Lying* to me? Jeopardizing our entire case?"

There's no small amount of judgment in his tone and I'm not in the mood for this. "Just say what you're dying to say."

Warner closes in on me, dropping his deep voice. "You did what you said you wouldn't. What you laughed at when I suggested it. You got too close to your target."

"No, I didn't," I deny, taking in Luke's hunched posture, his fingers locked behind his head, his elbows resting on the desk. He won't even look up at the glass. He won't look up at me. "I did what I had to do."

"So when were you guys meeting up? At night? In the park, while walking the dogs?" Warner pushes. "You weren't even in your room, that night in the yacht, were you?"

I set my jaw firm.

"You don't think that if I walk in there right now, he's not going to hang you out to dry? You don't think he's going to tell his lawyer *everything*? You're going to get crucified if this ever makes it to court. Your career is done!" Thank God these rooms have thick walls because Warner is borderline yelling. "You may as well stop protecting him and admit everything to me right now. Maybe we can contain this."

Warner's probably right. There's no reason to protect what I had with Luke because it died the second I stepped through that door. Hell, it's always been on life support, waiting for someone to pull the plug. I know that. I've always known that. Yet, I chose to ignore it. I chose to act with my heart and not my head. I chose to think that I could somehow change him.

Save him.

I need to try and save myself now.

And yet my jaw tenses at the very thought of divulging my most intimate moments with Luke. I don't fight it, turning to level Warner with a hard stare. "Is this an interrogation?"

"Dammit, Bertelli." Warner closes his eyes. "Don't make me prove it to you."

When I don't answer, he pushes past me, out the door.

And into the room with Luke.

Chapter 57

...

LUKE

"Her brother. Good one," I admit, watching the tall guy fold into the chair across from me. "I'm not talking to you without my lawyer here."

"I wouldn't suggest it." He slides the paper bag forward. "Come on, you should eat. You've been here a while."

Even the smell of the sandwich is turning my stomach right now. One bite and I'd no doubt puke all over this table. Then again, maybe then they'd leave me the fuck alone.

"Would you prefer Clara to cook for you?" he says very carefully, making a point of shifting and straightening all the pictures lying on the table. His dark, emotionless gaze lifts to meet mine. "Oh, I'm sorry. *Rain*. She really fooled you, didn't she?"

Clara.

I can't keep my eyes from flickering toward the one-way mirror, or prevent the roughness in my voice. "She sure did."

I've only ever felt that level of cold shock one other time in my life—a week ago, when two police officers showed up at my door to tell me that Rust was dead.

I had marked that day off as the worst day of my entire life.

But then that douchebag introduced Rain as she stepped into this holding room.

Rain knows everything that I know.

Everything.

I trusted her.

And now I'm completely fucked.

And Rust called it. He said she made him nervous. He saw it right away. Me? I saw nothing but pretty blue eyes. A gorgeous smile. A charming personality. A girl I couldn't get enough of. I'm a fucking idiot. What was Rust ever thinking, bringing me into this?

"She's good. That's why we picked her. I'll bet you've been sitting here for the past hour, replaying the last few weeks in your head. All the conversations you had, asking yourself how you fell for it."

Replaying the last few weeks? Try every last second of every day since the moment she stepped out of her car at the garage. All the qualities I admired in her—how she listened to me, how she never got angry when I had to take off, how she was so happy to see me, so willing to go anywhere with me . . .

The night on the yacht.

The day in the garden.

Was that *all* part of her cover? Are cops even allowed to do that?

"I'd be pissed if someone did that to me. Especially given how close she got to you." He draws a finger over his chest. "Just so the necklace around her neck could record everything."

"Fuck . . ." It slips out of my mouth before I can help myself. The necklace that she wore all the time.

Except . . . I frown. Except she didn't wear it *all* the time.

"What is it?" Special Agent Warner Briggs leans in.

I struggle to smooth my expression. She didn't wear it every time. I remember the day at the garden. She wasn't wearing it then. I noticed it missing. There were other times too, nights in bed, in the shower, when I stared down at her bare neck, wondering what the diamond raindrops would look like on her, wondering if it was too soon to give the gift to her.

But what does that mean?

Everything you've ever told me about Rust, the car stuff, every-thing, stays between you and me. That's what she said.

You'll make it through, I promise.

Holy shit. She knew they were bringing me in. She was warning me. My heart begins racing with confusion, with hope, with pain.

But why?

Chapter 58

...

CLARA

The observation room door clicks open and a man I am beginning to truly detest steps through.

"How's he holding up?" Sinclair peers through the window at Luke and Warner, who are facing off. Luke's face has grown at least four shades paler.

"Still not budging."

Sinclair exhales loudly, clearly frustrated. "Well, we have a twenty-four-hour surveillance detail on the garage manager now, but who knows if he's actually going to lead us to the drop."

I silently berate myself. Luke even told me that Miller was in on it. "I can't believe we didn't see the connection."

"Too many moving pieces. Sometimes the most obvious ones are the ones that get missed." He pauses. "What's Warner doing in there?"

"Playing good cop and trying to piss 12 off."

Sinclair hits a button on the wall, turning the audio to the room up a few notches.

Warner's thick Boston accent fills the speakers. "What? Do you think she fell in love with you? Come on, man. She was just doing her job. She'd doesn't fucking love you. She doesn't even like you!"

Sinclair snorts, seemingly unperturbed. "That's good cop?"

By the hard set of Luke's jaw, Warner's words are cutting him deep. My stomach drops when I hear him demand, "Let me talk to her. I want to talk to Rain."

"You mean undercover *Officer* Clara Bertelli. Really? Why? What could you possibly have to say that she might want to hear?"

Warner's so wrong. I want to hear it all. Every last reason why Luke hates my guts now. Maybe it'll make this hurt less. I swallow against the hard lump in my throat. "As soon as 12 lawyers up, he's going to find out that we have nothing on him and he's going to walk."

"Well, then you don't have a lot of time to get in there and convince him to help us, do you? Look." Sinclair steps in closer. "Busting this guy isn't going to do anything. He's a dumb kid who trusted his uncle and got mixed up in this stuff. I know that. He can walk. But I want the Russian mob. I want Aref Hamidi. And I will do whatever I have to to shut this entire operation down." He knocks on the glass and Warner turns his head toward us. "Did you see the look on the garage manager's face today? He was scared shitless. I'm guessing he doesn't want to be in whatever spot Vladimir Bragin has forced him in, especially after the last guy ended up with a bullet in his head. I've seen guys like Steve Miller before. They squeal like pigs when they're cornered. When we get him in here, he's going to give us everything we need, and that includes 12. So if this kid wants any chance of freedom, he'd better start spilling his guts."

"What if he doesn't know anything?"

"He knows a helluva lot more than we think he does." Sinclair's eyes narrow, boring into me. "And I think you know that."

Chapter 59

...

LUKE

"You're not getting another word out of me until I see my lawyer. Now, can you please ask Rain to come in here?"

A second knock on the window and Special Agent Briggs throws his index finger in the air, as if to signal "one minute." "I'll see if she wants to see you. I know she's getting ready to move on to her next case. Another decent-looking guy who's going to fall for her."

This guy knows how to aim his punches for impact.

He stands and then, leaning in so close to me that I can smell the coffee on his breath, he whispers, "There isn't a law that can protect you if you touch so much as a hair on Clara's body. Now, or fifty years from now. Do you understand?" Smoothing his shirt as he straightens, I watch him stalk out of the room, his back rigid.

His lethal warning completely unnecessary.

Another uncomfortable length of time stretches out in front of me as I now stare at that glass, unable to keep my fingers from drumming against the smooth table surface. Wondering if she'll show up. Wondering how different Officer Clara will be from Rain, the girl I fell for.

Finally, I get my wish.

Rain walks through the door, hugging a small stack of folders, a look that I've seen flicker across her face before now permanently etched. I didn't recognize if for what it was, then. Now I do.

Guilt.

Good.

"Your lawyer's on his way," she says in a strained voice, taking a seat across from me. "You don't have to say anything, and you shouldn't. But please listen." I notice her throat bobbing with a hard swallow. "Four months ago, Assistant Director Sinclair approached me. The FBI were trying to build a case against your uncle after an informant avoiding drug charges identified him as the leader in an international car theft ring involving the Russian mob. I was tasked to get close to you, so I could gather evidence that could lead to a conviction of the key players."

She sounds the same and yet so completely different. So much older, smarter. "We believe that this theft ring is responsible for several violent carjacks in the Portland and Seattle area."

"No," I interrupt, unable to control myself as my anger boils. "Rust wouldn't be involved in anything that hurts people." He wouldn't lie to me.

She doesn't argue or counter what I'm saying. "Cases like this one." She opens a folder with a picture of a blue Buick on one side and the badly beaten face of a man on the other. "And this one." Another folder. Another car, another picture, this time a beaten woman.

My head's shaking. They're not pinning this on Rust. No way. He's not even here to defend himself and he'd never . . .

"And this one." The folder opens to a cherry-red Ford F-250 truck with fuzzy dice hanging from the rearview mirror. Next to it is the picture of a male.

Very obviously dead.

A wave of nausea hits me. I remember that truck. That truck was in the warehouse.

"I believe you," she says slowly. "I believe you that Rust wouldn't *knowingly* be involved. But what if he wasn't knowingly involved? What if someone had been slowly working his way into his organization. Someone who wanted to take over. Who may have wanted to take over the network and cut him out. Who may not have been so smart or vigilant about the kinds of thieves and wheelmen they hired. Who wanted cars to sell, and fast.

"If we can get the right information, we can stop this from happening again. You're not betraying Rust anymore, Luke." She makes a move to reach forward but then freezes, pulling her hand back. "If you tell us everything you know, I'll make sure you walk away from this. Safe." She leans in, her eyes pleading with me, looking so honest. They've lied to me before, though. Many, many times. "Don't ruin the rest of your life protecting criminals. I know you aren't one. You've done the right thing before, Luke. Do the right thing again here. Don't let more innocent people get hurt."

Alex. She's using Alex against me. Did she know all along, when I drove up that driveway, who she was about to meet? Or did she just figure it out, because it's her job to figure things like that out? Did she use the whole abusive ex-boyfriend angle because she somehow knew that it was a soft spot for me?

Jesse passed on Alex's condolences, telling me that she didn't come because she was afraid of someone from that circle recognizing her. She'd rather remain missing in their eyes. The poor woman still lives with a cloud of fear over her. And now these assholes are about to drag her into this mess—and Jesse, and Jesse's dad—just to get at me. I know that's why Sinclair says he's launching an investigation. He doesn't give a shit about her.

Fuck, Jesse will never talk to me again if that happens, if I bring this disaster to his doorstep. To his father's doorstep. If they figured out how the sheriff abused his power . . .

The door bursts open and an old guy in wire-rimmed glasses storms in. "Get away from my client, now. All room recording stops immediately."

Rain moves to stand.

I should hate her. Maybe I will once the shock wears off. "Was any of it real?" I ask, my voice as hollow as my chest.

She only stares down at me, blinking away the tears that form in her light blue eyes.

Is that even real?

Not that it matters anymore.

■ ■ ■

"They don't have enough to make this fucking stick," Fred, my lanky and brash lawyer, who drops more f-bombs than I've ever heard before, promises. "Any judge would throw this case out the second it entered his courtroom. Now, what he may say about the investigative techniques used on you . . ." he mutters with a wicked gleam in his eye. One that says he wants to stand in front of a judge and publicly flay Rain. The excitement disappears just as quickly. "But I have to warn you, I get the feeling that they're working on a few other angles into this case. If they bring someone in and that person gives names up—which always happens—you could be facing some serious time." Fred's obviously past the point of wondering whether Rust and I were ever involved in a car theft operation. He hasn't even bothered to ask. "They're offering you a pretty good deal right now. Voluntary cooperation in exchange for confidentiality and immunity against all charges connected with this case. They don't want you, son."

Son. Rust used to call me that all the time. I have to remind myself for the thousandth time that he's dead. That I can't call him to help me get out of this mess. That, in a way, he got me into this mess.

Fuck . . . Flashes of those pictures hit me again, and anger boils inside.

Of that car seat that these very hands in front of me yanked out of the truck.

"But what if I don't know enough?" I counter.

He busies his hands with a stack of papers. "They seem to think you do."

How much did Rain tell them?

"They also seem to think that someone did this to Rust because they wanted him out of the way." The more I think about it, the more it makes sense.

Fred gives a half-shrug, half-nod. "There's a lot of money involved here. I've heard of a lot worse happening for a lot less. Listen, you give me the word and you'll be walking out of here. I just can't say how long before you're back. You need to decide if you want to risk that." He pauses. "You're a twenty-four-year-old guy who may or may not have gotten mixed up in the wrong stuff. If you did, you've still got a long life ahead. You can start over and lead a clean life. This deal they're offering guarantees that you can do that."

A clean life. I had never focused on it, but the life I've been living up until now has been dirty. It's come from dirty money that I've accepted greedily. But Rust's dead and none of it looks very appealing anymore. Jesse's words that day fill my head. Maybe this is my wake-up call. I'm definitely scared shitless.

"What exactly does this voluntary cooperation involve?"

■ ■ ■

"Is that everything?" Briggs rubs at his eyes as he scribbles down his final notes. I feel like I haven't seen the outside of these walls for weeks, though it's been more like twenty hours. Still, a painfully long time to be sitting in this suffocating room, on a hard plastic chair, having him and Rain—I can't think of her as anything else—squeeze every last bit of information out of me. Things I remember Rust saying, things I remember seeing. Anything and everything, damning and seemingly inconsequential. From the secret warehouse in the woods to the port security guard who's paid to look the other way.

I ratted out my own garage manager, who has three kids—one in a wheelchair. I named Aref as both the shipper and a new business partner.

I knew a lot more than I thought I did.

The only thing I don't know is the one thing they need most: the exact date, time, and location of the coming shipment for Vlad. Rust kept that close to his chest. Part of me wonders if it's because of the exact situation I'm in right now.

"I think so." The glass of water they gave me isn't helping soothe my throat anymore, which is raw from talking. I can't keep my eyes from flickering to Rain, who looks as tired as I feel. She meets my gaze for a moment before shifting away to focus on the floor.

We haven't said two words to each other.

"Okay. Let Officer Bertelli know if you remember anything else."

Officer Bertelli.

"And it'll be added to this document, formally, right?" Fred insists.

"Yes," Briggs confirms. "You've done the right thing today, Luke. So thank you." He actually sounds sincere. He glances over at Rain, his jaw tightening, like he's not happy about what he's about to say. "She'll take custody of you now."

When Fred told me that part of this deal is that I'll be released into "my girlfriend's" custody, to keep up pretenses of the loving couple for the next few days, just until they can track down and bust the shipment for Vlad—which they believe is still happening—I refused.

But I apparently don't have a choice.

"Your phone is being monitored, the condo is under full surveillance. If you disappear for so much as a second, this deal is dead and you'll never get a chance at another one." Dark, sharp eyes bore into me.

"Come on, Luke." Rain stands, her eyes tired and pleading. "Let's go home."

Chapter 60

■ ■ ■

CLARA

Luke kicks off his shoes and unsnaps Licks' leash, who bolts straight for Stanley, their tails wagging frantically. "Where am I sleeping?" The same vacantness in his voice that I've listened to for hours in the interrogation room still exists. He hasn't said a word to me since he demanded to see me. The car ride home was painfully silent.

"In the spare room, next to mine."

He begins heading toward it, duffel bag slung over his shoulder.

"I need you to leave your phones with me. I'll let you know if someone's calling."

I'm expecting some form of resistance, but he simply slides his hand into his pocket and tosses both phones onto a side table before continuing on.

"Just so you know, they've installed several cameras in here, as well as at the front door. They're being monitored at all times. We also have twenty-four-hour surveillance around the building." He's been nothing but cooperative—much more so than most people when their backs are against the wall. Most would have said "fuck you" and strolled out that door. "There aren't any in your bedroom, though." Or mine. "And I'm not wearing a wire anymore."

His feet slow for just a second, enough that I think he may stop, may turn, may say something to me. I'd take anything right now. Yelling, accusing, swearing. He can call me a bitch; I don't care.

But then he disappears behind a closed door.

I toss my keys onto the counter and answer my ringing phone.

"We have twenty-four-hour detail on 48, 60, and 72. 36 has already left the country."

Miller, Andrei, Vlad, and Aref. *Ugh* . . . Too many targets. The code names are getting confusing.

And Aref is gone. "Fuck . . . he's going to get off, isn't he?"

"Yeah. He probably will. We won't even be able to seize his ship. He'll just say that he has no knowledge of what ended up on there and the customs papers will all be falsified anyway."

It's not fair. "Otherwise?"

"We're in good shape. A crew is getting organized to check out 24's warehouse. We've got the name of two fences now, thanks to 12." Warner's excited. I could almost see the adrenaline pumping through his veins with each new piece of information that came from Luke's mouth. "Plus I'm guessing we'll get two more, if we bring in the registered owners of the storage spots that held the stolen Porsche. Rix is gaining headway at the low level. Those guys are getting sloppy in their rush to get this done. I'm going to bring in that port guard and set him up as an informant, and when we finally pull 48 in here, he's going to help us cripple their entire operation."

"Good."

There's a pause. "You could have said no to Sinclair. For the record, I don't think this is a good idea. We should have put 12 in a safe house for the next few days."

"And risk that shipment not happening because someone suspects he's turned?" Sinclair and the team went through a lot of effort to cover Luke's time being questioned. Of anyone, Luke would have the motive to want Vlad punished. "No. He won't hurt me."

"Are you sure? 'Cause you sure as hell hurt *him*."

I take a deep, calming breath. Amidst all the emotions assaulting me over the last couple of days, the sense of relief is the most overwhelming. Relief that the lie is over, that Luke knows what I am. I didn't realize just how much that guilt was weighing on my conscience until today.

"Bill had a floor safe added to your bedroom to hold your gun, along with the deadbolt. 12 doesn't have a lock on his door, and we bolted his furniture down, in case he tries to barricade himself in."

"You guys really think of everything, don't you? And his name is Luke, not 12." He's no longer my target.

Sinclair's sigh fills my ear. "Just keep an eye on that kid. He's been through a lot this past week. I wouldn't want him doing something stupid."

For a long time after I hang up the phone, I stare at his closed door. Fearful of Warner's warning. Wondering if there's truth to it.

Until I can't help myself anymore. Beckoning the dogs, I walk over to the spare room. My knock earns no answer, so I crack the door open. "Luke?"

No answer.

He's lying on his back, eyes closed. He's been up for nearly thirty-six hours and under extreme stress, so I'm not at all surprised he fell hard and fast asleep. I feel the urge to crawl into bed and wrap my arms around his body, rest my head on his chest, and somehow find a way to make him understand how I could do this to him. How I know he's a good person who was led astray by people who loved him, by his own, entirely human desires.

Make him realize that, while he probably feels like he's drowning in a torrential downpour of bad choices and consequences, this is all for the best.

That he will survive this.

I want him to know that I did everything I could to save him from the worst of it. In a way, I think I did. Maybe one day he'll see it. Right now, all he feels is guilt and anger and hurt.

Stanley and Licks push past me and run straight to him, as if they can sense the sadness in the air. I'll bet they can. Licks is on the bed with one leap, but my poor little mutt can only paw at the edge and whimper. With hesitation, I tiptoe closer, until I can lift him up. "Shh . . . Let him sleep," I scold softly, pushing at Stanley's backside until he stretches out along Luke's side.

It isn't until I'm closing the door behind me that I see Luke's arm shift to wrap around the affectionate dog's body, pulling him close.

Chapter 61

∎∎∎

LUKE

"He's two and a half. His name is Mason," Rain says, pointing out the little boy who dumps stones from the ground onto the slide, watching them fall and scatter. His mother stands nearby, rocking a stroller for the sleeping baby inside while talking quietly with another mom. "She just got a job at a twenty-four-hour supermarket deli counter, working midnights. Her mom looks after the kids while she's there."

So she probably got as much sleep as I did last night, which was next to none. Neither did Rain. I know because I kept hearing my door creak open. When she stuck her head into my bedroom this morning and told me to get showered and dressed, I figured it was to take the dogs for a walk. I didn't bother asking her where we were going. I'm not ready to talk to her. God knows what may spill out of my mouth, and there's no way I'm letting her know how much she hurt me.

If I had known this was the destination—watching that murdered guy's little boy play in a park and hear about how his wife is struggling, her face drawn, her eyes tired, her smiles sad—I might have refused.

"She's going to have it rough for a while. You can't raise two kids on minimum wage, not without a lot of help. But who knows, maybe she'll meet someone new one day down the road."

"Why are you doing this to me?" finally bursts out of my

mouth, my sore throat from yesterday's marathon confessional making my voice hoarse.

Rain—she'll always be Rain to me; I don't know that I'll ever call her anything else—stares at the little boy. "A few months ago, I sat outside this woman's window, her entire world crumbling around her, and watched her rock him to sleep. I wanted to punish everyone involved in the ring that killed her husband. They were scum. Every last one of them. And . . ." she hesitates briefly ". . . this was going to be my big break. I was going to win this case, impress Sinclair, and go Fed. It would open up so many exciting doors for me—all the resources at my disposal, the cases I'd be working on . . ." She studies her nails, usually polished, but bitten down to the quick in the last twenty-four hours. "I was eager and willing, and when Sinclair said jump, it wasn't too hard to get me doing all kinds of things that I never thought I'd do. That I'm not proud of doing."

I grit my teeth against the jab to my ego. Is she trying to make me feel better by admitting to this? "Was it really that bad?"

"No, it wasn't. That's the thing," she whispers, and I feel her eyes burning into the side of my face. "It was too easy because I wanted to."

I meet her eyes—so sincere, so deceptive—for just a moment before turning away again.

"I think I'm a pretty good cop and person, but I did things that I'm ashamed of. At first it was because of my ego and my career, and then . . ." She ducks her head, blushing. ". . . it was because of you. The entire time, I knew it was wrong, but I kept doing it. I couldn't stop myself. I didn't want to." She turns to focus on the little boy again. "You're a good person, too, Luke. I believe that."

Even though I don't trust her, her words temporarily soothe the guilt burning my insides.

A baby cries out and the woman reaches down to fuss over her other son, adjusting his soother and blanket. "Do you think they'll get an arrest for her husband out of this?"

"The truck is long gone, so not likely, unless someone confesses. Which they tend not to do," Rain says matter-of-factly. "But maybe we can uncover the stolen SUVs involved in the latest hijackings and get some arrests out of that."

"Aref's not going to go through with that shipment if Vlad is busted," I counter.

Rain doesn't answer. While I've spilled my guts about all that I know, I have no idea exactly what else they've gathered, or how far they've reached into Rust's organization.

Looking at the remnants of Wayne Billings's family across from me, I find myself hoping they have enough to bring it down.

Ringing sounds from Rain's purse and I recognize it as my phone. "It's Miller," she says, pulling it out of her purse to read the screen. "Act normal and don't try talking through code because I'll know right away." With that warning—reminding me that she isn't Rain, she's a cop—she hands it over to me.

"Hey, Miller, what's up?" Can he hear it in my voice? Does he know I've given him up?

Miller's usual gruff voice fills my ear. "I have some more checks I need you to sign. Can you make it in this afternoon?"

I look at my watch and then at Rain. It's noon and we're a good drive away. "Yeah, give me a few hours."

"What does he need?" she asks right way.

"I need to sign some checks." I sigh. "What's going to happen to him? It seems unfair that I get off and he doesn't. He's got three kids. One of them's in a wheelchair. Isn't there something you can do to help him?"

I see Rain's throat bob with a swallow, her eyes leaving mine. "Miller's going to help himself. Trust me."

Chapter 62

...

CLARA

"I'll make this quick," Luke mumbles as we step out of his car and head toward the garage. He keeps flexing his hands. I know he's nervous.

I am too.

We have a lot riding on everything going smoothly and, while we have no reason to suspect that anyone's after Luke, given that he's basically been cut out of the ring since Rust's death, we can't leave anything to chance.

Miller's on his feet as soon as we step in, dark bags hanging under his eyes.

He's not going to last long under Sinclair's glare.

"Thanks for coming, Luke." He moves quickly, collecting the sheets and a pen, and walking over to lay them all out on Luke's desk for him. "This one's for the repairs on one of the lifts. And this one's . . ." He goes on, explaining each invoice, that abrasive demeanor gone, replaced with only helpfulness. Some may say it's because he feels a strange kinship with Luke, for what happened. Others may say that he's worried about keeping his job.

I know that it's pure guilt.

But I keep my mouth shut, pulling my phone out to check my texts, because that's what a twenty-something-year-old girl standing in a garage would do, while her boyfriend sits down and signs away money.

"Is that it?" I watch Luke's face as he barely glances at Miller, like he's having trouble making eye contact. Of all the confessions he made, giving up Miller's name was the hardest. I saw it in his eyes; I heard it in his voice.

If he only knew what I suspected, he wouldn't feel so guilty.

Miller nods. "Yup. But, listen . . ." He checks his watch, clearing his throat several times. "I hate to do this to you, but I need to head out a bit early tonight. I've got to take Paige to an appointment." Eyes downcast, shifting on his feet.

Miller's a terrible liar.

"I can stick around and lock up." Luke turns to me. "You don't mind, do you?"

Anyone could explain Luke's reserved, overly calm temperament as the lingering effects of the shock of his uncle's murder, but this all feels way too awkward and wrong. Sliding my phone into my pocket, I plaster on my softest smile and stroll around the desk to lean against his side.

He stiffens immediately.

"Of course." Casually sliding my arm around his shoulder, I dig my thumb into his back in warning.

With a soft exhale, his body slackens slightly.

"Are you sure? Because I could ask Tabbs. He's good for it."

"Did I just hear my name?" A short, bald mechanic sticks his head in and tosses a set of keys to Miller. "Brakes are done on the Jeep."

The Jeep. Hearing that word reminds me of *my* Jeep—the one I left sitting at my parents' house months ago so my dad can drive it around the block every few days to keep the thing from seizing.

I wonder what it'll feel like, driving it again.

Being only Clara again.

Saying goodbye to Luke.

Tabbs grins, winking at me. "How's that clutch of yours doing, pretty lady?"

"Good, though I hardly ever get to drive it anymore because Luke's too in love with his to let it sit idle. Right?" Luke hasn't been in his car since the day he drove it home from the police forensics impound lot. When I suggested that we take his car today to keep up appearances, he immediately shook his head.

I think it's lost its luster.

I wait for Luke to respond, because normal, confident Luke always responds. It takes a moment. "Don't you know it." He ropes his arm around my waist and pulls me down, onto his lap. His grip on me tightens until I can feel his heart pound against my rib cage.

He's struggling with keeping up appearances, and it's in sharp contrast to how he used to be. How confident. How suave, when talking to Aref about "business." I can't figure out if it's because of everything, or because of me.

I know I shouldn't, but I can't help myself. Turning in to him, I lean forward and steal a kiss from his lips.

I doubt anyone else hears the sharp inhale that escapes him. I hold my breath and pull back just slightly, waiting for him to respond. Hoping he'll respond.

He doesn't. And when he turns his attention back to Miller and Tabbs, my stomach drops with disappointment. And hurt.

"Okay, lovebirds. Some of us have to work," Tabbs jokes, heading for the door. His voice turns sober. "Any news on Rust's case?"

Luke's body stiffens beneath me. "No. Nothing. The police are fucking useless. A bunch of liars."

That was for my benefit, I'm sure.

Tabbs shakes his head and disappears through the door. Miller trails behind him, his jacket slung over his shoulder, offering a gruff, "I'll see you guys later."

I stand from Luke's lap before he has a chance to throw me off, and dial Warner. "48's on the move. He says he's taking his daughter to an appointment."

"Got it. We just left the warehouse outside of Astoria. The gate was busted down and the storage shed emptied."

"What do you think?"

"I think they're taking precautions."

Or, it's all already on a ship and about to go out, and we're going to miss it.

I can feel Warner's adrenaline pulsing through the phone. Everyone's on high alert right now, armed and ready to move in on Sinclair's call. It'll likely be a sloppy bust, if we even manage to catch them, given we're working off Luke's knowledge, a bunch of tails, and the hope that Vlad hasn't had enough time to change everything we know. That he's too damn arrogant to think anyone's on to him. "Okay. Do you need me to do anything?"

"We're covered. You should get him back to your condo, though." Normally, I'd hate being relegated to what most cops would call "babysitting." It doesn't bother me now, though, because I know it's one of the last nights I get with Luke.

"What was my number?" Luke asks.

"12."

"Did you call in every time after we met?"

I find the courage to turn and face him. "No. There were a lot of times that I didn't call in. A lot of times that no one knew where I was." I take a hesitant step toward him, craving the feel of him again, after the brief one I just got.

"Do they know now?"

"Yeah. They figured it out."

"And they don't care?"

"This could be the last case I ever work on," I admit, voicing my fears out loud for the first time. Sinclair hasn't said a word to me about my "extracurricular activities" with Luke. Maybe Warner's right and he truly doesn't give a damn. Or maybe he's ignoring it until he no longer needs me. Right now, all I care about is keeping Luke safe. I'll take whatever punishment's coming after. "Can you ask Tabbs to close up?"

■ ■ ■

I've been sitting on my leather couch, staring at the same page of a book I couldn't even name for over an hour as my mind spins frantically, desperate for an update.

Vlad's shipment is going out tonight.

Miller didn't have a doctor's appointment for his daughter

yesterday. He didn't even go home. He led his tails directly to a commercial storage facility in NoPo. They photographed Miller unlocking the doors, his head bobbing this way and that, obviously on guard but not perceptive enough to suspect the beat-up cargo van across the road. Several cube vans showed up over the course of an hour, backing into the storage warehouse to unload before swiftly taking off. The team waited until Miller was locking the doors before they pulled in, flashing badges and the emergency warrant they had obtained.

Apparently Miller's face went so pale, they were afraid he had died on his feet.

But he was alive, his hands shaking so badly that he nearly broke the key in the lock. Inside they found a storage warehouse *full* of stolen car parts and even some cars. Hundreds of thousands of dollars that they could pin on Miller for the simple fact that he was holding the key to it all.

That's what Sinclair told him when he pulled him into an interrogation room.

It took only two hours and plenty of sobbing before Miller was ready to sign his life away in blood and tell us everything we wanted to know.

We guessed right.

Some months back, Vlad met Miller outside one of their shady money exchange spots, and Vlad began commenting on how reliable Rust's "team" was. Miller thought it was odd—how civil Vlad was acting. His questions and suggestions were casual enough, asking if Miller worked with any of the guys. Maybe some of the guys at the garage were helping to chop? Did Rust ever pass on orders to Miller to handle through the fences?

Miller wasn't involved in that side of things, and he told him as much.

About a week after that, Vlad showed up at Miller's house one night. He stood in front of the family pictures that Miller's wife, Marie, had hung all over the living room wall, studying each one of his daughters at length while sipping from the cup of tea

Marie had so graciously handed to him. Telling Miller that he had a beautiful family. That he must be worried, having three teenage girls in this world. That it must be hard, managing with Lauren's cerebral palsy.

That if Miller were to get more involved in "that side of things" with Rust's business, he'd make it worth his while.

Miller had never talked to Vlad about his family or his daughter's issues. He'd never invited him to come to his home. Vlad's tactic here was unmistakable: a veiled threat. Miller didn't trust this guy; he never understood why Rust got involved with him, seeing as he was so successful in his legitimate businesses. But Lauren had been in more pain lately; she needed more therapy, more injections.

Miller needed more money.

So he agreed.

It wasn't hard to convince Rust, who had suggested several times that he should get more involved. But Miller had always drawn a line. It was one thing to stop and grab a bag of money every once in a while. Calling guys and telling them which car they needed to hire someone to steal, though . . . Miller only needed to give Lauren's name for Rust to understand why he was now asking. Rust didn't suspect a thing. He trusted Miller completely.

It was easy enough at first, Miller said. Just a phone call to a guy named Leon on an untraceable phone whenever Rust swung by and wordlessly handed him a one-page printout with a list of cars, which Miller would shred immediately after making the call. A week or two later, he'd meet Leon and a few guys out at Rust's backwoods warehouse to exchange the cars for the money. Miller described how scared shitless he was every single time, expecting to end up with a bullet in his head.

Then it became a phone call to Leon when Vlad called to pass on an order. Miller didn't understand why both guys were feeding orders to him—but he didn't know how everything worked anyway. He figured the cars were going to the same place, the same pot of money was being divided, and he needed to keep his mouth shut about it.

Not long after, Rust had him working with another fence by the name of Kyle. Which meant Miller was sending orders to Kyle for both Rust and Vlad.

Then Vlad showed up at his house—again—with a bonus envelope of cash in exchange for bringing him along to the next meet with the fences.

Miller did, introducing him to both Kyle and Leon.

Vlad had a conversation with them that Miller didn't hear, and then he saw Vlad hand them envelopes. No doubt with cash in them. The envelope of cash Vlad handed him for "cooperating" and the way Vlad ducked down to avoid the cameras on the way in kept Miller quiet.

Two weeks later, Vlad told Miller that he *needed* to find out who the other high-level fences were. Vlad knew there were others, because his father was sending Rust orders and the orders weren't being passed through Miller. Miller had guessed as much anyway. He'd seen cars that he didn't order at Rust's storage.

So Miller asked Rust if he could do more.

But Rust said no. Someone else was handling those guys.

It wasn't hard for Miller to figure out who that someone else was. Rust's useless nephew, Luke, who would no doubt be owning the garage soon enough and firing Miller. Miller, who had to work his ass off just to fill a drug prescription for his kid, while Luke had just been handed a fucking Porsche.

Vlad was livid when he heard Luke was now involved.

The orders kept coming in for Miller to manage, only the ones from Rust were growing smaller while the ones directly from Vlad increased. At first Miller figured that Rust was passing his share on to Luke.

Miller began meeting Leon, Kyle, and a new guy who simple went by Smith—one of Vlad's additions—at a new location: the commercial warehouse just off Highway 5 in North Portland where we caught Miller.

At that point, it was pretty obvious to Miller that Vlad was using what Rust built to run his own ring. Still, Miller said nothing because now he was an accomplice to Vlad. If Rust found out, his steady, legitimate job as manager at the garage would be gone.

That's when the anxiety began to take its toll on him.

The day Vlad called him and asked if he had ever heard Rust talking about a guy named Aref Hamidi, Miller didn't think much of mentioning what he overheard at the office—Rust asking Luke to set up a meeting at Corleone's. That seemed to really piss off Vlad.

A week later, Vlad sent Miller an order for a ton of vehicles. All late models, all black, all SUVs.

All needed within the week, in shipping containers at an Astoria shipyard.

A few days after that, Rust ended up with a bullet in his head.

Miller doesn't have the context we have. He hasn't figured out that that last order was for Aref. That the deal Luke says was made with Aref that night in Corleone's didn't stick. That when Vlad found out about what Rust was doing, he must have gone straight to Aref and demanded the business. That the lead time Rust insisted on obviously wasn't ideal for Aref, but instead of telling Rust that, he simply smiled and nodded and agreed.

Which tells us that Aref knew what Vlad had in store for Rust.

Miller doesn't know all that, but Rust dying scared him enough. What I witnessed the day of Rust's funeral was Miller telling Vlad that he wanted out.

And Vlad telling Miller that Rust had wanted "out" too.

It's all great information, and exactly what we expected to get from him. But it's not enough. So Miller has agreed to wear a wire to his meet with Vlad tonight, in exchange for immunity and Witness Protection for him and his family.

By sunrise, we'll have that Russian asshole.

It's hard to be excited when I can't seem to dislodge this painful knot in my throat. Because by sunrise, I'll be saying goodbye to Luke.

"Licks needs a run."

I look up to see Luke wearing his track pants. *Luke* needs to run, is more like it. He's as much on edge as I am. I'm sure he's heard enough of my conversations with Warner over the past twenty-four hours—from the confines of his room—to figure out that something's happening tonight.

"I don't know if that's such a good idea," I offer as gently as I can, glancing over at the clock. One forty-five a.m.

"I run every single day. If anyone's watching us, they'll notice," he counters in a flat voice.

He's right. Except that he hasn't gone running in the past two days. Plus, it's in the middle of the night and therefore not the safest time to go out. Still, his hands are visibly shaking. He's as much on edge as I am.

"Okay. Just let me get changed and we'll go together."

When I leave my room, he already has both dogs on their harnesses. I walk toward him, feeling the weight of the hidden gun strapped to my ankle beneath my pants. "You're not going to try something stupid, are you? Like run away from me?"

"No."

"Are you lying to me?"

"I've never lied to you." Clear blue eyes stare hard at me. I can't read anything besides pain and accusation in them. So acute, though, that I'm forced to look away.

"You've hardly eaten in days." I gaze at the full plate of pasta he dropped on the counter, the one I brought to his room hours ago.

"You ready?" He ignores my concern. "I wouldn't want to be out of your sight and have you send me to jail on a technicality. Especially after I've given you everything."

He doesn't trust me. He'll never trust me again. I can't blame him.

But it hurts, all the same.

■ ■ ■

Water splashes against my pants as we jog through the puddles of the dimly lit path, lined with corners and shadows that are testing my anxiety limits. I've jogged with Luke several times before and it's now clear he always slowed down for my benefit. The punishing pace has my lungs burning and my heart pounding, until I have to call out, "Slow down!"

He does, finally, leaving me hunched over and struggling to catch my breath.

"You can hate me all you want, but don't try to kill my dog." I pick up a wet and wheezing Stanley, my eyes scanning the shadows. I don't like standing out here. Even in the darkness, I still feel someone could pluck us off like birds sitting on a wire.

"But I thought you loved this." A bitter chuckle escapes him and he throws his arms out, palms up, to accept the cold drizzle as it seeps into his clothes. "Or was that part of the lie too?"

"Say what you want to say, Luke. Get if off your chest. I can handle it."

Luke's breaths are just as ragged. He keeps his legs moving by walking in small circles, his head hung, his hands now on his hips. For what feels like forever, I just stand there, watching him.

Waiting for the accusations and insults to begin. I expect him to call me a two-faced, conniving bitch, a slut, a terrible lay. A dirty cop.

Anything to try and heal his pride.

"I'm getting exactly what I deserve." His eyes are focused on the trees, on the path, on the ground. On anything but on me. "I can't get those pictures out of my head. Every time I close my eyes, I see a red Ford pickup truck and fuzzy dice. And a car seat. *I* pulled that car seat out of that truck, Rain. And I just tossed it aside like trash, and now I can't stop thinking about the kid who sat in it."

The rain and the darkness mask a lot, but they don't hide the sheen in Luke's eyes. "How could Rust have been involved with that! How could I have let myself get involved in that?"

"You're helping stop it, now that you know it's happening," I offer. "You're helping to stop people who hurt others from doing it again."

After a pause, "Miller didn't hurt anyone," he argues, his chuckle bitter. "No more than I did. He's got a family to feed, a kid in a wheelchair, and now, because I ratted him out, they're going to lose everything. He should be the one with this deal, not me."

So that's what's weighing on Luke's guilt, on top of everything else.

I sigh. "We were putting surveillance on Miller anyway. He isn't going to lose everything." I step in close, because I'm about to say things I'm not allowed to, that can't be overheard. Even without a soul out here, I'm still paranoid. "Vlad wanted to take over Rust's operation and cut him out of it, and Miller helped him do it. He's not innocent."

"No." Luke shakes his head furiously. "You guys are fucking crazy with your theories. Miller was loyal to Rust. He's one of the only guys that Rust trusted. He wouldn't stab him in the back like that."

"We caught him with the stolen cars and brought him in. He admitted to it all last night."

Luke looks like I slapped him across the face. I reach out, letting my fingers graze his forearm, layered in raindrops and gooseflesh from the cold. "He fed Vlad information and introduced him to Rust's high-level fences. Vlad worked his way in, paying the guys off to keep quiet while they filled orders for him."

"But . . . why?" A heavy, disbelieving frown pulls at Luke's brow. "Rust was always so good to him."

"Because Vlad threatened him and his family."

Shock fills Luke's face as he processes my words. Maybe the shock is why he hasn't pulled away from my touch yet.

"And Aref made a deal for those SUVs with Vlad. The same deal he made with you guys, only I'm guessing it was for a faster delivery date. That's why he didn't care when you told him you were out. He never intended on going through with it." I pause, offering the last bit more gently. "I'm pretty sure he knew that Vlad was going to kill Rust."

Another slap to Luke's face.

Maybe Aref does have a redeeming quality, in that he tried to protect Luke from a bullet to his head through Elmira's warnings. Or maybe it was Elmira operating on her own, the entire time. I still haven't figured her out. Now, with both of them overseas, I probably never will.

"I can't trust anyone, can I?" All pretenses of a confident man are long gone from his voice. He sounds completely lost, hollow.

"Yes you can. You can trust your friend Jesse, and Alex, and Sheriff Gabe. They care about what happens to you." I hesitate before I add, "And though I know you don't believe it . . . I care, too."

Silence hangs between us. Finally he admits, "I don't hate you. But you broke my fucking heart, Rain. Clara." He wipes the rain off his face with an upward stroke, pushing his fingers through his hair. "I don't even know what to call you. You're not even real."

"I *am* real," I argue, my grip on his arm tightening. "You got a lot more of the real me than you ever should have. For what it's worth, I can't tell you how many times I wished that Sinclair was wrong, that you weren't involved. Then, when I figured out that you were, I wanted things to be different. I tried to make them different."

I get a glimpse of the Luke I knew before when he leans forward, pressing his forehead against mine. "But they never will be different now, will they?"

His tears burn against my cheeks, so cold from the rain. I'm sure he can feel mine too. I swallow, wanting so badly for him to lean forward more, so I can taste the ones that have rolled over his lips.

"How am I going to live with myself after all this?"

"You'll figure it out. You're a decent person. You just needed a good, harsh rain to remind you of it."

I feel his breath skate across my lips. "I knew that was a metaphor."

I smile at the weak joke, daring to brush my lips against his.

My phone starts vibrating in my pocket. I want nothing more than to ignore it for just a few minutes, but I know that's a bad idea.

"Yeah?"

"Where are you?" Warner's more abrupt than usual.

"Just out for a run with Luke and the dogs. Why?"

"72 wasn't at the exchange with Miller. Our guys tailed some other guy driving his car from his house to the meet spot."

"Where is he, then? At home?"

Silence. "We don't know."

My heart begins racing, pumping adrenaline into my body. My eyes are scanning the shadows with renewed fear. "Call you in five." I pull my Glock out of my ankle holster. "Let's go. Now."

Luke must sense that something's wrong because he doesn't ask questions, swooping down to grab both dogs under an arm. He sticks close to my side as we jog back, our pace even faster than the one Luke set before.

Only when my back is pressed against the inside of my front door, with the deadbolts in place, the security cameras on us, and a team of cops watching the entries from outside, do I allow myself to breathe again.

"What's going on?" Luke asks, his chest swelling with each ragged breath.

I'm past the point of caring what I'm supposed to tell him. So I tell him exactly what Warner told me.

"Do you really think . . ." His wary eyes shift to my gun.

I throw the safety back on and slide it into my holster. "Honestly? No, I don't. I think he just changed up the way things work, now that Rust is out of the picture. But I wasn't risking anything happening to you."

A flash of pain touches Luke's eyes with the reminder, but I see him working to push it aside. "So what does this mean now?"

I heave a sigh, the words bitter in my mouth. "That Vlad might get away." I pull my phone out to touch base with Warner.

I knew this was all too easy.

Chapter 63

■ ■ ■

LUKE

I feel like I haven't seen the sun in years.

Maybe that's why I've been lying in Rain's spare bed for over two hours—ignoring the fact that I need to take a piss—to stare at the broken lines of muted light stealing through the blinds to stretch over my sheets.

It sure as hell doesn't feel like it should be sunny outside.

I don't get all the legal shit that Rain was explaining last night, but I got the gist of it: that they've got a ship with cargo containers filled with stolen cars and car parts, one of Vlad's guys in a room identifying Vlad as the mastermind, and a bag of cash that I assume is Miller's payment but is only a fraction of what Vlad would have paid out to Rust.

But no Vlad.

And nothing to tie Vlad to anything beyond hearsay.

So basically, Vlad is going to get away with everything. So is Andrei, by default.

I hear a soft knock just a second before the door creaks open. Licks and Stanley tear out of my room.

"Coffee?" Rain holds up a mug.

"Yeah, sure." I think that cold rain seeped into my bones last night. Even after a hot shower, I still woke up shivering.

"I'll take the mutts out!" a deep male voice calls out from the living room.

"Thanks, Warner." Rain strolls into my room and places the mug on my nightstand. "Black, right?"

I can't help but stare into her light blue eyes. They're lined with dark bags, telling me she didn't sleep much. "Was that in my file, too?"

She smiles and her gaze drags over my body, stalling on the tent that my morning dick is making, before quickly turning away with a blush.

Part of me wants to tease her, just like I used to do. "What's he doing here? Does that mean we're not keeping up pretenses anymore?" Disappointment stirs inside me.

"I need a few hours of sleep. Otherwise, I may shoot you." A sly grin touches her lips. "I don't think you want that."

"No, that would suck after all this." Rain, with a gun. Sure, I know she's a cop. I know she has a gun, but actually seeing her pull it last night, right before ordering me to move, made it hit home.

"What would have happened last night, if Vlad had showed up?" Vlad wasn't waiting in the shadows to kill me. He probably hasn't given me two seconds' thought since the funeral. But for those five minutes between the phone call and getting home, all I could think about was keeping Rain safe. Ironic, considering she was the one with the gun, protecting me.

I'm beginning to understand that she's been protecting me for a lot longer than last night.

"If he was armed, I would have shot him." No hesitation.

I believe her. Something's shifted between us since last night. I think it has more to do with me than her. I spent hours lying in bed, trying to review every moment since the day I met her. All the ways she deceived me for her case.

But doing that made me realize all the ways she also helped me. This mess with Vlad was going down one way or another. If Rain hadn't been here, who knows where I would have ended up?

Maybe in that SUV with Rust.

In a sense, she saved me. So no, I don't hate her.

I miss her. She's standing a foot away from me and I miss her so damn much.

Her eyes flash. "What?"

I reach out to graze her knuckles with mine. "Thank you. I know you're doing it for the case, but . . . what's gonna happen now?"

With a sigh, she turns and sits down on the edge of my bed, her back to me. "They're searching the cargo containers for any evidence. But we're waiting on Sinclair to make the call. They may have enough to issue an arrest warrant for Vlad in Rust's murder soon."

"So that asshole wasn't bluffing when he told me they had something?"

She chuckles softly. "No, he actually was. But the guy they brought in last night for the money exchange with Miller was more than happy to offer information on Rust's murder. Apparently he knows exactly which Dumpster Vlad pitched the gun into."

That same chest pain that flares at mentions of Rust throbs again. "That was over a week ago. The Dumpsters would have been emptied."

"I know. The police are sifting through trash as we speak. They also have some surveillance video that they're looking into." She sighs. "It's not over yet."

"But what about this case?"

"Sometimes it takes months. Sometimes we get a lucky break." She pauses. "And sometimes we have to just be happy with scaring people into stopping without ever being punished. There are a lot of cars on that ship and we've gathered a lot of names. We'll get some arrest warrants out of this and do more surveillance, which will lead to more arrests. It's a long process."

"So . . . does that mean you're going to be here until it's all wrapped up?" *Hell*, three days ago I couldn't even look at her. Now I don't want her to leave.

"The case is going to go on for months. Maybe years. But for me . . ." She takes a deep breath. "Yeah. My part's pretty much done."

She'll go back to her life as a cop. Or not, if the way she's helped me gets her into trouble. "What's going to happen for you?"

"I don't know yet. They'll send me back to D.C., for sure. Then . . . I don't know."

No more Rain.

My fingers curl around the hem of her T-shirt, reveling in its softness, her slender figure now striking me as so much stronger than it ever did before. "You wore this that night on the yacht."

Her profile is so beautiful when she smiles. "You remember."

"Of course I do." With only slight hesitation, I slip a hand under to graze her back, letting my finger trail up along her spine, all the way up to see that she's not wearing anything underneath. She shivers but doesn't stop me, doesn't say a word when I slide my hand around, letting her right breast fill it.

"Rain?"

She turns to look at me, her lips parted, her eyes burning. "Yeah?"

The front door slams shut and the sound of paws on the hard-wood announce Warner's return.

I hear a soft "*shit*" escape Rain's mouth as her eyes close, her frustration so obvious it makes me chuckle. She stands, moving away from my touch. "I'll see you in a few hours, okay? I need to sleep." She can't peel her eyes off me.

Fucking Warner. "Okay." I know I shouldn't, but I'm running out of time with her. I can't help myself. I toss my bedsheet off and stand, earning her wide-eyed stare, before I head for my bathroom, feeling her gaze on me the entire time.

■ ■ ■

"Do you always watch this much baseball?"

"Yep."

One-word answers. That's what I've been getting out of Warner for the past four hours, when he isn't answering calls.

Sometimes he wanders off to the other side of the condo while he's talking, but he holds onto the damn remote so I can't change the channel.

I could just go back to my bedroom and watch TV there—and that's likely his aim by being such a dick—but I feel caged in there.

Plus, truth be told, I'm just waiting for Rain to wake up.

With a sigh, I head over to the fridge and crack open a beer.

"That better not be my IPA!" he barks.

I pour half of it down my throat before I hold up the can. "You mean this one?"

He glares at me.

"Want one?"

"Can't. I might accidently shoot you if I'm drinking," he mutters, eyes back on the screen.

"Everyone's talking about shooting me today." He's in a pissy mood. I wonder if it's because of me or because of losing Vlad. Either way, with a gun holstered to his side, I probably shouldn't irritate him. "When do you think Rain's going to wake up?"

"You mean Clara? I think I heard her shower running, actually."

I frown. I didn't hear a damn thing.

"You know that whatever you two had is over, right?" He watches me through those dark, shrewd eyes, like he can read my every thought. "She's a good cop and she's got a big future ahead of her, as long as no one drags her down."

"I'm sure she'll figure out what she wants." I take another sip.

And silently hope that what she wants involves me.

"She wants to make a difference in the world. She's not the kind of girl to play house. She wouldn't be happy."

"What are you two talking about?" We both turn in time so see Rain step out of her bedroom in those yoga pants that she knows I love, her hair dark and wet from a shower. Eyes still weary but more rested than before. And not carrying a gun, to my relief.

"Did Sinclair get hold of you?" Warner asks. There's excitement in his voice.

She frowns slightly. "Yeah. He did."

"Good news, right?"

She takes a deep breath and then nods. I could be wrong, but it doesn't seem like good news.

"What's going on?" I blurt out. "Is this about the case?"

"Sort of. Clara's heading home and you're free to go. Your Russian friend is no doubt aware of the investigation by now, so you two don't have to keep faking your romance."

My stomach sinks with his words. That's it? Just like that?

Rain takes a deep breath. Is it one of relief? Frustration? Does she feel any of the sadness that just washed over me? Stanley trots over to climb her leg. She picks him up and hugs him. "You ready to fly to your new home?"

He snorts in answer.

"Did someone book my flight already?" she asks, her eyes not leaving his bug eyes.

"Ten a.m. tomorrow."

Tomorrow?

"Okay." There's a long pause. "So I'm *officially* off this case and Luke is *officially* free?"

"Yup."

She takes a deep breath. "I want the cameras shut down." Warner opens his mouth but she cuts him off. "Please, Warner. Make it happen."

His jaw tenses as his gaze flickers between me and Rain. Finally, he nods. "I'll take you to the airport in the morning."

"Sounds great. Thanks, Warner."

Heading for the door, he stops a foot away from me. "I don't want to ever see your fucking face again, so stay away from trouble."

With that, he's gone.

"So . . ." Rain tucks a strand of hair behind her ear, her fingers trembling slightly. "You're free to go home anytime you want." Wandering over to the counter, her back to me, she unscrews a fresh a bottle of wine and pours herself a glass. I watch in silence as she takes a long, slow sip of her glass. An agonizingly slow sip.

Where do we go from here?

I don't want her to leave. That's all I know.

"Do you remember when I told you that I didn't like the idea of looking out my window and you not being there anymore?"

Her head bobs up and down.

I step forward, resting my hands on her shoulders, able to see the tears sliding down her cheeks. "I'm dreading tomorrow."

"Me too." She leans back and turns her face to rest against my chest, her eyes closed. This is the real girl. And I've seen her before. Rain may not have been real, but this person right here is, and I know her. I've known her this whole time.

"Can I show you something?"

Glossy eyes open to stare up at me. "Please."

Curling her fingers into mine, I lead her toward my bedroom.

Chapter 64

. . .

CLARA

When I answered the call from Sinclair, my stomach instantly clenched, dreading what he was going to demand from me now. The conversation was brief, and he did all the talking, telling me that the death of Rust Markov caused considerable challenges in this case but we still managed to get some impressive results. That line sounded like a formal statement to quash internal politics. Then he announced that my role in this case was finished and that I would be going home to resume my previous job on the MCU, but that I should fill out another application to join the FBI.

Apparently Sinclair is impressed by my tenacity, my intelligence, and most of all, my resourcefulness. He will make sure that my name rises to the top of the list.

I should be ecstatic. This is everything I wanted. And this could have—and by all rights should have—gone an entirely different way, ending with me working as a rent-a-cop, chasing twelve-year-old shoplifters at the local mall.

But the entire time he was talking, all I was thinking about was Luke. About how I went to sleep after our midnight run thinking that maybe there was a chance to salvage something here. That if I was going to lose my job anyway, then maybe we could make this work.

My career hasn't ended. I'm getting what I've worked so hard for.

Which means that I can't carry on a real relationship with my former target. I wouldn't get past the first levels of applicant vetting without raising major flags.

So this, right here, is everything I'm ever going to have with Luke.

He kicks the door shut before the dogs have a chance to join us, and then he doesn't waste a second, pulling me into a long kiss that has me finally breaking for air.

We become a tangled mess of limbs as our clothes fall to the floor, until there's nothing between us but skin and this mass of emotions that have somehow survived such a violent storm.

"Hold on a sec." He leaves me stretched out onto the bed to fish something from his duffel bag. I assume it's a condom, so when the first sparkles of diamonds catch my eye, I frown.

"I know you can't keep this," he starts, kneeling on the bed, his perfect naked form almost as overwhelming as the necklace in his hands. "But can you please just wear it for tonight?" He clasps it behind my neck and then straightens all the long strands, his fingers skating all over my breasts as he positions the diamond raindrops. "When I saw it, I knew it would be perfect for you."

I simply lie there, letting his eyes roam over me, letting my eyes roam over him. Drinking him up for the last time.

Until it's just too much to bear.

I wrap my legs around his hips, knowing he'll get the message.

His Adam's apple bobs with his hard swallow. "God, you're so beautiful."

So are you. That mess of wavy brown hair that somehow looks perfect, even though I know he didn't do anything to it today. That jawline that I remember staring up at the night I threw a drink at him. It feels like an eternity ago. Those full lips that are almost too pretty to be on a man.

Those sincere blue eyes that have never lied to me.

I give his hips a gentle tug toward me with my legs but he resists. "Is something wrong?"

He blinks several times, as if fighting tears. "You're never coming back, are you?"

I grit my teeth to fight my own tears as I climb to my knees, until my chest is pressed against his and my arms coil around his head.

Holding him tight to me.

I can feel his heart hammering against my chest. I wonder if it's hurting as much as mine is. I coax his lips with my own. And then he's stealing the air in my lungs with his mouth, consuming my body with such palpable emotion, it's almost suffocating.

I absorb all of it.

Reveling in the feel of being with Luke one last time.

No guilt.

No lies.

Telling myself that I can never forget what this feels like.

■ ■ ■

Tangled with Luke's body, I'm so comfortable that Stanley and Licks' howls don't register immediately. It's not until I feel Luke's body stiffen, and I know he's awake too, that it clicks.

I'm on my feet in seconds and peering around the door frame to see the dogs standing in front of the door, growling.

Luke's up and pulling on track pants. I run into my room to throw on the first pair of pants and T-shirt that I can find. And then my fingers make fast work of the safe so I can get to my gun. I check my phone for any calls from Warner, wondering if it could be him.

No missed calls.

This isn't him.

A knock sounds.

I punch Warner's number in and toss the phone to Luke. "Tell him what's going on." Right about now, I'm really wishing I didn't demand that they shut off the cameras. Tiptoeing toward the door, I flick the safety off my gun. I shoo the dogs away with a gentle nudge of my foot, and then call out, "Who is it?"

"Delivery." A deep, male voice. Not Russian, but still . . .

"At three a.m.?"

"It's special."

"Special my ass. The cops are on their way."

There's a long pause, and I hold my breath, listening for the cock of a gun. When he speaks again, it's with less confidence. "I was told that you needed to receive this now, or it will be too late."

"What will be too late?" *Dammit.* How do I ignore that?

"I don't know, Miss. It's . . . help."

For all I know, the guy could have a gun aimed at the door, waiting for a shadow to pass over the peephole. I wave my hand several times, holding my breath. No shots fired.

I know what the protocol is here: wait for backup.

As quietly as possible, I unlatch the locks.

And then I throw open the door, gun aimed and ready.

A middle-aged man in a baseball cap that hides half of his face lets out a yelp of surprise, holding the flimsy white envelope tight against his chest as if it can somehow protect him from a bullet.

"Who sent you?" I demand to know.

He swallows and, instead of answering, he slowly extends his arms.

I'm torn between refusing it and grabbing it. Until I see the small emblem in the top right-hand corner of the envelope.

A black orchid.

I snatch it out of his hand. "You need to stay—"

The deliveryman turns and bolts, leaving me with no option but to either shoot him or let him go.

"Yeah . . . An envelope . . . He's gone . . ." Luke is telling Warner. I didn't notice he had stepped up beside me. To me he says, "Warner says not to open it until he gets here."

I tear the seal open and pull several slips of paper out.

"Tell him he's going to have to reschedule my flight."

■ ■ ■

"Ready?" Warner calls from the black agency sedan he's using to get me to the airport. My things—a suitcase stuffed with clothes

I accumulated while undercover that they can't possibly use on another case, and Stanley—are already packed in the backseat.

"Yeah, give me a minute?"

"We've already rescheduled the flight once . . ."

"And remind me why again?"

Warner slides his aviator glasses on and smirks at me. "Because you're a superstar, Bertelli." He rolls the window up, giving Luke and me some privacy as we say our goodbyes outside my building.

Except it's not *my* building anymore.

I'm going home today.

Luke peers down at me with big blue eyes. "You seriously don't know who sent you that envelope?"

To everyone else, including Sinclair and Warner, my official answer all morning has been "I have no clue."

To Luke, I smile. "Do you want me to lie to you or just not answer?"

I can't tell anyone that Elmira's the one who sent me detailed instructions on where to find the stolen black SUVs, heading for Durban—on the coast of South Africa—at first light this morning, right down to the name and location of the ship in the Seattle port. Or that it was her prompting that led us to set up surveillance on Gold Bond to watch Vlad stroll in a few hours later, at exactly nine a.m., only to walk back out after fifteen minutes with a duffel bag full of cash. Or that it was Elmira who told us which port official would be receiving a call from Jerry Rosenthal, to confirm that the cargo was loaded and that he should release the money to Vlad.

The port official answered the phone with a shaky "yes," while Warner breathed down his neck. By that point, a fleet of customs officers had already been sifting through containers for hours. Thirty-six black SUVs were discovered. It'll take time to confirm that they're all stolen.

I can't tell any of them because I don't know why she'd sabotage her own husband's deal.

It'll take time to build a solid case. We already have Jerry

Rosenthal on handling the payment of the stolen Porsche, so we'll have to see how cooperative he'll be. It helps that Vlad pulled a gun when he saw the two cops approaching him outside Gold Bond. That gave us the excuse we needed to ask him what he did to deserve so much cash. With all the road blocks and dead ends we've dealt with on this case, it was almost a miracle that Vlad would be that stupid.

Luke shakes his head, but then smirks.

"So? What are you going to do now?"

He peers upward, squinting against the sun, as if the answer is up there. "I don't know. I guess I'll be figuring out life."

"That's my excuse."

He leans down to press his forehead against mine. "I don't know what I'm doing. Where I'm going. But I'm going to miss you so much."

The lump that's been sitting in my throat grows, pulling tears from my eyes. "I'm going to miss you, too. And Rain."

But Clara needs to move on with her life.

■ ■ ■

"Stanley!" I holler, dragging myself from my bedroom to brew a cup of coffee, my giant furry slippers sliding along the worn parquet floor.

He turns to glare at me from his perch on the windowsill, before continuing his incessant barking. I peer out at the window next door, perpendicular to us thanks to the L-shaped apartment building. Sure enough, the fat white cat is sitting there, glaring at Stanley, not amused. With the morning sun beaming down to warm its perch, I know it's not moving anywhere for hours. Which means Stanley will be barking for hours. I've had plenty of noise complaints since I came back from Portland.

"It's good we're leaving soon or else we'd be getting evicted." I shoo him off the windowsill with a pillow and then finish making my coffee and flop down onto the couch, eyeing all the boxes.

The moving truck will be here in a few hours to put my things into storage.

Stanley hops onto the couch and begins pawing at my chest. I know he needs to go for a run. "I'm going to miss you, buddy. You'll be good for my parents, right? It's only for five months."

He snorts in response.

"Well, I'm sorry, but they'd probably use you as target practice." I don't know that pets are allowed at the FBI Academy anyway.

After seven months of interviews and tests and more tests and *more* tests, I'm starting the next chapter of my life. I feel like I should be more excited. I *am* excited. It's just . . .

I grab my iPad and begin flipping through the pictures I loaded on there. My life on the West Coast. The case that taught me so much about myself—my strengths, my weaknesses—and about the good in people. I run my fingers along my greatest weakness, tracing the lines of Luke Boone's handsome face.

I dove headfirst back into local police work when I returned to D.C., allowing my mind to be consumed, the ache in my chest dulled. But I still miss him terribly. I still think about him strolling around his condo when my eyes first crack open at dawn. I still picture his perfect body as his feet pound against the pavement, a drooling bulldog trying to keep up behind him. I still smile when I think of his cocky smirk and his self-assurance. I've found myself recording hours of stupid reality TV, just so I can mock it with Stanley. I still close my eyes at night and imagine the smell, and taste, and feel of him in bed beside me.

My heart still clenches when I think of how badly his life could have ended up. I could arrest a hundred dirty criminals and it won't ever give me as much satisfaction as helping one genuinely good Luke.

A few months ago, the same day I received my conditional offer of employment from the FBI, after a few too many glasses of wine, I actually dialed his number. It's out of service.

I cried myself to sleep that night.

Then I woke up the next morning and reminded myself that

I'm doing something important. Something for me. And I can't throw that away for anyone.

My phone starts ringing. I almost don't get it, figuring it's my parents asking for the sixth time when I'm bringing Stanley over. They seem to have taken a liking to him. I may have a hard time getting him back.

"Bertelli!" booms the loud Boston-accented voice.

"Why are you calling me this early?"

"I never sleep. You know that. So, are you ready for school?"

"You know, you're so excited for me, I think *you* should just go."

He chuckles. "No, thanks. I'm just here to laugh at you. Hope you survive." Warner and I have kept in touch since the case so he could fill me in on the latest news, but also because we've become good friends. Much better than I ever expected.

"So, what's new?"

"We nailed another low-level fence from the ring."

"Is that all?" Between all the information we gathered, plus additional surveillance and Rix's undercover work, they're slowly picking away at the ranks, issuing arrest warrants. They've seen a significant decline in car thefts over the last six months, proving that we've made a big difference.

But Warner's calls usually come when there are bigger breaks. Like, a few months ago, when they handed a search warrant to Vlad Bragin's wife and she in turn handed them a pair of Vlad's pants and black gloves that, upon testing, revealed gun residue and Rust's blood. When asked why she was willing to cooperate, she told us it was because she married an asshole.

Sometimes all it takes is a bitter wife.

While it's not a smoking gun, it's another piece of the puzzle. Several others have fallen into place, including GPS tracking on Vlad's Suburban that proves where he was and when, such as at the location where Rust's body was found on the night of the murder, as well as street camera surveillance that captures him driving that night.

They're closing in on him for the murder. As for the stolen

cars, the corrupt jeweler documented and recorded much more than he likely was supposed to. Perhaps for the day he got caught and needed big-ticket leverage.

Warner snorts. "Actually, no, smart-ass. Have you looked at the news today?"

"No . . .?"

"Check out CNN. International news." He goes quiet, and I know he's waiting for me to tune in.

I open the browser on my iPad, following his instructions. "Holy shit!"

I quickly read the news article, with the picture of the wealthy, attractive man in the inset, my eyes zeroing in on the scar bisecting his lip that I've seen in person before. "Human trafficking?"

"It's disgusting. Do you know how many children they found in one of those ships?"

Though there's not a lot of information, and I always question the accuracy of anything I read produced by a reporter, according to the article, a complex investigation has been running for seven years, with evidence of human trafficking surfacing from many countries. Aref Hamidi was arrested and charged while visiting China.

"This is going to create a huge, international mess. China will give him the death penalty."

Which is exactly what he would deserve. It almost seems too good to be true. Like perhaps it was orchestrated. Otherwise how would Aref be stupid enough to get caught?

There's only one person I can think of capable of coordinating such a takedown.

"Makes you not so bitter about the asshole getting away on our case, right? I mean, it would have been a slap on the wrist compared to what's coming his way."

"It does," I murmur softly, my mind spinning with absurd, improbable speculation. "I wish there was more information. Can you find anything out?"

"I'll just wave my magic wand . . ."

I roll my eyes. "Seriously, Warner, don't we have any pull on getting dirt?"

"'We.' You're cute. You know as well as I do that there's shit going on over on that side of the world that the FBI will never catch wind of."

"Is his wife involved?"

"I don't see her mentioned, and they would have mentioned something like that. She has ties to Iranian royalty, after all. I hope she kept some money, because I'll bet everything gets seized." An entire empire . . . lost, for no reason other than greed.

Thoughts of the mysterious Elmira Zamani fade to the background as someone more important to me comes to mind with Warner's words. "Speaking of seizing assets . . ." I pause, waiting for Warner to fill in the blanks. He knows who I'm asking about. He's just been reluctant to tell me anything about Luke.

"Everything's been released. The kid hired good lawyers and, since we have no proof beyond hearsay that 24 was involved, we couldn't hold his assets anymore."

I take a deep breath. I'm not sure if I'm happy about this or not. That means Luke has a ton of money at his disposal now. All money earned through dirty dealings. And he fought the Feds to get it. What does that mean? Seven months later, where is his head at?

"Anything else . . . interesting?"

There's a long silence. "Yes." Warner hesitates. "Betty-Jo Billings received a check made out to cash by an anonymous donor last week. She called the police, because it was a lot of money, and she thought it was fraudulent."

"How much money?"

"Like, if you were to sell a million-dollar condo and your Porsche 911 . . . that much money."

My heart skips a few beats. "He . . ."

"He's renting a small place downtown. He's in the garage, from morning until night. Goes home, jogs with his dog. Spends a lot of time at the Japanese Gardens. At first I thought he was getting into something again, but he just goes to sit on a bench. Alone."

"You're still doing surveillance on him?" *God, please tell me they don't suspect him of something else.* "Did Sinclair tell you to do that?"

"Nope. It's unofficial."

I swallow. "Then why?"

Warner sighs. "Because I know you too well."

I smile. "Thanks, Warner."

I stare at the picture of Aref on my iPad long after I hang up the phone, rereading the article several times, Googling Elmira's name, looking for more news on her, finding only socialite-type posts and pictures about the beautiful wife of the heir to Hamidi Enterprises.

My gut tells me that Elmira suspected what I really was—the stunt involving Luke's car had to be her way of outing me. The hows and whys have remained a mystery to me.

But now . . . I frown, staring at her face, remembering her ageless beauty, her cool disposition, her shrewd gaze. She knew just what to say, what to do . . .

They always say a good undercover can spot another.

I'd like to say that I'll track her down one day and ask her who she really is, but my guess is that I will not cross paths with Elmira—or whatever her name is—ever again.

So instead, I'll have to thank her silently. That's fairly easy; all I have to do it is think of Luke Boone.

Epilogue

...

LUKE

The office walls rattle as someone—probably Tabbs—tests out a broken muffler by revving the engine in the bay.

"Fuck," I mutter, my ears ringing. I'm going to be deaf by forty if I have to listen to that every day. I glance up at the clock with a sigh. Already five. I was planning on ducking out early today and taking Licks for a jog along my usual trail. It's much nicer in daylight, especially right now, when the Japanese cherry blossom trees are in full bloom.

But the day has turned to dusk while I've been slaving away. The garage is a lot of work for one guy to run—especially when that one guy never saw himself spending six days a week in a tiny office, listening to broken mufflers and smelling engine oil. But I think I've got the place running smoother than Miller ever did.

It's for the best that he "disappeared" with his wife and daughters. I could never have kept him working here, but I would have felt guilty firing him because of his family. And because, out of all of us, he's the only one who had a truly redeeming reason for being involved in that world. A world that feels increasingly farther away.

I pick up the newspaper to read the ad I ran for a part-time office manager. It's been four days and, though I've had a lot of applicants, none of them are what I'm looking for. I guess I'm picky. I even tried to get Jesse to come and work for me. He laughed in my face.

A sudden and loud roar of pain has me running toward the bays, hoping to all hell that my employer insurance premiums are paid up.

"Son of a bitch. He bit me!" Tabbs roars. "Get that ugly mutt out of here!"

I round the corner in time to see a little dog square off against Tabbs like a bull, his giant ears turning back and forth like satellites.

My heart stops. If Stanley's here . . .

"I swear, he never bites." Rain stands in the bay door, her short black leather jacket zipped up to her chin to ward off the early evening chill.

Her hair's a few inches shorter than the last time I saw her, a year ago, but otherwise she looks exactly the same.

Beautiful.

And smiling broadly.

I don't waste a second. I take quick steps toward her and pull her into my arms. She comes willingly, her hands finding their way around my waist. She smells like roses, just like I remember. "What are you doing here?"

She points over her shoulder with her thumb. "I'm having a problem with my clutch. I thought I'd bring it here."

"Right." I chuckle and play along, throwing an arm over her shoulder. "Let's see this car."

"It's not so much a car as a Jeep."

"Yeah, I can see that," I murmur with awe, circling the matte black beauty. "Solid grill guard, four-inch lift kit . . . what are those, thirty-eights?" Definitely trail tires.

"Would you like some time alone with it?"

I chuckle. Passing the front, I notice the plates are from Oregon. "You rented this?"

"No."

I frown. "I'd like to think you know better than to steal."

"Funny." She pauses. "I bought it."

My heartbeat speeds up. "Does that mean . . ."

Maybe she sees the excitement in my eyes because she breaks out in a smile. "Portland was my first choice for assignments, and Sinclair pulled some strings to make sure it happened."

So many thoughts and emotions are racing through me that I'm left with my mouth hanging open, unable to speak. Just staring at her.

"So . . . are you seeing anyone?" She cringes as she says it, offering a very rare and brief glimpse of what Rain looks like when she's nervous. "I mean . . . what are you doing tonight?"

I can't help scanning her top-to-bottom—she's even more fit than she was before. It's been so freaking long. I've gone out on a couple of dates since she left, but none of them came close to holding my interest. And I never knew how to talk about myself, how to let anyone in.

"I thought this couldn't happen. I mean . . ." I'm nervous too. Or excited. Or petrified that she's only here to say "hi" because she's in town.

But, then, why would she ask to be located here?

"How is this happening?"

She reaches out, beckoning my hand. I take it, and then yank her into me, earning her slight gasp. She runs her knuckles against the light stubble along my jaw. "You look different."

"Yeah . . ." I gaze down at my dark jeans and T-shirt. I've kept the Rolex, but only because it's one of the few things, besides the garage, that I have left from Rust. "I'm living a more simple life."

"I like it." Her palm slides along my chest and stomach. My nightly workout routine has only gotten more obsessive since she left.

"Seriously . . . how is this happening? I thought you couldn't get involved with someone like me."

"Someone with a beautiful heart? Someone who paid a price for his mistakes?" Her face grows serious. "I know what you did for the Billings family."

I duck my head, my cheeks burning. "How'd you find out?"

"Because I'm an FBI agent. You can't hide anything from me.

Remember that." She winks, taking my hands and walking back-ward, pulling me to the passenger side. "Hey Tabbs! Can you lock up?" she hollers.

"Sure thing, Boss Lady!"

I climb into the passenger seat, Stanley perched on my lap. "I guess I'll just leave my car here until tomorrow?" I say, hopeful.

She glances at the silver '74 Porsche 911 that I paid Jesse to fix up for me. I actually love it more than the last one. Probably because I feel like I earned it. "I can drive you, on my way into the office."

"So . . ." I cover her hand, weaving my fingers between hers as she shifts gears. There's so much I want to say, to ask. What has she been doing in the last year? Is she seeing anyone else? What exactly is she looking for? "What's new?"

"A lot. But I'll tell you what's not new." Her face grows serious, causing a moment of panic in my gut. "The fact that you still don't cover your windows at night."

I smirk. "You've been watching me?"

"Kind of hard not to." Excitement flashes in her eyes "Wait until you see where I'm living."

ACKNOWLEDGMENTS

Getting into the head of an undercover police officer is difficult when you're not an undercover police officer. Telling a story that balances the excitement of fiction with legal realities is also difficult. Fortunately, I had a lot of help from a real undercover. I hope that Clara has done the profession and this world justice. Please note though, that this *is* fiction. As such, some liberties need to be taken to keep the plot flowing and readers interested. Characters like Sinclair and Clara—and their choices—are pure fiction. They are *not* based on what *does* happen or what *has* happened. They are based on what *could* happen. Because crazy things happen all the time.

I first want to thank my readers and the bloggers who continue with me on this journey. You know who you are—grabbing my books when they come out, chatting with me on social media, sharing my stories with friends, family, and your reading communities. You all keep making this dream possible for me.

To Sven Halle, for allowing me to interrupt your dinner to ask about sailing along the West Coast.

To Heather Self—always jumping to read my drafts in whatever shape they may be in, and providing sound input.

To my publicist, KP—for putting up with not hearing from me for weeks at a time because of a deadline, and then having me fire off question after question at all hours of the day and night through every method of communication available.

To my agent, Stacey Donaghy—for sitting in Pickle Barrel with me for hours, brainstorming this complicated story. For actually wanting to brainstorm with me for hours. And for leaving my face hurting from all the laughter.

To my editor, Sarah Cantin—for letting me run with this

complicated story and tolerating the many, many, *many* revisions that went along with it.

To my publisher, Judith Curr, and the team at Atria Books: Ben Lee, Ariele Fredman, Tory Lowy, Kimberly Goldstein, and Alysha Bullock—for continuing to package my stories so beautifully. The cover on this one is truly perfect.

To P—for suffering through all those bottles of wine and dinners out to discuss this plot. I know it was a real hardship. Okay, maybe the 700+ texts were a bit much, but you were a real trouper, answering each and every one of them without ever asking why I'd want to know such absurd things.

To Lia and Sadie—for asking me almost daily why I write books. Some days—when the words aren't flowing and the plot isn't working and all I want to do is watch five episodes of *The Walking Dead* back-to-back—answering that question is what keeps me going.

To Paul—for dealing with the never-ending deadlines. And for not punching any more of my author friends in the face.